"You're nsettling down 1 chest. "I don't care for city girls. Besides..." His gaze was lazy and lingering. "You're like my kid sister."

Kid sister. Right. Except her body didn't have sisterly responses to his. No. The handsome cowboy made her toes curl with his deep, sexy drawl, and her heart race should his brown eyes stare for too long. Yeah. *Not* sisterly.

"Then this should be interesting," Cole said, smile still hovering around his mouth.

Kerri watched Jordan turn to her fiancé and frown. "What?"

"The mistletoe, of course." Her future brother-in-law pointed to the branch hanging directly above Connor's head.

Kerri's gaze bounced from the sprig down to Connor, then to the others.

They were all staring right at her. *Oh, heck no.* They'd all lost their friggin' minds. "No way." She couldn't. She just couldn't. "You can't be serious?"

"Of course we are," Cole replied, looking from her to his brother. "You're the only single girl standing here."

"Then I'll go get another." She laughed and would have left if Connor had kept his pain-in-the-butt mouth shut.

"She's too chicken, little brother. Must be a city girl thing. No backbone."

What they're saying…

About Her Fated Cowboy:

"As always, this author perfectly blended an amazing storyline, which contained characters you just can't help but fall in love with and she worked her magic in creating a masterpiece of the heart. I even enjoyed her sense of humor sprinkled throughout, which was placed in all the right places. This is one story I highly recommend and one author I just can't read enough from. Since this is the first book in the Harland County series, I'm eagerly looking forward to the next book."
—**Night Owl Reviews, Reviewer Top Pick**

About Captive Hero (Time-shift Heroes Series-Book One):
2012 RONE Awards Nominee for Best Time Travel
"Captive Hero" is a compelling story about two star crossed lovers. They make an amazing couple. Their banter, chemistry and the deep love that is obvious in their interactions make them a true pleasure to read about! The story is full of twists, unexpected revelations interwoven with moments of peace and love. It's an amazing adventure that will tug at the reader's heartstrings and refuse to let go!"
—**InD'tale Magazine, Awarded Crowned Heart of Excellence**

About Cowboy-Sexy:

"A blend of military man and cowboy …ohh my. The connection between these two is electric. This book is full of real life struggles that military couples face. These details give the story a lot of depth and heart. Readers will race through this story and then preorder the next book in the series to see what is in store for outrageous Brett."
—**RT Book Reviews, 4 Stars**

Dear Reader,

Thank you for purchasing Her Unbridled Cowboy. This was the second book in my four book Harland County Series. Unruly cowboys and the women who tame them.

Connor McCall is Cole's older, laid-back brother. Tall and handsome, the cattle rancher loves the outdoors, but isn't crazy about city girls. Three times he was engaged to one, and three times the relationship failed. Connor turned out to be the sweetest, biggest, teddy bear hero I'd ever written, and it was going to take an understanding 'cowboy tamer' to help him overcome his trust issues.

Kerri Masters is exactly what the cowboy needs, and vice versa. Sweet and unsure, she's homeless and unemployed, hoping to stay in Texas only until her sister is married. But of course, the matchmaking parents have other ideas.

Once they give in the attraction, they stumble and grow, falter and blossom, learning a few things about themselves along the way. Another hot, heartfelt, sexy read, this story also includes some of the other characters in the series. Their participation rounds out this book and sets the stage for the next.

Thanks for reading,

~Donna

www.donnamichaelsauthor.com

Also by Donna Michaels

~Novels~
Captive Hero (Time-shift Heroes Series-Book One)
The Spy Who Fanged Me
She Does Know Jack
Her Fated Cowboy(Book 1/Cole)
Her Uniform Cowboy(Book 3/Kade)
Her Forever Cowboy(Book 4/Kevin)
~Novellas~
Cowboy-Sexy
Thanks for Giving
Ten Things I'd Do for a Cowboy
Vampire Kristmas
~Short Stories~
The Hunted
Negative Image
The Truth About Daydreams
Holiday Spirit
~Do-Over Series~
Valentine's Day Do-Over
Valentine's Day Do-Over Part II: The Siblings

UPCOMING RELEASES:
~Time-shift Heroes Series~
Future Hero—Book Two
~Harland County Series~
Her Healing Cowboy (Book 5/Jace)
~Citizen Soldier Series (Harland County Spinoff)~
Wyne and Dine(Book 1/Ben)

Her Unbridled Cowboy
Harland County Series
Book Two: Connor

By
Donna Michaels

HER UNBRIDLED COWBOY

Harland County Series/Book Two: Connor

Copyright © 2013 Donna Michaels
Cover Art by Ramona Lockwood © 2013
Excerpt from *Her Uniform Cowboy* Copyright © 2013 Donna Michaels

Excerpt from *Her Uniform Cowboy* Copyright © 2013 Donna Michaels

ALL RIGHTS RESERVED. No part of this book may be reproduced or transmitted in any form whatsoever without written permission from the author—except by a reviewer who may quote brief passages in a review to be printed in a magazine, newspaper, or on the web. For information, please contact the author via email at Donna_Michaels@msn.com

All characters in this book have no existence outside the imagination of the author and have no relation whatsoever to anyone bearing the same name or names. They are not even distantly inspired by any individual known or unknown to the author, and all incidents are pure invention.

ISBN-13: 978-1490323213
ISBN-10: 149032321X

Print edition June 2013
Book Two in Harland County Series

Dedication

To the fans of the first book, Her Fated Cowboy. I hope you enjoy the story of Cole's older brother Connor, the laid back cowboy and his bumpy journey!

To my husband Michael, my family, the HOODS, and most of all, to my fellow author and friend JT Schultz who's waited years for Connor's story. This one's for you, JT!

Chapter One

Homeless and unemployed.

West Coast Chef Kerri Masters silently summed up her current life situation. Her *sucky* life situation. *Will I ever catch a break*, she wondered as she stood in a roomful of people gathered at the Wild Creek Ranch, home of longtime family friends, the McCalls.

The last place she wanted to be.

Ever.

She had hoped not to suffer this fate again until, oh…say *never*. Okay, not true. She loved her parents, and since they'd recently moved back to Harland County, Texas and were currently staying with the McCalls until renovations were completed on their old homestead, *never* wasn't an option.

But, next summer worked for her. Yes, she'd had *that* timeframe in mind. Not *now*. Not the day before *flippin'* Thanksgiving.

Leave it to fate.

Fate.

She swallowed a sneer, but was unable to stop a slight twist from reaching her top lip. *Yeah*—leave it to fate to take another swing at her life with a blasted butcher knife. Felt more like a meat cleaver. *Two* meat cleavers.

Didn't she already have enough deep cuts? *Criminy.* Was she walking around with an invisible sign on her back blaring, *Come on, is that all you've got?*

"We're just thankful you and Jordan are all right," her mother, Hannah Masters said, pulling her into a hug.

Again.

This one made number seven since she'd arrived from California with her sister Jordan a little over four hours ago. She'd spent most of that time in her room avoiding…well, everyone, while Jordan did the same by saddling a horse and going for a ride.

But that was okay. She'd understood her sister's need to be alone. Coming here had been painful for Jordan until Cole had shown up and gone after her sister to profess his love. The happy couple had returned five minutes ago. Engaged.

Finally.

A good size helping of warmth invaded the almost constant chill in Kerri's body. If ever two people were meant to be together, it was Jordan and Cole. Both had lost a spouse, and it was that shared pain, plus a long history of attraction that had brought them together at last.

It did her heart good to know at least her sister would have a happy life.

She also understood her mother's worry and immediately returned the embrace. It couldn't have been easy residing several states away and hearing about the earthquake that had destroyed her youngest daughter's home and restaurant. *My home. My restaurant.*

The sweet fragrance of jasmine filled her nose and instantly calmed the aggravation from her soul. The smell of her mother's perfume always brought with it an invisible hug and strong sense of reassurance. Something Kerri hadn't realized she needed until that moment.

"I'm fine," she said, holding back a sigh.

"Thank goodness." Her mother tightened her hold and shook while they embraced. "Things would've been a lot different if you were home when the quake hit."

Her Unbridled Cowboy

Everyone in the gathering room knew Kerri's stilted house had crumbled in the disaster. Kind of similar to what was left of her life.

She would laugh if it wasn't so *flippin'* tragic.

"And we thank God both you and your sister got out of your restaurant before it blew up," her father, Nate Masters added from behind, his hand warm and reassuring as it closed around her shoulder in a soft squeeze.

God, if they only knew...

Kerri closed her eyes and recalled the image forever burned into her mind. The image of Jordan rushing across the pavement intent on turning off the gas to their restaurant despite the danger. Terror, unlike anything she'd ever felt before, had resembled a sharp skewer piercing the air from her lungs. All she had been able to manage was a panicked cry for her sister to stop.

It was the worst moment of her life.

"We certainly had a guardian angel watching over us that day. Didn't we, Kerri?" Jordan's voice from only a few steps away cut through her thoughts.

Kerri opened her eyes and smiled at her sister, now safe and sound, happily cocooned in Cole's arms. Matching expressions of love and wonderment adorned their faces as they stood in front of a stone fireplace, warm fire crackling in the background. The white bandage on her sister's temple was a stark reminder of last Sunday, but did nothing to dim the mood.

Jordan's long, wavy brown hair fell to her waist and dark eyes held the same happy gleam as her dark haired, dark eyed fiancé.

Okay, forget *love* and *wonderment*. Heck, given her sister's soft smile and relaxed posture—*extremely satisfied* was a better description. *Jeez Louise*, Cole had only taken off after Jordan an hour ago. Ride time alone was close to forty minutes. How the heck did they fit in sex, let alone satisfying sex?

It usually took Kerri that long just to concentrate when Lance used to…

"What do you mean?" their father asked, removing his hand from her shoulder.

Her mind stumbled a bit to get back in the conversation.

"What guardian angel?"

Jordan burrowed in a little closer to Cole, and he gathered her sister tighter. "Well, I just think we were both lucky that day."

"I don't know about me." Kerri stepped out of her mother's embrace to answer her sister. "But you definitely have a guardian angel. I remember calling out to you as you ran toward the restaurant. But you didn't stop. That's when the most amazing thing happened." She paused to glance around the room, a little uncomfortable with being the center of attention. That was more a Jordan thing. A trait the former cop embraced.

"Go on. Tell us what happened next," her father prodded.

Kerri swallowed, then forced herself to continue. "Something…or someone, I can't be sure, mysteriously yanked Jordan to the ground right before Comets exploded. No one was there. Just the two of us, but it was as if an invisible pair of hands had reached up from nowhere and pulled her down, out of harms' way."

"Oh my…do you think it was Eric?" her mom asked, eyes wide and unblinking.

Jordan's late husband, Eric, had died in a convenience store robbery almost three years ago. Kerri had to admit, the thought had crossed her mind more than once in the last few days. But she honestly didn't know.

"Could've been my Cole," Leeann McCall said, a look of pride lighting her brown eyes. "I bet he kept her safe through sheer willpower that day."

"True," her husband, Alex McCall chimed in, draping an arm around his petite wife. "No one's more stubborn than our boys."

Whatever it was, Kerri would be forever grateful for whatever caused her sister to hit the pavement at that exact moment. And she had to admit, now she was just a tad envious, too. Envious that her sister had found such a strong love twice in her life, while she couldn't find it even once. All she'd managed was a disastrous marriage that had left her hurt, confused and divorced, doubting there were any good men left in the world.

"That's not entirely true." A deep baritone with a hint of humor cut through the room, captivating the air into a silence of unadulterated anticipation. Her heart tail-spinned into her ribs, until she looked up and realized he was talking to his father.

Still, the captivation part was typical Connor McCall fashion.

There wasn't an unattached female in the tri-county area safe from his sex appeal. That's why Kerri kept her gaze glued to the worn-out sole of his left boot. She knew her place. He was way out of her league. She was under no illusion as to where she stood against such a virile man. Heck, she didn't even qualify to kiss the sole of his worn-out left boot. But that's where her gaze remained. Much safer than traveling upward.

She hadn't really said more than a quick hello. He'd headed to the stables shortly after they'd arrived, and she'd happily retreated to her room to regroup. To summon strength, because she was a vulnerable mess at the moment. If she could just gather some willpower, even just a smidge, in order to resist the gorgeous cowboy…because heck, he made her *feel* things she had no business feeling. Cripes, she was desperate. Had to be if she was stupid enough to let herself feel something for someone like him. He was too raw, too manly.

Yes, staring at Connor's boot was about all she could handle at the moment. Anything higher…

Heat shot through her body, settling in her face and other parts further south. Parts that liked to be called good, but she preferred to call them *closed for the season*. No way could she allow her gaze to take in the whole man. *Jeez*, the toned scenery of his northern terrain could make a girl want to get lost. And stay lost. Forever. Connor McCall sported a very sexy landscape restricted for equally sexy women…of which she was not.

The reality of those words hit her with the force of an icy, cold blast. She blinked until his boot came back into focus.

"There is someone more stubborn than us," he continued, that darn sexy drawl sending shivers to her toes, while an unwelcomed heat pooled low in her belly.

And she'd only just cooled off.

"Who?" his father asked.

"Jordan," came Connor's humorous reply.

Laughter filled the room. No one would argue the fact. Once her sister made up her mind about anything, she didn't let go. Kerri laughed, too. When the cowboy was right, he was right.

Smiling, she lifted her head, intending to snicker at her sister but…dang, it wasn't her sister who filled her view.

Tall, broad shoulders and chest, muscles bulging out from under his red, rolled up sleeves, brown hair, dancing brown eyes and those darn dimples…six-foot-four-inches of Texas testosterone. The equivalent of saturated fat. Tasted good but wasn't good for you.

Granted, she'd only had a little taste when he'd briefly kissed her at her parent's anniversary party back in September. But it had been enough for Kerri to scratch him off her menu—permanently. That small sampling promised to be as delicious as a fresh from the oven cannoli dipped in chocolate. How could she stop at just one? She couldn't, hence the permanent scratching off part.

Besides, she preferred men with class, who'd pick her up for a date wearing a suit and enjoyed the fine arts. Not a brash, long-haired cowboy whose favorite pastime was teasing and never took anything serious. One who thought dressing up was donning a new pair of jeans. Whose idea of culture was the black velvet painting of a pack of poker playing, cigar smoking, bulldogs hanging in his office.

A smirk hovered on her lips, while her gaze traveled up the tall Texan. Maybe she'd gotten this all wrong. Maybe *he* was out of *her* league…

Having put things into a clearer perspective, Kerri felt better and turned her attention to her father who'd started to speak.

"…yes, my daughters are beautiful and headstrong. Like their mother."

"And smart like their father. I'm sure it was quick thinking that kept them safe," her mother added, slipping an arm around her father's waist.

All thoughts of the troubling cowboy left Kerri's head as the events of that horrible day came rushing back again.

Absently rubbing her shoulder, she was thankful the only scar she suffered was of the skin and not of the heart. Her chest tightened, restricting her breathing. Jordan had come so close to dying. So close. No one in the room, not even her sister had any idea it had been a mere millimeter that had separated life from death last Sunday. Just a hair higher and the big chunk of plate glass would've sheared…would've killed her sister.

God. She couldn't get that moment out of her head.

"Maybe it's a sign you should leave California and move back here to Texas like we did, Kerri," her father said, his grin a little too mischievous for her peace of mind. "There's plenty of room at our house now that renovations are almost completed."

Her parents had repurchased the house they'd sold when they moved to California eleven years ago. She'd been fifteen, nearly sixteen, and Jordan had been almost seventeen when their father had gotten a promotion and moved his family to the west coast.

The place she now called home.

"No, dad. I love it out there, especially since Jordan and I opened Comets two years ago." Kerri swallowed. She still couldn't believe it was gone. All gone. The invisible vise gripping her heart hadn't eased since the explosion. The loss of their restaurant ran deep. Cooking was her life.

After graduating from the New York School of Culinary Arts, she'd been lucky to honeymoon and train a few weeks in Paris before landing a good job, along with her former husband, in one of California's premiere restaurants.

Life had been good...until she'd caught Lance cheating with a coworker. That's when her outlook on the world had changed. Her confidence in her feminine-side had changed. She'd changed. No longer seeing the world as a perfect soufflé, she left her job, and husband, and opened Comets with her recently widowed sister.

The restaurant had been a lifeline for them both. Her heart squeezed tighter. Jordan no longer needed that lifeline. She had Cole. But nothing had changed for Kerri. Other than life had gotten worse. What would she do now?

"What about Texas? Don't you like it here?" Alex McCall asked, coming to stand in the middle of the room.

All eyes turned to Kerri. Her face heated. Again.

"I-I love it here, too. Texas will always be special to me." She smiled. Texas did hold a lot of found memories...and a few embarrassing ones.

Like teenage Connor and Cole dripping naked at the water hole when she and Jordan had stolen their clothes. Her first glimpse of a full-monty male had been...*holy wow*.

"I guess it's true what they say. *You can take the girl out of Texas, but you can't take Texas out of the girl.*" Mrs. McCall grinned.

"I guess not." Kerri laughed, wishing they'd change the subject. They should be celebrating her sister's engagement, not wasting time on her. She lifted her chin. "So, are we going to toast the happy couple, or not?"

"You heard the little lady. Gather around." Mr. McCall handed out glasses of Dom Perignon. Her favorite. "Here's to Jordan and Cole. A marriage eleven years in the making."

A chuckle went around the room before everyone took a sip of the chilled liquid.

"I'd say it's more like twenty-eight years in the making," Connor corrected. "Cole was smitten with her right from the beginning."

Kerri found herself standing across from the cowboy and allowed her gaze to take a closer look, from under her lashes, of course.

Being five years older, Connor always appeared tall, and although she'd grown up and was by no means small at five-foot-eight-inches, she still felt that way next to him. He towered a good eight inches over her now, and his trim muscular frame had gotten broader and more defined, deliciously stretching his red flannel shirt to its limits.

The bugger.

Finally allowing her gaze to move to his face, Kerri's insides fluttered. *Holy cow*. He cut his hair.

The brown locks the sun loved to kiss with highlights in the summer and that would curl out from under his Stetson showed little evidence of either. She couldn't recall ever seeing him wear it this short.

Following his hairline, the cut came in front of his ears in a slight sideburn, giving him a more respectable look. Her fluttering increased. The style gave depth to his dancing brown eyes and emphasized a strong jaw sporting a five-o'clock shadow, which did nothing to disguise the sexy dimples that showed up with his ever-present lop-sided grin.

This new Connor didn't look like a reckless cowboy at all. In fact, she had no trouble picturing him in Armani. *Darn it*. Her gaze dropped to his left boot again. Forget the *Marlboro Man*, he could easily model for GQ.

Her Unbridled Cowboy

She took a long sip of the bubbly in order to calm her jumpy nerves. Why in the world did this uncouth, sexy, reckless...*cowboy* have this effect on her? She didn't like it at all. Not one little bit. Kerri always prided herself in being in control but *gosh-darnit*, whenever he was near that trait seemed to disappear along with her common sense.

Looking up, she caught her father and Mr. McCall studying her strangely before their gazes darted away.

Ah, great. Her throat dried. She knew that look. They were in match-making mode. Again. And this time she was the target along with...

Her gaze drifted back to Connor. Those darn dimples appeared, backing up the amused glint in his eyes. He'd definitely witnessed their fathers' exchange. Of course he was laughing. *Her and him?* Yeah, biggest mismatch of the century. The sexy, cowboy chick-magnet and the girl who was more at ease turning on an oven than men.

Well, whatever the case, she didn't want any part. No way. And figured Connor didn't either. As far as she knew, he'd been engaged three times, and after his last fiancée was arrested for murdering a husband Connor had no knowledge of, Kerri heard he'd given up on marriage for good.

She certainly had.

Just thinking about her former marriage and all her inadequacies brought a sour taste to her mouth. No thanks. She'd weathered enough self-depreciation storms, thank you very much.

A sudden need to escape the room became overpowering. She'd had enough. Needed a breather.

Placing her glass down on the nearest table, Kerri walked as nonchalantly as possible to the door and slipped quietly from the room.

Connor McCall's gut twisted tighter than a rope around a bull's horns as he watched the beautiful west coast chef close the door. Their fathers' were up to something. He'd seen their exchange.

Well, it wasn't going to work. Hell no. He'd already told them. Not on this cowboy. Just because they'd managed to help bring Jordan and Cole together, they now thought they were experts. But what the *experts* failed to realize was his brother and fiancée had a thing for one another since their childhood.

Not at all the case with him and Kerri.

Sure she'd been a cute, smart, sweet kid who'd grown up...okay, amazing. Still, despite her beauty, Connor had absolutely no interest in obtaining a wife. *Been there. Tried it. Failed miserably. Three times.* And each time it had ended in devastation instead of marriage. *Cripes.* After the last one, he had absolutely no wish to go for number four.

She sure grew into a looker though, Connor thought with a twitch of a smile tugging his lips. Long, straight, chocolate brown hair fell past her shoulders while a smattering of bangs covering her forehead and temple. All of this framed a heart-shaped face that held the most beautiful eyes he'd ever seen. Eyes that mesmerized and could stop a bull at twenty paces.

God, they were gorgeous. Big and brown with lashes so thick he doubted she used makeup. They drew him in, held fast, tugging deep in his gut. And her lips? Damn. His insides twisted tight. He'd never forget when he'd briefly touched them with his own a few months back.

Full and soft, she'd tasted like strawberries. Sweet, succulent strawberries. That was the good part. The dangerous part was the current that'd shot straight to his toes. His toes! *What the hell?* The unexpected sensation caused him to abruptly end the kiss, apologize and run away as fast as his cowboy boots would take him.

He was no idiot. That woman could hogtie and filet him in under eight seconds if he was so inclined. Which he was not. Hell no. Not him. Never again.

"How's Kerri really doing?" Mr. Masters asked Jordan, bringing Connor's attention back to the conversation.

"She puts on a good front, but she's hurting," his future sister-in-law replied. "That restaurant was her life."

Connor set his teeth and resisted the urge to rub at the unknown ache residing in his chest.

"I know. Poor baby." Mrs. Masters sighed. "I wish we could do something."

Jordan nodded. "Yeah, me too, but I don't think she's going to be here long."

"Really?" Her father's frown matched his dad's. "We'd hoped she'd at least stay until after the holidays."

Connor had to admit, half of him wished that, too. The stupid half.

Scratching the bridge of his nose, he fought a grin. Cripes. Some days he really was hopeless.

Until this year, he'd always regarded Kerri as an adorable little sister. One he enjoyed teasing and laughingly tolerated.

Boy, had that changed drastically in April. When he'd come out of the stables with Cole and saw the tall, elegant, curvy woman standing in the driveway next to Jordan, his stomach had gripped tight and his damn heart nearly beat a hole clean through his chest.

And now, jeez, now his foolish body suffered the same abuse every time the gorgeous cook was in his presence. Every. Single. Time. Connor didn't like it. Not one damn bit.

Kerri was a city girl.

A *city* girl.

That in itself was a big enough strike against her, and a hell-of-a-good reason for him to keep his distance. So then, why did he still entertain thoughts of doing exactly the opposite?

All three of his former fiancées were city girls, and he'd long vowed never to get involved with another one again. Ever.

Even though Kerri was born in Harland County and spent the first fifteen years of her life in Texas, her time in California had been almost as long and recent. Her west coast residency easily cancelled any redeeming qualities from the former. Take her jeans, for instance. As a youngster, she'd lived in them. As an adult? He had yet to see her in a pair. Did she even own any? Doubtful. All she seemed to wear were fancy dress pants and heels.

Yes. The cook was a regular city girl now, and despite her beauty and its affect on him, Connor wasn't going to fall for his father's well-meaning, if not totally misplaced, matchmaking attempt. And he could tell by the apprehension that sometimes flittered through her gaze that she wasn't interested or was afraid of him for some reason, which was unfounded…and unimportant. It didn't matter *what* put that look in her eyes. He wasn't interested.

Swallowing down what was left of his champagne, Connor walked over to the table and set his glass next to Kerri's. They needed to talk. And fast. Telling his body and his brain that the pretty cook was just his little sister and nothing more, Connor felt better able to seek her out and head this matchmaking off at the pass.

Her Unbridled Cowboy

As soon as the door closed, Hannah Masters turned to her husband Nate and smiled. "Well now, that was interesting."

"It certainly was, sweetheart," he said with a grin.

"I'll say," Alex McCall agreed, slapping Nate's back.

Cole groaned. "You're not seriously going to try to set Connor up with Kerri, are you?"

Hannah watched as Alex turned to his son, brows raised. "We didn't do so bad with the two of you, did we?"

"No," Jordan replied, hugging Cole close. "But we've always had a thing for each other."

"True," Cole agreed.

He looked at her daughter with so much affection it warmed Hannah's heart.

"There's the difference." Jordan smiled before kissing Cole's cheek.

Alex and his wife Leeann exchanged a look before Hannah turned to her daughter and frowned. "You don't think Connor and Kerri are attracted to each other?"

"Yes, I do," Jordan replied. "But that's not the point."

Nate stepped close and dropped an arm around Hannah's shoulders. "Then what is?" her husband asked, looking at their daughter.

Jordan exhaled slowly as she shook her head. "Kerri has a lot on her plate right now. The last thing she needs is to be badgered. Besides, I really don't see her staying past this weekend."

Not exactly what any of them wanted to hear, but Hannah had to admit, she'd gotten the same impression from her youngest the second she'd stepped foot on the ranch. They hadn't been here more than five minutes when her eyes took on a look of flight.

"We aren't going to badger," Alex insisted. "Just give a slight push when needed."

"Yes. That's all," Leeann agreed.

But Hannah knew her husband was going to do whatever it took to make sure their daughter stuck around long enough to realize something amazing happened to her whenever Connor was close. She lit up. Came alive, didn't walk around just existing. And even better was the fact the same thing happened to Connor when Kerri was near.

Those two belonged together, or at the very least, could help each other to head in the right direction. And none of that could take place if Kerri left so soon.

She wasn't about to let that happen. No. She just needed a little help.

Hannah smiled at Jordan and Cole. "Oh, I think we can guarantee Kerri will stick around."

"You do?" Her oldest blinked at her and frowned. "How?"

Hannah exchanged a quick look with a smiling Leeann then glanced back at her daughter and grinned. "Well now, that's where the two of you come in."

Chapter Two

It took all of five seconds for the jumbling inside Kerri to subside. She poured herself a glass of ice water and leaned against the counter feeling much better, much calmer. Looking around the McCall's quiet kitchen, she understood why. This room represented nothing but fun and happy times. A smile tugged at her lips as she recalled the many lessons their cook, Emma, had given to a young and eager protégé when Kerri had only lived ten minutes away.

Twirling an ice cube around in her mouth, she pondered her homeless situation. For the past three nights, she'd been staying with Jordan at their friend Megan's house, and now with her sister's engagement—which Kerri was sure wouldn't be a long one—her job situation was suddenly unknown.

Just happy to be alive, she hadn't given any real thought about her unemployment. She naturally assumed she and her sister would rebuild, but now that Jordan would soon become Mrs. Cole McCall, her sister wasn't going to leave Texas. And she wouldn't expect her to.

But, where does that leave me?

"I figured I'd find you in here, kiddo," Connor said.

Caught off guard, her heart kicked against her ribs like a bucking bronco while a startled gasp ripped up her throat, propelling the ice cube from her mouth.

Of course, it couldn't just land on the floor and make the situation only mildly embarrassing. No. The sucker had to shoot straight across the room and hit the handsome cowboy square in the chest.

"Well now, darlin', for a city girl, you've got a heck of an aim," he drawled.

The sexy dimples made an appearance, and her face heated beyond scalding.

"Oh, Connor, I...I'm so sorry." Hand to her throat, she blinked. Feeling like an idiot, which lately wasn't much of a stretch, Kerri grabbed a napkin from the counter, rushed forward and dabbed at the wet spot centered over his heart.

It leapt.

No, she had to be wrong. Why would his heart leap? It wouldn't leap. Okay, now she was imagining things, just like she was imagining the thundering taking place under her palm.

Thundering. How silly. *Her* heart was thundering. Not Connor's. She was such an idiot. No way would this virile cowboy's heart leap or thunder because of her. No way. Her rapid pulse was starving her brain for oxygen. That's what it was. She was hallucinating. Because if not, that would mean...that would mean he...and it couldn't mean...

He cleared his throat. "Ah, darlin', a little water isn't gonna hurt me none."

The deep timber of his voice had no business being breathless as well. Darn him. Now he wasn't the only one who was wet.

Big and broad and hard, the man smelled clean and fresh, like he'd just stepped out of the shower. And he was hot. Really hot. Steam rising hot. Heat emanated from his body, engulfing her in a searing, sensual embrace.

Suddenly tingling from head to toe, she realized just how close they stood. Very close. Too close. She had to fight the urge—really, *really* fight the urge—to lean forward and nuzzle his neck.

A tremor started at her toes, and before it could reach midway, she stumbled backward, and, *oh, look at that*, stepped on what was left of the ice cube.

As she slipped and headed for the floor, two strong hands clamped around her arms and held her upright. *Dang, he's quick and strong.*

Nervous laughter bubbled up her throat. "Found the ice cube," she said, staring at that neck still beckoning for a nuzzle.

His hold slackened as a chuckle rumbled through him. She chanced a quick peek at his face, and her pulse hiccupped. *Holy smokes.* The man was just too darn gorgeous. Amusement tugged at his tempting lip while laughter sparkled from his warm, brown eyes. Forget nuzzling his neck, she wanted to taste him.

"God, you're adorable."

And just like that, her urge to taste disappeared.

Adorable?

Lovely. First he called her *kiddo*, now *adorable*. Just what every woman wanted to hear while in the arms of such a potent male. Her knees stopped mid-buckle and pulse instantly leveled out. There was nothing like a good wake-up call. He just gave her one, loud and clear. She found him hot, like a red-blooded male, and he found her adorable, like a box of puppies. Yeah, they were definitely not on the same page. Worlds apart…cities apart.

She dredged up a smile and even managed a laugh. "Thanks for stopping my fall, and yep, that's me." Pushing free, she bent and swiped the remains' of the frozen culprit from the floor with the napkin still clutched in her hand, then tossed them in the trash. "Kerri the adorable. Adorable Kerri."

Cute, but not sexy enough to hold a man's attention. What was she thinking?

Silently, and for something to do, she walked to the sink and refilled her discarded glass with cold water. One sip turned into three and…

"Kerri, I wanted to talk to you about a few things."

She nearly dropped it in the sink when Connor spoke again. From right flippin' behind her. His sexy southern drawl sent goosebumps down her spine, and she stayed put not wanting him to see another flush heating her face. She really wasn't in the mood to hear that *adorable* remark again.

"What is it?"

"Well, for one thing, could you maybe turn around so I don't have to talk to your backside?" he asked, smile evident in his tone. "Not that it isn't a nice, well rounded backside, but right now, I'd prefer to talk to your face."

Taking a deep breath, Kerri willed her body not to respond to his nearness or his unexpected compliment about her backside, as she placed the glass in the sink then turned around. "What is it, Connor?"

"Ah, that's much better."

His dimple glared and her insides took to fluttering.

"You sure are beautiful when you're annoyed."

Oh, swell. She moved up from adorable to beautiful to annoyed. "Did you want to say something or not?"

"Relax, darlin'." He held his hands up, palms out. "There's no need to get your thong in a bunch."

She blushed. Again. *Darn it.* "My *thong* is of no concern to you, Connor," she replied with a little more attitude than she'd intended. "Now, if you don't mind, I am going back to the celebration."

Lightening fast, his hand snaked out and wrapped around her arm. "I'm sorry, Kerri. I didn't mean to offend you. Why do you have to take things so literally, and why can't the two of us have a civilized conversation?"

Why indeed.

She swallowed a snort. "I don't know, Connor. Maybe because when I look at you I don't see civilized."

Shoot. That was mean. What was her problem? And what was her body's problem? Darn thing tingled where his hand lay.

"Oh, now you've got me curious." He raised an eyebrow and leaned closer. "Just what *do* you see when you look at me?"

A naked 18 year old Connor coming out of the swimming hole. The thought caused the image to instantly materialize.

Shoot.

Her throat and face heated at the memory of him proud and built and smiling, stalking toward her and her sister wearing nothing but his dang dimples. Given his increased size and muscles, she knew that delicious view could only have improved. Big time.

Shaking her head, she focused on that dimple and swallowed hard before stammering, "A-a cowboy."

His chin lifted. "A cowboy."

She nodded. He didn't need to know about the naked part.

"So, you're saying you see a tobacco chewing, cattle roping hick that could only get a woman if he hog ties her and throws her over his shoulder? Someone who couldn't survive in a big city, only out in the open range?"

Whoa. Where in the world is all this coming from?

"I wouldn't exactly put it like that." Kerri tugged free and raised a brow at him. "Now who's got their boxers in a bunch?"

"Then what would you change from that statement?" He stared down at her, amusement and curiosity evident in his eyes.

The bugger. His teasing demeanor was contagious. A smile hovered over her lips. "You don't chew tobacco."

He laughed, full and boisterous, just like the man. A few seconds later, his gaze grew wicked. "And what makes you think I wear boxers? Maybe I wear briefs."

Images of Connor modeling underwear tried to form in her mind. She refused to let them. *Heck no.* He was dangerous enough as a cowboy.

"You're right, Connor. What was I thinking?" She smacked her palm off of her temple. "You, in conservative boxers?" With a smirk, she ran her gaze up and down his relaxed form, and of course, blushed, but still, she continued, "No, you are definitely a brief man. Fire engine red ones, I think."

Dimples appeared while devilment flashed through his eyes. "Well, now, why don't we check?" He reached for his jeans, undid his belt buckle and chuckled.

She stopped smiling. *Dear Lord.* Surely he wouldn't...

"What's wrong, darlin'? Don't you want to see if you're right?"

Heck yeah!

No... No, *you don't*, her mind insisted.

Her gaze met his amused expression, and she swallowed hard. Darn, sexy cowboy. She was no longer a young teenager. It was time to stand up to his teasing.

"No," she replied, relieved her voice sounded calmer than she felt. "That won't be necessary, Connor. Some things are better left to the imagination."

To her immense relief—okay, and a tiny shard of disappointment—he did up his buckle, and soon her heartbeats began to decelerate. The cowboy was just lucky she wasn't Jordan or his jeans would be hugging his ankles right now.

No. That wasn't true. Her sister had never been interested in Connor. It was Cole's bluffs Jordan had always called.

"All right then. I'll just let you think about it then. But," he said on a sigh, looking crestfallen. "I was hoping if I showed you mine, you'd show me yours."

She snorted. *Dang, incorrigible man.* She couldn't believe they were standing in the McCall's kitchen discussing underwear.

"At least tell me if you *are* wearing a thong. Come on. Throw a guy a bone." His eyes danced with the devil as he sent her an indolent grin.

Yes, dang incorrigible. And his teasing was *very* contagious. "Well, I could have on a pair of grandma underwear," she said, twirling a strand of hair around her finger. "Or maybe I am wearing a nice lacey black thong with red satin running through it." Her chin lifted. "I guess you'll never know...*cowboy*."

Silently applauding her attempt at bravado, she smiled. *There. Put that in your Stetson and wear it.* Happy at standing her ground, she stared, mouth drying as his smile disappeared and heat suddenly replaced the amusement in his eyes.

Shoot. No. No. This wasn't good.

With his simmering gaze now trained on her lips, Kerri's euphoria diminished along with her ability to breath or talk, and if she didn't move quick, she wouldn't be standing either.

Whether it was divine intervention or dumb luck, he

chose that moment to turn around and walk to the center island.

His potent gaze no longer visible, her brain began to function, and she drew in a long, overdue breath.

Idiot.

Exhaling, she watched him place his hands on the counter, and noticed his shoulders rising and falling while he took a few deep breaths.

Not even trying to contemplate what any of that meant, she found her voice and said hurriedly, "I think we should be getting back to the others now."

"Wait, Kerri." He twisted to face her. "Before we go back, we need to clear the air."

Clear the air? How? The air was charged and thick with…with…*something*. How could they clear the air if she couldn't name it?

"All right," she replied anyway, when what she really wanted to do was bolt from the darn room.

Still, she waited, heart beating out of control as he leaned his large frame against the island and folded his arms across his broad chest.

"I think we both know our parents are up to something, if those looks they were exchanging in there are anything to go by," he stated slowly.

So, he *had* seen them, too. *Dang.* She'd hoped she'd been wrong.

"Yes, they most definitely are." Her heart continued to beat out of control while she wondered just what he was getting at.

"Well, no offense to you, darlin', but I'm not looking to get hitched. And I got the impression you were done for a while, too. Am I right?"

His question brought instant relief.

"Oh, absolutely! I'm so glad you said that, Connor."

Her Unbridled Cowboy

She smiled as she tucked a strand of hair behind her ear, and her mind cleared. "I have to admit, you had me worried for a moment."

He smirked. "I take it being married to me would be like a death sentence?"

"Oh no. It's nothing like that." Horrified he'd come to that conclusion, she stepped forward and lightly touched his arm. His very warm, muscular, manly arm. It was…nice. "I'm sure you'd make a fine husband. You really would. It's just that with all my other worries, the last thing I need right now is a man," she stated, and was shocked to see understanding enter his warm gaze.

"I'm sorry about your home and your restaurant, Kerri. It can't be easy for you."

The sincerity in his voice brought a stinging to her eyes.

"I'm okay." She withdrew her hand and repeated her worn out line, "I'm just glad to be alive."

A single tear wet her face. Darn it. Why him? She'd had this conversation with both her parents and his, and yet, somehow, this cowboy with the smart aleck remarks and laughing brown eyes, got past her walls.

Shoot. She should've bolted while she'd had the chance.

Kerri peeked up at him thru her blurry vision and bit her lips to keep them from trembling.

A groan ripped from his *nuzzle-me* throat, and before she knew it, he pulled her against his warm, rock hard body, and held tight. Nice and tight.

"It'll be all right, darlin'," he said, running a hand gently through her hair.

Feeling safe and engulfed, Kerri momentarily gave into her emotions and hugged him closer, her tears soaking his chest. She missed this part of marriage.

Although they had hugged a lot, it never felt like this with Lance. Probably because he was only two inches taller than her, she reasoned.

"I'm glad you were with your sister that morning," Connor said gently, his chin resting on her head.

Sometimes, the incorrigible cowboy could be so darn sweet. She squeezed him a little harder while another round of tears fell.

Okay, Kerri, that's enough now, she admonished herself a minute later. *You don't need him or anyone else. You've been doing just fine by yourself for the past two years.*

Getting her emotions back under control, Kerri pulled out of Connor's embrace and looked up at him. "I'm sorry. I don't know what came over me, but...thank you."

"No problem, kiddo. Anytime," he replied with his trademark grin dimpling his cheeks. "So, as far as our matchmaking parents, are we good?"

Grabbing another napkin from the counter, she nodded then wiped her face. "Yes. Absolutely. You don't want a wife, and I don't want a husband. So we're real good. Besides, I'm hoping to fly back to L.A. this weekend."

"Perfect." His smile broadened. "That won't leave them much time to do anything."

She returned his smile. "Nope."

Whatever their parents had planned, it wasn't going to work. They were wasting their time.

"And even if Jordan needs me to stick around and help plan the wedding, you and I both know that's going to be quick."

"True." Connor chuckled. "Knowing my brother, he'll want it to take place by Christmas. Heck, probably by the end of *this* month."

By the end of November?

Oh, she liked that idea. A lot.

"That works for me." Sending him a smile and a nod, she turned around and walked to the door.

For the first time since stepping foot back on Wild Creek Ranch, Kerri felt good. Calm. Relaxed. If everything went right, she'd be back home this weekend. Worse case, she'd have to stick around a few weeks until her sister was married, and as soon as Christmas was over, Kerri would be back on a plane bound for California. Safe. Yes, safely away from matchmaking parents, and more importantly, the red-blooded, teasing cowboy following her back into the gathering room with his sexy darn dimples and fire engine red briefs.

"Valentine's Day?" Kerri couldn't help but bellow in total disbelief.

Her sister made the crazy announcement of the projected date of her wedding soon after Kerri and Connor returned from the kitchen. Maybe she'd heard wrong.

Please, God. Let that be it.

She couldn't possibly stick around for *three* months. *Crud. Not three months*. No. She'd never survive.

"Yes. February 14th. Why? Is there a problem?" Jordan asked as the others in the room stopped talking and waited for Kerri to answer.

Problem? No. Why would there be a problem?

Just because she'd be forced to stay in the same town—which would *not* be big enough—with the cowboy full of unbridled sex appeal? A sex appeal she was finding harder and harder to resist? Because her mind was a jumbled mess and not in clear working order, which made her close proximity to him a danger she couldn't afford? And, as it happened every time he was near, her body wanted her to chuck reason out to pasture and ride the cowboy 'til the cows came home?

See? *Those thoughts!* Kerri didn't have those kinds of thoughts. But she was on testosterone overload and didn't have a clue how to fight her body's need. And lately, she wasn't sure she wanted to.

That was it. *That* was the problem. Cripes. She'd never been easy. Ever. Yet, standing in the McCall's gathering room, all eyes upon her, she clearly saw the truth. She was undeniably attracted to Connor McCall.

Ah fudge!

That wouldn't do. No, it wouldn't. So, *heck ya!* She had a *problem*. Only about a million, and most of them centered around the cowboy whose trademark grin was nowhere to be found. Jeez, that earthquake shook her up more than she'd originally thought. Left her vulnerable. She was weak in both heart and mind. Why else would she find the cowboy so darned attractive?

Of course, none of that could be shared. At least, not with the entire room. Had she had this conversation in private, Kerri would be on her knees, pleading with her sister to up the date.

But, since the room was full of questioning gazes and frowns and matchmakers galore, she had to revise her response, and deal with a hefty dose of guilt. What was wrong with her? Goodness. What kind of sister was she? A few days ago, she'd nearly lost Jordan. Kerri's chest squeezed tight. She loved her sister, would do anything for her sister. She'd never felt more selfish. Poor Jordan and Cole had gone through so much. It was their time to be happy. She had no business giving them grief over their wedding date. None at all. If they wanted

Her Unbridled Cowboy

to wait for Valentine's Day, she'd do it. By God, she'd do it. Might be a blubbering fool by then, but she'd manage, darn it!

"Of course there's no problem," she rushed to say. "I-I'm just surprised you were both going to wait that long."

At least that much was true.

Jordan grasped Kerri's hands and smiled. "It's only three months away, and between the preparations for the engagement party and for the wedding, not to mention the holidays, it'll go by fast."

"True," Cole said, moving to stand behind her sister before slipping an arm around Jordan's waist. "But the main reason for the delay is Kade. We'd really like to wait so he can be one of my ushers."

The McCall's neighbor would be back from deployment with the National Guard in a few weeks. Between sports and rodeos, Connor and his best friend Kade, together with Cole and his buddy Kevin—Kade's cousin—had been inseparable in their youth. The Daltons and the McCalls. The four musketeers, or *caballeros* as she remembered the boys liked to call themselves.

Kerri nodded at the happy couple. "That's nice."

"We really want him to be a part of our wedding." Jordan glanced at Connor. "He'll be back in early February, right?"

"Yeah." The cowboy cleared his throat and stepped closer. "His unit is due in February 5th."

"That's what I thought," Cole said, and the whole room seemed to wear a matching grin.

Weird.

"It'll be so nice to have him back safe and sound in Harland County," Mrs. McCall exclaimed, her smile misting over. "I just hate it when he's deployed."

According to Kerri's parents, the McCalls had taken to watching over Mrs. Dalton's children, Jen and Kevin and their cousin Kade when Mrs. Dalton had passed almost ten years ago.

Mr. McCall ambled up behind his wife and squeezed both of her shoulders. "He'll be fine, and it's nice of Jordan and Cole to wait for his return."

"Wouldn't dream of letting Jordan make an honest man out of me without him." Cole smiled and let out an '*umph*' when his fiancée elbowed him in the ribs.

"And I wouldn't dream of having this wedding without Kerri as my maid-of-honor." Jordan turned to her and tipped her head. "What do you say?"

"Of course," she replied, hugging her sister tight. "Anything for you."

Jordan drew back and smiled. "Thank you."

It really did Kerri's heart good to see her sister happy, and not the *fake* happy she'd tried to pass off as real a few times the last two years. The sparkle in Jordan's eyes and flush to her cheeks were the real deal, and certainly enough to set Kerri's world right again.

At least, for the time being.

"What about you, bro?"

Cole's voice broke through her thoughts, and she focused on the younger McCall as he placed a hand on his brother's shoulder.

"Are you up to being my best man?"

Connor grinned wide enough to bare his twin dimples. "Absolutely."

Best man…

The urge to clap trembled through Kerri's hands when realization dawned. She resisted. Barely. *I get to stand up with Connor. Oh, goodie.*

Not.

As she took a sip of the bubbly that was once again shoved in her hands, she swallowed it down along with her apprehension.

So much for going back to California this year.

Still, she had to admit, Valentine's Day was an appropriate date for the happy couple. Theirs was a match made in heaven and brought together by fate. What better day for the two of them to pledge their love for each other than on the most romantic day of the year?

Truly perfect.

Now, if Kerri could just figure out how to avoid Connor for the next three months...

Her gaze shifted across the room to *Mr. Tall Broad and Manly* laughing it up at something his father had said.

Dang cowboy always seemed to turn her orderly world upside down. And she liked orderly. Liked it just fine. Thrived on it, even.

Lifting her glass to her lips, Kerri studied his broad back and narrow waist, and smirked as visions of Connor in red briefs filled her head.

Boxers indeed.

Chapter Three

It wasn't going to work.

Whatever the matchmakers had planned, whatever they thought they were going to accomplish by delaying Kerri's departure…it wasn't going to work. Connor's mind reeled several days later as he strode through the cattle barn on his way to see his foreman. Keeping the poor girl in Texas when she clearly wanted to run back to California was a mistake. A big mistake.

Who was he trying to kid?

It was damn brilliant. A few weeks of bumping into the beautiful, vulnerable chef he could handle, but a few *months*? Hell no. He was in trouble. Big trouble. *Standing in the middle of cow-patty pasture with no rocks in sight* trouble.

In other words, deep shit.

He was a strong man. Both physically and mentally, but he wasn't stupid. He was under no illusions that he could resist the strange pull Kerri had over him. But resist he would, until he was down for the count, hogtied and drew in his very last breath of freewill.

The visual his thoughts conjured soured Connor's gut and twisted his lips. Cripes. He was tired of being a pansy ass. No more. The last three females he let into his heart took advantage of his good nature, wrapped him around their little finger, siphoned out what they could get, then tossed him in a dumpster with last week's garbage.

He was nobody's garbage. And although he didn't lump Kerri in the *bitch* category, she *was* in the city girl category, and he wasn't taking any chances with his heart. Never again. Ever. Hell, his heart was off the market. Permanently.

Were the next three months going to be tough? *Hell yeah*. Was he going to give into his attraction to the west coast beauty? *Hell no*. Was he just whistling Dixie?

God, I hope not.

The sound of amicable voices broke through his thoughts.

"I know. And the rice pudding? She had some kind of spice in there. I ain't never tasted nothing quite like it before," Hank Thompson, his fifty-four year old ranch foreman stated to the four supervisors standing around drinking coffee. "My wife asked for the recipe."

Connor groaned inwardly and slowed his approach. No need to ask who or what they were all talking about. Only one cook could put a smile on a man like the one consuming Hank's weathered face.

Kerri.

He'd specifically avoided the stable knowing there was a small chance the dang visiting temptress could waltz in and disrupt his fledgling resolve.

Now he wondered why he even bothered.

"It was right nice of her to think of us and send food over on Thanksgiving when she had her own dinner to worry about at the main house," Joe, one of the supervisors stated.

She did?

Connor shouldn't be surprised. Kerri always did think of others. He remembered when she was young and Emma would offer her a cookie, she'd always ask if her sister or Cole and Connor could have one, too. Always.

He shook his head. Why in the world did that memory stick with him after all this time? And why the hell did it matter?

It didn't.

He straightened his shoulders and walked up to his men. Men who didn't necessarily need him to carry out their jobs. He'd handpicked and trained every one of them, and was replete in the knowledge his ranch could run without him. Exactly what he'd intended. This afforded him the leeway to participate in a rodeo or head to an auction without the added worry chores would go undone because he wasn't around.

That didn't mean he didn't work. No. Just the opposite. He worked his ass off. Could do any job on the ranch and did. Often working side-by-side with the men and women he employed. He believed in leading by example.

A quality he'd learned from his grandfather William McCall. The man, who for eighty some years, had given blood, sweat and tears to Wild Creek. Tall and lean, right up until his heart had failed him five years ago, Will had been Connor's mentor, and every day he strived to live up to his granddaddy's name.

Old Will had led the ranch through the depression, dust storms, droughts, wars and even a flood, and still he never once failed his family or crew. He ran the ranch with a fair and just hand, and now Connor carried on the legacy.

His father and Cole had a head and passion for business. But Wild Creek was in Connor's blood. He loved the open range, the livestock, hills, creeks, horses, cattle drives, auctions and the day-to-day trials that came with running the ranch. If he had to wear a suit and work in an office, he'd shrivel up and die.

Hell no. He tugged absently at his collar. No monkey suit or walls to pen him in. He needed the sky above him and God's green earth beneath his boots to keep him sane. Surviving long term in a city was beyond his ability. And not an option.

"There he is now," Hank said, bringing Connor's mind back around to the men. "The lucky stiff who got to partake in a full meal cooked by the little lady last Thursday."

The guys murmured things like, *"yeah"* and "good for you." while some even slapped his back.

"Imagine tasting her vittles every day," Pete, another of his men chimed in. "Lucky bastard."

Now, Connor knew they meant food. He *knew* it, but that didn't stop every muscle, bone and organ in his body to stiffen at once. Cripes. He was a six-foot-four-inch piece of hard wood. Throbbing wood.

The men stared at him, waiting. For a reply, or did they know he was about to blow? And it wasn't a gasket. Damn it. One beat passed then another. He blew out a breath before clearing his throat.

"True," he said, scratching the bridge of his nose. "Kerri's a great cook."

The men nodded again.

"You should hang on to that one," Joe told him.

"Yeah," Art agreed. "Don't let her get away."

Ah, hell. Not them too. The last thing he needed was his foreman and supervisors to jump on his parents' bandwagon.

"She's just a friend." He pushed passed them to get to the coffee pot in the make-shift break area set up in an empty stall. It was too early for this crap.

They were supposed to have their morning meeting where they discussed the day's itinerary. He may not want to work in an office, but he did see the merit of structure and teamwork. He had a foreman who watched over the supervisors who watched over the workers in their crews. Their morning meetings were to discuss issues and jobs, not sweet, sexy, unsettling cooks, dammit. So why the hell were they discussing Kerri?

"Bull," Hank said. "The two of you don't look at each other like friends."

"Yeah." Cal nodded. "You should do something about it."

Connor poured a cup and shook his head. "No."

Did his parents put them up to this?

"Why not?" Hank asked.

Ah hell, they'd all followed him into the break room.

"She sure is pretty."

Connor didn't need Joe pointing it out. Cripes. He knew Kerri was pretty. Hell, she was gorgeous. But that didn't matter.

"I wouldn't mind giving it a go, if she'd have me."

"Pete, even your mama won't have you," Art replied, and they all laughed, including Connor.

"Seriously, though." Hank cupped his shoulder and stared up at him. "We've all seen the way you look at her, and she looks at you."

He snorted into his coffee. There goes his foreman with that *looking* thing again. The past year during her visits, Kerri had looked at him, alright…but her gaze had been mostly friendly, sometimes guarded, sometimes apprehensive, and admittedly, that tore at his gut. It hadn't sat right with him. Made his chest ache.

He would never hurt her. Ever. Why would she be afraid of him? Was it because of her ex-husband? So help him, if that man had laid a hand on her, he'd hunt him down and…

And what?

Connor expelled another breath. Nothing. It wasn't his concern. *She* wasn't his concern.

And *he* wasn't their concern. "You're all imagining things. We're just friends," he said again. "Besides, Kerri's going back to L.A. after the wedding."

"Then make her stay."

"Yeah." Joe nodded. "Change her mind."

"Use the old McCall charm," Cal suggested. "Your brother did, and he hooked one of the west coast beauties."

Connor sipped his coffee and shook his head. "Forget it. It's not the same. Those two always had a thing for each other."

Hank folded his arms across his chest and studied him. "So, you're saying you don't have a thing for Kerri?"

"Are you dead?" Pete stared at him like he'd gone bonkers. "How can you not find her attractive?"

"Of course I do. And, no, I'm not dead. Just realistic," Connor replied. "Why start something that's going to end with her leaving in a few months?"

Cal frowned at him. "Who said it had to be something permanent?"

"Yeah." Pete's head bobbed like a troubled mare. "Why can't the two of you have a little fun?"

Fun? Kerri?

Connor's insides tightened again. He'd like to have a few months of fun with the beauty. Hell…he'd like that a lot. But, could they? His pulse galloped a few beats then slowed to a realistic trot. No. "She's not the type."

"How do you know? Ask her," Pete insisted.

Ask Kerri to have an affair? That was the stupidest suggestion he'd ever heard. Connor laughed in their faces. "You're all crazy."

Off their rockers. Off their meds. Maybe they needed meds.

Why the hell were they having this conversation, anyway? It was getting out of hand. He slammed his empty cup down on the wooden counter by the coffee pot. "Look, guys, I know you mean well, but drop it. She's a city girl, and you all know I'm allergic to them. End of story."

He turned around, and son-of-a-bitch if that city girl wasn't standing in the doorway turning a deep shade of red.

Ah hell. How much of the conversation had she heard?

"Kerri." He stumbled forward, and the guys turned to the doorway, guilt coloring their own faces.

"Hi," she said weakly, then thrust a paper at Hank. "I'm sorry to interrupt. I just wanted to give you the recipe I promised your wife."

The foreman took it and smiled. "Thank you. It's right nice of you to share. Meg says not a lot of chef's give up their secrets."

"Nothing secret there." She smiled as she backed out of the room. "Well, I've got to go. Have a nice day."

Connor sent his men an agitated look as he rushed out after the well-dressed woman, surprised to find her fancy shoes had carried her halfway through the barn already.

"Kerri, wait," he called, but she ignored him. "Dammit, Kerri." Rushing forward, he grabbed her elbow and pulled her to a stop. "Would you wait?"

"I—I can't. I'm supposed to meet Jordan and our mothers to go shopping."

Shopping? Jeez. He tried to keep the scowl off his face. She couldn't let a whole week go by without the need to hit the stores? What was it with city girls? Okay, that wasn't fair. Most girls, no matter where they lived liked to shop. Especially the weekend after Thanksgiving. But still, she hadn't even been on Wild Creek five days. "I won't keep you from your fun. I just wanted to apologize."

"For what?"

"How much of that conversation did you hear?"

Her gaze dropped to his boot while the flush reclaimed her cheeks. "Not much."

"Liar."

Her head snapped up, and heaven help him, righteous indignation sparkled in her eyes, turning them whiskey brown.

She stole his breath.

"For your information"—she yanked free—"this *city girl* isn't shopping for fun. It's out of necessity. Nothing I'm wearing is my own." She waved a hand at herself. "I had to borrow this coat from your mother, and the pants, shoes and top are Jordan's. Even the bra is hers. And you know what?"

Dear God, she unzipped the coat and held it open like a flasher. His heart rocked in his chest, and without looking down the walkway to see if his men were watching, Connor grabbed her arm and tugged her into the nearest stall. "What are you doing?"

"These clothes aren't me." She ignored his question. "It's too revealing. Jordan's just more comfortable with herself," Kerri said.

But he'd only half heard, thanks to the blood rushing through his ears at the sight of black lace peeking out from under a body hugging navy top. Damn she was mouthwatering. And he knew exactly how mouthwatering her body was. He'd seen her in a blue bikini last spring, a blessed scrap of blue material that hardly covered her luscious curves. Curves he'd fantasized about all year.

And now his mouth wasn't the only thing watering.

"So, you don't have to worry about being allergic to this *city girl*," she continued, zipping up her coat, covering the delectable view.

Damn. He liked that view.

"And I already told you, I'm not here to land a husband," she added.

That last part was delivered on a long sigh. He studied her slumped shoulders and downcast gaze.

"I know that," he said when he found his voice. "And I'm not sure what you heard, but I'm sorry. Seems my men have jumped on the matchmaking wagon."

Her gaze shifted to him before her eyes closed, and she shook her head and groaned. "I'm sorry, Connor. I didn't mean to disrupt your life like this. It's bad enough mine is disrupted." Her eyes opened and they locked gazes. "I've no idea what has gotten into everyone."

"My guess is they want to see us happy."

She nodded. "Yeah, but, we can be happy being single." Her spine straightened and chin lifted. "We *are* happy being single. Why don't they see that? Why do they have to make everything so hard?"

He shrugged. She was the one making things hard. Cripes. Unable to get the image of lace-covered cleavage out of his head, he was back to being that block of wood again.

"I mean, it's silly, really." A small smile tugged her full, luscious lips.

"What's silly?"

"You and me." She snickered.

Oh, now he was curious. "What exactly is so funny about you and me?" He frowned down at her. "You think I'm too much of a hick and couldn't attract a girl like you?"

"What? N-no." Her head shook vigorously, knocking a lock of hair in her face. "Just the opposite. Why would they think you'd be interested in me?"

Was she was being coy, fishing for compliments or actually that clueless as to her sex appeal? Either way, he decided to play along.

"Well now, darlin'," he said, lifting his hand to brush the strand of hair behind her ear. "That isn't much of a stretch."

Her eyes grew round. "It's n-not?"

"Nope." He shook his head, skimming his finger along her cheekbone to her lower lip.

Darn woman was soft. Real soft.

She sucked in a breath and backed up until she hit the stall wall. Hard. With his finger still stroking her face, he drew closer. Which was stupid. He should've let her go and walked away. Ran away.

But he couldn't. He couldn't break her wide-eyed gaze. That apprehension was back, and darn it all, he couldn't go...*wouldn't* go until she looked at him differently.

"Kerri." He bent slightly at the knee to make eye contact. "You know I would never hurt you, right?"

She blinked. "I—yes, of course."

"Then, darlin', why do you look at me like you're afraid."

"I-it's nothing like that. In fact...it's not you...it's me."

He dropped his hand and squeezed a fist as disgust soured his mood. *God, how he hated those words.* They've ruined his life on more than one occasion.

"I've heard that before and it's a bunch of bull." He turned around, ready to do that walking thing when slim fingers wrapped around his arm and stopped him.

"Connor, wait. I'm not sure why you're mad, but what I said was true. It's not you. I'm the one with the problem," she said again, coming to stand in front of him, gaze open and honest. "I'm the one who's a mess right now. Since my divorce, I'm…I've been…"

Her voice trailed off as if she struggled for words to convey her meaning.

His darn heart squeezed and compassion flowed through him. *Sucker*.

His hand lifted to touch the softness of her cheek again. "It's all right, darlin'. Relationships can get messy." That was an understatement, and he was living proof. "I don't know what happened between you and your ex, but whatever he did to put that look in your eyes, I hate him for it."

Her fingers tightened around his arm, and her eyes filled with tears.

Ah hell. What did I do to cause that?

"Thank you," she said.

Kerri closed her eyes for a moment, and he wasn't sure if he should crush her close, stay put or run like hell. A moment later, they reopened and were clear.

Thank God.

A genuine smile softened her expression. "Sometimes, you say the nicest things. I swear, Connor, you're the sweetest man I know."

Normally, he would've taken offense. He'd much rather be the sexiest, or strongest, or greatest, but when she lifted on tiptoe and kissed his cheek, he decided being sweet had its perks. It got her to put her lips on his body, and that was all right by him. More than all right.

Besides, it removed the apprehensive look from her eyes. Now, she stared at him through a warm gaze, rapidly turning hot as he stroked her lower lip.

When the hell had he given his hand permission to touch her again? *Jesus*. He had zero control when she was near. Zero.

"I think you'll find I can be full of sugar, darlin'." Might have come out corny, but it made her smile widen, and that was worth it.

Whatever kind of pull she had on him, increased, tugging him closer in a stranglehold he couldn't break. And maybe he didn't want to break it. Even though they both had issues, he was beginning to wonder if maybe they shouldn't give into this attraction and try to heal each other.

She wet her lips, and he swore he felt the soft swipe of her tongue as if she'd touched his flesh. He inhaled and let her berry scent wrap around him tight, filling his senses to the brim. Yeah, fighting something this strong was foolish. It was much smarter to give in.

Cupping her face, he continued to stare into her eyes, giving her plenty of opportunity to run. She didn't. Hot damn, he had to admit, he was a bit surprised. His pulse pounded heavily through his veins, to the point of vibrating.

Wait, not him, but her phone pressed against his ribs.

She blinked and stepped back, color rising in her cheeks as she fished the cell out of her coat pocket.

"Hello?" She inhaled again, keeping her gaze on anything but him. "Hi, Jordan. Yeah, I'm ready. I'm in the cattle barn giving Hank a recipe for his wife." She sent Connor a quick glance and an equally quick nod before twisting on her heel and heading for the door, phone still stuck to her ear.

As he leaned against the corner of the stall, Connor watched the sexy, vulnerable, sweet west coaster disappear, and battled a few emotions of his own. Disappointment and relief claimed top billing.

He drew in a breath and released it on a slow exhale. *That was close. Too close.*

A smile tugged his mouth. Saved by the bell. He'd have to thank his future sister-in-law later; she'd inadvertently halted the runaway steed. Thank God.

Connor didn't know what it was about the cook, but he needed to up his resistance. She was a city girl. No matter how sweet and innocent and vulnerable she may seem, he needed to remember that.

A trying feat when she was near. Much clearer when she was not.

Drawing in another breath, he straightened from the wall. Now, if he could just do something about his sudden hankering for strawberries.

The first week went by fast as Kerri obtained a new wardrobe, moved into the old homestead with her parents, and helped Jordan and Emma plan and prepare Cole and Jordan's Engagement/Christmas Party to be held that night at the McCall Ranch. In less than an hour.

She hoped she made enough food.

Since it was practically winter, the celebration would be indoors, although a few heaters were set up outside should the guests feel the need to wander onto the brightly lit patio.

White lights and red and white poinsettias decorated the large gathering room, and a huge Douglas Fir was ornamented then centered at the far wall.

One half of the room was set up for eating while the other half was sectioned for dancing. The band, having already put up their stage and checked their sound this afternoon, was due back in a half hour.

Her Unbridled Cowboy

The routine was becoming old hat, and Kerri discovered she enjoyed the challenge of preparing for parties and wondered if her sister felt the same.

Maybe catering and party planning was something they should check into, even though Jordan would be in Texas and Kerri would be in California. She ignored the pang in her gut and refused to think about her future away from her family. Catering still held possibilities. So did opening another restaurant. Or working as the top chef in one. But, right now, it didn't matter. What mattered was her sister's engagement party due to start in a little while.

The happy couple wanted to keep things informal, so a buffet table was set up along the wall opposite from the band, allowing enough room to use either side. Covered in red with green linen napkins, the tables each had a white poinsettia centerpiece. Festive yet simple.

Having promised her sister she'd take care of last minute details so Jordan could get ready, Kerri went back to the kitchen to put some finishing touches on the hors d'oeurves. Satisfied with the good variety of finger foods, she glanced at the desserts, and her mouth watered at some of the delicious concoctions Emma had made. A piece of the death-by-chocolate cake had her name on it. If there had been time, she'd sneak a piece now, but somehow time had gotten away from her, and she needed to finish getting ready herself.

The comfortable navy pants and lilac, short-sleeved sweater she wore was fine to cook in, but not formal enough for the party. Her party clothes were hanging up in her old room upstairs.

Her old room.

Weird. She now had two of them. One here, and one at the homestead. Although both comfortable, she was beyond relieved to be at the other house and away from any chance meetings with a certain virile cowboy.

Shirtless chance meetings.

Her stomach fluttered just thinking about the last time she'd unexpectedly bumped into the hunk. It had been right there by the sink. Just before she'd moved back to her parents' home. She'd rushed in one night to pull a recipe from the oven she'd been experimenting with, only to find the sexy distraction drinking a tall glass of water.

Shirtless. And bootless.

It was the beginning of December. Why the heck was he shirtless, and at eleven o'clock at night, she'd wondered, and made the mistake of asking.

He just smiled at her over his glass, dang lop-sided grin dimpling his cheek. She took in his bare feet, bare chest, and the slight rumple to his short hair. That's when it had dawned on her. Her heart had slammed into her ribs and face had heated. Dang man obviously just had sex and had probably escorted his 'date' to the door right before Kerri had come down.

Oh how she'd wished the floor would've opened up and swallowed her whole. Which was stupid. They were adults. So he'd had sex. Big deal.

But it had been a big deal, and she didn't know why. She also didn't know where to look, so she'd grabbed the oven mitts and pulled out her pot pie.

"That smells great, darlin'," he'd said, moving to stand behind her. "I worked up an appetite. I'm starved. Can I have some?"

She smirked as she rearranged a tray. She bet he'd worked one up. Probably went all out, got very physical and sweaty when he had sex. And that's when she'd nodded, putting a stop to that dangerous train of thought.

Her Unbridled Cowboy

His lips had twitched, no doubt reading her mind and laughing at her. She'd handed him a knife and told him to help himself before she'd exited the room like it was on fire.

The next day, she'd moved out and hadn't spoken to him since except for a quick answering wave during her visit with Emma and Jordan on Thursday, but they hadn't talked.

Tonight, though, tonight she wouldn't be able to avoid him. But that was okay. No doubt the opposite sex would surround him, and he'd be too busy to spare her more than a passing hello. And so would she, between seeing her old friends Jen and Kevin again, and dealing with the food. Although Emma made her promise to forget the prep once the party started, Kerri vowed to be too busy to pay attention to the red-blooded cowboy and his dang lop-sided grin.

That man's mere presence engulfed, fogged, made her do the stupidest things, and since she hadn't been firing on all receptors since the earthquake, she couldn't afford the fogging.

"Did they set up the Sterno?" Emma asked, breezing in from the pantry. The cook grabbed the hot pads off of the counter and opened the oven to check on her salmon.

Kerri nodded. "Yes, it's all set up and waiting for us to start."

She washed her hands and began to fill up the appetizer trays. Jordan had insisted on a simple menu, so Kerri opted to make Bacon Wrapped Shrimp, Cheesy Barbecue Popcorn and her own favorite, Strawberry Flowers stuffed with a cream cheese mixture of powdered sugar, almond extract and grated chocolate.

Her mouth watered at the thought. She loved anything strawberry, the chocolate was a bonus.

For the main course, Emma and Kerri had split up the duty by each cooking three different dishes. Perfect week to move into her parents' house. This gave each cook their own kitchen and space to create. Emma made Barbecue Beef Short Ribs, Chicken and Drop Dumplings and Salmon Croquettes, while Kerri made Beef and Beer Oven Stew, Catfish Provencale and Jordan's favorite—Three Cheese Lasagna.

Earlier today, she'd borrowed her dad's SUV and carted her food over to store in the McCall's industrial refrigerator. With a double oven and warming racks, it had been super easy to heat the food at the ranch.

Kerri just wanted everything to go well. Jordan and Cole deserved this celebration.

She started to fill the last appetizer tray when Emma shooed her away like an annoying fly.

"Leave that to me. You go upstairs and change for the party. Guests have already started to arrive. You should be out there mingling," the cook insisted. "There are plenty of servers here to help me. Now, go and enjoy yourself."

"All right." Kerri laughed. "But I'll take this last tray out and then go up and change." With a smirk, she scurried from the kitchen before Emma could take the tray from her.

Several people were already there, including her sister, wearing a beautiful, backless red dress. Her fiancé, equally dapper in black dress pants and white silk shirt, couldn't take his eye off Jordan. They were in the middle of the room, talking to the new arrivals. A few women and Connor, she noted with that dang flutter in her chest, were laughing off to the side.

Dressed in black jeans and a red western shirt tucked in and with the sleeves rolled up, he looked more handsome than a man had the right. He wore his black Stetson, and as she passed with the tray, she warned herself not to think about red briefs.

Intending to walk by, she was stopped when a hand with five ruby red polished nails wrapped around her arm.

"Well, if it isn't little Kerri? Oh, that looks delicious." The blonde standing next to Connor cooed as she took a bacon wrap off of the tray and plopped it into her ruby red mouth.

Little Kerri?

Chapter Four

Little? Kerri towered over the woman.

"Sure does," Connor responded easily as he winked at Kerri.

She nearly dropped the dish. *Holy smokes.* Was he seriously flirting with her?

"Careful there, darlin'." Quick as lightning, he steadied the tray enough for her to gain control again.

"Thanks, *darlin'*," she replied.

Connor chuckled, and Kerri rolled her eyes as she continued to the buffet table. She'd recognized the girl. Ashley. The same blonde Connor was supposed to take to a party when Kerri had been eleven.

That hadn't gone well.

Laughter tickled her throat. It really hadn't been her fault. Ashley made the mistake of making fun of her pigtails and braces while waiting for Connor. Kerri wasted no time in recruiting the two golden retrievers the McCalls had at the time, and as the couple stepped outside, she'd turned off the hose and let the wet dogs loose on Ashley—and her new white dress. She smiled at the memory. Wasn't white after that.

Reaching the table, Kerri placed the tray down and wondered briefly if Bullet was around. He'd help her bring Ashley down a peg or two if need be. Grinning, she turned around to see her sister summoning from across the room.

Keeping the grin on her face, she walked to the happy couple and gave her sister a hug. "You look stunning, Jordan. What's up?"

"Thank you, hun. I just wanted to make sure you weren't over doing it." Her sister eyed her with concern. "I want you to enjoy yourself at this party, not work."

"That was the last tray. Honest. Emma said the same thing and threw me out of the kitchen." Kerri laughed along with Jordan and Cole.

"It had better be," her soon-to-be brother-in-law warned, killer smile on his handsome face. He pulled her into a hug. "You are supposed to have fun like all the other guests."

She returned his embrace. "I will, I promise. I'm going upstairs to change now, then I'll be back for the fun."

"We're going to hold you to that." Cole drew back and smiled down at her before he pushed her toward the foyer. "Oh, and Kerri?"

She turned around and waited. His dark eyes were sparkling. Bugger was up to something. "Yes, Cole?"

"Lose the apron."

Crud. She glanced down at the forgotten garment. Great, she'd talked to Ashley and Connor in her apron. Oh well. No sense in getting flustered. She was training herself to not make a big deal out of little things.

"What? Not festive enough?" she asked. She held the apron away from her and matched Cole's grin before turning to head upstairs to get ready.

The party was in full swing by the time Kerri descended the stairs in a dark green, velvet dress that didn't cling, only brushed her curves to stop just below fingertip length. She felt sexier in a dress that hinted rather than revealed.

It wasn't always the case. Heck no. Just this past summer, she'd lazed around Wild Creek with Jordan in her bikini. Her very small bikini. So used to blending in on the west coast, she hadn't really thought much of her lack of clothes at the time. And she refused to think about it now.

What's done was done.

Keeping her new motto uppermost in her mind, she entered the room with a smile on her face. She actually felt good. Surprising what a new dress and new sexy, black, strappy heels could do for a girl's ego.

With no time to waste on her hair, she'd twisted and clasped it at the top of her head, while her bangs and a few pieces fell loose about her face. Going for simple sophistication, she probably only got the simple part right. Oh well. Didn't matter. *Insert motto here.* Her smile widened.

What's done was done.

The more Kerri said it in her head, the more she liked the motto. Between that and what her sister always told her—*don't sweat the little stuff*—her outlook on life had improved the past week. And Jordan was right. Time to stop *sweating*.

So she was homeless and unemployed. So what. She was also loved by her family and friends. That's what counted.

"Oh, hun, you look lovely," her mom said, pulling her in for a quick hug.

"Thanks." She stepped back, eyeing her mother's pretty navy and silver dress. "So do you."

Her dad kissed her cheek. "Well, I don't look lovely, but I am loving your appetizers," he said, before popping another bacon wrap in his mouth.

The McCalls readily agreed, lifting their plates.

She smiled. "Good. I'm glad. But save room for the entrees, too." Her gaze shifted back to her dad. "Emma's made the salmon you love."

"Not to worry." He winked, slapping his gut. "I've got room. But first, we're going to mingle."

People were already lining up at the buffet table, so she began to make her way there when a familiar voice called out from behind.

"Kerri, you look stunning as always."

She'd wondered when she was going to bump into their handsome neighbor.

"Hello, Kevi—" She turned to greet him and burst out laughing. Cole's best friend wore a headband that dangled a piece of mistletoe above his dark head.

The blue-eyed, black haired cowboy smiled down at her. "What?" he asked innocently.

What indeed. Kerri grinned. "Leave it to you, Kevin Dalton, to come up with a way not to miss out on the free kissing."

"That's because it's the only way he's going to get any," Connor teased, approaching from the side.

With her pulse suddenly leaping in her chest, she turned to watch the gorgeous cowboy lumber closer.

"You're just upset you didn't think of it first," she said before she could curb her tongue.

He laughed, dimple glaring, brown eyes twinkling. "True."

Breath hitched in her throat, and she wondered for the umpteenth time why she had such a reaction to the teasing hunk.

And was there a way to make it stop.

"Actually, he doesn't need it," Kevin informed. "Girls have been cornering him under the mistletoe his parents hung over there." He pointed to a sprig hanging near the window seat in the far corner of the room.

She looked at the corner, then back to Connor.

He shrugged. "What can I say? When you got it, you got it." A self-satisfied smile tugged his lips as he rubbed his knuckles in a back and forth motion across his chest.

Smug bugger.

"Well, be that as it may, I am the one standing here under the mistletoe so, unless you're going to kiss me Connor, I think it's time for Kerri to do her duty." Kevin smiled and added a wink.

Normally, she'd make an excuse and run for the exit. But not tonight. Not now. Not with the smug cowboy looking on. No way would she give Connor a reason to call her chicken.

Kerri was only too happy to oblige. "Don't mind if I do, Kevin." She grinned as she pushed Connor out of the way and stood in front of the blue-eyed dreamboat.

About to put her arms around his neck, she only got as far as his broad shoulders when Kevin reached down and lifted her right up off the floor.

"Oh," she gasped, and that's when he kissed her, a pleasant kiss, lingering a few moments before placing her gently back down.

"Mmm…Strawberries," Kevin murmured as he licked his lips and grinned. "You tasted like strawberries. Remind me to corner you again later."

She laughed, ignoring the fact her face heated and Connor hadn't stopped staring. Make that glaring.

"And you really know how to sweep a girl off of her feet."

Smiling, she nodded at the grinning Kevin and surly Connor as she left the two heartthrobs to join her sister at the buffet.

Wow. So that's what it felt like to do the teasing for a change…

"That was interesting." Her sister smiled.

Ah, swell. Who else had noticed? Her parents? Probably. *Insert motto here.* Knowing better than to play dumb, Kerri just shrugged as they loaded their plates with food.

"Are you sure it's wise to anger the big puppy dog?" Jordan asked when they were the only two left at the buffet.

Kerri frowned. "What do you mean?"

"I mean, the whole time Kevin had his lips on you, Connor's big paws had clenched into fists."

They had? Kerri blinked, her heart racing for some unknown reason. His reaction meant something, but she wasn't sure what it meant. Or if she should even care.

Realizing her sister was waiting, watching her, she shrugged again. "It'll be all right. Connor won't do anything. He's *allergic* to me."

Jordan's head snapped up, eyes sparkling. "What? Did he say that to you?"

"Not directly," Kerri replied, wishing they could get off the subject. "I overheard him telling Hank and his supervisors he's allergic to city girls."

Jordan nodded. "Well, he hasn't had the best of luck with them."

"True. But it seems his men, along with our parents, think the two of us belong together."

Expecting her sister to laugh again, Kerri was surprised at Jordan's lack of response. Then her heart froze as she studied her silent sister. "Oh, no. Not you, too?"

Crud. If her sister ever, ever got it in her head to play matchmaker, Kerri was sunk. Nothing would stop Jordan. Nothing.

"Relax." Her sister's palm closed over her hand. "Yes, I think you'd be good together, but now isn't the time. And I told both parents not to push you."

So, everyone *had* been discussing them. *Great.* "Well, I hope they listen because Connor and I have already talked about this."

"You have?"

"Yes, and we both agreed we aren't interested."

"Then he lied, because, honey, the way that man looked at you, is *still* looking at you…he's most definitely interested."

The urge to turn and look at the cowboy shook through Kerri, but she remained strong. No. Didn't matter how or if he was looking at her, he was off limits.

"It's just curiosity," she said. "Because once he had me, he wouldn't…" her voice trailed off. *Yikes.* She'd almost revealed her deepest fear.

"Once he'd had you what? Kerri. Look at me." Jordan touched her hand again. "Surely you weren't going to say he wouldn't want you, because that is untrue. So *very* untrue. Why would you think that?"

"Because I'm not good…" She snapped her mouth shut. *Dear Lord.* She almost said it. She almost said 'in bed.' Her face heated anyway. This wasn't the time. She was not going to get into this here. Not now. Not in the middle of her sister's engagement party. *Good Lord.*

"Of course you're good. You're great."

Jordan squeezed her hand, and Kerri had never been more relieved her sister hadn't picked up her silent meaning.

"Thanks, but let's drop this, okay? Tonight isn't about me. It's about you and Cole, and I'd much rather celebrate than debate."

Jordan smiled. "Okay. Me, too. But if you ever do want to talk, you find me. Promise."

"I promise."

"Okay. Good. Now, let's eat. I'm starved."

"When aren't you?"

"Exactly."

Laughing, they joined Cole who was sitting with Kevin's sister Jen and her husband Brock.

They spent an enjoyable half hour eating and laughing about old times. Even the addition of Connor and Kevin hadn't spoiled her fun. Memories brought back their childhood camaraderie .

Kerri was still smiling when, a little later, Jordan and Cole left to take the stage, arms around each other.

"We'd like to thank everyone for their well wishes and for coming to help celebrate our engagement," Cole said, smiling adoringly at her sister.

"We'd also like to thank Kerri and Emma for the wonderful job they did with the food," Jordan gushed. "Everything was absolutely delicious, especially the lasagna."

Kerri smiled and thanked the murmuring crowd, unable to stop the impending blush. Her gaze met and locked with Connor's. Brown eyes darkened, and heaven help her…heated. Okay, now she had a problem. Her body tingled. What was up with that? And what happened to the childhood rapport that had enveloped them? It disappeared…like her breath. And she had the oddest urge to move to his side of the table to…

She gripped the bottom of her chair and stayed put. No. *Bad body*. He raised his glass and nodded. Kerri had no idea if his response was to her inner battle or Jordan's praise. Body humming with an unfamiliar current, she managed a small smile, and with extreme effort, pulled her gaze away. Her breathing returned to normal.

Holy smokes, that man was dangerous to her sanity. But, she had to admit, she kind of liked the off-kilter affect he brought to her world. Maybe it was something she should explore. Just a little. She'd certainly never encountered it before.

Maybe because she'd always been with safe men. Never with such a virile, dangerous one. *What am I thinking?* Like she'd even know what to do with one.

Kerri gave herself a mental shake and forced her attention back to the loving couple on stage.

"Finally, I'd like to thank my beautiful fiancée, Jordan." Cole turned her sister to face him and grasped both her hands. "Honey, thank you for being patient and not knocking my head off even though I deserved it more than once this past year."

The crowd laughed.

"And thank you for bringing me back to life," he continued. "I love you. You've made me a better man. A happy man. The luckiest damn man in the world."

Kerri watched with a tear in her eye as Jordan lovingly touched Cole's face. "I love you, too, sweetheart. And I brought you back for purely selfish reasons. I told you more than a decade ago, you were going to marry me, and I intend to make that happen."

"So do I, Jordan. So do I," Cole stated softly just before he gave his bride-to-be a thorough kiss in front of everyone.

When the clapping and whistling stopped, Cole announced he had a song he wanted to sing to Jordan. Kerri laughed at her wide-eyed, open-mouthed sister.

"Jordan speechless. That's not something you see very often," Connor commented, dropping down next to her.

Dang. Why'd he move? Her heart was now residing in her throat so all she could do was nod. But soon she forgot about her discomfort as Cole began to sing a beautiful Garth Brooks ballad about coming back to each other and finally closing a circle.

Kerri was never more thankful she didn't use mascara, because she'd certainly resemble a raccoon. What an incredibly, fitting song. She swallowed past her tight throat, then started when a warm hand covered her own. Her gaze swiveled to Connor's and she was surprised to note the same emotions stinging her eyes shined in his gaze. She squeezed back.

No reason they couldn't share a kindred, happy moment for their siblings. And their siblings *were* happy. It beamed from their faces. Jordan and Cole were so much in love nobody danced. Nobody moved. They sat in their seats and took delight in the happy couple's joy.

When the song ended, Jordan kissed Cole, then clung to him, and the two just stood there, holding each other tight. That's when the biggest pang of envy stabbed at Kerri, mutilating her with invisible slash after slash.

If it was in the cards for her to find a love even half as strong, she'd be eternally grateful.

Everyone stood and cheered, and when the clapping subsided, the happy couple stayed to sing a livelier tune that had everyone dancing. That's when Kerri escaped to the dessert table. She was too emotional, too vulnerable, too unsettled to be anywhere near Connor McCall.

Besides, it was time for death-by-chocolate and a few other goodies. Telling herself she'd start worrying about the tightness of her jeans tomorrow, Kerri loaded her plate.

She was just finishing her stuffed strawberry when Kevin approached.

"What do you say, pretty lady? Want to go a few turns around the floor?"

"I'd love to."

He was a good dancer, light and sure on his feet. His arms didn't feel as secure around her as Connor's, but he held her tight, and she enjoyed the dance. So much so, she agreed to another.

They were making their third pass around the floor when she suddenly realized Kevin no longer wore his headband.

"Where's your mistletoe?" she asked breathlessly as he spun her around.

"I took it off when I sat down to eat. Why? Did you want to kiss me again?" he teased before spinning her away from him only to twirl her back into his arms and dip her as the song ended.

She laughed, but had no time to answer as another cowboy asked her to dance. Recognizing him as one of the ranch supervisor's named Pete, she accepted. The friendly Texan was one of Connor's men, and she found his shyness rather cute.

Relaxing, Kerri was just starting to enjoy herself when she caught Connor staring at them. No dimples. No twinkle in his brown gaze. Great. Why was he so annoyed? Kerri watched as Ashley, in her red mini skirt, sauntered up to him, grabbed his hand and pulled him out onto the dance floor.

Even though the bugger no longer stared, her dance was ruined. She watched as Connor wrapped his arms around the blonde, and her body immediately remembered what it had felt like to be cocooned in warm strength.

Kerri stumbled and stepped on her partner's toes. Darn it. Mumbling an apology, she tried not to remember what it had felt like to be the one Connor had twirled and whirled with an easy confidence when they'd danced a few times at one of Kevin's barbeques, and again at her parents' fortieth anniversary party in September. She failed. He'd felt strong and sure and powerful. Heaven help her, she'd liked it. Very much. But back then, she'd been happy with the way her life was finally going in California. She'd chalked up the experience as nothing more than finding a good-looking dance partner who didn't have two left feet. But now? Now she didn't know. She was confused. Weak. Her life was upside down. She had nothing left of her old life. And he made her feel good. Strong. He made her feel...

Too much.

Heat spread throughout her body, and no doubt, brought color to her face. Bugger. Even from across the room, his potency affected her. Crud. She was becoming a Connor whore.

When the song eventually ended, Kerri thanked her partner then escaped into the kitchen, telling herself she wanted to check on Emma and see if her mentor needed any help.

After downing a glass of water, she placed it in the sink and turned around to find Emma leaning against the counter with her arms folded across her chest.

"What are you doing in here?"

Kerri's chin rose. "I just came for a glass of water and to see if you needed anything."

Emma's plump brow arched. "I'm fine, child. And I thought I made myself clear. You are to stay out there and enjoy yourself. I can handle things in here."

"All right, alright I'm going." Kerri smiled on her way out the door.

She hadn't walked two feet when an annoyed blonde stepped in front of her, blocking her path. "Well, well, if it isn't little Kerri trying to act all grown up."

"Well, well, if it isn't Ashley acting like a child,"

Kerri countered and made to walk around the witch.

"You think you're so great with your fancy clothes and your fancy food. Don't make the mistake of thinking you can land a man like Connor, because he likes his women more experienced and receptive."

"Yeah, well, you ought to know."

Shoot. Did she really just say that? Kerri's stomach clenched tight. Never in her adult life had she said something so catty. Or acted so immature.

"That's right." Ashley smiled. "I *do* know, *and* I know how to satisfy him. So don't go getting any ideas," the haughty blonde warned, poking Kerri with one of her red tipped fingers.

She felt her lips tug into a smirk. "You don't have to worry about me, honey. I like my men more civilized. He's all yours." She walked away leaving a dumbfounded Ashley to stare after her.

Connor sure could pick 'em. Surely he wasn't that desperate?

Kerri walked back into the party seething with anger. Not like her at all. She wasn't normally an angry person. Still, she didn't know whom she was angrier at; Ashley, who after all these years still made her feel inadequate despite everything Kerri had accomplished, or at herself for stooping to Ashley's level and acting like an immature twit.

Both. Definitely both.

Out of the corner of her eye, Kerri caught Jordan motioning to her from across the room. Heading to her sister, she worked on getting her emotions under control, trying desperately to apply her motto. It didn't work. By the time she reached her sister in the corner, she realized, too late, Jordan wasn't alone.

Perfect. Why should things go easy? Cole, Kevin

and Connor were also there. *Goodie.*

"What's wrong, Kerri?" Jordan touched her arm while Cole frowned.

"Yeah." Kevin nodded. "You look like you're ready to spit nails."

The image of Ashley's red-tipped fingers came to mind.

Connor stepped closer, concern deepening the creases by his eyes. "Are you okay? Did someone bother you?"

"Yeah." She snorted. "Your *girlfriend*. You need to keep a rein on your women, mister. I don't appreciate being blindsided by them."

The worry left Connor's face, and as his shoulders visibly relaxed, she noticed his gaze sparkled with suppressed amusement.

"What are you talking about, kiddo? You know I don't have a girlfriend."

"Tell that to Ashley," she replied. "You need to set her straight. She just cornered me and warned me off of you."

Jordan reeled back. "That bitch! You want to borrow my dog?"

Kerri laughed. Great minds. "No, that won't be necessary."

"Ooh…I smell a cat fight." Kevin smiled, rubbing his hands together.

Smiling, Kerri shook her head. "Sorry to disappoint you, but that won't be necessary either."

Jordan's gaze narrowed. "Why not? What did you do?"

She shrugged. "I told her she could have him."

Kevin's bark of laughter was drowned out by Cole's, and together, the two men chuckled in unison.

A dark emotion skittered through Connor's eyes, but before she could name it, a neutral expression fell into place.

"You're not my type either, darlin'," he said, settling down by the window, arms folded across his chest. "I don't care for city girls. Besides…" His gaze was lazy and lingering. "You're like my kid sister."

Kid sister. Right. Except her body didn't have sisterly responses to his. No. The handsome cowboy made her toes curl with his deep, sexy drawl, and her heart race should his brown eyes stare for too long. Yeah. *Not* sisterly.

"Then this should be interesting," Cole said, smile still hovering around his mouth.

Kerri watched Jordan turn to her fiancé and frown. "What?"

"The mistletoe, of course." Her future brother-in-law pointed to the branch hanging directly above Connor's head.

Kerri's gaze bounced from the sprig down to Connor, then to the others.

They were all staring right at her. *Oh, heck no.* They'd all lost their friggin' minds. "No way." She couldn't. She just couldn't. "You can't be serious?"

"Of course we are," Cole replied, looking from her to his brother. "You're the only single girl standing here."

"Then I'll go get another." She laughed and would have left if Connor had kept his pain-in-the-butt mouth shut.

"She's too chicken, little brother. Must be a city girl thing. No backbone."

Chapter Five

Chicken?
City girl?
No backbone?

Okay, so Connor was right about the city girl and the chicken part, but Kerri sure as heck had a backbone. A strong one. She'd been through a lot the past two years and learned plenty about herself. Resilient. Tough. Strong and resourceful. She didn't need this smirking cowboy saying any different.

Her mind reeled. This was a good opportunity to show him, and her, just what she was made of. She'd survived a cheating spouse, a divorce, the death of her brother-in-law, an earthquake, explosion, and the loss of her home and business. It was about time she tackled her sexual inadequacy.

And what better subject than the man whose lips had barely touched hers last April, hardly giving her a chance to respond before *he* ran away? She needed redemption. *Deserved* redemption. Would have her redemption, darn it!

Besides, it's only a kiss. Nothing more. And there were others there. They weren't alone. She could do this. She *would* do this.

Mind made up, Kerri set her shoulders and walked to him. *Baby steps*. She could do this, she told herself again.

Connor just sat there, lazy amusement lighting his expression as he looked up at her, daring her to run.

She didn't. This needed to be done, as much for him as for her. She'd probably be sorry later—would definitely be sorry later when her mind was clearer. But with her anger still lingering, she drew on the strong emotion and forced herself to use Connor as a guinea pig to her 'recovery.'

Talking her knees out of buckling, barely, she looked down at the smug cowboy and sighed. "I take it you're not going to stand?"

"No." His dimples appeared.

Bugger.

From the corner of her eye, Kerri could see her sister shake her head and heard her say, "Big mistake, cowboy," under her breath. Jordan knew the strength of Kerri's backbone.

At least someone did.

Ignoring everyone, Kerri sat right down on Connor's lap causing him to unfold his arms and stare at her through startled eyes.

Good.

Unexpected move number one.

Aware that his arms were at his sides, and he appeared to deliberately refrain from touching her, Kerri decided her goal would be to make him touch her. Once he did, she could break the kiss.

Now, if only she knew *how* to make him touch her. She had no friggin' clue. With the exception of Kevin, the last person she'd kissed didn't even like women. How in the world to get a virile man like Connor to break his control was way out of her repertoire of experience, and exactly the challenge she needed.

Heart hammering in her chest, palms sweating, she told herself this kiss wasn't about what Connor wanted her to do to him…it was about what *she* wanted to do to Connor.

Finding herself face to face with the potent man for the first time in her life, she felt less intimidated. He no longer towered over her. They were…equal.

She liked *equal*.

Clearly waiting for her next move, he sat still, spicy aftershave tickling her nose, and she was so close she could see every gold fleck dancing in his brown eyes as amusement sparked with heat. When the warmth of his exhale hit her face, a swarm of butterflies settled low in her belly. Massive ones. Huge. The size of mutants.

But she refused to lose her nerve. Raising her chin and ignoring the incessant beating of her heart, she removed his Stetson and handed it to Kevin.

"Here, hold this for Connor," she said without looking at the dreamboat cowboy. "He doesn't need it right now."

Right now. Right. Because she was going to…what?

Lordy, what am I doing? She had no idea, but refused to panic. *Go with your instincts.*

Okay. Right. Instincts.

Her hands itched to touch him, so she palmed his chest and slowly ran her fingers upward to his shoulders, loving the feel of sinew and muscles rippling beneath. Darn man was walking testosterone wrapped in hard strength.

Even though he still hadn't touched her, Connor's eyes had darkened, so she took that as a sign she was doing something right. *Please God, let me be doing this right.* Using her need as a guide, Kerri ran a finger up the bare flesh of his neck, over his jaw then down to his chin.

Holy smokes, the man was hot. Heat emanated off the cowboy like an L.A. sidewalk in mid July. And she could feel him, *all* of him. She was very aware of the bulge poking her cradled butt.

The strangest urge to squirm and rock into him shook through Kerri. So she did.

He stiffened. "Kerri." His sexy tone was too low for the others to hear, but she heard the warning.

Holy sugar, he made her want things...things she couldn't name.

Completely unable to breathe, she ignored that minor annoyance and brushed her finger over his lower lip, watching, enthralled as his pupils grew large as she very slowly moved her face closer.

But he still made no move to touch her.

Didn't matter. It was no longer about him. It was about her. She needed to taste him. Now.

Holding his chin in her hand, she lightly ran her tongue across the seal of his lips, and *Alleluia*, he growled.

Growled.

In an instant, she was crushed to him as one large hand spanned her shoulder blade and the other held the back of her head, breaking her clip like she'd broken his control.

If Kerri had been firing on all cylinders, she would've jumped to her feet and celebrated her victory. But her cylinders and brain cells, and even stark reality, shifted out of focus as he deepened the kiss.

Her whole body tingled and felt alive. She'd never been kissed like this before—like she was the most important thing in the universe. Worshipped. Needed. *Desired.* Connor's mouth was hungry and firm, his tongue touching hers, and judging by the increase in the bulge she was now sitting on, the cowboy wasn't as allergic to city girls as he claimed.

City girls...

Reason returned to her muddled brain with a thud. She abruptly ended the kiss and scrambled to her feet, thankful her boneless legs somehow supported her. One look at his desire-laden eyes, however, and she nearly sat back down for some more.

Thankfully, Kevin cleared his throat.

"Do you want this back now?" he asked, handing her Connor's hat.

Sanity returned and brought with it the reason she'd agreed to kiss Connor in the first place. To prove to him, and herself, she was desirable and…and…for now that was enough.

Baby steps.

Kerri placed the Stetson back on the unbridled cowboy's head, then with shaky fingers, took his chin in her hand, forcing herself to complete her redemption. "Never underestimate the back bone of a young city girl again, Connor McCall."

With a wink, she spun around, and ignored the snickering happy couple to her right.

Cripes, she'd forgotten they were even there. Oh well, it would certainly be an engagement party they'd remember.

She wasn't likely to forget. Ever. Her mouth still tingled, and she had no idea how her legs were working. Must be the new heels.

As Kerri walked past Kevin, the blue-eyed cowboy grumbled about her not kissing him like that. A smile tugged at her mouth because she knew she now wore the same smug expression she'd just succeeded in wiping from Connor's face.

It hadn't gotten any easier. Not one damn bit.

A whole week had passed since Kerri had settled onto his lap and proceeded to kiss the tar out of him. *What had been with that?* Connor wondered as he sat behind his desk at the ranch.

He was supposed to be entering this week's expenses into the computer, but he'd only gotten as far as booting up the laptop when thoughts of a brown-eyed, brown-haired cook with her sinfully delicious kiss entered his mind.

Again.

It was his fault. He shouldn't have let it happen. Sure, he knew instinctively she'd knock him for a loop. But had he known she'd taste so damn hot and willing and…and so hot, or feel so soft and curvy and…and hot, hell he never would've goaded her into that kiss.

Never.

But he had. And she had, and damn, he couldn't get the incredible feel of her supple curves, or the sweet, sensual taste of her out of his head. All week, she'd haunted him, fueling fantasy after fantasy he had no business having of his former childhood neighbor.

But he had.

And dammit, now he was hard. Again. He swiped the hat off his head and tossed it far across the room onto a leather couch before shoving a hand through his hair. Cripes. It was going to be a *long* two months.

As if agreeing, his computer dinged, breaking the silence of the room. He glanced at the screen and expelled a breath, easing some of his tension in the exhale.

It was Kade.

Connor immediately accepted the invitation to Skype. Thank God he'd been sidetracked by thoughts of Kerri or he might not have been online to get the unexpected call.

Kade's image filled the screen. His buddy was in his Army fatigues, hat and wrap-around-sunglasses in his hand, giving Connor an unobstructed view of his friend.

Her Unbridled Cowboy

He looked good. Tired and a little dusty, but otherwise, good.

"Hey, buddy," he said.

"Hi, Connor." His friend cracked a smile. "Got a new look, I see. Suits you."

Connor frowned at the smirking face on screen. "What new look?"

Kade pointed to his own hatless head. "If you're going for an *I want to pull my hair out look*, I'd say you've nailed it."

Glancing at his image in the small box at the top right corner of his monitor, Connor saw what had his friend grinning. Thanks to his raking fingers, the hair on top of his head stood at odd angles. He laughed and smoothed it down with a swipe of his palm.

"You're just jealous 'cause I *have* hair," he teased, motioning to his buddy's high-n-tight military cut. "This is about as short as I'll go. Couldn't handle that peach fuzz you've got growing on your head."

Kade hadn't had long hair since his teens. Once his best friend had joined the National Guard, the long-haired rebel had disappeared, and the short-haired, upstanding, responsible citizen had emerged.

"Believe me, you wouldn't want it longer than this during the summers here."

"It's not summer there now, though," he said dryly.

Kade nodded. "True. But it *is* regulation. Maybe you've heard of it? A guideline, parameter, rule. Oh wait, never mind. Connor McCall doesn't follow rules, he breaks them or makes his own."

"Damn straight," he agreed, and they both laughed.

God, it was good to hear. Tough enough to go on one deployment, but four? Connor appreciated Kade's sacrifice and that of all the troops, but how much more did his buddy have to give? Hell, how much more did his buddy have *left* to give?

Not much. Kade hadn't been the same since his first deployment and each time he came back there was a noticeable piece missing. Kade had always been good at hiding his feelings and emotions. Except from him. Connor could always tell by the slight stiffening of his friend's shoulders—like he was bracing himself, shoring up to weather a storm.

Ever since they were kids, when Kade's father had died, then his mom ran off with some rodeo clown and later also passed away, Kade had mastered the art of concealing. His buddy had been eleven when his Aunt Sarah had taken him in. It'd been the best thing that could've happened to him, and Kade would readily agree. Living on Shadow Rock, then eventually running the ranch had given his buddy a sense of purpose. A mission. And Kade Dalton was all about missions.

Still, he hoped to God his friend didn't re-enlist when his contract was up after this tour.

"We got your mom's holiday care package." Kade's deep tone broke through Connor's dark thoughts. "Please thank her for us. These cowboy boot stockings were a big hit," his friend informed, holding up a brown leather sample.

Connor smiled. "I'll tell her. She and Mrs. Masters have been working hard on them the past few weeks."

"Everyone especially loved the little package of dirt they had tucked into the tips," Kade said, holding up a tiny clear bag of Texas soil. "It'll be nice to have a *piece* of home with us for the holidays."

"That was exactly their thoughts, and exactly what they did," Connor told him. "They went to your ranch, and your cousin Jen and nephew Cody helped out. Every speck in those bags came from Shadow Rock."

Connor watched as emotions skittered across his buddy's normally passive face, before Kade cleared his throat and nodded.

"That was right nice of them. It's much appreciated."

"Glad you liked it. I'll be sure to tell them."

"You do that," Kade said, then cocked his head. "We still on for the trail ride?"

"Absolutely," Connor answered immediately.

Every time Kade returned from deployment, he and Connor saddled up and hit the trail hard, camping out for a few nights on Shadow Rock land. This allowed Kade some private time to adjust back to civilian life and let go of some of the darkness that always followed him home. Connor could always judge the severity of the deployments by how long his buddy wanted to ride.

"How many nights you figuring?" He watched his buddy closely.

Kade inhaled and ran a hand through his barely-there hair before releasing his exhale. "Five would be great, but with the wedding so close, let's make it three."

Jesus. Five? Connor knew something had happened this tour. And he knew when, too. Mid July. Their Skyping had become less frequent, and there'd been a haunted look behind Kade's eyes ever since.

"Okay, three it is," he said, deciding not to prod.

His buddy gave a curt nod as if in thanks, then cocked his head. "So…Cole and Jordan, huh?"

Connor leaned back and smiled. "Yeah. 'Bout damn time, too."

"You weren't kidding about the transformation. I barely recognized him last month when he asked me to be in the wedding."

"I know. It's great to have my little brother back." Connor had had enough of the dark times, the dark Cole. It was nice to finally have him excised.

"Jordan's doing," Kade correctly observed. "She always did bring out the best in that guy."

"Definitely."

"He's lucky. She's a good woman."

Kerri's smiling face flashed through Connor's mind. He quickly pushed it back. She'd occupied more than enough of his thoughts this past week. "She sure is."

"Okay." Kade's tone turned curious. "I'll bite. Who is she?"

"Who's who?"

"The woman you're trying not to think about."

How the hell did he know that? "You're imagining things."

"Right." Kade folded his arms across his chest and leaned back in his chair. "So just how pretty is Kerri?"

Dammit, Cole. "My brother needs to keep his mouth shut."

A rare smile lifted his friend's lips. "He just wants to see you happy and thinks Kerri's the right fit."

"Well, he's wrong. I don't do city girls."

"No, you *do* city girls, you just don't try to marry them, anymore."

"Yeah, well, I'm not going to do *this* city girl."

Jesus, why the hell was he talking to Kade about having sex with Kerri? Why were the words *Kerri* and *sex* even in the same damn sentence? He needed to have his head examined. What the hell was he thinking?

About having sex with Kerri.

"She's that pretty, huh?"

Pretty? God, Kerri was gorgeous. Breathtaking. With her soft, silky hair and doe-like eyes. Damn, he could get lost in their warmth and—

Kade's chuckle stopped him mid thought.

"Ah, man. You are so whipped. You might as well hang it up now."

"What the hell are you talking about? Whipped, my ass."

Kade's damn smile widened. "Oh, buddy, if you could've seen your face when I asked if Kerri was pretty. It got all *dreamy and serene*." His friend's high-pitched tone echoed between them.

"Bite me."

"Sorry, dude." Kade snorted. "You're not my type."

Connor flipped him the bird. Now Kade was laughing out right.

Shaking his head, he released a breath and his agitation disappeared. It was great to see his friend so relaxed. He appeared younger, the hardened soldier look disappearing as amusement took him.

Big difference from the tired and tight features that had pinched Kade's face at the beginning of the call. So what if it was at Connor's expense. Hell, they could make fun of him all night if it kept the spark of light in his buddy's gray eyes.

"Seriously, Connor, why not just ask Kerri out?"

He shook his head. "Why bother? She's only staying until the wedding. Hell, she'll probably be gone the day after."

"So?"

Connor frowned. "What do you mean, so?"

"Is there a law that says the two of you have to have a relationship?"

"No."

"Is there a law that says you can't have a fling?"

"Well, no, but this is little Kerri Masters, for God's

sake. I can't have a fling with her."

"Why not? She's got to be what? Twenty-six?"

"Seven."

"Connor, twenty-seven isn't young, and she's divorced, so she's not a virgin."

Connor's heart stopped and squeezed at the same time. He knew these things. Even thought the same several times, but to hear them spoken out loud knocked him hard.

"And from what Cole tells me, Kerri's attracted to you, too. Though, Lord knows' why. She used to be so sensible."

Connor flipped Kade the bird a second time, and his buddy's laughter filled the room.

"You're developing a twitch," Kade said after he sobered. "You should get that looked at."

"Yeah, I'll think about it if it still happens when you're home."

"It had better be taken care of, and same goes for the itch a certain city girl needs to scratch."

Right. If only.

Connor had no idea why his men and Kade thought Kerri would be willing to have a fling. *She's too sweet, and, well, uptight.* He could never see her agreeing to such a suggestion.

But he had to admit, it sure was interesting that several people seemed to think otherwise.

Kerri was more than happy to see the year end. It was time to put the bad things behind her and concentrate on the good times.

Why an image of Connor jumped, no...*lumbered* into her mind, she had no idea. He wasn't a good time. Okay, yes, yes he most certainly would be a good time. If she was willing. More importantly, if he was interested. But she wasn't and neither was he.

Then why did his gaze follow her as she mingled at the Dalton's New Year's Eve party? And why had she agreed to come?

Because Jordan had insisted they meet up there, that's why. She glanced around the sea of happy faces. Where in the world *was* her sister? She had yet to see Jordan.

Unfortunately, she couldn't miss Connor.

Mr. *Tall-Broad-and-Sexy* had stood out amongst the crowd when she'd first arrived. Jen had taken her coat, and he'd nodded from across the room. So far, they hadn't spoken. Which was fine with Kerri. The more she was around that man, the more her thought process suffered. It would be nice to socialize with most of her brain cells intact. Of course, thanks to his steady appraisal, she still suffered from *numb-tongue*.

Jeez, at times, his gaze appeared to be heated. Like now. Good Lord, she could barely breathe, and if he didn't stop, she was going to hyperventilate. How embarrassing would that be? She could see the news feed now: *Meek woman passes out when sexy cowboy gives her the eye.*

Wouldn't that be swell? Not.

She watched with a mixture of relief and disappointment as Kevin approached Connor and said something that had the cowboy smiling as the two men left the room.

Taking advantage of the break, she inhaled and exhaled until her pulse quieted down.

"Your steak-ka-bobs are a great hit, Kerri," Jen said, approaching with her three-year-old son, Cody, in her arms. "Thank you so much for making them."

She smiled at the little boy clinging shyly to his mother's neck. "It was my pleasure."

"Speaking of pleasure, I hear your Christmas dinner was a big hit, too. Kevin said Cole raved about your ham and turkey all week, and now Connor's backing him up."

Warmth spread through Kerri at a rapid rate and could feel it settling in her cheeks. "Having the McCalls at my parent's house gave me a chance to break in the new kitchen. It was great."

Needing to keep busy, she had been thrilled to handle all the holiday cooking and baking. She'd cooked and served both a pineapple-baked ham and a twenty-pound turkey with all the trimmings to the two families gathered in the adjoining dining room.

Connor had been his usual self. Gorgeous. Dressed in new jeans and a chocolate brown Henley shirt, he'd lumbered into the kitchen looking completely edible, shrinking the large space to the size of a shoe box with his mere presence.

"May I have the salt and pepper, darlin'?" He'd smiled his dang lop-sided grin.

A few minutes later, he came back and asked for the butter. By this time, Kerri couldn't help but wonder if her mother had deliberately forgotten things so they could send Connor in.

Probably.

She'd stopped what she was doing for the second time and handed him the butter, wanting him out of the kitchen so she could resume breathing again. It was easier to cook if she could concentrate, and it was easier to concentrate if she could breathe.

She should have known better.

Just as she picked up the knife and began chopping the last of the celery for the salad he waltzed back in and asked if she had any mistletoe. Kerri had nearly dropped the knife.

Sexy bugger–she'd thrown a dish towel at him and shooed him from the room.

If only she could do the same to the memory of that mistletoe kiss.

"I bet those two McCalls didn't leave any leftovers, either," Jen said, regaining Kerri's attention.

Laughing, she shook her head. "Not much."

Only a small platter of each had remained, and she'd sent it to Hank and his wife and the other ranch hands the next day, along with some pumpkin rolls.

"Well, look at the little cutie pie," Jordan said, appearing out of nowhere with Cole at her side. Her sister touched the little boy's head and smiled. "I didn't expect to see you still up."

Jen transferred her gaze to the little fair-haired boy in her arms. "Yeah, Cody had an extra nap today, so he'll probably be up longer than us."

Cole chuckled. "Takes after his Uncle Kevin."

"Holy crow. Don't wish that on me, Cole," Jen joked before excusing herself to get her son something to drink.

Jordan turned to Kerri and whistled. "You look great, hun. I told you the little black dress was killer." She pulled her into a hug. "Sorry we're late."

Kerri drew back, taking in Jordan's flushed face and satisfied expression. *Yeah, you look sorry all right.* Probably sorry they had to work in a quickie and couldn't take their time.

And Kerri immediately stopped thoughts of her sister's sex life before any images had a chance to materialize. "No problem," she lied.

She was beginning to think maybe she should've stayed home. Between Connor's incessant staring and…and…that was it. Connor's staring. The darn man befuddled her. He was a befuddler.

Cole stepped close and pulled her in for a hug. "Jordan's right, you look terrific."

"Thanks."

"You really do," Jordan said, taking her hand, looking nothing short of a bombshell in a slate gray number hugging her curves to perfection. "Now, let's find somewhere quieter. Cole and I want to talk to you."

Talk to me?

Kerri's heart hit her ribs. *About what? Shoot. See?* She should've stayed home. Was this going to be a good talk? A bad talk?

An *Oh-my-God-I-don't-want-to-hear-it* talk?

She didn't think she could handle that kind of talk right now. God, they better not be trying to fix her up with Connor. She couldn't handle that either.

Sneaking a peek at their faces yielded no clues, as she was tugged through the Dalton's crowded house. Why did they have to rock the boat tonight? Their secretive, yet anxious expressions brought no relief.

Dang it. She'd almost made it. The New Year started in less than an hour, and she'd almost made it through this year on her feet.

Please God, let Jordan tell me something good like she's pregnant. Yeah, that Kerri could handle. Actually, Kerri would *love* that. She'd make a great aunt. An awesome aunt. What she didn't love was the fact they'd pulled her into the Dalton's quiet kitchen and there, by the big butcher-block center island, stood Kevin and Connor having a beer.

Oh, goodie, more of *Mr. Hot* and his sidekick *Handsome*.

"Ah, we were wondering when the two of you would

show up," Kevin said to the couple with a grin.

"Yeah." Connor nodded. "We were about to take bets on if you'd make it this year or next."

Everyone laughed, including Kerri, except hers had nothing to do with amusement, and everything to do with her crappy luck.

Cole dropped an arm around Jordan's shoulders and tugged her sister close. "You're both just jealous because I had a reason to be late."

"Yes, a very good reason. Me."

Jordan released Kerri's arm then snuggled into her fiancé.

The smug cowboys shook their heads, but Kerri knew they felt the same pang of envy tightening her chest. How could they not? The couple was so much in love it made you long for the same.

"Seriously, though, Kerri," Jordan turned to her and took her hand once more. "We wanted to talk to you."

Okay. So, it couldn't be too bad if they were willing to talk to her in front of Kevin and Connor. *Right?*

"Why don't we sit down?"

Shoot. Scratch that. Had to be bad if they needed to sit down. Now her legs were starting to shake.

"Okay," she said and followed them to the table.

Kevin and Connor remained where they were, looking curious.

"Do you want us to leave?" Connor asked.

Yes, yes I do, Kerri longed to say, but kept her mouth shut. Besides, she couldn't talk. Apprehension had dried her dang throat.

"No, that won't be necessary," her sister replied.

Kerri wanted to punch her.

"We just wanted to get Kerri's opinion about possibly opening a restaurant, here in Harland County."

Chapter Six

A restaurant?

Kerri blinked at her sister, then glanced at Cole. The pair sat in complete silence, warmth and hope mirrored in their expressions.

"I—a restaurant?" was all she could manage. Never, had she thought opening a restaurant was what they'd wanted to talk about.

"Yes." Jordan nodded, reaching across the table to squeeze Kerri's clenched hands. "I know you were hoping we'd open Comets back up, and we still can, if you want to, but I'd also like to open one up here."

A restaurant in Texas. She let out a breath. "H-how? We haven't gotten our insurance money yet."

"Me," Cole said. "I'm giving you the money."

"*Loaning* the money," Jordan corrected, softening her words with a smile at her fiancé before turning back to face her. "Cole graciously agreed to spot us the money we need, and we can pay him back in installments."

Kerri's apprehension eased a little. "Wow, Cole, that's awfully nice of you."

Her soon-to-be brother-in-law smiled broadly. "I'm a nice guy."

The cowboys by the island snorted in tandem.

"And the biggest bullshitter, ever," Kevin mumbled.

"Yeah," Connor agreed. "He's so full of shit his eyes are brown."

Cole chuckled. "So are yours, bro."

Now Kerri and Jordan were laughing. If you asked her, Connor owned that distinction. He could sweet-talk a child into giving up their lollipop and make them think it was their idea. A trait, according to her parents, he'd inherited from his grandfather.

"You'd better not try to say the same about me and Kerri just because our eyes are brown." Jordan gave each man a pointed stare.

Kerri watched and waited, a little shaft of expectation upping her pulse.

Cole spoke first. "No, never." He pulled Jordan close to kiss her quick on the lips. "You two have brown eyes from all the chocolate you consume."

A murmur of agreement echoed around the room. No one would argue that point. She definitely loved her chocolate dessert, and everyone knew Jordan had a huge soft spot for chocolate chip cookies.

"Well, if there was a strawberry eye color, then Kerri would have it," Kevin said, leaning against the counter. "Because she sure tastes like them, doesn't she, Connor?"

Heat rushed into her face so fast, she was betting her body didn't have time to adjust and turned straight to crimson. Darn it. If ever the floor needed to open and swallow her, it was now. *Please.*

With everyone's gazes on her, Kerri suddenly became acutely aware of her *killer* black dress and how it dipped low enough in the front for the girls to make an appearance, and down the back to just above the bra. And it clung, too. She didn't do clingy. That's why she'd bought it. To force herself to step out of the norm, and surprisingly had no problem with it tonight…until now. Until a certain cowboy's gaze lingered on her chest, making her tips tingle and reach out for his touch. Darn them…and him.

Connor cleared his throat. "Chocolate and strawberry," the cowboy replied evenly, although when she chanced a peek, he looked ready to strangle someone. Namely Kevin.

"Not that it isn't interesting to hear you two handsome cowboys discussing what my little sister tastes like," Jordan said with a grin. "But I think we need to get back on track and talk about the restaurant."

Kerri could've kissed her sister right then and there. She tipped her chin instead. "We couldn't have the same menu." A Texas palate was very different than a Californian.

"I know," Jordan agreed, an excited smile spreading across her face. "It would be more steak, chili, barbeque and Mexican."

A slew of dishes flashed through Kerri's mind in an instant slideshow. She'd longed to tweak some age old recipes, and try her latest barbeque concoction. Not something she could do in California.

Now that she'd opened up that door, dang it, ideas and recipes flooded her mind. She glanced at her still smiling sister. Oh, she was good. So very, very good. The bugger.

"I thought we'd put in a pit where you could cook steaks over an open flame right in front of the customers."

It was official. Her sister was a bitch.

"You"—Kerri pointed to Jordan and narrowed her eyes—"you, my sister…you play dirty."

"No." Jordan sat back, smug expression, eyes sparkling. "I play smart. I play to win."

Cole leaned forward and grabbed Kerri's hand, his expression as light as his touch. "I'm living proof of that. What about you? Did she win?"

Win? God, she didn't know. Kerri wanted to reopen the restaurant, very much. The image of cooking for a crowd of eager people filled her with joy. Immense joy. Yes, she wanted to open a restaurant with her sister.

But not here.

"I—I don't know," she stammered. "That would mean I'd have to stay in Texas after the wedding."

"Yes." Jordan nodded, face devoid of any sparkle or mischief. Her sister really was serious. "I'd like your help with this, Kerri. To get it started, create a fixed menu, routine. The works. Once it takes off and has found its own momentum, if you still want to open up Comets, I promise I'll go to the coast and help you the same way."

She'd come to the coast...

Breathing instantly became easier. Kerri wasn't sentenced to stay in Texas. She could still go home. That actually made a difference. A big difference.

"Leave the permits and legalities to me. I'll take care of all that." Cole squeezed the hand he still held. "So, what do you say? Are you going to stick around to help my fiancée open up the best damn steak and rib joint in Texas?"

Oh, ribs. She'd forgotten about them. There was a recipe she'd started to fool with on her laptop...

"Yeah, Kerri," Kevin spoke up. "Come on. Lord knows Harland County could use one. Hell, every last one of those steak things you brought tonight are all gone."

"Really?" She turned to study him.

He smiled. "Really."

"But...I made over five dozen."

"I know, and they're all gone. Everyone loves your cooking. Take pity on us," Kevin pleaded, blue eyes rounded. "Harland County needs you."

She snickered. Another bull-shitter. Jeez, the man

should run for office. Between his incredible looks and smooth tongue, he'd be a shoe-in. No matter the position.

Her gaze shifted to the silent cowboy at his side. Connor just stared at her, jaw working, mouth shut, gaze neutral except for what could almost be mistaken for…fear? No, couldn't be. See, now her anxiety was making her see things again. Connor McCall scared? That was laughable.

So she did. She laughed, then turned to her sister and Cole. "Okay," she said, squeezing her future brother-in-law's hand, her gaze bouncing between the happy couple. "I'll help you open a restaurant here, then you can help me re-open Comets."

"Deal." Jordan stood and pulled Kerri to her feet so they could hug. "Thank you."

Kerri drew back and smiled at her grinning sister. "No, thank *you*."

"You're already going through recipes in your mind, aren't you?"

"Yes, you bitch."

They were still laughing when Cole shoved a glass of champagne into their hands. Where in the world that came from, she had no idea.

"I'd say a toast is in order." He lifted his glass, and Kevin and Connor drew near, holding up their beer as well. "To Harland County. Future home to the best steak and ribs Texas will ever see."

They toasted and drank, and Kerri refused to dwell on the fact she'd just committed herself to staying in Texas a good half a year—if not full year—longer than planned. *Crud. Nope, not thinking about that*…or the great smelling cowboy standing so close behind her she could feel his intoxicating heat.

"So, when do we start looking?" she asked, slowly

moving toward the door and away from Connor.

Jordan laughed. "In a hurry, are you?"

Kerri wasn't sure if her sister was referring to the restaurant or the cowboy. Either way, the answer was the same.

"Well, yeah." She smiled. No reason to lie. About the restaurant, anyway. They all knew her stay was temporary. Besides, she was actually starting to get excited.

"I'll have Stella find you a good realtor so you can start scouting locations this week," Cole said.

Cole's secretary was a shrewd one. The woman would find them a top-notch company, Kerri had no doubt. She and Jordan both nodded before they all rejoined the party.

An hour later, with only mere minutes left until the end of the year, all the party goers crowded into the Dalton's living room to watch the live action from Time Square on TV. The ball would soon drop. And the crowd was breaking into couples, no doubt getting ready to ring in the New Year with a kiss.

Kevin had two beauties under his arm. Jordan and Cole were cuddling in the corner. Jen and her husband Brock held a bright-eyed Cody, smiles on all their faces.

And Kerri had never felt so darn alone.

Intent on escaping to the porch, she made her way through the crowd, but couldn't get to the door thanks to the multitude of bodies blocking the path. So she did the next best thing—snuck into the Dalton's laundry room.

Another year alone.

She leaned up against a wall and sighed. But at least she wasn't being hurt or cheated on. The truth eased some of the ache from her chest.

Kerri started to feel a little better, until the door

opened and Connor walked in, sucking all the air from the darkened room. Oh, wait, that was her. She'd inhaled and pressed her back against the wall, hoping he wouldn't see her in the dark.

"Are you all right?" He stepped right to her.

Bugger. What does he have, night vision? Friggin' cat's eyes? Jeez. She'd forgotten he never needed a flashlight when they'd played flashlight tag. *Bugger.*

"Yeah. I'm fine." She sighed, trying not to notice the great scent of his aftershave. Fail. Or the heat from his hot body. Fail. Or the fact he now stood directly in front of her. She cleared her throat and grabbed at the first random thought to enter her mind. "Do you think I was just duped?"

Moonlight filtered in through a small window on their right, illuminating his face enough for her to see his expression. Contemplative. He removed his hat, set it on the washer to her left then ran a hand through his hair.

"I'm not sure," he said after several beats. "Jordan did appear sincere, but well, let's face it. Your sister's good."

Kerri smacked her head back against the wall a few times, closed her eyes and groaned. "I know. That's the problem."

Smack. What if this was all a ruse to get her to stay in Texas? *Smack.*

"Hey."

She reopened her eyes only to discover she had a bigger, sexier problem standing so close, she couldn't think, couldn't breathe, could only feel. The big, hot, sexually potent man crowded her space and she liked it. A lot. But he made her body consider things, want things, needy things she had no idea what to do about.

Smack.

Her Unbridled Cowboy

Then the bugger stepped closer still, easing his hand between her head and the wall, being sweet again. Making her heart melt. His other large, strong hand settled ever so lightly on her hip.

"Easy there, darlin'." His voice was soft and low, their gazes only inches apart in height thanks to her high heels. "It's not worth hurting yourself over."

Hurting myself? No. Hitting her head off the wall was meant to knock sense into her, not hurt. But the need and want and hunger suddenly raging inside, that sure as heck hurt. In a fierce way. If she had any sense, she'd run out of the room and not stop until she was miles from this man who could sometimes be so sweet, he had her chest aching with a longing that scared her witless.

She swallowed and opened her mouth, intending to tell him God knows what, when they heard the crowd in the other room start to count backwards from ten.

The New Year was upon them.

With each number called out, his face drew closer, his breath warm on her skin, her heart pounding louder and louder. Three. Two. *One.* Connor's hold on the back of her head tightened, and his other hand lifted to gently brush his thumb across her jaw.

"Happy New Year, Kerri," he breathed.

When she opened her mouth to reply, he covered her lips with his.

And that's how she rang in the New Year, in the Dalton's dark laundry room, sharing heat and touches and soft murmurs with Connor McCall.

Oh wait, the murmurs came from her, but man, he felt so good. And kissed even better. A mad rush of sensations engulfed and she was lost. Just utterly lost.

Warm, and tasting like beer and sin and long forgotten desire, his mouth moved over hers in a slow, lazy, open-mouthed kiss. She shuddered and slid her hands up over his broad shoulders to play with the short hair at the back of his neck. He groaned low in his throat, then pressed her against the wall, his body hard and deliciously warm. A zing of heat sliced straight to her core.

Their kiss under the mistletoe had been incredible, but this, *this* went beyond. Their bodies were lined up, touching, pressing, stroking…

Oh God, his tongue entered her mouth removing all thoughts of the party, their past, the future, everything from her mind.

Only the *here and now* mattered. Connor, and how he made her feel.

And boy did he make her feel. All sorts of things. Feminine, and desired, and needed. He rocked into her, nipping, tasting, drinking her lips like a man thirsty for days.

It was all so incredible and sensuous, and suddenly, she wanted more. *Needed* more, and with that need came boldness.

Giving her tongue permission to explore his mouth, she swept the roof, soft cheek, sliding against his, delighting in the low groan that rumbled from his chest yet again.

His hold tightened and, *sweet mercy*, he rocked against her, his arousal thick and hard, making her wet.

Kerri trembled with need. That was new. She'd never trembled with need before. Ever. The sensation was exciting and frightening and made her just a wee bit naughty.

Heaven help her, she wanted him to hike up her skirt, pull her panties aside and take her against the wall.

She should be appalled at her thoughts, and probably

would be tomorrow, but right now...*God, right now* she wanted what she wanted.

Connor McCall inside her.

Apparently, he had other thoughts, because a second later, he pulled back abruptly and removed his hard, pulsing warmth from her grasp. She nearly cried out. Okay, she did, but he ignored her, his expression a mixture of hunger and heat and...fear?

After shoving the hat back on his head, he lightly touched her lower lip. "Definitely, strawberry," he said.

And in the next heartbeat, he was gone.

Like her breathe...and her legs. Did they still exist? Kerri reached for the washer, clinging to the side as she worked on regulating her pulse.

What the heck just happened?

He saved you from yourself.

Too bad. Just when she'd decided she didn't want to be saved.

By the middle of January, Kerri and Jordan still hadn't found a suitable property for their restaurant. Over the past two weeks, they'd gone out repeatedly to a few of the local restaurants at the Gulf, as well as several well-established ones in the Houston area. Having tasted the varied cuisine and experienced the ambiance of those places, the two of them had come up with a game plan.

Their menu would consist of beef, seafood and chicken, and they needed a place big enough for an open barbecue pit. It was also important for the building to have an area that could accommodate a stage for the locals to come out and show off their talent. A part of Comets' legacy they wanted to continue in Texas.

So far, none of the properties they'd looked at had that expanse.

"Well, sis, today's the day. I can feel it," Jordan said as Cole drove them to meet their realtor at a location Cole had spotted on his way to work the day before. "You've cooked and pleased New Yorkers, the finicky French and are highly regarded for the magical things you can do with tofu in So Cal. Are you ready to bring pleasure to the palates of Texas?"

"Yes, I am, actually," she replied, and meant it.

The excitement of the challenge had already started to take root. She'd even begun to experiment in her mother's kitchen, thrilling her parents night after night with her concoctions.

Even Mr. and Mrs. McCall had stopped by, and Jordan and Cole.

But not Connor.

Kerri hadn't seen the perplexing cowboy since the party. Since *the kiss*.

Absently running a finger across her bottom lip, Kerri recalled his taste. The way he felt all hard and masculine, and how that made her feel all soft and feminine. She never had that reaction with Lance. Ever. And they'd been married for fifteen months.

Actually, she'd never felt the fierce need to be taken that had hit her when she and Connor had kissed.

Kissed.

Goodness, it was just a kiss, but boy she'd felt more in that little spec of time than she had her whole marriage. Correction, make that the whole relationship with her ex-husband.

They'd both been eighteen when she met Lance while working together at a restaurant. The two of them had a lot in common and became fast friends, eventually best friends. After a year, they'd both applied and were accepted at The Culinary Institute in New York, making her time away from her family not such a hardship. In fact, it had been wonderful. Lance had understood her obsession and love for cooking because he had it, too.

They'd shared an apartment while in New York, and eventually, the small confines had led their relationship to the next level. After graduation, he'd asked her to marry him, and it seemed like the natural thing to do. Within a month, they were husband and wife working in Paris where they furthered their experience as cooks in many of the smaller cafés and restaurants all throughout the beautiful city.

Lance had been the only lover she'd ever had, and although they didn't make love every night, they did it often enough that she was unaware there was a problem.

Looking back on it now, there were signs leading up to *the incident,* but at the time, she'd been clueless.

"Well, it's time for a change," Cole said, bringing her mind back to the present.

She gladly switched off thoughts of the past.

"This place looked big enough on the outside for what you girls have in mind. Apparently, it just went on the market yesterday. I'm glad Ms. Harper was able to get such a quick appointment with the listing agent."

"Me, too," Jordan said as Cole pulled into the parking lot of a large two-story, cinder-blocked building, and next to their realtor and a large truck.

Kerri's pulse increased. They were in Bay Beach, a quaint Gulf community she'd often frequented as a child. They were a few miles east of the bigger tourist locations, and she loved the area for its small shops and boardwalk with an equally small pier and beautiful beach. And although it had been hit by a recent hurricane, as usual, Texans bounce back. So far, the property appeared promising. The building had weathered well, and the size was right. More than right, and the parking lot could easily accommodate a big crowd.

Oh please let the inside be doable, she prayed as Cole turned off the ignition and groaned.

"What's wrong, honey?" Jordan narrowed her eyes.

"That's Duke Carver's truck. This must be one of his listings," he answered with a shake to his head.

"And?" her sister prompted.

"And he's always had a problem with the McCall brothers...especially Connor."

Kerri was a little surprised. Connor generally got along with everyone. A little too well. She turned to get a better look at the guy in question, but their realtor's car was in the way.

"Really? Why?" Jordan asked.

"One of my brother's fiancée's used to be Duke's girlfriend, and although they were through before Connor and Tiffany started dating, Duke got it in his head that Connor stole her from him."

Her sister placed a hand on his arm. "Do you want to leave?"

"Yeah, Cole." Kerri leaned forward from the back seat. "I'm sure there are places still out there. We don't need to make this uncomfortable for you."

But...*darn*, she really liked the look of this place, and the seaside area.

"No, that won't be necessary. Duke has some of the best property, and we'd only have to deal with him eventually anyway." Cole turned and smiled at her. "And *he* was wrong, not Connor. Although, my brother should have let him have the woman." He cocked his head, then added, "Besides, a McCall never runs from a Carver," before he got out.

Her Unbridled Cowboy

Kerri glanced at her sister and laughed when Jordan rolled her eyes. She silently agreed. *Men*. She'd never understand their need to chest-pound. Seemed like a waste of energy.

She slid out of the passenger side of the car and greeted their realtor Marcy with a nod and a smile before turning her attention to Connor's nemesis.

Duke Carver was six-foot-one and all man. He wore a black Stetson, western shirt, jeans and snakeskin cowboy boots under a long black coat she could envision a gunslinger wearing a hundred years ago.

"Well, Cole McCall. It sure has been awhile." The man in black was on the other side of the car, extending his hand to Cole.

"Duke." Her soon-to-be brother-in-law shook the man's hand, eyeing him warily.

"I hear you're engaged. This must be the lucky lady now." Duke turned his attention to Jordan rounding the car to slip her arm around Cole.

Her sister sent him a killer smile to go with her handshake. "Yes, it is. I'm Jordan. Jordan Masters."

Kerri tried not to laugh as Duke's eyes nearly popped out of his head.

"It's a pleasure to meet you, Jordan. Is this the same Jordan that used to follow you around, Cole? The one you used to talk about when you started college?" Still shaking Jordan's hand, Duke glanced at Cole, waiting for a reply.

"Yes."

The enigmatic man released Jordan and nodded. "I see why you've stopped running. Good for you," Duke said, his tone earnest before turning his gaze on her as she neared. "And you must be Kerri. Marcy said the two of you were looking for commercial property for a restaurant, and that you were a great chef, but she never told me you were beautiful."

His blue eyes flashed their approval as he eyed her up and down before bringing her hand to his lips.

Chapter Seven

A little unnerved and intimidated by his directness, Kerri blushed and quickly pulled her hand away. "Thanks."

He stared a little longer before shaking his head and got down to the business of showing them around.

"It definitely has enough parking space," Kerri remarked.

"Yes, and room for more if you need it." Marcy pointed to the weeded area to their left. "That land is also part of the listing."

"It is," Duke confirmed. "As well as another acre out back."

Turning their attention to the building, Kerri felt the stirrings of hope and excitement coursing through her yet again. A steak and seafood restaurant with ribs and barbeque would fit in great in this town. She remembered hanging out with her friends here often, going to the beach, renting bikes, eating ice cream, and even playing miniature golf, which were all still offered across the street.

She turned to look. From where she stood, Kerri had a beautiful view of the Gulf and a wave of nostalgia hit her full force.

She'd been happy here. Very happy back then. Maybe it was a good sign. Maybe this was a good place to open their restaurant.

Their *Texas* restaurant.

She was still going back to L.A., but having committed to helping her sister, this area wouldn't be such a hardship on Kerri.

The locale was quiet yet well-traveled even in the off season. Foster's Creamery was open year round, and she made a mental note to stop in for some ice cream real soon.

"It looks big enough on the outside," Jordan said, stopping next to her.

Kerri turned back to survey the big concrete square. "I agree. I just hope it's workable on the inside."

"Well then, ladies, what do you say we check it out?" Duke asked with a knowing smile.

"Yes," they echoed each other and laughed.

Duke unlocked and held the door open for them. As they stepped inside, Kerri knew the instant he turned on the lights they'd found their future restaurant.

Big enough for both a barbeque pit and a stage, and a fleet of buses or maybe two private jets, the building did indeed have promise. The walls were wired but mostly unfinished. A pile of two-by-fours and sheetrock each sat in the middle of the room. Perfect. The place was practically a blank canvas.

"How's the building codes?" Cole asked Duke.

"Everything that has been done so far is up to code. This place was originally built last year. The owner I represent was going to open up a feed store, but the economy tanked and then the hurricane hit, he ran out of money and decided not to go any further." Duke waved a hand around. "The electricity, heat and plumbing are started down here, but the upstairs is finished."

"And what's upstairs?" Jordan asked.

"A huge storage area, or whatever you'd want to use it for, as well as a two-bedroom apartment."

Kerri's heart leapt. *Holy smokes*. She turned to Duke and grabbed his arm, forgetting her shyness. "Are you saying there's an apartment, and it's finished?"

He smiled. "Yes, ma'am, I am. The owner just moved out last week. Would you like to see it?"

"Yes, please." Kerri removed her hand and followed the grinning realtor out the back door.

She loved her parents and what they'd done to the old homestead, but…an apartment? The thought of having her own place, regaining her independence brought such a rush of joy, she knew it showed on her face.

Marcy smiled at her as they ascended a set of outside stairs. "As I understand it, the new appliances are included, too."

"They are," Duke confirmed, unlocking the door and standing aside so they could all enter a hallway that ran the length of the whole side of building. "The first door is to the storage area and the other is for the apartment."

"Cole and I will check out the storage area while you show Kerri the apartment," Jordan said.

Duke nodded. "Sure thing. Let me just get the door for you, then."

While he unlocked the first door for her sister and Cole, Kerri walked down to the other, excitement upping her pulse. Behind this door could be her new place. Never had she imaged when she woke up this morning that checking out a location for their restaurant could possibly lead to a new home.

"I think you're going to like this," he said, with a grin.

Smiling, she nodded as he unlocked the door, then sucked in a breath when she walked in. He was right. The apartment was huge. It ran the whole length of the building. Much bigger than her New York apartment. Heck, she could fit two and a half of them in this space.

"The storage area is the same square footage, but it's all open," Duke informed.

Nodding, Kerri walked through the modern kitchen into the opened living room and looked out the window over-looking the front of the property. She had a gulf view.

"And how much square feet is it exactly?"

"Eighteen hundred. Each," Duke replied.

Kerri didn't know if that was good. Didn't really care as she continued to walk through the apartment. She was too busy falling in love, already seeing the place as her own, adding colorful touches to the functional smaller bedroom, picturing purple bedding in the master bedroom that had, *alleluia,* its own bathroom. And boy, what a bathroom, complete with a huge walk in shower. It had a corner. *A corner*. She had to walk around a tiled corner to find the showerhead, which was in the ceiling. The *ceiling.*

"Oh, that is too cool," Jordan said, walking in behind her.

Kerri turned to her and grinned. "I know, right?"

Smiling, her sister dropped an arm around her shoulder and guided her back to the bedroom. "So, what do you think?"

"I love it," Kerri gushed. "The kitchen is a little on the small side, but I'd be right above the restaurant and could always go down there to create…"

Jordan chuckled. "I meant about the place in general, but I think I get the picture. It's great to see you happy and excited again."

Her cheeks heated as she nodded. "I liked the feel of the place, even before I heard about this apartment."

"Me, too." Jordan turned to Cole as he entered the bedroom, leaving the two realtors in the kitchen. "What do you think, hun?"

"Well, this building is certainly big enough for what you want, and I like that most of the downstairs is unconstructed. Keeps the renovation costs down."

"Yeah, it's like a blank canvas," Kerri spoke her earlier thoughts.

Jordan nodded. "Exactly. We can hire a designer straight away and work on a plan."

Cole turned to Kerri and smiled. "I guess I don't have to ask you if you like the apartment, or what you girls are going to do with it."

"I'm going to help my sister regain her independence and have fun in the process." Jordan winked at her.

Independence and fun. Both had been scarce for far too long. Kerri could hardly wait to change that.

"Well now, Kerri," Cole said, leading them out of the room with a hand on their backs. "It looks like you are no longer homeless or unemployed."

Re-shoeing to some was a chore, but not to Connor. He found the job relaxing and sometimes therapeutic. Like now. Lord knew he needed the therapy. A double session twice a week and he still wouldn't be right.

What the hell was wrong with him, kissing Kerri like that last month?

On his final hoof, he rasped the last stub of nail, filing it down before he used a pair of clenchers to seat the nail in the groove to keep the shoe from slipping. Done. Connor released the horse's foot and straightened.

He knew Kerri was trouble. He knew she made him forget reality when they touched, and still he'd followed her into that damn laundry room and kissed her.

Idiot.

After putting away his tools, he washed his hands at the utility sink and grimaced. Had that kiss been any different than the mind altering mistletoe kiss? No, well, yes, damn it. It had been worse. Better. All-consuming. The very reason he'd avoided Kerri for the last month.

A wuss move.

The intoxicating city girl was turning him into a coward. Connor McCall never turned tail and ran in his life, until she stepped her pretty little foot back on Wild Creek soil last spring. Twice now, he ran from her. And each time after a kiss. The only reason he hadn't run after the mistletoe incident was because she'd been sitting on him.

Yeah, a wuss move.

He was ticked off.

It had to stop.

It was going to stop.

Tonight. At Kade's welcome home dinner here at the ranch. Kerri was cooking. No way could he get out of this one. And why should he? His best friend's homecoming was a long time coming, and Connor had to admit, at times he'd wondered if it would take place at all.

He'd kept up with the news feeds and events most television stations didn't air, and knew this deployment was tougher than Kade's last one. But it was officially over. His best friend was officially home. Kevin and Jen had gone to the armory and brought their cousin back to Shadow Rock this morning. Though Connor had already talked to Kade on the phone, it would be great to see his buddy in person.

Leaving the stable, Connor was walking toward the ranch just as Kerri pulled up. She got out and popped the back of the SUV, and his gut tightened at the sight of her in a light purple ribbed turtleneck, black leather jacket and jeans—*jeans*—hugging a drool-worthy bottom.

His mouth dutifully watered. *Damn it.*

It was early February, but the sun was out and glinting off of her long dark hair that formed a curtain around her face as she reached into the back and pulled a long covered tin toward her.

"Need any help?" He asked as he came around to stand next to her, noticing the back was full of tins identical to the one she almost dropped just now.

"Connor! You startled me." Kerri stared up at him through rounded eyes.

"Sorry, didn't mean to." He sent her a slight grin.

She was so beautiful. And he was such a wuss. But he didn't care. No. Right now, his mind was full of all the indecent things he wanted to do to her.

"Yes."

He blinked. "Yes?" *Good Lord.* It was his turn to be startled as his heart hammered out of his chest.

She frowned at him like he'd lost his senses. "Yes, I could use the help."

"Oh, sure," he stammered. She was right, he'd lost his senses. They were stolen, and she was the damn thief.

"Emma asked me to bring these over to put in the refrigerator so we can get an early start on them tonight," Kerri graciously informed while he managed to juggle the trays and open the front door. "Jordan will be by shortly with the rest."

"You mean there's more?"

"Of course." Her tone indicated she now thought he was crazy.

Again, she was right again.

Connor lifted the tins he carried and inhaled as he followed her into his kitchen. Barbeque. "Mmm...smells good."

"Thanks."

A blush colored her beautiful face. The woman really was making a habit of stealing his breath.

Damn thief.

"Some of these Jordan and I are thinking about putting on the menu of our restaurant."

"Well, if it tastes half as good as it smells, I'd say you have a winner." Connor smiled down at her as he placed his trays on the counter.

Her blush deepened, adding a sparkle to her eyes. Like he needed that. Cripes. He had to hold back to keep from touching her.

He failed.

When the tray wobbled in her arms, he had every intention of just grabbing the damn thing and placing it near the others on the counter. But no. His knuckles had to brush the soft inner side of her arm. And her lips had to part in a soft gasp.

One he could maybe—*maybe*—fight, but both? Hell no. He was sunk. Connor set the food down as planned, but then reached out and wrapped his fingers around her wrist, rubbing his thumb over her pulse point. It leapt.

His pulse jumped in response.

And then her eyes, God, those big, beautiful chocolate brown eyes stared up at him, brimming with uncertainty and, heaven help him, blatant need.

She swayed toward him.

"Connor." Emma smiled as she walked into the room. "I was just going to call to ask you to help Kerri, but I see you've already started."

Kerri jumped and would've backed up, but Connor held tight, grin tugging his lips.

"No problem. I'm all over it," he informed, never

taking his eyes off the beauty, and he stood fascinated as her blush deepened.

"I'm sure you are, big guy." The older cook chuckled as she slapped his back and pushed him toward the door. "Now, go get the rest."

A few more trips and they were done. Emma already had most of it neatly stored in the industrial size freezer by the time Jordan arrived with the rest.

"Hi, everyone," she greeted with a cheerful smile and her hands full of trays.

"Let me help you with that." Connor quickly took them from her and placed them on the counter where Emma and Kerri were standing.

"Thanks, big guy," Jordan said. "You sure are handy to have around."

"You bet I am, sweetheart. I'm the master of many talents." He winked, and then grinned when the three ladies smirked. "Where's my brother? Shouldn't he be helping you?"

Jordan shook her head. "No. He's at work finishing up his codes." Her smile turned wicked. "I want his undivided attention on our two week honeymoon."

He chuckled. "Jordan, believe me. With you in a negligee, my brother is *not* going to be thinking about codes!"

"Negligee? Do you know something I don't, Connor?" His soon to be sister-in-law studied him with a curious gaze.

He held in his grin. "Could be."

"I guess I'll have to wait and see."

Connor kept his expression neutral as he went out to grab the final two trays. He had no idea if his brother had gotten Jordan any type of negligee, but she didn't need to know that, and he loved that he had the clever woman guessing.

"That's the last of them," he informed Emma and Kerri as he placed the final tray down.

"Thanks again, Connor. You can go now. We don't need you anymore," Kerri told him.

As he watched her place the last tin in the refrigerator, he couldn't fight the urge to tease. She might reward him with another blush.

Dropping his shoulders and pulling his brows together, he hoped to come across dejected. "What? That's it? No kiss? Just wham bam thank you ma'am? You use me for manual labor, and once you got what you want, you just discard me without giving thought to what I want, or my needs?"

"Your *needs*? Oh Lordy, Connor. It would take all of the Dallas Cowboy Cheerleaders to satisfy *your* needs," Kerri stated, then promptly turned a deep shade of red.

God, she's adorable. He wanted to eat her up, and well, maybe just start with the eat part. Yeah, he liked that part.

"Now, darlin', you are seriously underestimating your powers."

Connor watched as a flash of sadness skittered through her brown eyes. What the hell? He stared at her, but the puzzle remained. She gave nothing away. Just what the hell went on between her and her ex-husband? Surely the guy knew what a beautiful, vibrant and passionate women he had there. Cripes. If she were his woman, he'd never let her doubt that, and he would show…

"He's right, Kerri," Jordan agreed, and he felt some of the tension ease from his body. "Oh, I almost forgot to tell you, Duke Carver called just before I left the house. He said he'd call you back later."

Connor sucked in a sharp breath, and his head snapped in Kerri's direction. To his horror, he watched her blush as if pleased with this news. *Hell no*. She was not going to have anything to do with that man.

"Kerri, you can't go out with him," Connor told her. The man was the biggest jackass in Harland County. No way was he going to let him anywhere near Kerri.

"Excuse me?" Her gaze narrowed, and a shaft of anger flittered through her eyes.

"I said you can't go out with him."

"Oh, well then, that's different. Since Connor said not to go out with him, I won't go out with him." As she spoke, she tossed her hands in the air and turned around to look at her sister and Emma who remained silently smiling.

Not sure where Kerri was heading with that statement, he waited for her to face him. "Good."

"Good?" She blinked.

Okay, maybe not good.

"I'm sorry, I must have missed something, Connor. Since when did you own me?" she asked while walking toward him finger pointed. "I can go out with *whomever* I want."

"Just not Duke Carver." *Or any other man I know*.

Shit, where'd that thought come from?

"Whatever happened between you and him and Tiffany has nothing to do with me." Her eyes were really flashing now.

How the hell does she known about Tiffany?

Cole. Damn man needed a muzzle.

He stepped to the angry woman, determined to make her understand. "It has everything to do with you, Kerri. Don't you see?" He lifted his hand to lightly trace her chin. "Duke is just using you. He doesn't care about you;

he just wants to get back at me."

She swallowed before taking a deep breath and knocking his hand away. "Why is it so hard for you to believe he might find me attractive?"

Pain rippled through her eyes and his gut tightened. Cripes. She was hurt. *How the hell did I do that?*

"Maybe I want to be used." Her chin lifted. "Why is it alright for you to use women, but I can't use men?"

Jesus. Did she even know what she was saying? He glanced at Emma and Jordan, but they just shrugged.

Shrugged!

Blasted women.

Before he could reply, Kerri stomped out of the room, and his heart beat out of control at the thought of her sharing Duke Carver's bed. Damn, fool woman had no idea what she was doing.

Or did she?

His insides turned cold. Maybe Kerri knew *exactly* what she was doing. After all, she was a city girl.

In the process of sprinkling mozzarella cheese to the top of her pizza pasta bake, Kerri heard the commotion in the hallway and knew the guest of honor had made an appearance. Kade was the only reason she was there. After her earlier run in with Connor, she'd had no wish to return to Wild Creek, but did for Kade.

After nearly thirteen months away, the soldier deserved a home-cooked meal. And she'd pulled out all the stops. Okay, maybe went overboard. By a mile. But, hey, the poor guy's palate had suffered overseas. And she was in the business of exciting and pleasing palates. There would be no suffering tonight. Only joy. So Kerri had made several traditional Texas beef and rib entrees along with a few trusted favorites.

Her Unbridled Cowboy

And she was happy Emma had relinquished the kitchen to her without any fuss or hard feelings. It was actually kind of weird. But Kerri hadn't had time to ponder.

"Something sure smells great in here." The deep, authoritative tone brought a smile to her lips.

Kerri shut the oven door, twisted around and gasped. *Holy Guardsmen. Had he filled out. Big time.* She knew her mouth was open. Probably similar to last year when she'd first seen the other three cowboys after that eleven year span. Still. *Wow*. Kade was solid, and dangerous. And gorgeous. He always had been. Now he was…more.

He removed his Stetson and smiled. "It's great to see you, Kerri."

She returned his smile as she rushed across the kitchen to his opened arms.

Estimating the cowboy to be somewhere around six-foot-two, she discovered he appeared solid because a mass of coiled muscles resided under his civilian clothes. The man fit the bill of a lean, mean machine. Dressed in jeans and a slate gray, button-down shirt, he oozed fitness. And authority. And danger.

When they drew apart, Kade was still smiling down at her, his thickly lashed eyes full of warmth, but she sensed a darkness in the gray depths. Her heart constricted at the thought of what had caused the shadows.

"You sure grew up beautiful," he said, releasing her to set his hat back on his head.

Right on schedule, her face heated like a bad habit. Because it *was* a bad habit, darn it. She smiled and touched his arm.

"Thanks, and you've grown out. Jeez," she said, squeezing his bicep. "I don't think you have any more room to add muscle."

Surprised at how at ease she was around the virile man, Kerri took stock. She was comfortable enough to get close and touch and be touched without any anxiety what-so-ever.

Unlike his best friend.

Her gaze shifted to the silent cowboy who came to stand just inside the room, swallowing up the doorway…and her breath. *Darn him.* His expression was neutral, which was another surprise, since she half expected him to tell her to back away from Kade.

She still couldn't believe he had the gall to forbid her to go out with Duke. Who did he think he was? He *didn't* own her. They weren't an item. Just because they shared a few kisses. Okay, a few *incredible, bone-melting kisses.* Still, that didn't give him the right to tell her who she could and couldn't see. The fact she had no intention of dating the realtor was moot. Connor had no right to order her around.

He's just worried about you, her conscience insisted. Deep down, Kerri knew this, but it still hurt that he didn't think she was attractive enough to catch Duke's attention on her own.

Kade chuckled. "Probably not."

She blinked and turned her attention back to the guest of honor, trying to get her mind back to their conversation. *Muscles.* Right. "Well, tonight I'm going to load you up with enough carbs your muscles will weep with joy."

"I can hardly wait," he said, then motioned to his silent friend. "According to Connor, I'm in for a real treat."

She glanced at the quiet cowboy, still leaning against the doorframe. He'd talked to Kade about her cooking?

Her Unbridled Cowboy

When? And darn him. She wanted to be mad at the condescending bugger for longer than an afternoon. He had no right to go pulling a sweet move so soon.

Connor nodded, gaze still glued to hers. "Kerri's the best cook I've ever tasted."

Holy crow. He did not just say that! Heat shot to her face, and her stomach fluttered without mercy. Bad body. She was still mad at him.

A lazy smile spread across his lips and dimpled his cheek.

Stupid fluttering increased.

She searched her mind for something flippant to say, but due to the limited amount of brain cell activity, she was operating on auxiliary power.

Shifting her gaze to Kade, she noted amusement brought a much needed light to the soldier's eyes.

She smiled. "Kade will just have to taste and judge for himself."

Chapter Eight

When Kade's eyebrow shot up in time with Connor's sharp inhale, Kerri realized her mistake. Her face, of course, did the heating thing again while she blamed her stupid lack of brain power on Connor.

"I mean the food," she stammered. *Friggin' brain-cell-sucking giant.* "I was talking about the food."

The Guardsman touched her arm and smiled. "I know."

"Good." She was pretty sure her mouth turned up. Hopefully. Good time for a subject change. "I-I heard the two of you were going on a trail ride for a few days."

"Yes." Kade released her and stiffened, some of the light disappearing from his eyes.

Connor straightened from the door. "We leave at first light."

According to Mrs. McCall, this was a ritual whenever Kade returned from deployment. Kerri's heart melted a little. Connor was a good friend.

She bounced her gaze between the cowboys. "I'll pack up some food for you to take. Including beef jerky."

"You know how to make beef jerky?" Kade asked.

Her mouth definitely turned up this time. "Yes. You'd be surprised what I can do."

"Well now, darlin'," Connor said before his buddy had the chance. "That's where you're wrong, because I know you're full of surprises."

Unsure if that was a compliment, she decided it was best just to agree. "Exactly."

He stared at her, gaze dark and serious, but the smirk remained. The longer he stared, the harder breathing became, until she eventually stopped. A second later, the oven timer dinged, saving her from herself, and spurring her into action.

Kerri sucked in a breath. "If you'll excuse me," she said with a slight nod. "I need to finish up."

She also needed to get a grip. A tight one. On her emotions, not the tall cowboy lumbering from the room. Although, that held much more appeal. Turning her back to them, and her attention to the food where it belonged, she used hot pads to pull the pizza bake from the oven.

"It does smell good," she heard Connor say in his sexy drawl. "But how could it not? Kerri made it."

Her heart stopped mid-beat while warmth engulfed in a swift wave. He just had to keep playing the sweet card.

Darn him.

The trail ride, so far, had been a success. At least Connor hoped so. Kade certainly looked better than when they'd first set out on Shadow Rock land three days ago. They rode hard, hiked hard, shot the shit out of targets, but tonight…tonight was the topper. It was always on the last night they participated in letter burning.

"Here," Connor said, passing Kade a notebook and pen.

As they sat around the campfire, Connor put pen to paper in order to participate in their version of 'cleansing.' Their way of releasing the shit weighing them down. Knowing his troubles paled in comparison to his buddy's, Connor wrote anyway. He didn't want Kade to feel singled out, even though these outings were clearly for his buddy to regroup, find his feet.

Transition from combat boots to cowboy boots.

Kade had been writing silently for nearly an hour

when he eventually stopped. By this time, alarm had tightened the muscles in Connor's back. His buddy had never taken that long before.

Death by indirect enemy fire...

The news report had said a Texas soldier had died during this deployment, and Connor knew the death haunted his friend. Kade had never brought it up and neither had Connor, although he'd wanted to, many times over the past several months. It'd just seemed awkward over the damn internet.

But now Kade was home, face to face. It was time to open up and shake the shadows out. To let them be seen and addressed and put away for good. Not that one's demons ever truly go away. But Connor would do whatever it took to tip the scales in his buddy's favor.

Oh, they'd talked the past few days. Sure. About Wild Creek, Shadow Rock, family, Cole and Jordan, auctions, rodeos, horses...hell, even the damn weather. Anything and everything but what really needed addressing. This past deployment.

Connor watched, noting a slight shake to his buddy's hands as Kade folded the papers then tossed them into the fire. Silence. Not a word. As a matter of fact, his best friend had gone still, just stared at the flames engulfing the confession or promise or whatever the hell it was Kade had written, sealing the words in ashes.

The fire wasn't the only thing that crackled. Ripping out his solitary page, Connor could feel stress and pressure building around them. The cool night air was ripe with it. Something was going on inside his best friend.

Tossing his note into the flames, he waited. Tension rolled off Kade's still form in wave after wave.

Another minute went by. Connor watched, waited.

Nothing. He had to break the silence. "You okay?"

Mouth thin, jaw tight and cracking, Kade shook his head. "No," he replied, voice so low, so raw Connor felt it in his bones.

The suffocating energy spiked until Kade shot to his feet, grabbed the metal bat from his pack and began to beat a nearby boulder into submission.

That was new.

And not good. Connor's gut tightened and alarm returned tenfold. His buddy had always brought the bat along, but had never used it.

Until now.

Christ. What? Was he making up for lost time? Kade kept hitting and hitting and hitting, the incessant ding echoing into the night without end.

God, how much more could his friend dish out?

Not much, apparently, because a minute later, sweaty and exhausted, Kade dropped the bat, then fell to his knees, silent tears streaming down his face, chest heaving from the exertion.

Connor knew the man code. Stay away. Keep a distance. Let the guy handle it on his own. In his own way.

But that hadn't worked so well for his brother last year, and it sure as shit didn't work for his best friend right now. No way in hell could he stand by and watch Kade suffer any longer.

Connor walked over and clamped a hand on his buddy's stiff shoulder, but did nothing more. He didn't say anything or do anything other than squeeze to show his support.

After a minute, Kade nodded and Connor released him.

"Is this about the Specialist?" he asked.

His buddy nodded again, then twisted to sit back against the boulder he'd just tried to crack in two, swiping the wetness from his face.

"It's not fucking fair," Kade grumbled. "He wasn't even part of our unit. Just an attachment, a fill in from up north. He had a fiancée and a six-month old little girl."

Christ. Connor inhaled, wishing he had the wit or knowhow to say the right thing. But was there a right thing? He decided probably not, so instead, he handed Kade a cold beer, dropped down next to him and together they stared at the flickering flames.

"You write about Kerri?" his buddy asked, surprising the shit out of Connor. Again.

He stilled, bottle touching his lip, waiting for him to tip and drink. He nodded. "Yeah." Then took a long pull. He wasn't about to say more. Not because he felt weak, but because his troubles were so minor compared to what his friend was going through. All he had written on the damn paper was that he was going to make an honest effort to try and not lump Kerri into the same category as the other city girls he'd known.

He'd never felt lousier in his life. Lousy because he practically had it all. A job he loved. Money. A loving family. So what if he had rotten luck with women. The rest of his life was perfect. He was blessed. He slept at night. There were no nightmares. He didn't have memories of combat. Or death.

No way would he insult his friend by even considering his troubles to be paramount. They weren't. Far from it.

"You going to ask her out?"

Beer flew from Connor's mouth as he choked. "What? No!" He emphatically shook his head as he wiped his face on his sleeve.

"Funny, I never took you for a fucking fool," Kade said matter-of-factly before he swallowed more beer.

Was the man looking for a fight? Probably. Connor smiled. *Not going to happen, buddy.*

"I'm not. That's why I'm staying away from her. The woman's going back to L.A., end of story."

"Right." Kade nodded. "That's why she's opening a restaurant with her sister here in Texas."

He swallowed back a curse. Why the hell where they talking about this? Oh, yeah, right. To keep his buddy from the pit of despair. He relented. "*Then* she's going back to—"

"L.A." Kade cut him off, his tone bored. "Yeah, I know. So you keep saying."

"Then why the hell do you keep asking?"

"Because I don't understand why that's stopping you." Again, he used a matter-of-fact tone.

It was beginning to irritate.

"Bullshit. You know I have zero luck with city girls. They always choose their career over me. Why beat that old horse? I'm right tired of it," he said, lifting his bottle to his mouth.

Kade nodded, took a pull of beer then met his gaze. "You don't mind if I ask her out, then?"

Beer spewed from Connor as, once again, he choked. Kerri and Kade? No way in hell. Surely his buddy wouldn't do that to…

Kade's chuckle echoed softly into the night. A gift considering the poor guy's mood not ten minutes earlier.

Damn man had been yanking his chain.

"Not funny," he grumbled.

"Oh, I disagree." Kade smirked. "I think it's fucking hilarious. You should've seen your face. Man, you are so whipped. You might as well stop fighting it. Something tells me it'll go much easier if you don't fight it."

"Fight this." Connor flipped him the bird, and they were both laughing by the time they finished the rest of their beer.

It was the week of the wedding, and Kerri couldn't believe how fast the time had gone. Not that she'd admit it out loud. No. But it did seem like yesterday she was standing in the McCall's gathering room with Jordan dropping the bomb that the wedding would be on Valentine's Day. At the time, the news had felt like a death sentence to Kerri.

In actuality, it hadn't been that bad.

And, although she still wasn't free to go back to the west coast, she was essentially, marginally…happy.

Especially now that she had an apartment.

"Where do you want this?" Cole asked, helping Kevin carry in a large dresser.

"In the master," she replied, a little thrill shooting down her spine at the thought of finally sleeping in her own place tonight.

Since it was a cash deal, they'd closed on the property within two weeks. Cole and his legal team had made everything painless. She and Jordan had spent the past week freshening up the apartment with a thorough cleaning, a coat of paint and new curtains, while taking time out to meet with possible designers for the restaurant.

So far, they hadn't found the right fit. Much to their surprise. They truly hadn't expected to have trouble, but apparently, local designers didn't quite get the Texas beach vibe they were going for. The designers would give one or the other, not both. So the search continued.

Kerri glanced at her watch. They had another

interview in two hours. This one was a transplant from the east coast. Kerri and Jordan figured the woman couldn't do any worse. Besides, they liked her name. Brandi Wyne.

"Where do you want this, darlin'?" Connor asked, setting down the large armoire he carried in with Kade.

Muscles bulged under their T-shirts. Her heart skipped a beat or three as her gaze wondered over the rippling Connor had going on across his back while he straightened to stand and stare. His hair was growing in. It flopped haphazardly on his forehead and she had the strangest urge to step close and brush it back.

Yeah…he…wow…

"Uh, Kerri? Did you want to leave it right here in the kitchen, because Connor and I would be happy to move on to something else."

Her gaze snapped to the man on the other side of the large cupboard. Funny, his muscles bulged and rippled, too, but the skipping had ceased in her chest.

"Actually, I'd be happy to stay here. What smells so good?" Kade asked, inhaling with a smile on his face.

Kerri couldn't believe how much better he looked since his trail ride. Whatever the two of them had done, it was good. The shadows she'd seen at his homecoming dinner where almost all gone. The gray of his eyes appeared lighter, piercing, almost smiling. And the set of his shoulders was definitely more relaxed, although he still walked with a lethal grace she knew he'd never lose. It was a cop thing. A soldier thing. Anyone who'd seen action. Her sister had it. Her late brother-in-law had had it. Their friend Shawn had it. All cops. Of course Kade would have it. Anyone who'd been deployed would carry himself with a dangerous, capable air.

"Yeah," Connor agreed, inhaling. "Sure smells great,

darlin'. What is it?"

She smiled. "Lasagna. My way of thanking Jordan for her help this week. She's fixing up my guest room right now."

"Mmm…lasagna." Kade smiled outright. "Dare I hope to ask if we get to try some?"

"Of course. I made it for you, too."

Connor shot a look at his friend, then back to her and frowned. "For him? What about me?"

She laughed. "Yes, you, too, ya big baby. I'm making it for everyone. You didn't think I'd let you slave for me all day and not make sure you were properly fed, did you?"

"Well, all right. I look forward to it."

Dimples appeared and brown eyes gleamed, warming her from the inside out.

"Now, if you could just tell us where you want this monster, we'll get back to work."

"In the master. Down at the end of the hall."

His face fell.

"Sorry."

"No problem, darlin'," he said. "We'd be happy to carry this seven ton slab of oak to the furthest room. At least we're done with the stairs."

"Quit your belly-aching, McCall and get a move on," Kade said, gripping the armoire.

"Sir, yes, sir." Connor saluted his friend, then tipped the heavy piece of furniture, and together the two men slowly made their way down the hall.

Kerri was grateful she had such good friends. Good *strong* friends. In and out all morning, they'd carried, moved and placed the furniture her parents and the McCalls had donated, along with the bedroom suit she'd bought. A smile tugged her lips. Smiling was something she'd done a lot lately. It felt good to be in control of her life again.

She had just finished unpacking the last box marked *kitchen* when Jordan called out.

"Hey, Kerri come here. You need to see this."

Weaving around the stack of empty boxes in the living room, she joined her sister at the end of the hall. "What?"

"What do you mean, what?" Jordan blinked, then motioned to the men putting her bed together in the master bedroom. "That! You are one lucky woman. Four gorgeous, muscle-bound men working on your bed."

Kerri's face heated before she drew her next breath. And of course, all the men now stopped to stare at them. Yeah, she really wanted to punch her sister. And to think, she'd gone most of the day without embarrassing herself.

Thanks, Jordan. Not.

"Kerri, I have to admit, I'm a little surprised," Kevin said, devilment lighting his eyes. "I never took you for a king-size bed, type."

"I'm not," she rushed to say, because she had actually wanted the queen. "Jordan's the one who talked me into it."

"True. And someday you'll thank me. That extra room comes in handy," her sister informed, winking at her grinning fiancé.

Just kill me now.

She could feel Connor's stare, and there was just no way she was going to look at him. No way. Just the talk of king size and extra room in conjunction with Connor was enough to keep her body heated 'til next winter.

"Well, if you'll excuse me." She turned around without waiting for a reply. From any of them. "I've got more unpacking to do."

And now she was thinking about Connor and king size and unpacking. Yeah, she definitely wanted to punch her sister.

A little while later, after the men finished in her bedroom and were working on the living room—at a good, safe distance—Kerri started to fill the vanity in the master bath.

On her knees, stuffing towels way in the back, she was concentrating on her task when she heard someone walk in.

"Kerri, Jordan tol—" he sucked in a breath. "Holy hell."

Barely avoiding a head smack as she jerked and backed out, Kerri glanced up at Connor. Gaze trained on her butt, he stood in her doorway stalk still, a look of fierce hunger darkening his eyes.

Holy hell is right.

Body instantly heating, she was thankful to be on the floor because her legs literally shook. No one had ever looked at her with so much hunger before.

She cleared her throat. "D-did you want something?"

A low growl rumbled from his chest, and she thought she heard him say, "*Hell yeah,*" but wasn't sure thanks to the pulse pounding in her ears. A second later, he was gone.

Kerri drew in a breath and sat back on her legs. *Okay, that was intense*. And he never did tell her what he wanted…needed…why he came…oh for crying out loud, she couldn't even think a thought without it making her hot.

Needing a distraction, she scrambled to her feet and started to load the remaining towels into the linen closet next to the vanity. Her New York apartment had been the size of the linen closet. She snickered. It hadn't been *that* bad. In fact, she'd always thought of it as cozy. And her stilted house on the west coast had been…perfect.

God, she missed that house. It had been her refuge. Her home. The place where she'd been regrouping, discovering who she was, finding herself again. And she'd actually started to like what she found.

A sigh pushed the strands of hair off her face that had fallen out of her ponytail. *Enough of those thoughts.* There was no reason she couldn't continue to discover new things right here.

Running out of space, she stretched on her tip-toes, trying to shove the last towel on the top shelf when sudden heat and sin and temptation surrounded her from behind.

"Let me help you, darlin'," Connor's deep murmur rumbled from his chest straight through her as he took the towel from her fingers and set it on the top shelf with ease.

"Th-thank you," she managed, eyes squeezed shut, willing her body to stop shaking.

And wanting, and needing. She failed.

"You're very welcome," he replied in a tone barely above a whisper.

Why didn't he move away? *Please, go away.*

He stilled, as if realizing their positions. Heat warmed her back, and heaven help her, a large hand curled around her hip, while his other slid slowly down her upstretched arm. Yeah, see, now this created a problem with her shaking legs. And her thundering pulse, and don't forget her hitched breath. Breathing became less of a thought when his hand continued down her side, lightly skimming her breast.

That's when need took over. *Holy smokes.* Desire pooled low in her belly and led to a delicious ache between her legs. Darn man felt good. So darn good. Her nipples tightened and breasts felt heavy, hoping, wanting, needing a visit from his big, wandering hand.

"Damn, Kerri," he breathed near her ear, sending shivers down her spine. "I can't seem to stay away from you."

Which was fine with her since he started to place open-mouthed kisses on her neck. A feat he couldn't perform if he stayed away.

A moan sounded low in her throat. Yeah, he felt really, *really* good. He pressed closer, and she answered by pressing back. That's when things got wild. Those large, callused, wonderful hands roamed all over, cupping, tweaking, kneading her breasts while his mouth continued to kiss and nip at her neck.

She'd never been so hungry, so turned on—so wet in all her life. Kerri threw her head back, grinding her hips against the large erection pressing into her lower back. God, he felt so great. He was so hot and hard, and had her wound so tight she nearly came undone when he shoved a hand between her legs and brushed a finger over her throbbing center.

"God, you drive me crazy," he said next to her ear again, voice low and husky, vibrating straight through her.

"Connor? Where are you, man?"

Before she had a chance to reply, or climax, Cole's voice cut through her foggy haze.

"This couch isn't going to move itself."

He stilled.

No. Don't do it, she willed. *Don't leave*. But with a curse on his lips, he pulled his hands from her and stepped back, taking his hot, rock hard body and talented hands with him.

Darn it.

And since she not only had mush for brains but legs too, she grasped the closet doorframe to keep from falling.

"I'm coming," he called out, voice a bit gruff.

Wish I had, her mind added.

Was that good or bad? She didn't know. God, she was so confused. And completely turned on. Not a good combination.

This was insane. They were fully clothed, and yet, she'd been close. *Really* close to going off, and judging by the bulge she'd felt and the gruffness of his tone, he'd been there, too.

"Good," Cole said from the doorway. "Because we require a giant's expertise out here."

So did she.

Kerri continued to clutch the doorframe with one hand and straightened towels with the other, while she hoped she brought what resembled a smile to her lips.

Forget looking at them. Either of them. It wasn't happening. Thankfully, it wasn't required because the men disappeared a second later.

She slowly slid to the floor. *Holy crow.* That was nuts. *And exhilarating.* She'd felt desired. And heaven help her, she loved it.

Which wasn't good. No. No. Not good at all. They couldn't just become lovers. Their families where lifelong friends. It would be too awkward. And they certainly wouldn't become more. How could they? She wasn't staying in Texas, and Connor had made it perfectly clear he didn't trust city girls. No, they didn't have a future together, no matter how strong the attraction.

And he apparently concurred a little while later

when they sat down to eat. Though he was polite and didn't ignore her, he also barely made eye contact. Which actually, made her breathe a little easier. She was caught somewhere between embarrassment and need. And she didn't like it at all. His non-attention helped her gain her perspective.

They were friends who were attracted to each other. No harm in that.

"Well, thank you for such a wonderful lunch, Kerri," Kade said, pushing back from the table after eating his plate clean. "I hope you enjoy your new place. If you don't need me for anything else, I have to get back to the ranch."

"Me, too," Connor said before she could reply.

Kevin smiled, rising to his feet. "Me three."

"You've got that right." Cole snickered. "Sometimes you do act like you're three."

Kerri laughed and rose to her feet with everyone. "Thank you all so much for your help."

"Yeah," her sister said. "We appreciate the use of those muscles today."

"Well now, you girls feel free to use me anytime," Kevin offered, devilment backing the twinkle in his blue eyes.

Cole stepped closer to Jordan. "The only one Jordan will be using is *me*," he said, kissing her sister full on the lips. "But, since I drove, I guess that means I'm leaving, too."

Kerri gave them each a quick hug, and a half hour later, as she made her way downstairs with her sister to interview the next designer, she was still pondering her body's reaction. She'd hugged four very impressive, very handsome cowboys, but her body had only tingled when she'd made contact with Connor.

"Chemistry," Jordan said as they stepped outside to wait for the east coast designer. "Don't you agree?"

It took Kerri a second to back pedal through her sister's words. She got nothing. Darn. She'd completely zoned out.

"I think that's what's been missing from the one's we've interviewed," Jordan continued.

Ah, yes, chemistry...with a designer.

Kerri caught on. "Yeah, I think you're right. Chemistry is important."

It was also very dangerous when it came to a certain brown-eyed cowboy.

Cole's bachelor party was in full swing, two nights before the wedding. A night Connor had been dreading.

He hated stag parties ever since his second attempt at marriage had been ruined by one. An excuse for the groom and his buddies to have a bit of raunchy fun had lost its appeal. But since he was the best man, it was Connor's duty to see his little brother had one.

Kevin and Kade were generous enough to offer up their ranch for the festivities, and Kevin had even helped to procure the entertainment. A fact that admittedly made Connor nervous. He shrugged. Too late now. The party had started. He put on a game face for his brother's sake, but he already couldn't wait to leave.

Kerri had made a big batch of chili and three dozen chicken enchiladas, which the men obligingly devoured. All Connor had to do was take care of the snacks and drinks. He'd gotten off easy.

Having made it thru the food, which was like the cook—mouthwatering delicious—he was leaning back against the bar in the Dalton's den watching his brother open up prank gifts. Tonight would be different. Tonight would be fun. He was not going to think about Kerri and her sexy body, or prior bachelor parties. This was all about Cole. He was going to enjoy his younger brother's long deserved happiness.

Kade passed him a beer and settled next to him. "I have to admit, I'm a little nervous to see what my cousin added to that pile."

Connor eyed the gifts littering the coffee table in front of Cole. "You and me both."

With Kevin, there was no telling what he'd wrapped, but they were about to find out as the groom-to-be read the prankster's name on the card attached to the gift in his hand.

"Why am I suddenly afraid," Cole said, looking warily at his smiling friend.

"Cause you're a wuss," Kevin replied, smile broadening. "You know, if Jordan tires of you and needs a real man—"

"I'll be sure to contact your cousin," Cole countered, causing the guests to whoop and shout and turn to Kade with big grins.

Connor watched his buddy stiffen next to him. Yeah, Kade was as happy as he was to be there. He couldn't help smiling, though. His little brother had landed a good zing to Kevin. Apparently, Kade agreed because the guy relaxed a second later and lifted his beer.

"Happy to help," his buddy said. "I always pick up my cousin's slack anyway."

"Yeah, I got your slack right here." Kevin made an obscene hand gesture and the guys laughed.

Kade snorted. "No you don't, or you'd be using two hands."

The laughter got louder and Connor found himself joining in. He'd forgotten how much fun it was to listen to the Dalton's spar. God, it was good to have Kade back, and he could see that sentiment mirrored in Kevin's eyes.

"Now I'm really worried about opening this," his brother said, unwrapping the odd shaped gift to reveal a set of handcuffs.

Damn, they looked real.

Cole grinned at his buddy. "I think you know she already has a set."

"Yeah." Kevin nodded. "This is for backup. Besides, it can't hurt to have two."

Wait. Jordan uses handcuffs? He glanced at Kade who raised a brow, then turned back to look at his smiling brother. *Jesus.* Yes, she must if Cole's blissful expression was anything to go by.

And that expression remained on his brother's face by the time Cole got to the last gift. "It's from Jordan," his brother announced, face alive with excitement.

Connor smiled. He wasn't surprised. Jordan would never miss out on contributing to Cole's fun.

"Come on, open it," someone shouted.

"Yeah," another agreed. "What is it?"

Everyone leaned closer and waited, the room suddenly quiet as Cole reached into the gift bag.

Chapter Nine

Connor watched as his brother lifted out the sexiest damn piece of lingerie he'd ever seen. *Hot damn.* It was sheer white net and crisscrossed lace with the back cut out and a g-string and garter and stockings...and damn, if it wasn't the other Masters sister he pictured wearing the sexy number.

And she looked good, too. Damn good.

"Your brother's one lucky son-of-a-bitch," Kade mumbled before drinking his beer.

Connor nodded, thankful his buddy had dragged his mind away from thoughts of Kerri and white lace. He was so not going to go there.

Lifting his beer to his lips, he acknowledged he was halfway through the night. Only the stripper and movie remained.

The worst parts.

A second later, the doorbell rang.

Oh great. Let's jump right in then.

"Ah." Kevin smiled. "Right on time. That would be the entertainment."

Cole's gaze fastened to his from across the room as Kevin rushed to get the door. Connor shrugged.

"Kevin was in charge of entertainment," he told his brother.

Cole made a face. "I'm suddenly afraid again."

Kevin returned with a pretty blonde in a tan raincoat. "Everyone, this is Charity."

Connor barely held back the smirk.

"Hi, Charity," the men chorused.

She smiled and said hi, her blue eyes clear and bright

as she pulled an iPod from her pocket and set it on the coffee table near the lingerie and handcuffs.

"And this is the groom-to-be, Cole," Kevin told her, slapping Cole on the shoulder, forcing him to sit down when his brother made to stand. "No need. You just relax and enjoy, buddy."

Connor and Kade chuckled at the look of fear on Cole's face, but his brother was a good sport. He smiled and settled back in his seat, waiting for the show.

The blonde promptly sat on his brother's lap, laid her head on his shoulder and made a remark about a baby and a diaphragm. Connor had no idea what she was talking about, but the look on Cole's face as he threw his head back and laughed told him that his brother certainly understood the joke that had Kevin and the guys from McCall Enterprises in stitches. They were all laughing uncontrollably.

He exchanged another look with Kade. His buddy raised a brow and shrugged. Good. He wasn't the only one who had no damn clue what was so funny.

A smiling Kevin came over and explained an office visit Jordan had made last spring when Cole had refused to take her calls.

Connor couldn't catch his breath, he was laughing so hard. Damn, he would've given his right nut to have been in that boardroom last year. Leave it to Jordan.

"Oh man, you should've seen your brother's face," Kevin said, glancing at him and Kade. "He looked like he wanted to either strangle her or kiss her. It was priceless."

Yep, leave it to Jordan. God, she was so good for his stubborn brother.

"Cole should've known better than to piss off a Masters," he said with a shake of his head and smile still on his lips.

"True," Kevin agreed, then turned to walk toward the stripper. "Well, time to get this show going."

He helped Charity to her feet, and she slipped out of her shoes then ditched her raincoat to reveal a belly dancing outfit.

Okay. They were actually going to get something different than a biker chick routine. Connor watched the blonde hit the play button on her iPod and soon the sound of a flute, symbols and drums filled the room.

So far, Kevin had done pretty good.

After dancing an exclusive dance for Cole, she started another routine, swaying and jiggling around the other smiling men. Connor was finishing his beer when the blonde turned her attention to Kevin who eagerly danced with the woman.

The guy had moves, he had to admit, almost as good as his own. Almost. When she started dancing seductively in his direction, Connor watched in amusement as the cute little blonde gyrated her hips in front of him, but when she didn't move on to Kade, he raised a brow.

"You know," he began, as she tried to put a bright pink scarf around his neck but couldn't reach and ended up putting it around his waist instead. "I'm not the groom," he finished with a smirk.

She smiled up at him. "I know, but he said you would enjoy the dance more than he would. So, who am I to complain, cowboy?" She winked while shaking her goods, jingling the chains around her neck and hips.

Connor glanced at his brother. Cole gave him a puckish grin and raised his beer.

Yeah, ah, no thanks. Not that she wasn't pretty, because she was, and stacked, but he wasn't interested.

Her Unbridled Cowboy

Which should've alarmed him.

Normally, he would've been happy to enjoy all the delectable delights the blonde in front of him possessed, but for some reason, he wasn't in the mood. Probably due to the premise of the party and past party nightmares. He refused to believe his reluctance had anything to do with a certain dark-haired, dark-eyed cook.

"That's right nice of you, darlin'." He tipped his hat then clamped a hand on Kade's shoulder. "But this is the guy who deserves some attention." The look Kade gave him had Connor smiling. Time for his buddy to enjoy life. "He just got back from Iraq."

"Oh." The blonde's eyes lit up, and she swayed to Kade, managing to wrap that pink scarf around his friend's neck. "I'm always happy to take care of our troops. *Extra* care."

Deciding his buddy was in good hands, Connor left the room for more beer, even though there was plenty behind the bar. Best to give the girl room to work. He knew from Kevin that Kade hadn't been out with anyone yet. So, yeah, it was past time his friend got some pleasant action.

When he returned from the kitchen, the stripper was gone and so was Kade. Good. Maybe this party wasn't so bad.

"Okay. It's movie time." Kevin grinned, and as the men cheered, Connor groaned inwardly.

And maybe it was.

It had been during this activity at his second bachelor party that things had gone astray. Big time. The guys had rented the video, *Tiffany does Texas*, picking it out purposely because the girl had the same name as his fiancée. The joke had turned out to be on him when he watched in horror as images of his future wife and several men came on the screen. He'd been devastated.

Not because of her secret career, but because she'd never told him, not to mention he later found out she didn't plan on quitting once they were married.

Yeah, he fucking hated this part of the party. He was about to leave the room again when Kevin popped the movie in and images of young Jordan and Cole filled the screen.

His brother gasped in delighted surprise. "Where did this come from?"

Kevin frowned. "I don't know. This wasn't the one I rented," he grumbled, riffling through a stack of nearby DVD's.

Images of the happy couple growing up in both video and print flashed before them. Starting from childhood right to present day, the tape had images of Jordan and some of Kerri that they'd never seen. Connor's gut tightened at the carefree, bright eyed Kerri in a graduation cap and gown…and then a wedding gown. Shit. His jaw cracked from teeth he hadn't realized he'd clenched.

"Ease up there, buddy," Kade said quietly. "You might crack a molar."

When the hell had he returned? Damn ninja.

Connor grunted and the tightness eased from his jaw when the video moved on to shots from both 40th anniversary parties from last year. Cole and Jordan were singing for his parents, but that wasn't what caught his attention. No. It was the dark-haired beauty in his arms, moving with a sensual grace as they danced around the floor. She was smiling up at him in one of those unguarded moments when it actually reached her eyes.

"Damn, Connor, the two of you move like one," Kade remarked, tone serious. "You gonna do something about that?"

Connor grunted. Cripes. Now his mind was jumping onto the *move like one train*, supplying images of him and Kerri doing a naked tango. Damn. He didn't need this, or want this. But his body did. Hell yeah. His body immediately remembered how she'd felt in his hands while he'd explored her curves in her bathroom. All soft and warm and responsive.

He chugged the rest of his beer and set the empty bottle on the bar behind him. Dangerous territory, and that train needed derailing. Fast.

"So…" He looked sideways at his friend. "Did you give a donation to Charity?"

Kade smiled. "Nice try changing the subject. But you still didn't answer my question."

"No, I didn't," he said. "And you didn't answer mine."

"No. I didn't."

Connor smiled. Neither one said any more. Instead, they turned their attention back to the television and watched the rest of the movie. A movie he was increasingly convinced was there courtesy of his future sister-in-law. Exactly the kind of move that woman would make.

When it ended with Jordan sitting on a chair at the girl's new restaurant, acoustic guitar in her hands, he was certain. Yeah, Kevin could kiss that porno good-bye. She'd replaced it with this tape. *Thank God*. She said a few sweet words for his smiling brother, and Connor's chest tightened at the love he could see on her face and hear in her voice which continued as she sang a special song for Cole.

And Connor had to admit, for the most part, this was one bachelor party he'd actually enjoyed.

Valentine's Day dawned with a bright, cloudless blue sky, ready for Jordan and Cole to profess their love and their lives to each other in front of a handful of family and friends and one very happy dog.

A gazebo was erected on their land overlooking the ocean where their house would soon reside.

Connor felt like he took a hoof to his ribs when he glanced past Jen and Megan, Jordan's west coast friend he'd meet last September, and saw Kerri walking toward him in cloud of red sin. Darn woman was the prettiest, sexiest thing he'd ever seen. And he'd seen plenty.

Cripes. The gown clung to her upper torso with some kind of fancy detailing across the top, cupping her breasts, while the bottom had layers of thin, red, gauzy material he wanted to peel off her luscious hips. One by one.

With his teeth.

Watching in anticipation, Connor's heart stopped for a beat then slammed into his trampled ribs when her gaze finally found his. She looked at him with such longing his groin instantly tightened. Damn. His body clearly remembered how incredible those curves had felt. How exquisite her skin had tasted when he'd kissed her neck in that master bathroom.

Ah hell. He was standing in front of friends and relatives, next to his brother *at his brother's friggin' wedding* wearing the biggest damn hard-on of his life. Thank goodness for his monkey suit. The jacket concealed the fact he brandished equipment hard enough to pound a horseshoe straight.

He was a glutton for punishment. An idiot. A foolish risk-taker. He knew he should tear his gaze away and calm himself down, but she was taking him on a wild ride, and Lord help him, he was not ready to stop.

Never had a woman brought him to this state of desire with just a look, and he had to hold back a groan at the thought of what would happen if they did more than just kiss.

If the ride was this wild already, what would happen if he took her down to the beach, peeled the material off her tempting curves and sank into her on the sand?

They'd be arrested for indecent exposure.

Christ.

He needed to get a grip. Fast. *Down boy*, he silently admonished. *This is Cole's wedding.*

But still, he watched her. He couldn't help it. She was addicting. He felt alive. He felt...*everything* when she looked at him. *Which was not necessarily a good thing*, his mind reminded.

But he didn't have to worry about looking away because the desire in her eyes turned to sadness and what he thought looked like uncertainty before Kerri pulled her gaze from his and never glanced his way for the rest of the ceremony.

The pulse eventually slowed through his veins, and he brought his attention to the happy couple as they exchanged the vows they wrote.

"Jordan," Cole began as he faced his bride and held both of her hands. "I love you. And I know you slipped through my hands not once, not twice but three times."

That startled a few people, including Connor who made a mental note to ask his little brother for clarification later.

Smiling down into Jordan's face, Cole continued, "But I have you now, and I swear to you I will never, *ever* let you go again. I will always love you even through death. And I promise here and now in front of

God and our families that I will use this second chance to make you happy, and to love you and our children for the rest of my life."

Connor watched Cole use his thumb to gently brush the tears from Jordan's face. His chest tightened at the magnitude of love his brother had for his bride.

"Cole, first of all I want to say"—Jordan grabbed his hands and a mischievous grin crossed her face—"I told you so."

Laughter bubbled up Connor's throat and his chuckle mixed with others.

"A long time ago I told you we were going to do this, and as you can see, I meant every word. Just like when I say I've always, *always* loved you and always will. You are my life and I want to have your children." A tear ran down her cheek and, Cole wiped it away as she continued, "And I promise here and now, in front of God and our families that I will love you forever, even in death…as you will see when I come back to haunt you." She winked and touched his brother's smiling face. "And lastly, I promise you this Cole McCall, I will spend the rest of my life making you happy that the chase is finally over. And I won."

Jordan kissed Cole's hand as his brother touched her lips and said, "Me, too."

She looked up at her soon to be husband with such intense love that pain gripped Connor's heart, and he wondered what that must feel like.

All three times he'd been engaged, the ladies had professed their love for him. But he now realized they had never said it with their eyes. How would it feel to have a woman as faithful and fabulous as Jordan look at him that way? How would it feel to experience the complete joy his brother must be feeling right now?

Connor's gaze was inexplicably pulled to the brunette in red.

The head table at the reception being held at the McCall Ranch had Jordan and Cole in the middle with Connor, Kevin and Kade next to the groom. Kerri sat with the corresponding bridesmaids, Megan and Jen to her sister's right.

"I'd like to propose a toast," Connor said, rising to his feet.

God, he's gorgeous.

Heart fluttering, Kerri watched the Best Man pause as he lifted his champagne filled glass and waited until everyone was standing with flutes raised.

"To Jordan and Cole, health and happiness, and may you always be as joyful as you are at this moment." He turned to look at her sister. "To, Jordan, my beautiful new sister-in-law, for never giving up on my brother, and for waiting for the stubborn SOB even though he made it tough on you at times." The cowboy's gaze shifted to his brother. "And to Cole, for helping fate to accomplish its mission by allowing Jordan to finally catch you after twenty-eight years."

Once the laughter and clapping quieted down, Connor added with a mischievous gleam, "Now, you two need to work on giving me some nieces and nephews."

Kerri almost choked on her champagne as laughter and hooting roared throughout the room.

"Okay," Cole said, pulling Jordan to her feet.

"Yeah, no problem." Her sister smiled and the laughter raised a pitch, then turned to more hooting as the couple shared a passionate embrace.

Twenty minutes later, Kerri was concentrating on the food in front of her when the tinkling of silverware onto glasses brought her attention back to her sister and new husband. The tradition was calling for the couple to kiss again, so she glanced at them with a ready grin, expecting them to willingly comply.

Oh shoot. The grin slowly fell from her face as the couple smiled expectantly at her, instead.

"Your turn, sis," Jordan said, knowing smile on her darn smug face.

Note to self, punch sister upon return from her honeymoon.

Kerri had been hoping to be spared this part of the tradition when the couples standing up for the bride and groom had to kiss as well. No such luck. Not that she minded kissing Connor. No. Quite the opposite. She liked it too much. But...*dang*, not in front of everyone.

Maybe he'll let her get away with a peck on his cheek. Yeah. She felt comfortable doing that in public. Not as much chance of getting carried away with a quick kiss to his cheek. Right?

Wrong.

Glancing at Connor, she could see amusement lighting his eyes and tugging that dang delectable mouth into a grin. Yeah, she could kiss that cheek peck good-bye.

Not wanting to repeat the mistletoe incident...or New Years Eve incident...or master bathroom incident...Kerri rose to her feet and met the tall, gorgeous, grinning cowboy behind the happy couple.

"Yeah, Kerri, it's your turn," he said, gaze full of pulse-pounding heat dropping to her lips then back to her eyes.

Her heart slammed into her ribs. Shoot. If she even tried to just aim for his cheek, she just knew he was going to turn into the kiss. Bugger.

Her Unbridled Cowboy

Reaching out, he gently cupped her face and immediately brought his lips down to hers. Prepared to weather the passionate storm he always had brewing, Kerri was taken by surprise as they shared the sweetest kiss of her life.

Her pulse fluttered along with her eyelashes as the tenderness in the embrace brought a flush to her face and a severe longing for that type of relationship straight to her heart.

As catcalls filled the room, she slowly pulled away and made the mistake of glancing up into his eyes. The amusement and teasing she expected to see were not there. The cowboy's face was as flushed and confused as hers.

How Kerri made it back to her seat was a mystery, and she was only vaguely aware of Megan kissing Kevin's cheek, followed by Jen kissing Kade's during their respective turns.

With her appetite for food gone, Kerri reached for her champagne and took several small sips as her heartbeats returned to normal. Okay, something just happened, but what?

She wasn't supposed to share tender kisses with Connor. Hot, wild, heart-pounding ones, *yeah...hell yeah,* even, but not tender ones. No. They were connected to emotions—and emotions were dangerous. Way too dangerous. Emotions needed to stay out of it.

Connor was on a totally different plane. Very different. Completely different. Heck, he traveled *the* plains and she traveled *on* planes. Yeah, their lives were just too different.

Right. So, try telling that to her still tingling lips.

Emma shut the drawing room door and nodded. "Okay.

All the guests are gone. Kerri's washing out pans in the kitchen and I saw Connor go upstairs."

"Good," Hannah said, glancing at her husband and friends. "What's our next move?"

"Well, now that one of my sons has shown good sense and married one of your daughters, we can concentrate all our efforts on my thick headed oldest boy." Alex let out a determined sigh.

Nate slapped him on the shoulder and smiled. "Not to worry my old friend. We had our work cut out for us with Jordan and Cole, but we prevailed. Right? This match can't be any harder."

"Oh, I think you are wrong there, my dear," Hannah said. "You're forgetting about fate and the bond that has always been there between Jordan and Cole. That made our job *much* easier. This time we're working on our own."

Leeann nodded. "Yes. It would do us good to remember that." Her friend settled down next to her on the brown leather sofa, and Alex sent his wife a strange look.

"Surely you don't deny those two are attracted to each other," he said.

Nate straightened next to his friend. "Yeah. It's like the same kind of fireworks Cole and Jordan sparked off each other last spring."

"Oh, I'm not denying they're attracted to each other, but those two have serious issue to work through. And the sooner they realize the answers to their issues and path to healing lie in each other, the sooner we can get to planning another wedding," Leeann said with a firm nod of her head.

"Amen to that," Emma said quietly, and the others agreed.

"Well then, what we need is to throw them together," Nate stated. "I think it's time to put 'Plan A' into motion."

"You do realize we just might have to go all the way through to 'Plan Z' with these two," she noted, linking her fingers together on her lap.

Her husband smiled down at her. "Whatever it takes."

"Whatever it takes," the others echoed back.

Chapter Ten

It was an unusually warm February day, so Kerri decided to take Bullet for a walk and enjoy the promise of spring that was in the air. Jordan had asked her to watch the dog until she returned from her honeymoon next week. She loved the German Shepherd so she was thrilled, and he seemed to enjoy the plethora of scents in the field behind her apartment and on the side of the road.

They were on their way back when Kerri heard a truck approaching and stepped to the side to let it pass. The road was fairly busy, which would be a plus for business. *For business*. God, it felt great to think those words again.

Her mind wandered over the renovations she and Jordan had discussed with Brandi, who had officially been signed on as their designer. The woman had walked inside the building and without one word from Kerri or Jordan, sat down and sketched furiously for ten minutes, then showed them a design she got from the vibe of the place.

A Texas beachy design.

They hired her that night.

Lost in thought, Kerri forgot about the truck she'd heard until a horn sounded on her left, and she nearly jumped out of her skin.

With a hand on her chest, she glanced into a red cab from the passenger side to find a lop-sided grin and a dimple staring back at her.

"Hello, darlin'."

Kerri had stern words for her heart and the way her

Her Unbridled Cowboy

tempo increased at the sight of sexy cowboy under his Stetson. "Connor."

"You're just the person I was looking for. I need you," he said.

She sent those same stern words to her pulse as it accelerated at *his* choice of words. Clearing her throat, she placed her hand on the truck and asked apprehensively, "What for?"

He shoved the truck in park and leaned across the seat toward the passenger window. "Hmm... Well now, let's see..." Rubbing his chin, he made a pretense of contemplating while his wicked brown eyes danced with delight. "The possibilities are endless."

Incorrigible.

Kerri reached in and pulled his hat down on his face and said as sexy as she could manage, "In your dreams cowboy." Then called to Bullet and resumed her trek home.

Undeterred, Connor drove up and kept pace with her. "Come on, Kerri. Give your big brother a break."

"Oh, big brother is it now?" Kerri stopped and turned toward him, placing her hands on her hips. He had no clue how her recent thoughts had put him as far away from *big brother* as possible.

He halted the truck and sent her his sexy smile. "Of course. What else would I be?"

"What indeed?" She raised her eyebrows and smiled despite her attempt to remain stoic.

"Seriously though, darlin', Cole asked me to check on the progress of the construction on your restaurant while he was away. Since I haven't seen it before, I need you to accompany me to let me know if things are on schedule."

Narrowing her eyes, she searched his face to see if

this was just another ploy to annoy her. Satisfied all she found was sincerity, Kerri moved closer. "All right. I'm curious myself. I've heard them working like mad this past week."

"Well, then, ma'am." He tipped his hat. "What are you waiting for? Hop in."

Kerri nodded and opened the door. Bullet eagerly jumped in first, settling between them, licking Connor's arm as he got a belly scratch.

Barely a minute later, Connor pulled into the parking lot of her soon-to-be restaurant. A thrill still ran through her at the thought. The excitement and challenge of establishing a clientele got her adrenaline pumping. She couldn't wait to serve her Texas public. Unfortunately, there were still at least two months before they would be anywhere near opening, but she was excited nonetheless.

Stepping out of the cab, she could hear the evidence of work being done inside. "Let me just run Bullet up to the apartment, then I'll be right back," she said, and didn't wait for a reply, mostly because she didn't want the sexy guy to invite himself along.

The last thing she needed was to be alone with Connor in her apartment. A tremor raced down her torso at the thought. Yeah, alone with that cowboy was a very bad idea. Another tremor shook through her. And apparently her body had a thing for very bad ideas. So it was a good thing he was outside, and she was opening her apartment for Bullet. Alone.

She patted the dog's head. "I'll be back in a bit." Another pat, then she shut him in and rushed to join the cowboy.

Kerri couldn't wait to get a glimpse inside her restaurant. She'd deliberately stayed out so as not to get in the workers' way, and hadn't stepped foot inside all week. Excitement flowed through her veins.

"You ready?" Connor pushed off the truck where he'd been leaning when she rounded the building.

"Yep."

"Then let's go check out your restaurant." He opened the front door for her, then followed her in.

To the untrained eye, it looked like a multitude of chaos with wires hanging and wood and sawdust everywhere, but Kerri saw several aspects of the restaurant coming together.

Excitement increased and her face heated from the rush. She grabbed Connor's arm and began to show him around. "The stage is going to go here. And a fish tank behind the bar there, with freshwater fish." She leaned in close, and bless him, he bent down to hear the details of her vision for the restaurant. A funny feeling fluttered through her chest. It warmed her that he seemed genuinely interested.

After Connor talked to the foreman, and she was satisfied that everything was on schedule, they walked outside.

"Thanks, Connor," she said, heart suddenly clogging her throat. Now what? Normally, out of politeness, she'd offer a cup of coffee. But that would mean taking him up to her apartment.

No. She needed to steer clear of the apartment. In fact, now was a real good time to head to the store.

Kerri turned to him and smiled. "Thanks, Connor…for checking on the progress."

"My pleasure, darlin'." He tipped his hat, but made no move to get in his truck.

Darn it. Now what?

She cleared her throat. "Well, if you'll excuse me, I've got to run to the store. I want to try a new recipe and need a few things"

"Let me drive you," he said, rushing to open his passenger door.

Okay, see, she knew what he'd meant. Really, she did, but dang, his offer put all kinds of images in her head. And they had nothing to do with a vehicle.

He smiled expectantly at her, waiting for her to climb in. Shoot. She couldn't very well refuse now.

"Thanks," she mumbled, cursing herself for not coming up with a viable reason to refuse.

Connor was unusually quiet, but she didn't pry. It was a short drive, and although she glanced at him a few times, Kerri remained silent, enjoying the peace.

Once inside the store, he disappeared, but Kerri shrugged figuring she'd meet up with him eventually; the place was tiny. Grabbing a cart, she wheeled through the aisles, picking up the things on the list she'd had in her pocket. She was examining the green peppers when a shadow fell across the vegetables.

"Hello, Kerri," a deep voice said from behind. "I've been trying to reach you."

Surprised, she nearly dropped the pepper, but recovered before it tumbled to the floor. Meeting Duke's blue gaze, she smiled weakly. "Hello. I didn't see you there."

He was so big and male, and she felt shabby despite the approval in his eyes and soft smile on his lips.

"I didn't mean to startle you, but I couldn't believe my luck in running into you here. I just left a message with your mother." He grinned.

"Oh. Is there something wrong?" Kerri asked, concern washed away some of her nerves.

He shook his head. "No, there isn't anything wrong. I just wanted to ask…"

He didn't get a chance to finish because another shadow crossed over her, and the voice belonging to it rudely cut into their conversation.

"Don't go getting any ideas, Carver."

Connor's voice was grim, and Kerri had all she could do not to jump at the venom in his tone. Turning to face him, she was shocked to see fury emanating from his every pore.

Holy cow. She'd never seen Connor so angry before. Heck, she never would've associated Connor with the word *fury*. The cowboy was usually just too laid back.

"Stay out of it, McCall. This is between Kerri and me," Duke growled out a warning.

"She doesn't want to go out with you."

"How do you know? I haven't even asked her yet!"

As the two cowboys squared off, gazes locked, Kerri wondered briefly if this was what a showdown was like in the old west.

"I know because she has better taste than the likes of you," Connor said, tone steely cold. "Your problem is with me." He pointed to himself and then nodded to her. "Leave her out of it."

"You do *not* have dibs on every woman, McCall." Duke narrowed his eyes. "This isn't college. You can't bully me around."

Kerri's neck was getting sore looking from one to the other. A few customers stopped shopping and were eyeing the men with interest. Disgusted with their juvenile behavior, she set the pepper in her cart and silently pushed her items, along with her embarrassment, to the checkout, leaving the men to continue with their squabble.

She was putting her bags in the truck when Connor finally came out of the store. He didn't have any marks on him, so it must've only been words the idiots exchanged.

She didn't know whether to laugh or be angry, so she kept her voice void of feeling. "Oh, you're finally done."

"Yeah. Look, Kerri—"

She cut him off with a wave of her hand. "I don't want to hear it. Whatever your problems are, they're between the two of you. Leave me out of it."

"It's just that—"

Again she silenced him with her hand and shook her head. "I mean it, Connor. I'm not interested."

And she wasn't. She didn't care who the best chest pounder was or who had the bigger penis. None of that impressed her. She liked her men civilized. Ones who didn't have shouting matches in the middle of a flippin' market.

She hadn't had problem with Duke. He'd been civilized and polite until Connor had barged in.

Kerri climbed into the truck and slammed the door, putting an end to their conversation. At least, she hoped so.

The ride home was done in total silence. She kept going over the events of the squabble in her head, and by the time Connor stopped the truck, she was angry.

What right did he have to interfere? She could take care of herself. Did he do it out of concern for her, or just because he didn't want Duke to have what he couldn't? The more she contemplated, the angrier she became.

Getting out of the truck, Kerri drew in a breath and grabbed a bag. She was so ready to put some distance between them. Her mind knew he had only been trying to protect her, but it still rankled that he'd treated her like a head of cattle. She reached for the second bag, but

Connor grabbed it first. Fine. No sense in arguing over groceries. She trudged up the stairs, down the hallway and fished the key out with her free hand. He could drop the bag off and leave; she really didn't want his company right now.

"Kerri, will you let me explain?"

"No." She set her bag on the counter, and he did the same, while she bent to pat the greeting Bullet.

"You're being childish!"

She laughed and reeled around to face him. "I'm being childish? I can't believe you just said that!"

"Well you are. Miss high-and-mighty cultured Kerri is acting like a baby." Connor looked down his nose at her.

Her anger rose so high she couldn't decide what to say first. So she repeated him. "*I'm* acting like a baby? *You* were the one causing a scene near the vegetables, not me." Her finger poked his firm chest. "I wasn't the one acting all territorial and making a fool out of myself."

"Of course not. Miss *Priss* would never stoop so low, would she?"

Miss Priss? Her head began to pound as they stared at each other. Is that really what he thought of her?

"She would never show any passion! Hell no, that's a dirty word." Distaste covered his face as he continued, "I don't know what I was worried about. You wouldn't know what to do with a red-blooded cowboy anyway!"

The sting of his words cut so deep she swallowed back tears. Her whole body alternated between numb and shaking. About to retaliate, she had her mouth open when her phone rang. Happy for the interruption, she didn't bother to look at the caller.

"Hello?"

"Hi, Kerri. It's Duke."

She glanced at Connor. "Hi, Duke." She didn't think it was possible, but the cowboy stiffened further. "What can I do for you?"

"I'm really sorry about that mess. All I wanted to do was ask you to have dinner with me tonight at the Gulfport."

With her gaze glued to Connor's furious face, she straightened her shoulders and smiled. "I'd *love* to go to the Gulfport tonight. I've wanted to try their food." At least that last part was true. She'd worry about the first part, later.

Kerri watched Connor's eyes narrow and lips thin before he spun on his boots and stalked out the door. She vaguely heard Duke tell her he'd pick her up at six before he hung up. Her attention had been drawn to the sound of tires kicking up gravel in Connor's haste to leave.

She slumped down into a chair, her legs no longer able to support her. As if sensing her emotional state, Bullet whimpered and set his head on her thigh. Kerri absently stroked his fur as the reality of what just happened hit full force.

Two men had verbally fought over her in public. She'd accepted a date with a cowboy she didn't want to go out with and was told by the one she did that he didn't think she could handle a red-blooded cowboy.

And wasn't that just it. He'd nailed it. Her biggest fear shouted out, made public right to her face. By the one cowboy she'd hoped would prove her wrong.

As six o'clock grew nearer, Kerri's apprehension grew stronger. More than once, she'd picked up the phone to bail out of her date with Duke, but each time she stopped because she saw Connor's face and heard his troubling words.

You wouldn't know what to do with a red-blooded cowboy.

Her stomach still gripped tight. The words hurt so much because they were the truth. In fact, Kerri wasn't sure she had what it took to keep the sexual interest in any man any more.

That wasn't always the case. She'd dated throughout high school, shared heated embraces with the quarterback and might have even done more if he hadn't headed to Harvard. Then there was the cute lifeguard she'd met through Jordan when her sister had been life guarding. Tate had been fun and sweet, and he'd taught her the merits of making out under a blanket on a moonlit beach.

So, yeah, her young adult years had been fine. It was since her marriage that her 'problem' surfaced. Maybe if she hadn't toned herself down so people would pay more attention to her food. Maybe then she would've been more attractive and sexy, and Lance wouldn't have looked elsewhere. Maybe if she'd been more responsive.

God, she didn't know. But she couldn't help but feel a failure when it came to sex. Why else would her husband have…strayed?

Jordan and Megan had insisted it wasn't her. God, she wanted to believe them, but they didn't exactly know the full story.

Sure, Connor couldn't seem to keep his hands off her, although, she didn't think she'd have that problem with him anymore. And he didn't actually count. He was almost as bad as Kevin. Those two cowboys weren't picky when it came to women. They didn't seem to care about size, shape or color. Which was a good thing. She actually admired them for that…it was just that it didn't say much for her, then. If they dated anything in a skirt, it didn't quite prove her desirability.

No. She needed to test the waters with someone not so…easy. Her date with Duke was a good place to start.

The doorbell rang as if to confirm her thoughts. She glanced at her watch. Six o'clock. Prompt. Kerri put that in Duke's favor. Opening the door, she had to add his sense of style to the list. He was wearing a charcoal gray suit with a black silk shirt underneath and sported a matching gray tie. He didn't look like a cowboy at all. He looked like a gentleman right down to his leather shoes.

So it was odd that Bullet let out a low *woof*. She bent to pat the dog and told him it was okay. He remained quiet, but didn't budge.

"These are for you, Kerri," Duke said, handing her a darling bouquet of tiny, red roses. "You look lovely."

She smiled at the sincerity in his gaze, and was glad she'd decided to wear her simple but elegant black dress with a boat neck and small slit up the back. She'd also pulled up the sides of her hair, and even dusted gray eyeshadow across her lids.

"Thank you for the roses and the compliment," she replied, feeling her face heat.

An appreciative gleam entered his blue eyes. "You're more than welcome."

Nerves began to invade her body. *Calm down, you can do this.* She smiled. "I'm just going to put these in water, then we can go."

After placing the clear vase on the credenza, she grabbed her coat off the back of the chair.

"Allow me." He took it out of her hands and held it open for her.

Another plus in his favor. He looked and acted like a perfect gentleman. She only hoped he continued to do so throughout the evening. Her mama didn't raise an idiot. Connor had to have had a reason to dislike Duke. And since she had foolishly stopped Connor from explaining, she was on her own.

When they arrived at the Gulfport restaurant, Duke told the maitre d' his name, and they were led to a corner booth with a wonderful view of the place.

He ordered their wine as she looked over the posh menu. Many of the entrées were either steak or seafood, and having received rave revues for their seafood, Kerri chose the grilled salmon. Since that would be on her menu as well, she wanted to taste the competition.

After they placed their orders, Duke sat back and gave her a curious look.

"What?" she asked with a shy smile.

"I was just wondering what a cultured woman like yourself is doing opening a restaurant here in Texas instead of New York or California," he replied, tilting his head.

"Well, I did go to school in New York and studied techniques in Paris. And my sister and I did own a restaurant in California." Pride sent heat to her face.

Duke stared at her, as if mesmerized, which only caused her face to heat further. He shook his head slightly and his gaze cleared.

"You said 'did own' as in past tense. What happened to make you want to open one here?"

"An earthquake."

His brow furrowed in concern. "You weren't in there at the time, where you?"

"Yes, Jordan and I were both in there, taking inventory and making a list of things we needed for the upcoming Thanksgiving holiday," she informed, before taking a sip of her wine. She really hated to think about that day.

He leaned forward and touched her hand. "Were you hurt?"

"Cuts and bruises mainly, but a spark set off the gas leak and reduced the place to a pile of ashes."

She pulled her hand away and sat back as the memory of her sister's body being thrown to the ground and the deafening sound that preceded flying glass and debris flashed through her mind.

With a shudder, Kerri took another sip of her wine and placed her glass back down when she heard a familiar giggle.

"Look, Connor, isn't that your cook?"

Kerri knew whom that voice belonged to before she lifted her eyes to see a red dressed Ashley standing by their table with her arm possessively through Connor's. The cowboy wore black jeans, a solid white shirt neatly tucked in, a black leather belt and cowboy boots, but no hat. Her pulse leapt at the sight of him.

Stupid body.

"I'm not his cook, Ashley," she said. "Whatever gave you that idea?"

"Didn't you cook that meal for Cole's engagement party?" the blonde asked with a finely arched brow.

She smirked. "I cooked some of it, but not for Connor. I did it as a favor to my sister. You know, the one who married Cole? And I seemed to recall there were other people there too, who enjoyed the buffet. Not just Connor."

Ashley's eyes darkened, and two twin spots of color marked her cheeks. The blonde looked anything but pleased about being put in her place in front of two men.

Too bad. Kerri looked from Duke to Connor and found both men wearing an identical look of amusement on their handsome faces.

Shoot. Now who was involved in a public pissing match? With a sigh, Kerri changed the subject and directed her question to Connor, knowing full well he'd overheard her phone conversation with Duke. "So, what brings you to Gulfport tonight? You get a sudden hankering for seafood?"

"Yes, their grilled salmon is top notch," he answered smoothly.

"And their lobster," Ashley added, before tugging at Connor's arm. "Come on, honey, our table is ready now."

Kerri watched as they were led to a booth across the restaurant. Great. Right in her line of sight. A second later, the blonde's annoying giggle reached her ears, and Kerri promptly lost her appetite.

Turning her attention back to Duke, she felt compelled to say something. "I'm sorry about that. If you want to leave, I would understand."

Duke reached across the table and took her hand gently in his. "There is nothing to apologize for, and I don't want to leave. But if you are uncomfortable, we can go somewhere else."

That was sweet. She looked down at her hand in his, which was undemanding yet warm, and when she glanced up, his eyes held the same signal. Until Connor and his date had arrived, she had actually been enjoying herself. No. Kerri was not going to allow them to ruin her evening.

Defiance tilted her chin and crept into her voice. "I'd like to stay, too. I was looking forward to the salmon." She smiled, her annoyance at their intrusion easing a bit.

The rest of the meal went surprisingly well despite the few times her gaze had met Connor's disapproving glare. And thanks to Ashley's irritating laughter, occasionally Kerri's salmon tasted as if it had been marinated in gasoline instead of lemon juice, thyme and oregano. Yeah, her gut burned. In those rare instances, she found her wine helped wash the seafood down.

After strong coffee and delicious baked Alaska for dessert, they left the restaurant and Connor and his date behind without a backward glance.

Duke took her to a small nightclub where they enjoyed some dance music and a few drinks. Kerri switched to soda and was placing her glass down when Duke pulled her back out onto the floor. It was a long time since Kerri had this much fun. The last time had been when she and Lance were in New York at school. Every Friday they'd go out with a bunch of students to the local clubs and dance all night long.

Nope, Kerri hadn't felt this carefree in years. All the old moves were coming back, and she was loosening up, dancing between Duke and a few other admiring males. Then she bumped into an angry eyed cowboy.

Chapter Eleven

Instant awareness and anger vibrated through Kerri's swaying body. She stopped and put her hands on her hips. "What is wrong with you, Connor? Are you following me?"

"I'd like an answer to that as well," Duke demanded coldly from behind.

Connor ignored Duke and looked directly at Kerri. "It's a good thing I am here. You're making a fool of yourself, acting like a tramp."

Tramp?

She lifted her hand, intending to slap his insolent face, but he caught her wrist with ease, and instead of releasing it, he yanked her off of the dance floor.

"I'm taking you home right now."

Digging her heels in, she stopped dead and jerk from his grasp. "You most certainly are not. I came here with Duke, and I will be leaving with Duke," she told him, moving closer to her date.

Who does he think he is? She wasn't doing anything wrong. Duke wasn't doing anything wrong. Heck, she was having a great time. No way was she leaving now, and certainly not with the gorgeous jerk.

"Kerri." Connor clenched his teeth, then took a step toward her, but Duke intervened and put his body between them.

Uh oh. The last thing she wanted was another round of public shoulder knocking.

"She said she wants to stay here with me, Connor." Judging by the rigid way Duke was standing, she was afraid fists would fly if she didn't do something.

Glancing at the red-faced woman silently standing on the outskirts of the dance floor, Kerri frowned. "Ashley, why don't you take your cowboy and get out of here?"

The blonde shrugged her shoulders. "Connor is a big boy. I learned long ago to let him do what he wants."

That didn't help her situation at all. She stepped around Duke to confront Connor. "Look, I don't know what you're thinking, but I am fine and having a good time. You don't need to play the big brother."

Brown eyes narrowed. "You're drunk and don't know what you're saying."

Oh, for the love of...

"I am not drunk! I'm drinking soda, see?" Anger made her grab her glass from the bar a little too hard, and as she thrust it at him, the force sent her cola onto his shirt.

With her hand to her mouth, Kerri barely suppressed the snicker that threatened as she tried to apologize. "Sorry, Connor. I didn't mean to do that."

"I'm sure you didn't," he ground out, ignoring the napkin she grabbed off the bar and thrust in his direction.

She lifted her chin and calmed her voice. "As you can see, Duke is not trying to get me drunk, so you can leave, and I can go back to having a good time."

The cowboy stared at her for a moment, then shifted his gaze to Duke. Kerri shivered as a deep freeze took over his features. It matched the expression on her date's face.

"She had better be home at a reasonable hour and unharmed or I will hold you responsible. Do I make myself clear, Carver?"

He sounded like an irate father dressing down a teenager taking his daughter on her first date. If the two men hadn't had clenched fists and looked like they wanted to brawl, Kerri would've found it comical.

"I'll be fine, Connor. Really. Now *go*," she said, turning him around and pushing him toward the door.

Five minutes later, she had a fresh cola in her hand and the dancing had resumed on the mopped up floor. But, try as she might, Kerri couldn't get Connor's angry face out of her head, or the way Duke had held such vehemence for the cowboy.

Was this still about Connor's ex-fiancée that Cole had mentioned? She was really beginning to wonder what exactly had transpired between the two alphas.

An hour later, Duke pulled up to the side of her apartment and let out a muffled curse.

A red pickup sat in the shadows.

He doesn't quit!

Connor was leaning up against the hood with his arms folded and one knee bent. With his booted heel hooked on the bumper, he silently watched them.

"I can't believe him," Duke exclaimed. "What does he think I am going to do?"

"I don't know, but I don't appreciate his interference." Kerri sighed, then smiled as an idea began to form in her mind. "I think we need to teach my *big brother* a little lesson. What do you say?" She focused on Duke's face semi visible in the moonlight.

He grinned and sat up straighter. "Sure, I'd love to. What do you have in mind?"

"Well, first I think I need to do this." Too busy wanting to teach Connor a lesson to worry about her inadequacies, she cupped his chin and brought her lips to his.

Duke kissed her back gently, then pulled away with a smile. "I think I'm going to like this. Now what?"

Not exactly a declaration of passion, but it wasn't a rebuttal either.

"Okay. Now you need to come around and open up my door, then put your arm around me and walk me to the stairs," Kerri explained.

Duke's eyes sparkled with mirth. "It would be my pleasure." He got out and rushed to her side and did as instructed. Stopping at the bottom of the outside stairs, he turned her to face him and grinned. "Now what?"

"Kiss me again."

If she'd been in her right mind, Kerri would've been appalled at her actions, but she was beyond right, she was pissed. She caught a glimpse of Connor's scowl through the corner of her eye and inwardly smiled.

Good for him.

Kerri found Duke very obliging and not a bad kisser either as she threw herself into the pretense.

When they finished, her heart was racing, but not from Duke's lovemaking. It was pounding because of the charade they were pulling on Connor.

As they broke apart, she noticed the cowboy was no longer leaning against his truck. He was now standing a few feet from it, squinting and watching them intently.

Shoot. He was supposed to get mad and leave. Now what was she going to do?

Darn, stubborn cowboy.

Since he refused to leave, Kerri had no choice but to take the game up a notch.

Smiling sweetly, she pulled out her keys and looked up at Duke. "Looks like we'll have to go inside. He's not leaving."

"Yes, ma'am." Her date smiled, then set his hand lightly on the small of her back to guide her up the stairs.

In the hallway, she glanced through one of the

Her Unbridled Cowboy

windows and watched Connor stare at the door for a few seconds before raising his hands in the air and walking around in a circle. Stopping, he looked at the door again, and then angrily kicked at the gravel, spewing it in all directions before finally getting into his truck.

Good. He's leaving. Kerri thought she'd won until he settled back in his seat and made no attempt to start the darn truck.

Her heart fell. Bugger was calling her bluff. She was stuck. Had no choice. She had to take Duke into the apartment.

"He is one stubborn *brother*," Duke said from behind.

Turning around, she laughed as nervousness started to set in. "Yes, he sure is. And I can't very well send you out there now. How long should we wait…an hour?" she asked, leading them into her apartment.

A wicked gleam entered his eyes. "How about two?"

She smiled. "Oh, I don't know if I can be that mean." Although, after his *tramp* remark, maybe she should.

Duke helped her out of her coat, then jumped when Bullet let out a low bark.

Kerri bent to pet the dog. "Hey, it's okay, boy."

Bullet didn't bark or growl again, but he remained by her side. She straightened and turned to Duke. "You might as well have a seat. I'm sure we can find something to watch. If not, I have a few DVD's," she told him, then smiled. "How about some popcorn?"

"Buttered?" he asked with a hopeful gleam in his eyes.

"Of course."

"Sounds good to me." He smiled, then walked away, but turned around. "Aren't you worried what people are going to think with one cowboy sitting outside and one in the apartment?"

She snickered, highly doubting anyone would take notice at all. They were pretty much in a commercial area with all the shops already closed. "No. People can think what they want. I know nothing's going on."

Kerri didn't miss his raised brows, so she pointed a finger at him. "Don't you go getting any ideas or I'll be forced to use kung fu on you. I do hold a black belt, just so you know."

Well, almost. Jordan had insisted Kerri learn self-defense before she had gone to New York. Her sister taught some great moves and that had sparked Kerri's interest. After her divorce, she'd started lessons and was currently a second degree purple belt. Her training would have to wait until she returned to the west coast.

Another casualty of the earthquake.

"I won't. I promise." Duke backed away, hands up with a smile on his face, while Bullet never took his eyes off him. "Beside, you've got the Terminator sitting out in the parking lot, and Cujo right here."

True.

A bag of popcorn, a comedian's videotaped routine, two cans of cola and one hour later, Kerri and Duke headed for the stairs.

On the way down the outside hall, Kerri carefully peered through the window. "I wonder if he fell asleep yet."

"Connor? Not a chance." Duke's scathing voice filled the space between them. "Will you be all right when I leave? McCall can be a bastard," he spat, contempt filling his gaze.

"I'll be fine," she reassured. "But I need to do something first. I'll be right back."

Her Unbridled Cowboy

She headed back into her apartment, kicked off her shoes, removed her pantyhose, then took the clips out of her hair. Shaking her head upside down, she ran her fingers through it before standing up again. A quick glance in the mirror confirmed it looked wild enough, so she rushed back to the long hallway.

Duke's eyebrows rose and mouth dropped. "Wow. You don't play fair, do you?"

"Nope." She grinned. "I learned from the best."

Yes, Jordan would be quite proud.

"It's about damn time," Connor muttered inside his truck when the building's door finally opened after an hour of pure hell.

A half a dozen times, he'd been ready to rush up to the apartment, but managed to hold back. Barely. The last time had been ten minutes ago. He even had his hand on the door knob as images of Duke forcing himself on Kerri had finally gotten the better of him. They had him out of his truck, up the stairs, down the hallway and in front of her door. The sound of her laughter was the only thing that had stopped him from bursting inside. The only thing.

Relief had washed over him in waves as her giggles signaled her safety. It was on his way back to the truck that raw fury took over.

How could she make love to Duke knowing he was outside worrying about her?

Connor pressed the button to illuminate his watch and his anger increased. She took her damn time, too!

Thrusting a hand through his hair, he expelled a breath, trying to get a handle on his temper before the lovebirds reached the bottom of the stairs.

What the hell was wrong with him? Seriously. He

needed his head examined. Kerri's love life was none of his damn business.

He'd had no intensions of following her tonight, but before he knew it, he was pulling up in front of the Gulfport restaurant with Ashley, and the rest was history.

Christ. The thought of Kerri with Carver made him fucking sick.

Visions of Kerri being made love to filled his mind. Her hair down and tossed about, a soft flush to her cheeks and her luscious lips moist and swollen from passion. Connor's gut clenched at the thought of Duke bringing Kerri to that state.

It should be him.

Maybe they didn't do anything. Maybe they just talked. He got out and leaned against his truck, watching the couple walk to the bottom of the stairs.

His wishful thinking disintegrated in the moonlight. *Shit*. Her hair was now loose and tangled down her back, and the fact she stopped at the bottom step brought his attention to her lack of shoes.

Jealousy ripped through his gut as he bore witness to their kiss and lingering embrace. If possible, smoke would've come out of his ears. Duke caressed Kerri's face before leaving her to walk to his car. Then the bastard saluted him.

Carver fucking saluted him!

Connor's knuckles cracked into fists as Duke got into his car and drove off with a honk of his horn.

No good rotten bastard!

Expelling the breath he hadn't known he was holding, Connor focused his attention on Kerri who was half way up the stairs. *Oh, hell no*. As swift as sin, he raced up the stairs and beat her to her door. No way in hell was she going to just go inside and ignore him.

"Oh no you don't," he ground out, using his body to block her.

She sighed. "Connor, move out of the way. I am not in the mood."

The woman had some fucking nerve to say that to his face after keeping him waiting outside while she fooled around with Duke.

His fury was insurmountable, and as she pushed passed him, he quickly followed her in before she had the chance to shut him out.

Kerri stared at him through weary eyes. "Connor, please leave."

"No," he said. "We need to talk." As if knowing this, Bullet got up then disappeared down the hall.

"Talk?" Her voice rose. "After the way you acted tonight, I have nothing to say to you." She dismissed him, and then walked further into her apartment.

"The way I acted? *You* were the tramp tonight, Kerri, not me." He followed closely behind and nearly bumped into her when she stopped dead.

Twisting around, her hair was wild about her face, and browns eyes flashed with temper. *Christ*. He knew he shouldn't be thinking this, but God, she was beautiful.

"That's the second time you called me that tonight, Connor." Her chest rose at a rapid rate. "Don't make the mistake of doing it again."

His temper returned to unsafe. "Yeah, well if the shoe fits, darlin'."

She smiled a damn wicked smile. "But I'm not wearing any shoes." Then stuck her foot out for his inspection.

"Exactly," he grounded out as a fierce emotion took over. One he didn't recognize.

Her eyes lost their mirth and grew even darker, and a

second later, her hand made contact with his face. Catching her wrist on its decent, he ignored the stinging of his cheek and pulled her to him.

"Let go."

She tried to yank free, but he held on and backed her up against the wall before she could strike again. Trapped, she glared up at him, eyes wild, hair wild, cheeks flushed, and his groin tightened at the erotic sight. She was so damned beautiful and sexy that his hunger grew out of control, as did the bulge in his jeans. It was too much. Just too damn much.

He grabbed the back of her neck and brought his mouth down on hers. Hard. She resisted for a mere second until he ran his tongue over her lips. Hot damn, her moan granted him access to the sweetness he knew she had hidden inside.

Pressing his body to hers, he groaned when she swept her tongue into his mouth. His whole body was on fire. He picked her up and carried her to the living room, making sure not to break contact with her mouth.

Once there, he followed her down onto the couch and pulled his lips away so they could drag in air. She stared at him through dazed eyes, and God, he knew exactly how she felt. Off kilter. Hungry. Hot. He lowered his lips to her neck, and as she moaned and clutched his back, his need to feel more of her intensified.

Things got crazy. His hand glided over her dress, enjoying the feel of her breast against the silky material as he teased her nipple into a tight peak. She wiggled underneath him, tugging his shirt free so she could run her hands over his bare back. God, she was so responsive. His mouth sought the bared flesh of her cleavage, and she arched into him while pressing his head to her chest.

Her Unbridled Cowboy

So damn responsive.

Blood pounded through Connor's head, and his heartbeats drummed an A*lleluia* he'd never heard before. He knew he should stop. Things were way out of hand, but he couldn't. God, no. He needed to touch more of her.

His hand reluctantly left her breast and made its way over the delicious curve of her hip, down to her thigh. She let out a little whimper that nearly did him in. He pulled her dress up and his palm met with warm, soft, supple leg.

Bare leg.

Shit. Her stockings were gone.

He jerked back, and for the first time since entering her apartment, he took in the details of the room. There were pillows on the floor.

He didn't put them there.

Her shoes and missing panty hose were lying in a heap near the chair.

He didn't put them there either.

Son-of-a-bitch.

Looking down at her surprised face, the reality of what he was doing hit him hard.

Once again he was taken in by a city girl.

Not more than a half hour ago, she was in this very room having sex with Duke, the evidence was all around them, and now she was allowing him those same privileges. Well, he sure as hell didn't want them.

He sprang from the couch, barely able to breath, he was so fucking angry.

She reached for his hand. "What's wrong, Connor?" Her voice sounded innocent.

Oh, she's good.

He shook her hand off. "*You* are what's wrong,

Kerri! I must have been crazy to think..." his voice trailed off as anger with himself boiled over.

How could he allow himself to be taken in by a girl like her? Again.

He looked down at the hurt expression on her face. It was so intense, he almost believed it was real, except the events of the evening spoke for themselves. She had played him for a fool, and this was the last time this cowboy was going to let that happen. The very last time.

"What's wrong, Kerri? Did I spoil your plans?" He continued to stare down at her, anger shaking his limbs. "Well, take a good look, darlin', because *this* is the look of a man you won't have." And after giving her body a quick dismissing glance, he headed for the door and didn't look back.

Chapter Twelve

Kerri glanced at the German Shepherd sitting in the passenger seat happily staring out the window. She was going to miss Bullet. He'd been a godsend this past week, seeming to sense her desolation and didn't leave her side for much of the time. Still, she could tell he missed Jordan, and she was happy to be the one to reunite them.

So much for being spared the humiliation of seeing Connor again.

Maybe tonight her sister would be so overwhelmed with happiness she wouldn't catch on to Kerri's deceit. Her ruse that nothing was wrong, that deep inside she didn't feel cold and raw and like such a failure.

At least, she hoped her sister wouldn't catch on.

Fooling her parents was one thing, but trying to pull something over on Jordan was near impossible.

Sighing, she parked the car and crossed her fingers for luck before getting out with her excited companion.

The front door opened before she got there, and Cole ushered them in as the wind picked up. Her chest tightened. God, he looked so happy. Kerri hugged him and then her sister before taking her coat off and putting it into the coat closet while the couple reunited with their happy dog.

Kerri watched the newlyweds and could sense right away a difference in them. They had been happy before, but now...wow...their warm expressions and loose posture just oozed contentment and pure bliss. Total serenity.

Kerri fought the urge to sigh. She wanted that, too.

"Thanks for watching him for us," her sister said, still on her knees as Bullet continued to lavish her with welcome home kisses.

Kerri smiled. "It was my pleasure. He kept me good company."

"I hated to leave him again, especially after I promised him I wouldn't," Jordan confessed and rubbed him behind the ears before standing up to look at Kerri. "How about you? How've you been? Mom said you weren't feeling well."

Shoot. Now her sister was studying her carefully.

"Yeah." Kerri shrugged. "I had some kind of bug, but I'm on the mend."

Cole stepped next to Jordan, dropping an arm around her sister's shoulder while looking at Kerri. "Must be something going around. Seems Connor's been out of sorts this week, too."

"Could be." Hoping her expression appeared neutral, Kerri turned and headed for the drawing room where she heard voices.

After saying hello to the families, she avoided eye contact with Connor and thanked her father when he handed her a glass of wine.

She was ready for the whole darn bottle.

Dang, the cowboy looked good enough to snuggle up to in his red flannel shirt and jeans. Granted, she didn't allow her gaze to move passed his neck, but her body wasn't complaining. In fact, it was straining against her sweater, already responding to his nearness.

Stupid body. Yeah, she was going to require more than one glass of wine in order to get through this visit. Emma, thank the Lord, came in a few minutes later and asked to speak with her in the kitchen.

"Sorry to pull you away," Emma said, looking a little nervous as she twisted her apron. "I wanted to tell you…well…the community fair is coming soon, and I hope you don't mind, but I signed you up for a few things."

Kerri's heart stopped. "What sort of things?"

"Just the Chili Cook-off and the Lunch Basket Raffle."

Now her stomach rolled. "Oh, Emma I wish you hadn't."

"Why?" The cook frowned. "This is a good opportunity for you to show off your cooking skills *and* advertise your restaurant. It'll be opening up soon afterwards, right?"

"Yes." Kerri sighed. "It would be good advertising, I'm just not sure about the raffle. Doesn't that mean I will have to share lunch with whoever bids the highest for my basket?"

Emma smiled broadly. "Yes. Won't that be fun? All those young, handsome men vying for your goods."

Kerri groaned. "That's what I'm worried about."

"But why, for goodness sakes?" Now her mentor was frowning. "Just think about all the good that money will do. You know each year a charity is chosen to receive half of the fair's proceeds along with all the money from the raffle."

Actually, Kerri had forgotten about that, but she nodded and continued to listen.

"This year, all the proceeds will go toward building a gymnasium and indoor swimming facilities for the local physical rehabilitation center." Emma's eyes misted over. "Some of the children there will finally be able to go swimming for the first time in their life. And they're going to be adding some veteran's programs in the fall."

Ashamed, Kerri's stomach soured at her selfishness. Her discomfort at having to share a lunch with one of the local males was nothing compared to what the veterans or those children had to go through on a daily basis.

"You're right, and that's a great charity this year. When is the fair?"

"It's the first week of April. Thursday thru Sunday." Emma's voice was filled with pride as she'd been on the committee for decades now.

"Okay." She smiled. "Then that gives me a month to come up with a killer lunch."

"Oh child, I suspect the men will be bidding on your basket to spend time with you, not so much to eat your lunch, no matter how delicious it is." Emma's eyes twinkled.

Kerri's stomach turned. That was exactly why she didn't want to do it. She was so unsure of herself, and even more so since her disastrous encounter with Connor. The cowboy's reaction to her kisses once he'd gotten her on the couch confirmed what she'd suspected. She didn't live up to expectations. Her lack of sensuality left little to be desired. Literally. First, with her ex-husband, and now, with Connor. She'd been looking for validation, and boy, that was it.

Cripes. She wished with all her heart she could fly back to California and leave that cowboy and his words behind.

"I'd better get back," she said, and left Emma and headed to the dining room where everyone had settled.

Kerri took her usual seat. Unfortunately, it happened to be right across from Connor. Another sip of wine was in order. Maybe two.

Content to let the newlyweds relate a few details of their trip, Kerri discovered they'd also stopped off in

L.A. afterward so Jordan could pack up her belongings.

Homesickness for the coast hit Kerri full force, tightening a band across her chest. She'd been happier there.

No, not true, but that's her story, and she was sticking to it.

Another sip and she managed to ask the right questions at the right time. But Kerri's nerves began to increase with the pointed glances her sister kept throwing her way.

Since she and Connor were noticeably quiet tonight, Kerri guessed they looked suspicious. Probably...*hello*...because they were. She bravely stole a few glances at him, but was relieved he had his gaze on his food and not her.

God, she really couldn't bear it if he looked at her with disinterest in front of everyone.

Kerri was not surprised when, an hour later, her sister asked her to join her upstairs. Yeah, busted. At least her sister had the decency to grill her in private.

Once Jordan shut the door behind them, she motioned for Kerri to sit on the loveseat near the lit fireplace, which cast a soft glow about the bedroom.

Jordan sat down next to her and placed her hand on Kerri's knee. "All right, we're alone. Spill it. What's going on, Kerri?"

Raising her brows she managed to ask calmly, "What do you mean?"

"I mean, you and Connor barely ate a thing, barely said a word and didn't once look at each other," Jordan replied firmly. "Now, please tell me what is going on. Did something happen between the two of you?"

Kerri snorted. Yeah, nothing.

Her sister's sigh mingled with the crackling from the

fireplace. Jordan gave her knee a squeeze. "Kerri, tell me what happened. You can't keep it bottled up."

Yes, she could. In fact, she was real good at it.

"Kerri, come on."

She shook her head. "No, Jordan. I have to keep it in, otherwise, I'll fall apart."

Jordan's frown deepened. "What in the world did Connor do to you?"

"Nothing." That was all she could manage and could see it only worried Jordan all the more.

"Maybe I'd better go have a few words with my handsome but clueless brother-in-law." Jordan stood and turned to the door.

"No!" Kerri jumped to her feet and placed a hand on her sister's arm. "Please, Jordan, don't."

Her sister turned and looked her straight in the eye. "Kerri, honey, something is terribly wrong, and if you can't tell me then I am going to ask Connor. I can see you're in pain, and you know I won't stand by and watch you suffer."

"It...It isn't Connor's fault," Kerri stammered.

"What?"

"I said it isn't really his fault."

Jordan took her hand and led them back to the loveseat. "Okay, I think you'd better start at the beginning."

Kerri looked at her sister's concerned face and a tear trickled down her cheek. "Jordan, I can't." She closed her eyes, pushing out a multitude of tears in the process.

Jordan squeezed her hand. "Kerri, you're scaring me. What could be so bad?"

She opened her eyes and shook her head. God, she just couldn't voice it.

Her Unbridled Cowboy

With a sigh, her sister wiped Kerri's cheek. "I also brought you up here to tell you that Lance wants to talk to you."

Kerri's stomach lurched.

That was the last thing she needed. Hysterical laughter bubbled in her throat, working its way out, startling Jordan who looked at her like she'd grown two heads. No. just two *un*-admirers.

"Well, that's just great. I can make it a convention then." Kerri laughed some more. "We can hold a contest to see who could humiliate me the most."

Jordan's frown scrunched her whole face. "What are you talking about? Both Lance and Connor did something to humiliate you?"

Hearing her sister say it out loud sobered Kerri, sucking the smile from her face faster than steam through an overhead fan. "Something like that."

"Kerri." Her sister's voice was soft. "Lots of women are cheated on."

She couldn't help the snort that escaped.

"I always thought there was something more to your divorce than you told me. I'm right aren't I?"

Jordan tried to look in her eyes, but Kerri shot to her feet and walked over to the fireplace, staring at the blaze. Her sister was in bulldog mode now. Her teeth were sunk in with no easing in sight.

Sure enough, Jordan followed her, then laid a reassuring hand on her shoulder. "Kerri, it's okay," she encouraged softly. "Whatever it is, it will be okay. You need to get it out."

She knew this to be true. She really did. And cripes, she was so darn sick of carrying the secret around. So sick in fact, Kerri found she suddenly needed to tell it and get it off her chest.

So, with her eyes trained on the orange tipped flames, Kerri did just that. "You were right about Lance and me. I told you the truth about finding him in bed with someone else that day, but what I didn't tell you was with whom." Kerri paused for a breath, and Jordan remained silent, just squeezing her shoulder to give her the courage to go on. "I found him in bed with Ian, the man that managed the restaurant we both worked at."

The shock and humiliation came back full force. She drew in a shaky breath, then continued in a wobbly voice, "And do you want to know what the worst part was? I needed my best friend, but couldn't go to him, because *Lance* was my best friend. God, Jordan, I never felt so alone or desolate before."

Once she finally said it, Kerri felt sad, but also a little relieved, like a weight lifted off her shoulders. Jordan turned her around, and Kerri noted tears in her sister's eyes.

"Oh, Kerri, why didn't you tell me this sooner?"

"You'd just lost Eric a few months earlier," she replied. "You barely knew what month it was, and I didn't want to burden you with that kind of nonsense. God, what you were going through was so much worse than what I was."

Jordan inhaled and squeezed Kerri's shoulders at the same time. "Don't you ever think that, Kerri. Do you hear me? Your feelings and problems are just as important as mine." Her sister pulled her in for a tight hug. "God, I am so sorry I wasn't there for you. I let you down."

Kerri squeezed her sister back. "You could never do that."

"Well, I sure screwed up big time then." Jordan drew back, but didn't release her. "My gut told me there was more to your divorce back then, but I didn't push, and now I find out you've been going through this all by yourself for over two years now." Her sister took an unsteady breath. "I'm so, so sorry I let you down."

"Stop saying that. It was my choice, and I can be just as stubborn as you."

They both smiled at that. And why not? It was a known fact.

Jordan put both hands firmly on Kerri's shoulders and stared intently. "I don't want you to think, even for *one minute* that you were the reason that Lance is gay."

It felt as if someone had shoved a fist into her gut and twisted. Her face must've given her away because Jordan's pressure increased on her shoulders.

"I mean it, Kerri. It had nothing to do with you."

"How can I think that, Jordan?" She snorted. "The man wasn't gay before we got married. I must've been so undesirable, so horrible in bed that he went looking elsewhere." She pushed out of her sisters' grasp and flopped back down onto the loveseat. Finally, she'd revealed her dark secret—spoke the words aloud at last.

"If that were true, wouldn't he have just found a stripper or something? I mean, why would he look for a man?" Jordan asked as she sat down next to her.

"Because I was a lousy lover," she repeated.

"No honey, that's not true." Jordan smiled and put her arm around her. "Don't you see, if it were, he would've found another woman. Not a man. Lance obviously had some of his own issues to deal with."

Kerri blinked. Jordan's words made some sense, but after believing herself to be the problem for so long, it was hard to think otherwise.

"You need to talk to Lance."

Kerri stiffened. "No way. I-I couldn't."

Wouldn't that be a fun conversation?

Hi, Lance. So, um, is it true I was such a horrible lover I turned you off women?

Yes, Kerri. Yes, it's true. You should seek some professional help.

Kerri shuddered. *Talk to Lance? No thank you.*

"It's the only way you can move on, Kerri. Don't you see that?" her sister implored.

Kerri sighed. Jordan made a lot of sense. Darn her. "I guess you're right, but I'm not ready."

"Well, I hope you are by Sunday, because he is coming in then," Jordan informed quietly.

Kerri's heart rolled in her chest. "What?"

"He's coming to see you on Sunday. Cole and I ran into him in L.A., and he said he's been trying to contact you and offered to drive the moving van that has my things. He's on his way now," Jordan told her gently. "I knew you two had some unfinished business so I agreed. And after what you just told me, I am so glad I did."

Kerri sat there in stunned silence as the news sunk in. Her ex-husband was coming to Texas to talk to her. Her chest hurt. She was having trouble breathing. Talk to Lance? God, she didn't think she could do it.

As if sensing this, Jordan took her hand and squeeze. "Kerri, you can do this. You are strong, and you need to hear him out if you are ever going to get on with your life."

She closed her eyes, drew in a breath, then opened them. "I know you're right. I really do, but what if he confirms what I've been thinking all along?"

There, she voiced her strongest fear.

"Honey, he is not going to do that. He wouldn't drive through several states, hauling someone else's junk just to put you down. Think about it. You know I'm right."

Kerri managed to nod, though she was still a little unsure.

"Now," Jordan said firmly as she squeezed her hand again. "What went on between you and Connor?"

Images of the sexy cowboy standing over her and scowling, invaded her thoughts. Closing her eyes, she willed them to go away. They didn't.

"Kerri, what happened?"

"I…" Her voice was suddenly hoarse with emotion. She cleared her throat and proceeded to relate the events of her date with Duke, finishing up by briefly skimming over the part about the couch and Connor, and ended with his despairing remarks.

"Wow." Jordan sat back, then smiled.

Smiled. Why was she smiling? *I'm here dying inside and she's smiling.*

"You have that man hogtied."

Now it was Kerri's turn to look at Jordan as if she'd grown two heads. How could her sister have possibly come to that conclusion from what she just told her?

Kerri cocked her head and frowned. "Are we talking about Connor or Duke?"

"Connor you goof." Jordan playfully punched her arm.

"Did you not hear what he said to me?"

Jordan nodded. "Yes, I heard everything you told me, but I don't think you see the picture as clearly as I do." Her sister smiled smugly. "Kerri, that man is so besotted with you, he's not thinking straight."

Oh, that's different then. That clears everything up. Not.

Looking into Jordan's smiling eyes Kerri sighed. "You're going to have to tell me then, oh wise one, because I was there and that man was ranting and raving, slinging hateful words and…and…glaring at me like I was garbage."

"Exactly." Jordan slapped her leg. "Connor followed you because he was worried about what Duke might do to you. Then, after you made him sit outside while the two of you were inside, his jealousy ran rampant so that by the time Duke left, he was out of control."

Kerri narrowed her eyes as she tried to believe those words. They just didn't explain why he stopped and said those hateful things. It could only mean that she was right about being undesirable.

"No," Jordan remarked as if she could read her mind. "He said what he did because he was angry with himself for *being* so attracted to you."

Kerri laughed at that. "Yeah, right."

"I am right," Jordan said, cocky grin on her face. "He was trying to convince himself that he wasn't interested, when in fact, he was way interested to the point of obsession."

Now her sister had jumped into nutville, without a cape. Kerri stared at the woman sitting next to her because she made no sense.

"What did Connor do before he said those words to you? It's very important, so think."

Not knowing where Jordan was going with this, Kerri thought back to that horrible night. "He pulled away and looked around the room."

"What did he see? What did the room look like?"

Kerri closed her eyes and tried to envision it as best she could. "I hadn't cleaned up from Duke yet, so our popcorn and soda cans were on the coffee table. Pillows were on the floor and so was my…"

Her eyes flew open and she sat up straight.

"So was your what?" Jordan asked excitedly.

"My panty hose and shoes."

Her sister's eyes widened then narrowed.

"I took them off before walking Duke out to his car."

Jordan dropped back against the loveseat and laughed hysterically for several seconds before she sat up and smiled. "Oh my God, I love it! You are one sneaky bitch. You made me proud."

Kerri smiled back. "Well, he got me angry by staying out there. He should've gone home."

"Do you see what happened to Connor now?" Jordan asked, and when Kerri shook her head, she continued, "He thought you'd just made love to Duke, and you were giving him the same treatment."

Oh my god! Kerri's mouth dropped open. *Could Jordan be right?* Possibly. After all, that was the whole reason she took off her nylons and let her hair down.

"Do you really think so?"

Jordan nodded. "Yes."

Wow. Kerri stood and walked back to the fireplace. *He thought I...he thought...*

Turning around, she looked at Jordan and shook her head. "You mean I didn't turn him off?" *He was angry with himself for finding me attractive because he thought I'd just had sex with Duke, then sent Duke home and proceeded to lure him in for the same...*

"Definitely not." Her sister walked over to her and smiled while taking both her hands. "Now do you see? Lance was attracted to men, and it was *not* because of you. And Connor is so attracted to you, he's trying to push you away because he's afraid of getting burnt for the fourth time."

Sucking in a deep breath, Kerri squeezed her sister's hands. "If all of that is true, then that would mean there's nothing wrong with me," she said more to herself than Jordan,

"Of course there is nothing wrong with you. Except that *you* seem to think so." Pushing Kerri's hair behind her shoulder, Jordan continued, "You are a very beautiful and attractive woman. You have a wonderful sense of humor and wit, and I think it is about damn time that girl showed her head around here."

"Okay. But don't expect it to happen overnight," Kerri replied. She needed to take these new revelations and let them soak in.

Connor was working on the fence in the southern corral the next evening when he heard hoof beats in the distance. He'd already told his mother not to expect him for supper. Not because he had a lot of work, which he did. The spring cattle drive was coming up. But that wasn't what kept him from calling it a night.

No. It was desire to keep busy. To not think. Work hard. Drop into bed too exhausted for anything but sleep. Yeah, that suited him just fine.

"So, this is where you've been hiding," Cole said, approaching from the east on his horse. "I thought so."

Connor stopped pounding the post long enough to see his brother dismount and walk toward him with a bag in his hand.

Great. That meant Cole was here to badger. If an emergency had been the reason for a late evening ride, his brother would've stated it outright. Or called. Cell phone reception was actually great on the ranch. So, no, the reason for his brother's interruption was definitely to badger. He knew because he'd been guilty of it more than once. Hell, just last year their roles had practically been reversed.

"I'm not hiding. I'm working," he said, continuing to pound the latest post deep into the ground.

Cole snickered. "Yeah, I can see that. You're the reason I'm out here having a roast beef sandwich instead of a roast beef dinner." His brother pulled two wrappers out of the bag, tossed him one, along with a bottle of water. "Compliments of Emma."

He didn't want to eat. He wanted to work, but knew the sooner he placated his brother, the sooner his brother would leave.

Connor grunted, unwrapped part of the sandwich and began to eat. It was good. Real good. He had half of it gone before Cole opened his mouth.

"We need to talk."

Looking at his brother's broad smile, Connor's insides churned. "Whatever it is, Cole, I'm not in the mood." Ignoring him, he finished his sandwich and opened his water.

Cole chuckled. "Oh, boy. Avoiding family, skipping meals, doing physical labor could only mean one thing."

The goof was trying to get at something, but Connor wasn't about to help. He set his water on the ground, picked up the hammer and began to pound in a nail.

"Has to be a Masters."

It would've been fine if his hammer hadn't slipped off the damn wooden post and slammed into his friggin' knee. *"Son-of-bitch!"* Connor stumbled around, alternately rubbing then shaking his leg.

"Yeah. *Definitely* a Masters." Cole nodded. "Looks painful, bro. That's gonna leave a mark."

"I'm gonna mark you if you don't shut it, Cole," Connor ground out between curses.

Backing away, his brother held up his hands. "Hey, just payback from last year when I smashed my thumb, thanks to you."

Connor grumbled, bending over to rub his leg. "You don't know what you're saying."

"Oh, I know, Connor, because I've been there." Cole slapped him on the shoulder. "Last year, I took a bottle of Jack, locked myself up in my office and proceeded to empty it."

He glanced at his brother in surprise, wondering if that was during the Masters' sister's first visit or second. Cole had been a bear both times.

"It didn't work, by the way. Jordan still continued to haunt me, and that only stopped when a very wise person made me see things clearly." Cole squeezed his shoulder, then released him to lean against the fence and stare intently at him.

"That was totally different. My feelings for Kerri are not the same as yours are for Jordan." He swiped his water from the ground and proceeded to drain the bottle.

"Oh, so you don't feel a tightening in your gut when you look at her? Kerri's kisses don't haunt you at night and the thought of her making love to someone else doesn't make you want to punch something?"

Well, hell.

Connor stared at Cole, then lied through his teeth. "No."

He could tell his brother didn't buy it. Yeah, the way Cole threw his head back and laughed his ass off was a dead giveaway. Connor watched as his brother sobered and shook his head.

"That's exactly what I would've said last year, and *I* would've been lying, too."

Grumbling, Connor stuffed his garbage in the paper bag, then shoved it into Cole's gut. "My love life is none of your business."

"That's where you're wrong, bro. It is my business when I see you hurting."

He held back a snort. No way was he getting roped into this conversation. Shaking his head, he walked away to pick up the hammer.

"What happened between you and Kerri while I was gone?"

Jesus. Doesn't the guy quit?

"The two of you can barely breathe, and you won't even look at each other. Why is that, Connor?"

Pain-in-the-ass, that's what Cole was. And as tenacious as his bride. They were peas in a pod. *Two tenacious, pain-in-the-ass peas in a pod.* And because of that, Connor knew he wouldn't get away with remaining quiet.

"Look, you don't understand."

"You're right," Cole agreed. "I don't understand. So, why don't you enlighten me?"

Chapter Thirteen

Enlighten him?

Connor expelled a breath. Fine. If his brother wanted to hear the whole sordid soiree then so be it.

"She went out with Duke last Saturday after I asked her not to."

"That sucks. Did you ask her nicely?"

He must've given something away in his expression because Cole smirked. "I didn't think so," his brother said.

Hammer gripped tight in his hand, Connor walked to Cole, shaking his head. "You know, I had no intentions of following her that night, either, but after I picked Ashley up, I drove to the restaurant I'd overheard Kerri mention."

"And?"

And, Jesus, yeah, the and *part.*

"And then he took her to a club afterwards where I found her dancing seductively with Duke and three other guys!"

"Kind of like you at my Engagement party?"

"Yeah, but that was different."

"Oh, sorry, my mistake. I forgot it was okay for you to dance harmlessly with a bunch of women, but Kerri can't do that with a bunch of men."

"Right! They were undressing her with their eyes."

Cole laughed so hard he had to hold onto the fence to steady himself.

Connor's grip tightened on the hammer. "I'm glad you find this so funny."

Her Unbridled Cowboy

"Sorry, Connor, but you should see your face." He took a deep breath. "What happened next?"

"I tried to get her to leave with me, but she wouldn't."

Cole nodded. "I bet you were very tactful, too."

His stomach clenched. "I sort of called her a...tramp."

"Oh, man, you didn't..." Cole blinked. "What did she do?"

"She went to hit me, but I stopped her."

"Naturally."

"Yeah, but she got me back when I accused her of being drunk."

Cole dropped his head into his palm and groaned.

"She insisted she was drinking soda and threw it on me."

"I see."

Bastard brother was biting his lip now, and damn shoulders were shaking, too.

"So, I took Ashley home and waited outside Kerri's apartment until Duke brought her home."

Cole inhaled and shook his head. "Oh, shit, bro. Bad move. You don't undermine a Masters."

Now he tells me.

"I learned that the hard way that night." He pointed the hammer at Cole. "Do you know what she did?"

"I'm almost afraid to ask."

"She kissed him in his car, then again on the porch—with me there in the driveway!"

"No?"

"I kid you not. Then, as if that wasn't bad enough, she took him inside the house where they remained for a whole damn hour, knowing full well I was sitting outside in my truck." He slammed the hammer into the nearest post, twice, as the frustration of that moment came rushing back. Then he stopped and turned to point the hammer at his brother again. "And I'll tell you, Cole, I went to that door prepared to bust in if he was hurting her, but I only heard Kerri laughing, so I didn't."

His brother wisely remained silent.

"And then," he said, whipping the hammer near his pile of tools. "When they finally did come out, her hair is all down and shoes are off and she kisses him…and that bastard salutes me! He fucking salutes me!"

Anger took over. Connor reached for a nearby sledge hammer and went to town on the post as he vividly recalled that awful moment. Several whacks later, when the muscles in his arms went from strained to numb, he stopped and sucked in air.

"Carver's an asshole," Cole commented quietly.

Nodding, Connor dropped the sledge hammer and turned to his brother. "Oh, believe me, it's a good thing he drove off when he did, because I'll tell you, Cole, I swear I could've beaten the pulp out of him right then."

"I don't doubt it." His brother handed him another water.

Connor drained the bottle, then wiped his mouth with the back of his hand. "As if that wasn't bad enough, Kerri turns to go in without saying a word to me. Can you believe that?"

"Really?"

"Yeah, she was going to try to go in without saying a stinking word. But I wouldn't let her, and ended up inside before she could shut the door." He smirked, remembering the shock in her beautiful brown eyes. They'd widened to the size of a shot glass. "Then we argued, and she slapped me."

"Now, why would she do that?"

Her Unbridled Cowboy

Connor looked down at his boots, and then at his hands before replying. "I sort of called her a tramp again."

Cole whistled as he shook his head. "Bad move buddy. Then what happened?"

He remained silent. He may be angry at the woman, but he wasn't a kiss-and-tell kind of guy.

"Okay, so you kissed her and wanted more," Cole stated with surprising accuracy.

Connor's head snapped up. "How did you know?"

"She's a Masters." Cole shrugged. "They seem to have that effect on us McCalls."

"Well, that's what happened. Before I knew it, we were on the couch. I looked up and noticed pillows on the floor and her shoes and panty hose near the chair, and *I* wasn't the one who took them off her." *Christ*, it still rotted his gut. He sucked in a breath, then released it. "When it sunk in, I got up real fast. She asked me what was wrong, and I told her *'she'* was and that *'this is one man you won't have.'* Then I hightailed it the hell out of there, I can tell you that!"

He threw down the empty bottle, ripped his hat off and thrust a hand through his hair. God, he was such a fool. Suckered by another city girl.

"Tell me, Connor," Cole began, and waited until their gazes met. "Was I this big a fool last year?"

"What?" He strode to his brother and grabbed him by the shoulders. "Didn't you hear what I said?"

"I heard you, but apparently you aren't seeing things too clearly."

Bullshit.

"I'm seeing things just fine." He let go of Cole and began to pack up his tools. "Kerri had sex with Duke, then sent him packing and was willing to take me on right afterwards."

Cole's laughter echoed in the evening breeze. Cripes his brother was an idiot. Why the hell would he laugh at him after what he'd just revealed?

His hands tightened into fists. "You'd better stop that, Cole, or I swear I won't hesitate to wipe that grin off of your face."

"Calm down, bro. I'm sorry, it's just that the thought of Kerri actually being capable of such a thing is ridiculous."

He stared at Cole. Nope. He didn't see anything funny about it.

"Look, you can't possibly think Kerri would allow Duke those privileges, do you?"

A month ago, he would've said no. But now… "I don't know." He shrugged. "It sure looked like she did."

Cole stepped close and grabbed his arm. "Connor, this is important. What else did you notice about that room?"

He closed his eyes and grit his teeth. *Christ*, he was tired of thinking about that night. For the past week, that was all he'd done. It was a constant reminder he'd been fooled again. By a city girl. Again. He was such a patsy. An idiot. He should change his name to Sucker McCall.

"Connor, come on. What else did you see?" Cole squeezed his arm.

Whiny ass bastard.

With a sigh, he opened his eyes and thought back to last Saturday. "There were two cans of soda on the coffee table and a…"

"What? What else was there, Connor?"

He looked at Cole as if the fog had cleared. "Popcorn. There was a bowl of popcorn, too."

"There, see? They watched television while you sat

Her Unbridled Cowboy

outside." Cole moved his hand to Connor's shoulder and grinned. "Oh man, she is good. You, my brother, don't stand a chance."

An invisible band began to tighten around Connor's chest. "Are you telling me she only *pretended* to fool around with Duke...even going so far as to take off her shoes and stockings just to make it look like...?"

Cole nodded, still grinning as he slapped Connor's shoulder. "Yep, and don't forget her hair. You said it was down too."

Shit. Connor slumped against the fence, his mind back in a dazed state. "Jesus. You mean she did all of that to fool me?"

"Yes, although I'd say it was more to teach you a lesson for not trusting her. And, Connor?" Cole waited until he made eye contact. "You blew it. Big time. Whatever you did and said must've really hurt. She doesn't deserve it. You owe her an apology."

Christ. Not only was his chest tight, now his whole entire body ached. And Cole was right. He *was* still an idiot, but for an entirely different reason. Now all he saw was the wounded look that had come into Kerri's eyes when he'd delivered his parting shot.

"And you'd better make that apology soon, big brother, because Kerri's ex-husband is on his way here to see her as we speak."

In the middle of calling himself all sorts of names, his heart stopped at Cole's Texas-sized bomb.

Late Sunday afternoon, Kerri was helping her mentor prepare supper in order to channel her nervous energy. She needed an outlet. Cooking and baking were an ideal way to help take the edge off life. At least, it always had for Kerri, and today was no exception. Emma thankfully asked no questions and allowed her to work it off while she waited for Lance to show up with Jordan's belongings.

A little after three o'clock, the moving van pulled up out front—with her ex-husband at the wheel.

Oh Lordy.

All the nerves she'd managed to keep at bay hit her full force. She ripped off her apron, tossed it on the counter, then rushed from the kitchen to the half-bath down the hall. A deep breath or two helped slow the drum solo going on in her head.

"You can do this," she told her reflection, then double-checked her appearance.

She was wearing a chocolate brown, ribbed turtleneck, black jeans and boots. Neat, clean, comfortable. Perfect. *Whatever*. Kerri didn't want to dress fancy and appear over anxious, so she'd kept it simple and casual, and the heels of her boots gave an advantage since Lance wasn't much taller than her.

Another quick glance in the mirror told her everything was as good as it was going to get. Sucking in her third deep breath, she silently chanted, *I can do this,* then exhaled and left the room to join the commotion in the foyer.

Kerri arrived as Jordan finished introducing Lance to Connor. The cowboy was there to help Cole carry the things her sister wanted upstairs, while the rest would go into storage until their house was finished.

Okay, one awkward moment averted. *Thank you, Jordan.*

Now, it was her turn. She glanced at her ex husband, and other than the nervous strain she saw on his face, Lance appeared the same. As usual, he was dressed in a polo shirt and khaki pants. His short, dark hair was neatly

Her Unbridled Cowboy

in place and his green eyes looked at her with what she recognized as...love?

What?

Kerri swallowed hard and walked toward him, nerves knocking at her knees. *I can do this*. She hoped her expression was full of calm, serene, wonderful, fantastic coolness, because, *oh, Lordy,* that was not how she felt.

She stopped in front of him, well aware of three pairs of eyes watching their exchange. "Hello, Lance."

"Hello, Kerri." His gaze fastened on her face and looked...sad. "It's good to see you again."

She couldn't bring herself to say the same. Because it wasn't. It was so damn awkward and painful her mind reeled. "You must be thirsty after your drive. Would you like a drink?"

Connor hovered nearby, and when she finally glanced at the brooding cowboy, he opened his mouth as if to say something, then closed it and headed outside to the moving van.

"Yes," Lance replied. "As a matter of fact, I am thirsty. Thank you."

Kerri nodded. "Then come with me."

As she led the way to the deserted kitchen, she couldn't help but wonder about Connor's strange behavior. They hadn't really spoken since he'd slammed the door of her apartment, angry and hateful. Yet today, he seemed...different.

Instinctively grabbing Lance a bottle of water, she had to hold back a laugh. It was official. She was losing it. Yep, her head needed major examination. Here she was, meeting with her cheating ex-husband for the first time since their divorce, and her mind was on the unbridled cowboy.

"Thanks, Kerri, and thanks for agreeing to see me," Lance said, regaining her full attention. "I've been trying to talk to you for two years now."

Oh crud. Not yet. Nerves tightened her chest in a choke hold. She held up her hand. "Not here. Finish your drink, then we'll get out of here and go somewhere private."

Understanding warmed his gaze as he nodded.

Wonderful. That bought her a small reprieve. Maybe she could figure out a way to loosen the stranglehold in her chest enough to allow easier breathing. Wouldn't that be great?

She waited while he finished his drink in strained silence, and when he was done, they headed for her car. Whatever it was he had to say to her, it was not going to happen on Wild Creek.

Since it was Sunday, Kerri knew there was no work being done on the restaurant, so she figured it was a good spot. There was no way she'd take him to the apartment, though. Just the restaurant, and then the airport to catch his eight o'clock return flight.

The twenty minute car ride gave them a chance to talk pleasantries, and he inquired about Jordan and Cole. Happy to talk about her sister's relationship and not theirs, Kerri briefly told him their long history, some of which he'd already known.

Then he asked about Connor. Kerri hesitated slightly, and he must have picked up on it.

"Do you like him?"

Can you say awkward?

Kerri could. And she could spell it, too. Backwards, even.

She cleared her throat. "Sure. I-I've known him all my life." Yeah, nothing like discussing her feelings for

Connor with her ex-husband. Priceless.

"That's not what I meant," he said quietly.

Yeah, well...too bad. She pulled into the parking lot and parked before facing him.

"Look, Lance, Jordan said you had something to say to me, so let's not waste time discussing Connor. Okay?" She got out of the car without waiting for his reply.

Rude? Yeah, but she was entitled, dammit. Unlocking the front door to the restaurant, she stepped inside and flicked on the lights.

"Wow, Kerri, this is great," Lance said, voice full of enthusiasm.

Her pulse, admittedly, sped up at the sight of her restaurant starting to take shape. "Yeah, you think so?" She smiled as she looked around at the finished wooden paneled walls and wooden floors. "It's hard to believe that in little more than a month this place will be open for business."

"I have no doubt you and Jordan will make a success out of it. I'm just sorry Comets was destroyed. I know you two did well there." Emotions darkened his expression. "I'm so glad you're both okay. I nearly died when I saw it on the news."

He drew in a breath and looked like he wanted to hug her.

Oh, Lordy. No. She wasn't ready for that, so she moved to a table in the corner and dusted off two chairs for them before sitting down.

Lance joined her, and she noticed his hand shaking as he struggled for somewhere to start. Her throat jumped on the tight bandwagon her chest had going on. Dang. Her heart went out to him despite herself. He'd been a dear friend and a jerk only that once in the seven years she'd known him before the divorce. She couldn't just sit back and watch him suffer, so she made it easier for him by starting the conversation.

"Jordan encouraged me to meet with you."

He blew out a breath and looked up at her. "I'm glad she did, Kerri. I needed to try to explain to you about what happened."

Okay. I can do this.

Part of her wanted to run, and the other part wanted to hear it. The latter won. She remained where she was and sat nervously waiting for him to continue.

"Kerri, I swear I never meant to hurt you. You've got to believe that."

A troubled green gaze bore into hers, looking, searching…hoping. It hurt, but she knew he was telling the truth. When she nodded, he went on.

"I loved you, hell…I still do, but I should never have married you. I see that now. I always felt…odd inside, but didn't know what that meant."

What could she say to that? Nothing, so she remained quiet. And hurting.

He shot to his feet and began to pace as his confession spilled from his lips. "My mother was pressuring me to marry and have kids, and since I already loved you, I thought we could make it work. And we did for awhile. It wasn't until Ian got hired as manager that I started to understand why I had felt different all those years." He paused to take a deep breath, then he looked at her. "Kerri, I was wrong. I know that now. I should've told you, but I just didn't know how, and by not doing that the unthinkable happened." He closed his eyes and shuddered.

Tears streamed down her face as she found her voice. "Yes, Lance, you should have. What did you think I was going to do? I mean, sure, I would've been devastated, but at least you could've explained things, and I would've been spared walking in on you."

Closing her eyes, she shuddered, recalling the devastating moment her life had irrevocably changed. The moment her husband had forsaken her for another. For a man. She opened her eyes and stood, hugging herself in an attempt to keep the pain and humiliation from reaching the surface. "Do you have any idea what that did to me, Lance?"

He stepped closer. "Kerri, I'm so sorry. You're right. I should have, and if I had it to do over, I swear I would've told you. I swear it." He grabbed her by the shoulders and forced her to look at him.

Misery lived in his eyes, darkening, haunting, eating at him, and she realized she wasn't the only one who'd spent the last two years in wretchedness. A fresh round of tears trickled down her face. He wiped them away.

"I'm sorry."

She sniffed. "I thought that you...that you went looking in the opposite direction because I was doing something wrong," Kerri confessed haltingly, and felt some of the tightness loosen around her chest.

"Oh, God, Kerri, *no*. I am so sorry."

He hugged her then. Hugged her tight, and she hugged back, letting the pain out. Freeing it. And in doing so, she realized all the pain she felt wasn't for the loss of her husband. It was for the loss of her best friend.

It still felt good to be embraced by him, but it lacked something she couldn't quite put her finger on.

After a minute, he pulled away slightly to look her straight in the eyes. "Listen to me, Kerri. *You* did absolutely nothing wrong! Do you hear me? You did nothing wrong. It wasn't you. It really was all me," he told her firmly and waited until she nodded. "By not understanding my confusion, I hurt and lost you. You were my best friend...and I miss you," he said, voice cracking. "And I'm so, so sorry. I hope you believe me."

His gaze was troubled, but earnest. She knew him to be telling the truth, so she squeezed his arm. "I've missed you, too, Lance. And I'm sorry you had to go through all that by yourself. I only wish you would have confided in me."

He pressed his forehead to hers. "God, so do I, but I think subconsciously I was fighting it."

Not much she could say to that, so she remained quiet.

"I hope, somehow, some day, we can still be friends," he said, straightening to look into her eyes.

She inhaled, then let it out slow. "I want that, too, Lance, but...I...it's going to take time. Baby steps."

"I can do that." He pushed her hair behind her shoulder.

She smiled at the familiar gesture, and felt a lightness around her heart for the first time in years. "Good."

He smiled.

"So," she began, a little curious about his life. "Are you and Ian still together?"

A guarded expression fell across his face. "Yes."

"Are you happy?"

He studied her a moment, as if trying to decide if he should answer. Apparently, he must've seen something in her gaze because he nodded. "Yes."

Surprisingly, the news didn't hurt. So she smiled. "Good, I'm glad." And found she really meant it.

"Thank you, Kerri, for hearing me out."

They stood there and hugged for a few minutes before finally breaking away.

Her Unbridled Cowboy

"So," he said, holding her hands. "What about you?"

She frowned. "What about me?"

"Do you want to talk about…what was his name, Connor?"

Heck no. *Cripes*, especially with him. "No." She managed a small smile. "I don't."

"Well, take it from someone who knows," Lance said. "That man was looking at you as if he'd just lost something special."

Kerri reeled back and stared at her ex. "I-I doubt it. He doesn't go for city girls, and besides, me with a cowboy?" She shook her head and let loose with another small laugh.

But Lance knew her too well. Green eyes stared unblinkingly at her. "He is yours for the taking. And why not a cowboy? You were always a little reckless."

"Me?"

"Yes. You." He laughed outright. "You, who used to add certain ingredients to your recipes behind the teacher's back."

She shrugged, holding back a grin. "Yeah well, that teacher did rave about my quiche as I recall."

They laughed, a good laugh. Genuine. And just like that, she took an unrestricted breath, and her first step toward healing.

"Now." He dropped an arm around her shoulder and looked around. "Tell me about this new restaurant of yours."

"Did you apologize to Kerri yet?"

Connor glanced at Cole as they unloaded what was left of the van into the rented storage bay. "No," he replied, going back for another box.

"Do you think it's wise to let it go any longer?" his

brother asked, passing by with his hands full.

No. And he didn't think it was wise for his brother to pester him like a little girl about it, either.

"There hasn't been a right time yet," he grumbled instead.

Cole chuckled. "Oh, bro, anytime is the *right* time to apologize to a woman. You should know that by now," his brother proclaimed, joining him inside the van.

"Yeah, well, I'll apologize soon." Picking up the last box, he made a mental promise to seek Kerri out and apologize this week.

Maybe even today. If she was up to more company after the cheater from the coast left town.

With determination pushing away his uncertainty, Connor deposited the last box on the pile and looked around. "I'm glad Jordan sold her furniture or we'd be here another hour."

Cole laughed. "Yes, I know. I think I married a pack-rat."

His brother pulled the door down on the bay and locked it, while Connor did the same to the van. His mind strayed to Kerri. Again. He wondered how she was doing.

God, she'd looked so frail, so fragile back at the ranch. He'd wanted to grab her hand, pull her close and reassure her everything would be all right. Wipe away her uncertainty. Protect her from…

From what?

Ah hell. He shook his head, rubbing at the ache in his chest. He was just as guilty of causing her pain. Of dulling the light in her beautiful brown eyes.

"Okay," Cole said, slapping him on the back. "I just need to drop off the van."

Happy to have something to do, Connor climbed in

his truck and followed his brother to the designated drop off in town. It would be great if he could turn off his thoughts. Shut them down. Run on automatic. Then there would be no reason for his mind to shift to a certain sexy, cook.

God, he wished he knew what the hell it was Kerri's ex wanted to talk to her about.

He stiffened.

What if the guy wanted her back?

After all, his green eyes had been full of affection for Kerri.

Damn. That had to be it. The ache in Connor's chest intensified. Her ex must want her back. Why else would the guy drive someone else's belongings across four states?

He didn't have time to contemplate anymore, thank God, because his brother came out of the building.

"Thanks, bro," Cole said, getting into the cab. "Do you mind going down the road to the restaurant? I promised Jordan I'd check on the building while we were out this way."

"Sure. No problem," he replied, careful to keep the gloom from his voice.

He had no right to feel that way, but he did. Okay, he had the right to feel lousy, but not worthy. It wasn't like he even had a chance with Kerri. And it didn't matter if he did. She wasn't sticking around.

As he pulled into the parking lot, Connor realized the whole point was moot. His jaw clenched tight. Kerri and Lance were laughing as they walked out of the restaurant.

Chapter Fourteen

"Sorry, bro." Cole sighed, glancing sideways at him. "I didn't know she was coming here, honest. I thought she was going to drive him straight up to Houston to catch his return flight."

"Not a problem," Connor lied, angling his truck so the passenger door faced the happy couple.

Cole rolled down his window as Kerri approached. The closer she got, the more Connor noticed a change in her. She looked relaxed. Peaceful.

Happier.

It felt as if someone lodged their fist in his throat, via his stomach.

She smiled, placing her hand on the door to peer in. "What's up, guys?"

"Jordan asked me to check on the place, but I didn't realize you were coming here," Cole replied. "Sorry to intrude."

"You're not intruding," she said, turning to wave at the building. "I figured it was a good place for privacy, but we're done now. We're going to head to Houston. Feel free to look about."

God, her face, her smile…they were radiant, and Connor couldn't take his eyes off her.

"Lance, I'd like to thank you for driving the truck here from California. My wife and I appreciate it," Cole said, sticking his hand out the window to shake the man's hand.

"No problem. And, thank you. I appreciate the opportunity to talk to Kerri," *Slick Dick* replied. "And congratulations, again. Jordan is a real gem."

"I know." His brother nodded. "I'm very lucky."

The Californian slung a damn arm around Kerri and grinned. Like he had the right to touch her. Deserved to touch her. Well, he didn't. Damn it! He deserved Connor's fist upside his cheating head. Twice.

The damn man *cheated* on her. *Forsook* her.

"Kerri is a gem, as well," *Lance-can't-keep-it-in-his-pants* remarked, looking pointedly at Connor. "Worth any risk."

Well, hell. *Did he just...* His heart slammed against his ribs. Hard. Connor transferred his gaze to Kerri whose face rapidly turned pink.

"Okay, so, ah…time to go," she said, pulling her ex away from the truck. "Got a plane to catch. Bye."

"Bye." Cole waved, until Kerri pulled out of the parking lot. Then he slowly turned to Connor. "Holy shit, bro. Kerri's ex-husband just gave you the go ahead to date his former wife."

Son-of-a-bitch... if Connor had gotten that same message.

Tuesday evening, Kerri shut off her stove, intent on taking a break from perfecting her chili for the upcoming cook off. Foster's Creamery was open. And their ice cream was calling. Loudly. She'd slaved for two hours on this particular batch, and had high hopes. This could be the recipe she entered next month.

So, now was a good time to venture across the street and down the boardwalk to fetch an ice cream cone. Or, better yet, a pint.

It would give her chili a chance to sit and cool and stew, allow it to marinate and soak up all the flavors from the spices she added.

And Kerri the chance to feed her sadly neglected chocolate addiction.

Slipping into her jacket as she opened the door, Kerri nearly jumped out of her skin when she found Connor standing there, hand raised as if to knock.

"Hey," he said, recovering first.

Placing a hand to her pounding chest, she nodded. "Hey, yourself. You scared me."

"Sorry, darlin'. Didn't mean to."

She shook her head. This was becoming routine. "It's okay. Is something wrong?"

"No…well, yeah. I wanted to say I was sorry about the other night. And I brought a peace offering." His mouth twitched into a slight grin as he brought his arm out from behind him.

Ice cream. *Foster's* ice cream. A pint. Of chocolate. *Glory be*, he'd read her mind. Or taste buds.

She smiled and stood aside. "In that case, come in."

She'd wanted to talk to him, too. Ever since her conversation with Jordan last week, Kerri had been meaning to call the cowboy, or drop by the ranch…or something. Thanks to her sister enlightening her on the role she'd played that disastrous night, Kerri owed the man an apology. Between working on the chili, perfecting her menu, and trying to cook up the courage, time had gotten away from her. So, now, was good.

Besides, he had chocolate ice cream. Foster's chocolate ice cream. She'd let a pack of wolves in if they had chocolate.

He nodded and walked in.

Hiding a snicker, she hung up her coat then followed the cowboy into her slightly messy kitchen.

"Mmm…smells good in here," he said, setting the offering on the island while he shed his coat and hat on a nearby stool.

Kerri smiled. "Working on my chili for the cook off."

His brows rose. "You entered?"

"Yeah." She nodded. "Thanks to Emma. She's got me doing the basket raffle, too. Says it'll be good advertisement for the restaurant."

"She's right," he agreed, easing down on a stool. "And, hell, as for the cook off…" He closed his eyes and inhaled, then reopened them. "Darlin', if you could win on smell alone, you'd take the grand prize."

"Thanks. I'm excited about the cook off. I'm glad it's opened to professionals." Kerri sighed. "But not about the raffle. I'm just not crazy about having to eat with a stranger who bought my goods."

A low laugh rumbled from the handsome cowboy. "Bought your goods, huh?"

She smiled. "Emma's words."

"Ah." Again he nodded, gaze glued to her face.

The intensity of his stare made her blush, and it wasn't just her face that heated. Darn it. What was with her body and this cowboy, anyway?

Nothing. That was the problem.

Whoa. She shook her head. *Not even going to…*

Ice cream. Right. She rushed to the cupboard, grabbed a bowl, then two spoons and headed back to the island.

"Here." She handed him the bowl and a spoon.

He frowned. "Aren't you going to eat any?"

She opened the ice cream, then glanced at him. "Oh yeah." Scooping a few mouthfuls into his bowl, she smiled and pulled the pint closer. "I don't need a bowl."

He chuckled. "Oh, I see how it is."

"That's right," she said, shoving her spoon into the

ice cream, her mouth dutifully watering before she tasted. "Mmm…" Kerri closed her eyes and savored the flavor as the cold treasure slid down her throat. Old man Foster sure knew how to blend his chocolate. She opened her eyes and enjoyed another spoon before looking at Connor. The heat in his gaze set her stomach a flutter.

She pointed her spoon at him. "The way I see it. You owe me a bigger apology, so I get more."

He looked down at his small helping before glancing back at her. "Then here," he said, pushing the bowl her way. "This is yours, too. I owe you a huge apology, Kerri, and you do *not* owe me any."

Stupid watery eyes. She sniffed. "Dang it, Connor. Why do you have to go and be so sweet?" She jammed her spoon in the ice cream in order to swipe the wetness from her face.

"Ah, hell, darlin'. I'm not sweet," he claimed, an uncomfortable look pinching his face.

But she knew differently. He was sweet. And he probably tasted sweet about now, too. And chocolatey, because, like her, he'd already had a few spoonfuls of ice cream.

What a combination. Shards of heat sliced low in her belly. Connor and chocolate ice cream…

Holding her gaze, he lowered his spoon and swallowed. "Jesus, Kerri. What are you thinking right now?"

That I need my head examined.

Or him, covered in chocolate so she could lick it off.

She shook her head and cleared her throat, neither helping to dispel the desire now coursing through her body at mach speed.

"Nothing," she replied. "Just that I'm sorry about the other night. About making you think Duke and I…that we…because we didn't. I swear."

God, she hoped he believed her. She didn't know why it was so important, only that it was.

He slid off the stool and stepped to her, grabbing her hand and tugging until she looked up at him. "It's okay, Kerri. I know. I do believe you. But at the time…not so much." He drew in a breath and slowly exhaled. "I'm sorry. I was such an ass. The things I did. The things I said. I should've trusted you."

Wow. She stared up at him, unable to tear her gaze away from his troubled face. She hadn't expected the *T* word. According to Jordan, he had trust issues. It was a good sign that he recognized his faults.

"If it had been anybody but Duke, I would've let you alone. I wouldn't have liked it, but I would've let you be."

Her heart rate increased. He wouldn't like her to be with someone else… What did that mean?

"Kerri, Duke is bad news. I just didn't want him to hurt you." He gave a derisive laugh. "But in the end, it was me who hurt you. And I am *really* sorry."

She freed a hand to touch his face. "It's okay. I understand, now. And like I said, I'm to blame too. I'm the one who made you think I'd slept with the guy. I just never thought you and I'd end up on the couch…"

Her voice trailed off. It felt weird to say *making out*. And the way her heart was slamming against her ribs, she couldn't really get any more words out.

"Me either," he said, reaching up to cup the hand she still held against his face.

She should've dropped it, let him go, but dang, he felt good. Slight scruff from his five o'clock shadow scraped her palm while rough calluses scraped the back of her hand. A tremor started at that hand and raced straight down to her toes, increasing the tingle in all her good parts.

The next thing she knew, they were stepping into each other and kissing. *Oh, dang me, kissing.* His mouth was warm and seeking and tasty. Yeah, he tasted of chocolate and man. All man.

She shifted closer, practically climbing up him, which he helped by lifting her right off the floor without ever breaking the kiss.

He had an arm around her back, cupping the back of her head while the other cupped her butt, holding her in place. And what a place. A great place. Her new favorite place. He was hot and hard, and she felt every incredible inch of him pressing into her, right smack low in the belly.

By the time they broke for air, and he let her gently slide down his body until her feet hit the floor, she was a trembling, panting, wet heap of need. His arms remained around her, thank goodness, or she'd be a trembling mass on his boots.

Kerri dropped her forehead to his thundering chest and drew in a few ragged breaths. "Okay…wow. I don't even know what that was."

His chuckle rumbled against her head before he cupped her chin and tipped her head back until their gazes met. "I'd say that was pretty incredible."

Dang. Yeah, it was. But she didn't know what she was doing. She nodded, then closed her eyes. This was just too much.

"Don't you think so?" he asked, his tone troubled.

Again, she nodded and opened her eyes. "Yes, I do. It's just…I don't want to give you the wrong impression."

"What do you mean?" Now he was frowning. "Are

Her Unbridled Cowboy

you saying you're not attracted to me?"

"No." She shook her head. "I am. Very much so. It's just…" She sighed. God, this was hard, especially with his thumb caressing her chin. "Look, Connor, you've been with…you've had…lots of experience. And…I haven't." She laughed a small, cynical laugh. "I've only had one lover, and he didn't even like…"

Crap. She pulled out of his embrace and strode to the sink. *Holy, crud.* She almost told him. *God, how embarrassing.*

"Kerri. Hey," he said, big hands caressing her shoulders from behind. "What is it? What didn't your ex like? Surely you don't mean you, because I saw the way he looked at you, and he most definitely has feelings for you."

She nodded, drawing in a shaky breath. "I know. It's not that."

Connor turned her to face him and bent slightly at the knee to look into her eyes. "Then what is it?"

She squeezed them shut as if that would keep the secret in. "Please don't make me say it," she whispered.

Two warm hands cupped her face. "Say what?"

Eyes still closed, she shook her head.

"Come on, darlin'. Get it out. You'll feel better," he gently urged.

She'd already *gotten it out* with Jordan and had her little talk with Lance. And he was right. She had felt better. But telling this big, virile, hunk of a man she'd been having sex with a guy who preferred guys, was more than she could handle.

"Kerri, open your eyes. Look at me," he said, still lightly caressing her face.

She inhaled and forced her eyes to open, and was staggered by the amount of compassion warming his brown eyes to a delicious caramel hue.

"Are you trying to tell me Lance is gay?"

Her sharp inhale and obvious clenching of her body as she did her impression of rigor mortis should've answered his question. But in case that wasn't confirmation enough, she gave him a curt nod before the sudden onslaught of tears rolled down her cheeks.

He groaned and crushed her tight against him. "Ah, darlin'. I'm sorry," he said, stroking her hair, while she burrowed deeper into his accepting warmth. "I really am, but it makes sense."

Okay, poke her with an electrode, she was shocked.

Kerri drew back. "W-what do you mean?"

He brushed her tears aside and smiled. "The guy had to be gay to let someone as hot and gorgeous as you get away."

Her mouth dropped open and eyes widened. She was channeling that darn electrode again. "Y-you think I'm hot?"

"Hell, yeah, darlin'." And to prove it, he pressed her against the sink and ground into her. "I'd love to show you how much. In fact, I'd love to show you a lot of things," he said, running those big, wonderful hands up and down her body, bringing with them a trail of heat, while his mouth lowered to kiss a path up her neck. "I can guarantee you, you've been missing out."

Kerri clutched at him as sensations rushed through her body in wave after delicious wave.

"What do you say, darlin'? Want to let me show you how a cowboy makes love to a woman?"

She shook. Literally shook at his words. Well, that certainly made it clear what her body thought about his offer, but Kerri wasn't sure. She was afraid.

"What are you afraid of?" he asked as if reading her

Her Unbridled Cowboy

mind.

The bugger.

Drawing in a deep breath, she fought the urge to cross her eyes as he sunk his teeth into the curve of her neck. "Th-that I'll disappoint you."

There, she said it. It was out there, floating in the miniscule space between them.

He drew back and locked gazes. "Darlin', you could never, *ever* disappoint. Trust me."

She shook her head. "But I wouldn't know what you'd want."

"*You*, Kerri," he said, wrapping his hands around her hips and drawing her up close against him. "I just want you."

She backed up a little. "But what about our parents? Won't it make it awkward at family functions?"

"Isn't it awkward now?"

She laughed. "Yeah, I see your point."

"Good." He drew her close again.

But she put her hands on his chest to stop him. "Wait. Connor, you do know I'm not staying, right? Once this restaurant has an established clientele, I plan to head back to California and reopen Comets, or maybe look for a Top Chef position."

Last thing she wanted to do was hurt this guy. To become another city girl who left him. "I just want to be as honest with you as possible."

He nodded. "I know. And I appreciate it, darlin'."

"And you're okay with me leaving?"

"Sure."

"You don't have a problem with me being a city girl?"

He smiled. "Nope. This time it's different. This time I know up front you'll head back to the city."

She searched his eyes. They appeared to be earnest, and heated and *dang*, she was not equipped with the ability to fight the strong attraction flowing between them any longer. Not when they'd laid out all their concerns and considerations.

And why the heck should she fight it? They both wanted a *friends-with-benefits* relationship. A mutually satisfying one.

"So…what do you say?" he asked, forehead pressed to hers, lightly running his hands up her arms again, gaze hopeful, and yeah, still heated.

"Okay."

He stilled, then drew back. "Okay?"

"Yes, but don't say I didn't warn you. I really don't know what I'm doing."

His smile broadened until his dimples glared. "Don't worry, darlin'. I'll teach you. Starting right now."

And her heart nosedived into her ribs while her pulse soared sky high. The combination made Kerri sway and clutch at his shirt. Apparently this was okay with him because he lowered his mouth to hers and kissed the rest of her senses into oblivion.

If possible, he tasted even hotter, hungrier, more potent now that they'd dropped all their barriers. And heaven help her, she was sunk. She moaned and did that climbing thing again, to which he cupped her bottom and lifted while she wrapped her legs around his waist.

Hot dang, it felt good.

Still kissing, he turned them around and walked to the island where he set her down near their forgotten ice cream. Breaking the kiss, they drew in air, still touching and feeling. His forehead met hers again.

"You take the lead, Kerri. What do you want to do to me?"

"Me?" she practically squeaked. "I-I told you, I-I don't know."

He smiled that dang sexy, lop-sided grin as his hands ran up and down her thighs. "Oh, but you do. Listen to your body. Trust me. A guy is going to enjoy anything you do to him. So, what do *you* want?"

She wanted…her gaze traveled over him. She wanted him naked. She wanted… "To lick my ice cream off your chest."

Oh crud. She hadn't meant to say that out loud, but a second later, he'd ripped off his shirt and between her dangling legs, a glorious, bare torso awaited her pleasure.

Her mouth watered—and other parts further south—at the sight of him. With a wicked grin, the sexy cowboy shoved the pint of melting ice cream into her hand.

"Have at it."

So she did.

Tentatively at first, then she got both of her hands in on it, reaching into the pint before slathering the sticky, cold, delicious confection all over his broad chest and each individual ridge of his abs. God, he looked good enough to eat.

So she did,

Kerri leaned forward and began to lick that magnificent chest, delighting in his inhales and the way his hands tightened on her thighs as he stood while she licked him clean.

"Are you done?" he asked, voice strained, gaze dark and hungry.

She shook her head. "No." Then wiped a fresh coat of ice cream across his bottom lip. "There's still a little left," she said, then cupped his face and pulled his mouth close enough to lick.

His control snapped. He groaned and grabbed the

back of her head while his mouth devoured hers, eating, drinking, plunging until she quivered with so much need she didn't know what to do with herself.

Then his hands were on her shirt, unbuttoning, driving her wild with each brush of his knuckle across her breasts. She wanted his whole hand there. And…and maybe his mouth. Yeah. Definitely his mouth. He eased the shirt off and stood back. Her body shivered under the heat of his gaze.

"Purple. Nice," he said, then tugged the bra straps down her arms until she sprang free.

He inhaled, and reached behind to unhook the bra and toss it aside. "God, you're beautiful," he muttered, lowering his head. A second later, he was kissing her cleavage, a nipple, and when he caught the other between his thumb and finger and squeezed, she cried out and arched into him.

Lance had never done these things. He'd touched her, but not so lingering. Or greedily.

Connor lifted his head, eyes dark and practically glowing before he took her mouth. She nearly climaxed from the erotic sweeping of his tongue while his hand tweaked her nipple and the other strayed further south to stroke between her legs.

Kerri moaned and let him lay her back, tensing briefly when her bare skin met the cool counter.

He pulled away to look down at her. "Gorgeous," he said, gaze traveling down her body then back up. "But you have on too many clothes."

Strong, sure fingers were undoing her jeans, and before she could change her mind, or help, he had them down to her ankles while he removed her shoes. Which he did with startling efficiency, before he yanked off her jeans and socks.

Her Unbridled Cowboy

Now that heated gaze of his devoured her purple lace bikini. "They're not grandma panties," he said, a smirk tugging his lips.

She smiled. "Nope. Not today."

"Wouldn't matter. These aren't staying anyway," he said as he hooked both sides with his forefingers and slowly tugged them down her legs until they joined the rest of her clothes on the floor.

Can you say, self conscious? Heck yeah. Big time. She swallowed, and her face heated. Cripes, she was practically laid out like a buffet on her own kitchen island.

Ew, she was going to have to disinfect later.

"God, you're so damn beautiful, Kerri," he breathed, his gaze slowly running up her body and back down again.

It sent all thoughts of cleaning from her mind.

Okay, seen it once, no reason for another pass.

Her entire being screamed for her to cringe, to curl up and cover up. And *because* she wanted to roll away and hide under the quilt on the couch, Kerri forced herself to remain where she was and waited.

Forget breathing. That wasn't possible. Not with the gorgeous Connor McCall taking in every inch of her.

"Mouthwatering," he said, his gaze finally reaching hers. "God, Kerri, the things I want to do to you…"

Chapter Fifteen

Kerri could feel Connor shake as he gripped the counter and bent down to kiss her lips. The fact he was so turned on caused her to shake in response.

Something cold and sticky hit her chest. She gasped, and he drew back and smiled, holding up his ice cream covered hand.

"My turn," he beamed, and proceeded to slowly drive her mad with a barely there touch that circled her breasts, but not the nipple.

She inhaled and gripped the counter. *Not fair.* He did it again, each time coming closer, but never quite touching her firm peaks. She grit her teeth and held back a groan while she squeezed her thighs shut in an attempt to block the aching need.

It didn't work. The hunk of a cowboy was standing between her legs.

"Connor." The need forced his name from her lips.

"What, darlin'? Tell me what you want."

God, she couldn't. But then his tongue was on her, licking, teasing, hovering, yet never taking her into his mouth until she thought she'd scream.

"Connor, please."

His head lifted. "Tell me."

Lance had never touched her like this or teased or licked. It was incredible and annoying and if he didn't put his mouth on her nipples soon…

His warm lips closed over a tight peak, licking, sucking until she writhed about.

"Is this what you want?"

"Yes, yes, that's what I wanted. Thank you."

Her Unbridled Cowboy

He stiffened, then lifted his head. "Hey, hey, darlin' you don't have to thank me. Surely you know all of this foreplay is for me, too."

But she didn't know. Lance had never done it. Had never seemed to need it, and since he'd only touched her a little, she never knew there was more.

God, had she ever been wrong.

"Give me your hand," he said, taking the one nearest him to rub over his thick arousal.

She gasped again. He was so hard. It had to hurt.

"Trust me, darlin'. I am enjoying this every bit as much as you. Maybe even more, knowing this is your first time." He smiled down, tenderly brushing a piece of hair off her face. "I like that I'm bringing you pleasure."

She reached up to touch his face. "You are. I can barely catch my breath."

His smile broadened. "Good, then I'm doing it right."

She laughed. "Yeah, like there was ever any doubt."

He leaned down and kissed her, long and slow and deep. *Hot chocolate.* He tasted hot and like chocolate, and she closed her eyes and moaned. One big, calloused hand closed around her breast, all of it, even the nipple.

Yes, she silently rejoiced. The other skimmed her belly, over her hip, then thigh, thumb brushing her center. He released her mouth to kiss her neck and she stilled, then moaned when he slid a finger inside. His hand was big, his finger was thick, and she was so close to climax she was already seeing stars.

He groaned against her neck. "You're so wet."

No kidding. He was making her crazy.

His finger circled, then slipped inside. Yeah, no, Lance never did it that way. Too bad. It felt so much better.

Now Connor was kissing a path down her shoulder, her breast, lingering on her nipple before heading down her body toward his wicked hand, his slight scruff feeling like a little bit of heaven on her skin.

He pulled his finger out and stood back slightly, still between her dangling legs. Kerri's stomach clenched. He spread them wider and stared down at her. Jeez. He was looking at her practically spread eagle. His gaze lifted to meet hers, and *oh Lordy* were his eyes hot and fierce.

"You're beautiful. I can't wait to taste you."

Taste me? Dear God, surely he didn't mean...

But that was exactly what he'd meant, because a second later, his hands slid up her thighs spreading her even wider for his shoulders to fit.

For the first time since they'd started, uncertainty washed through Kerri. She'd never done this. The thought was actually kind of gross.

"Connor," she said, not sure what she wanted.

"It's all right," he said.

His finger was back, brushing over her, spreading her open for…

At the first touch of his warm mouth she lifted right up off the counter. He drew back, and a large hand palmed her belly and gently held her down.

"Easy there, darlin'," he said. "Just relax."

Relax? Easy for him to say. This was all new to her. She was spread wide open and all her good, tingly parts were there for…*oh, man*. His tongue tickled and licked. He felt good. *Real* good. In fact. If he didn't stop…

"Connor." She touched his head. "If…stop…I won't be able to."

He lifted his head, and the sexiest, wickedest grin crossed his handsome face, and her heart literally rocked against her ribs.

Her Unbridled Cowboy

"I don't want you to stop. I want you to come for me, darlin'."

And before she could respond, his mouth was back on her, licking, stroking, sucking, then he added a finger, causing her to moan.

Eyes closed, she lay there, uncaring that she was completely naked and he wasn't. That they were sticky with ice cream and sweat. That she was on the counter, wide open for him to explore, and *oh Lordy,* was he exploring.

Heat was building, her body was trembling, and she was enjoying all the new sensations he introduced. And when he reached up and caught a nipple between his finger and thumb, she felt the erotic sensation straight down to her center where his mouth and finger pleased.

That was all it took. She exploded into a shattering climax, and the talented cowboy drew it out for several beats before he let her down slowly.

When it was over, he kissed a path to her neck, where he lifted his head to look into her eyes. "Better than strawberries," he said with a grin.

Then he kissed her, long and deep, and again she should've been repulsed by the fact she could taste herself on his lips. But she wasn't. She kissed him back, running her hands up over his warm shoulder blades, then down around to the front of his jeans where she traced his bulge with her fingers.

He groaned and broke the kiss. "You're killing me."

She smiled, still touching him. "You have on too many clothes." Her initiation into such blatant intimacy made her bolder. "I want you naked."

His dimples appeared with his lop-sided grin. "Yes, ma'am." He backed up, kicked off his boots and stripped down right in front of her in her kitchen.

Holy Texan, he was bigger than she'd remembered seeing in her youth. And magnificent. Well proportioned for his large frame, and heaven help her, she wanted him inside her.

"Not boxers," she said when his briefs hit the floor.

He stepped out of them and shook his head, his grin broadening. "Nope. Not today." Bending down, he fished a foil packet from the pocket of his jeans, then stood and set it next to her on the counter. "Now, where were we?"

She reached for him, needing to take him into her hands. Hot, hard, smooth, he was like satin over steel. "We were about to take care of *you*."

He hissed a breath. "Me? Darlin', make no mistake, we're about to take care of us both."

"But…you already took care of me." She blinked, her pulse hiccupping at the heat in his eyes. "Didn't we?"

He shook his head, wicked grin returning. "Not by a long shot," he replied.

Connor kissed her again, his tongue growing bold, his hand daring as he skimmed over her breast, lightly grazing her tightened peak while his other slid further south and he slipped a finger into her wet center.

She moaned and rocked into him. He was right. She was ready for more. She'd never been ready for more. Her hand moved up and down his hard length still in her grasp, and a new, inner feminine something rejoiced when he pulsed in her hand.

A groan sounded deep in his throat before he drew back. "There's only so much I can take, darlin'." He ripped the foil packet, sheathed himself, then pulled her to the very edge of the counter, where he eased the tip inside.

Gripping his shoulders, she threw her head back and moaned while her body got used to him. He pushed further, then further still, and she inhaled at the feel of him. He was so big and filled her so good…

"You okay, darlin'?" he asked, eyes, half closed.

She nodded. "Oh, yeah. But I'm going to need you to start moving."

His smiled appeared. "Yes, ma'am." He gripped her hips and began to thrust.

Things got a little wild. She slung her arms around his broad shoulders and captured his mouth. Hungry and frenzied, they kissed, his tongue matching his thrusts, driving her mad.

Heated pressure built and enflamed and *oh yeah*, she was close again. Kerri had never had two orgasms during sex before. Heck, she never had two in one night. But she was almost there. Yeah, the pressure built with each delicious thrust.

When he broke the kiss and lifted her off the counter, Kerri decided then and there gravity was her new best friend because she sank onto him even more.

She moaned, then gasped as her back met with the cold wall. Blinking back surprise, she frowned at him. "We're not going to the bedroom?"

He shook his head, expression strained as he began to thrust again. "Won't make it. You feel too damn good."

His words, his praise, the way he felt driving deep inside had her right back at that incredible edge again. He was plastered against her, mouth on her neck, magnificent chest brushing her nipples with each thrust. Little mewls panted up and out of her throat.

She'd never made that sound before.

His body was hot. So hot. She wrapped her legs around him tighter and he groaned against her throat. God, he felt so good. He filled her completely. She was done.

"*Connor.*"

He lifted his head and looked into her eyes. "I'm right with you, darlin'," he said, then kissed her hot and rough, and with so much need, she shuddered, bursting clean over that edge to experience her first ever double orgasm.

A second later, with a fierce thrust and a sexy, rough sound rumbling in his throat, he followed her over the edge.

Unable to remain standing, he slid them down to the floor, holding her tight, still buried deep inside her. Air rustled around them as they stayed that way a few moments, working to catch their breath. Head resting against his collarbone, she'd never felt so relaxed, so boneless in all her life.

"Connor?"

Spurts of warm breath fanned the side of her face and neck as his forehead rested against her temple. "Yeah?"

"Is there a time frame on when you get the feeling back in your legs? Because mine are kind of gone."

His chuckle rumbled through her. "Not to worry, darlin'," he said, drawing back to look in her eyes. "It'll return." A long finger traced her face and pushed a strand of hair behind her ear. "You okay?"

She knew what he was fishing for. Some sign as to how he did. If she'd enjoyed sex with a straight guy. If she enjoyed sex with a cowboy. If she enjoyed sex with *him*. Well she did, *big time.* Surely he could tell by her moans and panting.

"Better than okay," she replied with a smile. "That was…wow."

His lips curved into a very satisfied grin. "I like

Her Unbridled Cowboy

wow."

"Me, too. But I think you know that."

"Yeah. You're screams kinda gave it away."

She smacked him. "I didn't scream." Yeah, she did. She totally did.

"Then you have a bad memory," he said, detangling from her before he brought them to their feet. "What do you say we head into that big shower of yours so we can wash off chocolate heaven, and I can refresh your memory?" He ran a finger down her chest, lightly grazing a hardened peak.

She shuddered and heat pooled low in her belly. *Holy smokes*. She was so easy when it came to him. Her hand skimmed up his taut abs to his muscled chest, and the thought of soaping up his hot, hard ridges made her ache.

"Yeah," she said, leaning forward to lick a spot of dried chocolate from his pecs. "I think I need a few more lessons."

In a swift move, he swept her off her feet and strode down the hall toward her bedroom. "Then we'd better hurry," he said. "We don't want to be late for class."

March was nearly over and Kerri had spent most of that time going through the applications and résumés in order to fill the staff for the restaurant. And trying not to think of Connor. Dang him. Darn cowboy had his way with her body and now he was in her head.

Last week, his visit had been unexpected and well, magnificent, but they were supposed to keep it casual friendly. They'd talked it out. Discussed a few simple rules that would help keep things free and easy. No sleeping over. No consecutive visits. Staying all night in either of their beds was a no-no. That was a sure way to form an attachment neither of them wanted. So, after their shower and another round of incredible sex—proving Jordan's theory about a king-size bed correct—Connor had left.

Surprisingly, she'd been fine with that. Sore as heck, but fine. Parts of her body she didn't even know had muscles hurt for a few days. She'd even walked funny. Trying to keep that from Jordan had been a big challenge.

And now, staying away from the cowboy was proving another. Six days without his kisses, without his touch was a test of her resolve. But she'd had the restaurant to keep her occupied, and she knew he was busy getting ready for his spring cattle drive.

"Earth to Kerri," her sister was saying, snapping her fingers. "Uh oh, Brandi, I think my sister's out in orbit, again."

Kerri blinked, and the two smiling women came into focus. They were sitting in a booth in the restaurant, having coffee and brownies, discussing the remaining renovations and upcoming inspections.

Brandi's design was coming to life and was just amazing. The wooden walls were completely done and stained, as were the floors. The tables, booths, and bar were complete. A big barbeque pit was ready for firing up. The kitchen was glorious with state-of-the-art industrial-size everything, and Kerri never wanted to leave her own little bit of heaven. *Texas Republic*, the name they chose for the restaurant since the public would have a say in the music and menu specials, was just about done. Only the stage area and restrooms needed to be finished.

"I'm here. I heard you. I was just thinking how nice it'll be to have everything complete," she told them, sipping her coffee.

Jordan snorted. "Yeah, right. That dreamy look had nothing to do with a certain brother-in-law of mine."

Brandi's brown eyes widened. "Oh? Really? You and Connor?"

"No." Kerri shook her head, knowing the designer had met him when he'd stopped in with Cole a few weeks back. "There's no me and Connor."

Not really.

"So, it wasn't his truck I saw parked here the other night. The same night he got home at four in the morning." Jordan raised a brow.

Cripes. Really? How the heck did her sister see all that?

Kerri sighed. "We had a one-time thing."

She wasn't sure there would be another. So it wasn't a lie. Sure, he'd called her once and texted a few times, but they'd never made any definite plans.

Jordan's palm hit the table. "Hah. I knew it. That explains why he's walking around with a smile on his face again."

Connor was smiling?

Darn, if that didn't put one on Kerri.

"Kind of like that?" Brandi asked, pointing to her.

Jordan nodded. "Exactly like that one."

"Ha ha. All right. Funs over," Kerri said, opening the folder on the table. "We still have applications to go through." She turned to pretty designer sitting next to her. "Thanks for helping, by the way."

"No problem," Brandi said. "Your place is almost done. I've got your mandatory inspections all lined up and my next project doesn't start for another month. I'm glad to help."

"Well, since you won't let us pay you for this extra

time, at least have one of my sister's to-die-for chocolate peanut butter brownies," Jordan said, pushing a piece to the designer.

Brandi eyed it with longing, but shook her head. "I'd better not."

"Why?" her sister asked. "Surely you're not worried about your figure. You look great."

"Yeah." Kerri nodded. "If I had your curves…"

"You'd be ten pounds heavier," Brandi said, cutting Kerri off. "I'm almost to my goal weight. The past year I've lost forty-two pounds and would really like to get back down to where I was before my thyroid quit working."

Oh wow, Kerri never would've guessed the woman had trouble with her weight. Brandi was a little shorter than her and Jordan, probably around five seven and looked wonderful. The designer had big, brown eyes, golden strands in her caramel color hair that fell past her shoulders, and curves, not rolls, that turned the construction crew's heads.

"So you're hypothyroid." Jordan nodded. "I had a cop friend in L.A. whose wife had to take a pill for it every day."

Kerri frowned at Brandi. "Is that what you do?"

"Yeah." The designer nodded. "But it doesn't help me lose weight. It just controls my TSH levels. I have to watch my diet and eat smart and small every two to three hours to keep my metabolism going." Her gaze rested on the brownies. "So, as much as I'd love to devour that beauty, I'd better not."

"Must be tough to eat out," Kerri said, mind beginning to run with possibilities as she sipped her coffee.

Brandi snorted. "You've no idea. Sure, I can pretty

much eat anything I want, but in such small portions I'd end up wasting money and food."

"Really?" Yeah, her mind was running rampant now.

Jordan smiled. "Okay, sis. What's cooking?"

Now Kerri smiled. "Well, it's just a thought, but you know how some restaurants will have an under 500 calorie dish? I was thinking we could maybe do that, but tailor it better." She glanced at Brandi. "Could you help me? Maybe make a list of acceptable food and portions so I can put together a few meals to add to the menu?"

Brandi's face lit up. "Oh, wow. That would be great. I'd love to."

"Thanks." Kerri nodded. "You can either email it, or stop by when you're ready and we can concoct."

"Sounds good," Brandi said.

"Then I guess we'd better get to work." Jordan divided the applications and they each took a stack.

An hour later, they had a nice pile of hopefuls sitting in the middle of the table and were fleshing out a training schedule when the door opened and four handsome cowboys strode in.

"Hi, husband." Jordan scrambled to her feet and met Cole halfway, causing the remaining cowboys to step around.

"Hi, wife," he said, crushing her sister in for a kiss.

"Hi, bathroom while I puke," Kevin muttered, without missing a beat.

Kerri stood and laughed with the others, while her heart pounded in her chest as her gaze strayed to Connor. This was the first time she saw him since they'd shared more than ice cream.

Dang, he looked good. All tall, and lean and smiling.

Did he tell anyone? Had any of the guys guessed like Jordan? Her gaze studied the others as they approached.

Friendly smiles, warm gazes, no knowing glances. Her secret was safe. Well, it wasn't a secret, but she was relieved she didn't have to fend questions.

"Hi, guys," she said, moving aside as Brandi scooted to her feet. "Brandi, you already know the McCalls. The other two handsome cowboys are Dalton's. Guys, this is our designer, Brandi."

Kevin, of course, stepped forward first and held out his hand. "Well, what do you know? I could go for a Brandi right about now."

Half the room groaned the other half laughed.

"All right, Kevin. Let her go," Cole prompted, stopping at his side.

"What? She has soft hands," Kevin said, reluctantly releasing their designer.

Kerri motioned to the silent man at his other side. "And this is his cousin, Kade."

Brandi held out her hand, and when Kade shook it, Kerri could feel the designer tense next to her.

"Nice to meet you," Kade said, slight frown on his forehead.

Brandi nodded. "Likewise." Then tugged free.

Connor stepped closer, placing a hand on Kerri's shoulder and one on Kade's. "They own the Shadow Rock Ranch on the other side of town," Connor said, thumb brushing Kerri's shoulder in a slow, circular motion.

Pulse hiccupping from his touch, she ordered her body not to sway into his yummy, hard, lean warmth. But her body remembered that motion all too well, when his touch had strayed to all her good parts...and lingered. *Shoot.* He was making her damp.

Kevin nodded. "Yeah, but, Kade runs it. I only help out when the *bossman* doesn't need my expertise with the keys at McCall Enterprises," he said, nodding toward Cole.

Brandi looked at Kade. "What kind of ranch is it?"

"A horse ranch," he replied.

Her friend's brown eyes warmed. "Do you board?"

He nodded. "Yes, ma'am. We do. Why? You have a horse needs boarding?"

The designer nodded. "Yes. I do. He's up north until I can find a good place around here."

"Feel free to check us out," Kevin, said, handing Brandi a card. "We're on the net. I designed the site myself. And the card."

Jordan chuckled. "Okay, down boy. Give the girl some room."

"Sorry. My bad. Is lunch ready?" Kevin asked, smile lighting his eyes. "I know the restaurant isn't open yet, but I heard it through the grapevine Kerri has several batches of prototype chili on her hands."

"True," she said, gaze straying to the tall cowboy with warm brown eyes standing next to her, still driving her crazy with that moving thumb.

After their shower, having worked up a bit of an appetite, they'd sampled her chili. He'd proclaimed it perfect, and since she'd agreed, she made up a few more batches this week. Just to make sure she got it right.

"You're in luck, I happen to have a pot simmering on the stove," she told the blue-eyed devil. "I'll go get a few bowls."

"And I'll help," Connor said, falling into step as she made her way to the kitchen, body tingling in anticipation.

Stupid body.

It was just a friendly gesture. He was helping her out. And it didn't mean anything except…

Oh boy, it was about to happen. Her first private meeting with the cowboy since they slept together.

Chapter Sixteen

Kerri had never been in the situation before. Was this the walk of shame? No. She didn't think so. She'd always thought that was right after sex. Not several days later.

What was this, then? Because she was certainly walking and well, not ashamed, but…nervous. Yes, she was very nervous and anxious. But was he?

She pushed through the swinging doors with one wish in her head…*Please don't be awkward.*

It's only awkward if you make it awkward. And she wasn't going to make it uncomfortable. Everything would be fine. And it was. Better than fine.

As soon as the doors closed behind them, Connor gently shoved her into the nearby pantry and shut the door. Before she could ask what was wrong, he had her up against the wall, bodies pressed tight, mouth on hers in a hungry, demanding kiss.

All thoughts of anxiety, lunch and the people in the other room shot from her mind as heat and need took over. *Dang, the cowboy can kiss.* She clutched him, her knees buckling, moan low in her throat as she rocked into him.

He broke the kiss and buried his face in her hair. "God, I thought about doing that all week."

She trembled, forehead resting against his collarbone. *Then why didn't you come over*, she wanted to ask. But didn't. "Me, too," she said, instead.

He began placing open-mouthed kisses on her neck, while his hands started to roam. One skimmed over her hip and the other cupped her breast, brushing the tip back and forth through her bra, and sending a wave of heat straight to her core.

"Sorry I didn't get to see you this week, darlin'," he said against the curve of her neck, nipping, biting, licking, until she could hardly breathe. "I've been busy at the ranch, and now I'm about to head to a horse auction with Kade for a few days. I only agreed to come into town with the guys because I heard they were stopping here."

Her hand found its way under his shirt, and she was enjoying the feel of his skin quivering under her touch. "I'm glad you did," she managed to say before he completely stole her breath by slipping a hand down her pants. "Connor…"

"I know," he said, kissing her lips, his tongue dipping inside her mouth in slow, languid thrusts.

Both of his hands were on her jeans, unbuttoning, and the rasp of her zipper pulled her out of her daze. She freed her mouth and sucked in air.

"W-what are you doing?"

"You," he replied. "In a few seconds."

Sexy, sneaky bugger turned her around, positioning her back to his chest, pushed her jeans to her knees, and slid a hand in her thong. Her heart about stopped. Then he reached further down and slipped a finger inside her.

His inhale cooled the back of her neck. "So wet…"

Kerri gasped and would've fallen, but he shoved his knee between her and guided her onto his leg.

"Relax," he said, holding her up with his body, kissing her neck, hand under her shirt cupping her breast through her bra while his wicked, wonderful finger slid in and out of her at the perfect pace. Her pace. He knew it already, and within no time he had her shuddering and panting his name.

"God, I love to hear you say my name."

His hold on her tightened, and she could feel his erection pressing against her backside as she rocked against him, matching the rhythm of his magical hand.

And as he captured her nipple with his fingers through her bra, crazy sensations shot through her body. He had her leaning back against him, supporting her completely because she was lost. Done. Couldn't feel her legs. She just trembled, and shuddered, and rocked. A deep, sexy sound rumbled in his throat as he bit her neck while he brushed the outside of her wet folds with his thumb.

And just like that, Kerri went off, clenching her jaw to keep the moan inside so the others wouldn't hear. Her body shook, and she had a death grip on his hips.

When she finally came back to herself, she turned, needing to see him. But her legs were still shaky, and she slid to the floor.

"Careful, darlin'." He caught her and pulled her close.

She was okay with that, because he was hot and hard. And even though he'd just given her a mind-blowing orgasm, she wanted him inside her. Now.

Sliding her hands down his chest and abs, reveling when he groaned, she trembled at the feel of firm, solid ridges under her palms. Lifting on tip-toe, she brushed her mouth over his jaw while her hands traveled south to her prize.

"Your turn," she said, outlining his erection, and she smiled when he sucked in air.

"Hey? How's that chili coming along?" Kevin's voice wafted in from the dining room, stopping her cold.

Holy crow. She'd forgotten about them. And their

lunch. Dang, sexy cowboy zapped her brain cells with startling efficiency.

Connor cursed and held her away from him. "We'd better get that lunch."

"But." She glanced at the bulge in his jeans. "What about you?"

He brushed her lower lip with his thumb, face strained, but his eyes were warm. "What about me?"

"It's your turn. I can't just...leave you in this state."

"You can if you don't want them to find us in here."

She blinked, not at all happy about leaving him hanging. Or the prospect of the others walking in. Still, she'd never let her ex down. Sure, *she'd* gone without, but she didn't do the hanging. And she didn't want to start with Connor.

"I'm not—"

"Shh…" he said, finger to her lips. "I'll be fine. Let's fix you up and get out of here before Kevin comes looking."

And because she knew she couldn't handle the feel of his big, warm, calloused hands on her skin, Kerri quickly righted her clothes, then followed him back into the kitchen.

He bent down and gave her a quick kiss. "Where are the bowls?" he asked, gaze full of heat, regret, and affection.

She pointed him in the direction and smiled as he limped away. The man was something else. Giving. That's what he was. Connor gave without taking.

It tugged at her chest. Softened something inside.

And as they left the kitchen, each carrying a tray, Kerri was struck by how something as common as a pantry could hold such significant moments in her life.

Two different restaurants.

Her Unbridled Cowboy

Two different states.

Two different pantries, and yet she'd felt the earth move in both. Knocked her off kilter. Turned her world upside down.

Changed her.

Given a choice, Kerri had to admit, she'd much preferred the Texas *earthquake*.

It wasn't working.

No matter how busy he was, how many chores he did himself, Connor couldn't stop thinking about Kerri and the look on her face yesterday as she gave Jenny's son Cody a piggy-back ride. He'd run into her on his way back from the horse auction when he'd helped Kade unload his stock.

She'd smiled over her shoulder at the little boy, her expression happy and carefree and so damn natural it tore his gut in two.

She'd be a great mom. And thoughts like that were killing him. Because he wouldn't be the dad. No. Some slick, city dude would have that honor once she moved back to the west coast.

But she's not there yet, his mind whispered. And although it was true, he knew it was also inevitable, so pretending otherwise was foolish.

He had to think of her as his current...what? *Special* friend? Lover?

Christ. He ripped his hat off and shoved a hand through his hair while he walked back into the cattle barn Saturday afternoon. The sexy cook was driving him nuts. He needed his head examined.

Sure she seemed to fit in and get along. She was born a Texan, but the newness of her re-acquaintance of her hometown would soon wear off. It always did with city girls.

And that's what she was. He'd do well to remember that the next time he was lost in her heat and softness. The woman had real talent. She belonged in the big city, creating dishes for the famous, not slinging barbeque in some small Texas town.

Their time together was temporary. It was simply a fling. She didn't fit in with this lifestyle. Didn't belong here.

So imagine his surprise when he walked into the break room to find the city girl sitting down eating chili with his ranch hands.

But that wasn't the most startling part. No. That would be the fact she was wearing jeans, cowboy boots, plaid shirt and a white cowgirl hat.

A hat!

His insides fisted so tight he stopped dead in his tracks. And, oh yeah, he was hard. Very hard, damn it. Not the best state to be in with five other guys in the room.

"There's the boss now," Pete said unnecessarily.

"Yeah." Joe nodded at him. "Look who stopped by with enough lunch for everyone."

Again, more unnecessary talk, but he was grateful because it gave him the chance to get his head out of his ass and move like he had a purpose. He headed to the sink to wash his hands, then to the old fridge in the corner for a bottle of water. Right now, he needed a gallon he was so friggin' parched.

"I see," he said, smiling at the grinning woman. "Hi, darlin'. This is a nice surprise."

Okay, that was good. It was true and didn't reek with overt sentiment. He took his water and sat down across from her since the spot miraculously became vacant

Her Unbridled Cowboy

when his back had been turned.

He wasn't about to look a gift horse in the mouth. He'd much rather look at hers. Touch hers. Taste hers. God, she was beautiful. Her face flushed and his insides warmed at the sight.

"Hi, Connor," she said, her gaze briefly dipping to his mouth before meeting his gaze once more.

His insides fisted again. Heat lurked in her warm brown eyes.

"I brought over the last of the chili." She motioned to the pot in the middle of the table. "I think everyone's going to be chili'd out by the time the cook off comes around next week."

"No way," Pete said.

Hank shook his head. "Not a chance."

The rest of the guys agreed.

Connor helped himself to a bowl. "See? There you have it. Never too much chili in a Texan's diet."

She laughed, a light, happy sound that filled the building with cheer. He found himself smiling for the first time that day.

And a half hour later, when he was done eating and knew he should leave to get back to the hundred and one chores on his list, Connor lingered.

Most of the men had gone back to work. Only Hank remained with them in the lunch room, talking to Kerri about one of her recipes his wife had tried.

"It was delicious, and she was so happy with the results she's going to make it for her family reunion next month," his foreman told her with a satisfied grin. "Thank you, miss. She'd been sweating this reunion, but now she's looking forward to it."

Kerri smiled broadly. "That's wonderful news. I'm only too happy to help."

"Speaking of help." Hank rose to his feet and nodded. "I'd better go help Cal check on the cows. It's birthing season and several of them are getting ready to go."

As soon as his foreman left, Connor reached across the table and grabbed Kerri's hand. He'd only waited because he didn't want to make her feel uncomfortable.

"This was a nice surprise. Thank you." He watched her blush again and smiled. "The chili was great as usual, but you taste so much better, and darlin', I really need to taste you."

He tugged her to her feet and held onto his control. "Not here," he told her, voice sounding strained. Because he was. Big time. "It's too open, too public."

Still holding her hand, he tugged her into the walkway, then over to the ladder leading up to the loft. Once there, he continued to lead her to the far corner behind a pile of hay.

"This is better," he said, pulling her into his arms and getting his first taste of her since their hot foray in her pantry earlier in the week.

Seemed like forever. Because it was. Much too long for him to go without her sweetness. And apparently, she felt the same because damn, she was kissing him back with such hunger and demand he was having a hard time keeping up.

Christ, her hands were everywhere, sliding under his shirts and over his skin in a frenzy that had him groaning and needing more.

She broke the kiss and blinked up at him. "Are we safe here?"

He nodded, reaching for her. "Yes. It's private."

"Good." She took off her hat, then pushed him onto the hay pile and followed him down. "The chili wasn't the only reason I'm here." Her hands fisted his shirts and lifted them while she licked a path up his chest.

"Oh?" He was having trouble concentrating on her words. His mind barely registered the hay poking his back as he gripped her sweet ass and rocked against her. He was so damn aroused, he could barely think and almost didn't hear her reply.

"Yeah. I'm here to make us even," she said against his abs a second before her hands made quick work of his belt and zipper, and had his jeans and boxers down to his knees. "Much better."

His heart literally stopped, then jumped orbit when she gripped his throbbing erection and made the sexiest purring sound he'd ever heard.

He must've died and gone to heaven. This was insane. He was supposed to taste her…not…

"Kerri," he groaned, trying to grab her shoulders and lift her up, but she pushed his hands aside.

"Oh no, cowboy."

She glanced up at him with the sexiest, wickedest grin on her lips and he nearly came right then.

"It's your turn to lay there and take it."

Kerri's warm breath washed over Connor's aching arousal a moment before she licked him and kissed the very tip.

A deep, guttural sound rumbled in his throat as she ran her tongue down his length. He gasped.

"Kerri…"

"Relax," she said before her mouth closed around him.

Ah, hell yeah, that feels good. So damn good. He laid back, squeezed his eyes shut and tried to hold on as long as possible. But he knew it wouldn't be long. Hell no. It'd been almost two weeks since he'd been inside her warmth, and this was exquisite.

Opening his eyes, he watched as she went down on him, over and over, her hands gripping his hips. She felt incredible, and watching her kneel between his legs, hair brushing his skin, mouth hot and wet on his erection, was like something out of his fantasies. Better than his fantasies.

And, Jesus, she knew his rhythm.

Heat skittered down his spine. His body tensed. Damn, he was close. He lay back, trying to hang on. Wanting to enjoy the erotic, incredible things she was doing to him with her tongue for as long as possible, but when she made that same sexy, purring sound as before, it vibrated around him and he was done. Hands on her head, he thrust up into her warmth and growled out her name as everything tightened, and he exploded.

His heart rate was still somewhere in the outer atmosphere when he opened his eyes and watched her rise to her feet, her expression so serene, so satisfied you'd swear she was the one who'd just had her boots knocked into the next county.

He held his hand out to her. "Come here," he said between breathes. "I don't know what you did to me, darlin', but my bones seemed to have melted away."

She laughed as she crawled up his body and set her forehead to his. "Hi."

God, she's adorable.

Able to at least move his arms, he cupped her face and stared into her beautiful, happy gaze. "Hi," he replied. "And thank you. But, Kerri, I don't want you to ever think you have to worry about keeping us even."

She pulled a piece of hay from his hair and tossed it aside. "Yes, I do. You're the one who has to learn to take once in awhile. You give so much in everything you do.

It's time you got to take...and to realize you're not the only one with a magical tongue."

She leaned down and kissed him, long and deep, and he crushed her close, loving how she fit against him. His heart gave a little jerk and snagged. Who would've thought a city girl would understand him so well?

His hands sought her warm, soft skin, and he skimmed over the curve of her waist, around the front to brush her quivering belly. She was sweet. But when he slipped his hand inside her pants she stiffened then rolled off him.

"Oh, no." She shook a finger at him as she stood panting a few feet away. "What part of *take* don't you understand?"

He groaned. "None of it. Come on, darlin'. Let me take care of you."

She seemed to have trouble standing, but dammit, she didn't come back.

"Sorry, *darlin'*," she said, straightening her clothes, checking her hair for straw. "You have work, and I'm meeting Brandi in a half hour to discuss a few menu items, so…" She paused to swipe her hat off the ground, dusted it off, then shoved it on her head. "It's my turn to leave all pent up."

He stilled. "Are you wet?"

She sucked in another mouthful of air and nodded. "Oh, yeah. Big time."

He groaned. "Damn it, Kerri, come here," he said, trying to reach for her, but his useless damn legs felt like lead. "Let me see."

She laughed. "No can do. Got to go. Next time, we'll have to make sure we're both taken care of." She tipped her hat at him. "Bye." And left.

"Kerri," he called and watched and waited, but she

never came back. He blew out a breath, and a moment later he chuckled. Damn, sexy woman tells him she's wet then leaves. He put his arms behind his head, laid back and closed his eyes.

Who does that?

Apparently his sinfully sexy cook.

"Sold! To the man with the longhorn tattoo!"

Kerri heard the announcer raffle another basket while she waited nervously in the back. The morning of the fair was unseasonably warm and brought in a good crowd.

She'd arrived with Cole and Jordan. They'd helped her cart her chili and the basket. She hadn't expected Connor to offer to give her ride. After all, they weren't an item. But she had hoped.

And she wasn't going to think about it right now. Her basket was up next.

Kerri sucked in a breath. She was expected to go out there and stand as if on display while people bid on her goodies. Kerri didn't know if she could do it. After all, she wasn't Jordan.

Sure, she had enough confidence in her food, it was in herself that she lacked. Although, she had to admit, she felt better about herself since Lance's visit, and a heck of a lot better thanks to Connor's…whatever you call what he'd done to her, and for her.

Fluttering commenced in her stomach. She hadn't seen the sexy cowboy since she'd left him half naked in the loft last week. Even now her body heated at the image of him laying back, shirts pushed up, jeans down, muscles—and other parts—gleaming, thanks to her. Just the thought that she'd put that look of pure satisfaction on the virile cowboy's face was enough to make her wet,

Her Unbridled Cowboy

and had her inner feminine goddess beaming.

Kerri couldn't believe how lucky she'd gotten when Connor had pulled her up into the loft. She'd gone to the ranch hoping to find a way to even their slate, and he went and provided it for her. Perfect opportunity, and she took it...and him.

She smirked. Yeah, she'd gotten lucky...and so had he.

But dealing with this challenge was different. This was public. People. Strangers.

As if sensing her dilemma, Jordan came to her rescue.

"Stop worrying. You got this. Just go out there and have fun," her sister said, placing her hands on Kerri's shoulders. "Besides, you're doing this to raise money for the children at the rehabilitation center. It isn't going to hurt if you cause a little mayhem amongst the single cowboys in the process."

Kerri groaned. "Jordan, I can't do that."

"Yes, you can, and you will. Plus, you're allowed to plug the restaurant, too. The raffle committee said it was fine." Her sister smiled with all the confidence Kerri was currently lacking. "Thing will be fine. You already know Duke is going to bid on your basket."

They'd bumped into the realtor on the way in, and he'd told Kerri point blank he planned to win her basket. She'd gotten a weird vibe from the guy today. He didn't seem like the same man who'd taken her to Gulfport. Hopefully, someone else would win.

"And I spotted Connor out there," Jordan informed with a grin. "This will give you an opportunity to strut your stuff. Drive him crazy. Or am I wrong in thinking your one-time-thing with him has turned into multiples?"

Her sister was fishing. And correct, darn her.

"Maybe." Kerri smirked. Her sister was good. Jordan knew what buttons to push all right.

She squared her shoulders, and with a determined lift of her chin, headed for the makeshift stage.

"And here she is, Ms. Kerri Masters, the owner and creator of all the delicious aromas that are coming from this basket." The announcer, a jolly man with a straw cowboy hat smiled broadly. "Not only is she a wonderful cook, but she is beautiful to boot, as I'm sure you young men have already noticed."

Okay, see? It was one thing to boast about her cooking. That was good. She could do that. But when the talk centered on her, she turned nervous. Uttered stupid things. Blushed. Like now. Darn it.

With her face heating, Kerri kept her chin high and bravely scanned the crowd in front of her. *Jeez*, there were a lot of people in the tent. She spotted Connor right away. Tall and big and hot. She warmed at the sight. He stood out. Hotly. And the urge to walk straight up the aisle and press into his sexy body was surprisingly strong.

She forced her gaze to the man next to him. His best friend wore fatigues with his hat in his hand. Another hotty. Several women were eyeing Kade like the cowboys were eyeing her. Hungrily.

Since Kade had told her at his ranch the other night that he didn't have drill this weekend, he must be working one of the military stands. There were a few; one for recruitment, one for veteran support, and another for rehab. Whatever the case, women couldn't take their eyes off him. Kerri held back a grin. The guy was oblivious.

She wished she was.

Her Unbridled Cowboy

Both Connor and Kade folded their arms across their chests and smiled.

At least *they* were having fun.

It took her a moment, but she noticed Emma, her parents and the McCalls smiling encouragingly at her. Cole and her sister gave her a thumbs up, and she grinned when she realized they were all wearing T-shirts advertising their new restaurant.

"Now, this lovely lady has packed this basket full with a feast fit for a king...or should I say a hungry cowboy?" the announcer joked as he looked over the paper she'd been required to submit, naming the contents of the basket. "Well, fellas, the winner of this basket is in for a treat. It seems this here little lady is the cook for the newest restaurant in our county. The grand opening is next Saturday. What is the name of it, sweetheart?" He held the microphone in front of her.

"It's called *Texas Republic* or *Texas Pub* for short." She smiled, then feeling more confident because she was talking food, Kerri took the microphone. "And what's in the basket is just a small sampling of what will be on the menu."

"Are *you* on the menu?" someone shouted, causing the crowd to hoot and a certain tall, sexy cowboy to scowl.

Kerri smiled. "Nope. Sorry, I just cook it," she replied, then continued with her pitch. "Every Friday night *Texas Pub* will feature local talent, and on Saturday will have live bands and plenty of dancing, so be sure to come in and check us out for some good food and good fun."

Still smiling, she handed the microphone back to the jovial announcer, pleased with herself for managing to get in a good plug for the restaurant.

"Sounds good to me, folks. I'll certainly be there," the announcer said, then inhaled and smiled. "You don't have the pleasure of smelling the delicious aroma coming from this basket." He motioned toward the table where it sat along with her cooler and blanket. "But trust me, it is smelling mighty fine." He grinned. "Now, let's just see what's causing it." And he held up his paper and began to read off the contents. "Lemon-Lime Chicken, onion and bacon crostatas, red potato salad, grilled peppers and apples, crusty French bread, cheese, banana slices, grapes, cherry pie, and the one that's got me curious, champagne soaked strawberries."

The crowd moaned and groaned their approval after each dish was mentioned. They especially liked the strawberries. Kerri grinned. That was a personal favorite of hers, too.

"And as if that wasn't good enough, Ms. Masters has also made a batch of Casa Grande Sangria to wash all that wonderful food down." The jolly man held the list to his chest and sighed. "Wooweee! I tell ya, if my wife wasn't in the audience today, I would've bid on this basket myself."

The crowd chuckled and Kerri smiled her thanks. She was glad he liked her list, but she really, really wanted off the stage. Too bad she had to stand up there and wait until he hollered, *Sold*.

Her heartbeats quickened as he opened the bidding.

"Remember now, people, this money is going toward those children and their gymnasium and much needed rehabilitation equipment for returning veterans. So, who will start the bidding at fifty dollars?"

"One hundred dollars," Cole called out from the front of the crowd, receiving a poke from Jordan.

"Two hundred," Duke offered from the side.

"Five hundred," Connor spoke up from the back.

Kerri's heartbeats quickened as she caught the determined gleam in his eyes.

Oh, yes…she'd love to share the basket with him. Heck, she'd love to share *more* than the basket with him. Okay, so she already had, but she was hoping for more shared orgasms. Cripes. Her face heated. What was wrong with her? This was certainly not the time to be thinking those thoughts.

"One thousand dollars," Duke countered with an equally determined gleam.

Unlike Connor's, she didn't like that gleam. After their date, the realtor had called a few times, but she'd turned him down. Kerri thought he'd gotten the message. Apparently not.

Connor straightened, and his arms dropped to his sides. "*Five* thousand," the cowboy said without blinking.

And that's when her lightheadedness began.

Chapter Seventeen

What is wrong with these guys? She glanced from Jordan to Cole to Kade as if their smiling faces held the answer.

They didn't.

"Six thousand," Duke hollered.

The look he gave her sent a chill down Kerri's spine. Okay. This was not good. He looked at her as if she were a trophy he was competing for instead of a human being. Cripes. She sure hoped Connor would out do him because she suddenly didn't want to be alone with Duke.

The dimpled cowboy smiled at her. "Seven thousand."

Relief flowed through her, and she mentally sent him a thank you.

Duke shifted in his seat. "Eight thousand."

Kerri automatically looked at Connor. It was like watching a tennis match. And she felt like the dang yellow ball. Only in a lilac sundress.

Dimples appeared and Connor touched his hat and winked at her. "Ten thousand."

Holy smokes. Kerri thought she might faint.

"Well, I've got to say, you two are making my job easier," the announcer said. "I haven't had to do anything. In fact, you two are so fast that no one else has had a chance to bid. Is there anyone who is willing to go over ten thousand?"

No, because obviously those two men were nuts. Her basket and her company were not worth anywhere near that amount of money. She was only happy the recreation center would reap the rewards.

Her Unbridled Cowboy

When no one else spoke up, the jolly man turned to Duke. "How about you?"

Kerri held her breath. *Please say no...please say no.* His gaze darkened, and he sent Connor a look filled with so much contempt, a small tremor ran through her body.

"Nope. Too rich for my blood," Duke claimed. "I'll just have to wait for the grand opening." He smiled, but his expression said he was not done with her.

Kerri shivered despite the warm temperature.

"Then I shall proclaim this basket and lunch with the pretty lady *sold* to the cowboy in...well we all recognize the cowboy," the announcer said with a grin. "Connor McCall. He always donates the best darn bulls for our rodeo. We look forward to the competition later this afternoon."

Connor tipped his hat, and Kade slapped him on the back while Cole, Jordan and both families cheered. Kerri was still in a daze over the amount of money her basket had pulled in as her lunch date ambled down the aisle and up onto the stage to pay at the table in the corner.

"Bless you, young man." The elderly lady had a tear in her eye as he handed her a check. "You will be making a lot of children happy with your donation."

He tipped his hat and showed the treasurer his dimple. "It was my pleasure, ma'am."

Who pays ten thousand dollars for lunch with their fling?

Was there more going on? Had they turned a corner when she wasn't looking?

"I'll get that." Connor quickly seized the basket and blanket and would've grabbed the cooler, too, if Kerri hadn't beaten him to it.

"You have enough to carry. I can handle this. It isn't heavy." Kerri glanced up at him and smiled, deciding to just enjoy the day.

Maybe she was reading more into the bidding. It was a donation. Heck, the two alphas were just competing. Probably would've tried to outbid one another on old man Foster's basket.

Okay, no, she'd want that one if it had his chocolate ice cream.

"All right then, where do you want to eat?" The dimpled cowboy looked down at her questioningly.

There was nothing extra behind the bidding, she kept telling herself. No secret motivation. They were just friends—with benefits—who hadn't had an hour or two of alone-time together in weeks.

Feeling better, and all sorts of excited at the prospect of that alone time, she looped her arm through his and tugged. "Follow me."

Kerri led them away from the crowd and into the meadow beyond the parking lot. There were several families and couples laid out on blankets, and she had to admit, this was a much quieter spot than at one of the many picnic tables in and about the fair grounds.

Five minutes later, they were sitting on the blanket Connor spread out, and she was busy setting out the food. Already, her body was heating and tingling in response to his closeness.

"I'm not sure what you want, so I'll let you help yourself."

He nearly choked on the grape he popped into his mouth.

"Hey, cowboy, are you alright?"

"Yes," he said between coughs.

Her Unbridled Cowboy

She smiled. "Good, I'd hate for you to choke on a meal you bought for ten thousand dollars."

He grinned, and their gazes held for several beats. She felt as if something needed to be said, or maybe he could just put his mouth on her. Yeah, she voted for that, and so did her body. See? It was unanimous. And dangerous.

She cleared her throat and asked him what he wanted to drink instead.

"I'll just have the water for now and the sangria with my dessert." Kerri handed him a bottle of spring water before turning her attention to her own plate of food, and the two of them ate in a companionable silence. When they finished, they tossed their plates in a small garbage bag she'd had the sense to bring.

"That was delicious," he said, gaze lazy and appraising. "But seeing as you were the cook, I'm not surprised."

His compliment warmed her whole being, and the heat in his eyes made her hot. She cleared her throat. "Thank you. Now, how about dessert?"

"Hmmm. What to have? What to have?" He grinned and tapped his mouth with his index finger. "I'll start with you."

Kerri smiled. "It might be too public for me to be on the menu."

Although, that was exactly what she wanted. Memories of the cowboy devouring her on the island flashed through her mind. Great. Now she was wet.

His gaze dropped to her chest, and her nipples tightened under his scrutiny. It'd definitely been too long since he'd had his hands on her.

When his gaze eventually lifted, his eyes had darkened to a rich, deep caramel. "But it's you I want most of all."

Air tried to funnel into her lungs, but clogged in her throat as fierce need and desire rushed at rapid speeds. "Jeez, Connor," she said in a hoarse whisper, hand trembling over her thudding heart. "You make me crazy."

"Ditto, darlin'." Eyes smoldering, he traced a delicious line down to her ankle.

She cleared her dry throat, and needing something to do, cut him a piece of pie. "There's nowhere we can go right now where we won't be seen, so we'll just have to save that thought 'til later."

His chin lifted, and a new light entered his eyes. "Later? You mean you're not going to leave after your cook off?"

Kerri's head snapped in his direction, and she frowned. "I'm supposed to sing with Jordan and Cole," she told him. "Then afterwards, I-I was going to stay…"

Maybe he didn't want her to. Maybe he was meeting up with someone. Her back stiffened as thoughts of him with another woman soured her stomach.

Warm fingers tightened around her leg. "I'd love for you to stay. I just didn't think you'd want to."

Her gaze shot to his face. "Why ever not?"

"I don't know." He shrugged and released her to grab his plate of pie. "Most city girls don't care for the sounds and smells the rodeo will bring later."

This time she reached out to touch his leg, brushing a thumb over his knee. "I think you know me better than that, Connor. You know I'm not like most city girls."

"I'm beginning to see that."

Holding his gaze, she squeezed his leg to make sure he knew she was serious. "I'd very much like to stay. In fact, just try and get rid of me."

He reached for her hand and smiled. "Yeah?"

"Yeah." She nodded and watched as his hand swallowed hers. Delicious warmth flowed through her, quickening her pulse to an unsteady beat. *You're in public*, her mind reminded. *Don't do anything...stupid.*

After a quick shake, she pulled her hand away and busied herself by pouring them each a serving of sangria. It was best if she didn't touch him.

With a hand slightly shaking, she offered him a glass along with a toast. "Here's to your generous donation." Kerri left out the part about him rescuing her from being alone with Duke. The realtor was not worth mentioning.

"And to the delicious rewards I've gotten in return." He grinned, and they clinked glasses before drinking the tasty mixture.

Connor's brows rose as he pulled the glass away from his mouth and gazed at the liquid. "You were right. This is by far the best tasting sangria I've ever had."

"I thought you might like it."

"I do, and I have to admit, I am dying to try your champagne soaked strawberries."

His gaze lowered to her mouth, and she had all she could do not to lick her lips. They tingled as if touched.

Sexy bugger.

She set her glass aside and offered the plate of fruit to him. Holding her gaze, he took a strawberry and bit into it.

Kerri knew the instant his taste buds registered the culmination of berry and bubbly by the slight narrowing of his eyes. Brows raised, she waited for his response.

"Mmm." He smiled his approval. "Who would have thought?"

"You need to broaden your horizon, cowboy." Grinning, she placed the plate back down and was about to grab one for herself when he pushed her hand away.

"Allow me." Leaning close, he lifted the strawberry to her lips.

A tremor hiccupped through her pulse on contact, and she didn't know what she savored more, the sweet taste of one of her favorite decadent desserts or the feel of his fingers touching the inside of her lips as she bit into the strawberry.

Her senses were in an uproar, and she could feel the invisible pull of attraction and unspoken command of desire as she lifted her gaze to his. God, it was so easy to get caught up in the moment, to give in to the unbridled feelings the cowboy brought out in her.

From somewhere deep inside, she knew she should stop. This was Connor, and he played in the major leagues while she was still dabbling in the minors, building up her confidence and working on her pitches.

But all thoughts of pulling away disappeared along with her surroundings as Connor's fingers left her lips to gently trace a path to her chin.

"I've got to have a taste," he murmured.

His touch was feather light, the complete opposite of her pulse. And slowly, very slowly he brought his face within inches of hers.

"Tasting's good." She expelled a breath and he captured it as his mouth came down on hers.

Awareness shot out in all directions, and Connor groaned as she ran one hand up his back and the other around his neck bringing him closer. He deepened the kiss, and her moan caught in her throat when his tongue entered her mouth as he pressed her back on the blanket.

Apparently, they weren't going to worry about being seen.

The urge to touch places and do things to him was as strong as it was confusing. This one kiss had filled her with more passion than she had ever known. In fact, Kerri never thought in a million years she was capable of such a thing. Instant burn. Instant longing.

Though Lance was the only other man she'd ever made love to, Kerri had had several boyfriends throughout her life and had shared a lot of embraces, but none had even come close to bringing her to this body-shaking, inferno state.

Every kiss she shared with Connor awoke something in her more and more. She was beginning to realize her body only had this reaction to Connor, and it flourished under his touch.

It was overwhelming, and she was still unsure if she was happy with that revelation. She didn't like the thought of this cowboy having so much power over her, but it became irrelevant when he ended the kiss, and she stared up into his dazed eyes.

They appeared just as mystified, just as…sunk.

"Sorry, darlin'." With a long finger, he pushed the hair off her temple and continued in a rough voice, "I didn't mean to get so carried away. I can't seem to help myself around you."

The confusion muddying his brown eyes confirmed the sincerity she heard in his words. Kerri reached up to trace the hard line of his jaw.

"It's alright. That same wave was carrying me, too."

"Yeah?" His gaze twinkled as it traveled down to her mouth again.

Taking a deep breath, she ignored her hammering

heart and gently pushed him back so she could sit up. "Oh no, cowboy, if we do that again, I'll probably miss the chili cook-off, and I don't want to disappoint Emma. She deliberately abstained from the event so I would enter, and I can't *not* show up."

He sighed. "You're right. I seem to lose all track of time when I kiss you." He grinned as he helped her up, but didn't let go of her hand.

She answered his grin with one of her own, then reluctantly pulled her hand from his. "Guess we'd better clean up."

Within minutes, everything was packed, the blanket was folded and Connor took her hand again. Connecting with him felt right. It felt…good. She allowed herself to enjoy the warmth and tingling sensations that spread throughout her body. *Yeah, really good.*

He tugged her close. "Thank you for a wonderful lunch, Kerri." He smiled down as he gently brushed a stray lock of hair from her face. "Everything was delicious, especially the cook."

She felt the blush. Couldn't stop the heat from invading her face, but she could control her lips, and they slid into a wide smile. "You tasted pretty good, too."

He had tasted great. She would never again be able to eat champagne soaked strawberries or drink her sangria without immediately thinking of the wildly hot, Connor McCall.

"There's more where that came from."

God, I hope so.

He lowered his head toward hers and Kerri dropped the blanket she'd been holding to put both her hands around his neck while standing on her toes to meet his lips.

Ignoring the chaotic thoughts that whirled in her

Her Unbridled Cowboy

head about him being a cowboy and experienced and a diehard Texan, Kerri instead listened to her body, and his, and gave herself up to the kiss. It was high time she took a chance and lived a little, starting by silently agreeing to everything promised by his embrace.

Slow and lazy and deep. He took his time driving her out of her mind. And she was. Delirious and crazy and shaking. But Connor was the one to pull away first, and her insides quivered at the sight of undisguised desire burning in his eyes. Desire she felt to her very core. It was shocking what he made her feel, and want, with a single kiss.

She had zero control when it came to him, and the fact he had the same problem when it came to her made it all okay. Very okay.

"That alone was worth the ten thousand dollars." He grinned, eyes warm as he brushed a thumb over her bottom lip.

"I still think I owe you a few hundred dollars worth, though."

He raised a brow, and her temperature, when he cupped her face and drew her bottom lip between his teeth. But instead of taking advantage of her opened mouth when she gasped, he soothed her lip with his tongue, then gently but firmly held her away.

"I think I'd better collect them later, darlin'," he said, voice rough. "I don't trust myself right now."

Right there with him, she drew in a shaky breath and nodded. Fingers entwined, they walked to his truck, dropped off the blanket and basket, then headed back to the fair and the cook off.

As she walked hand-in-hand with the handsome cowboy, she had to admit, it was fortunate Connor had had the sense to break the kiss, because Kerri found she was, for the first time in her life, senseless.

A few hours later, they finished their private supper on the blanket in the back of his truck. Connor was happy. He glanced down at the woman resting back in his arms, a content expression softening her face; yeah, Kerri was happy, too. The brilliant chef won first place in the cook off. Like there was ever any doubt.

The woman sure could cook. She'd wowed the judges, and a line of tasters had wrapped around the booth down the fairway eager to sample the winning chili. The committee, and a beaming Emma, had presented her with a trophy that now sat near the empty basket.

All that was left were three delicious strawberries. She picked one up and smiled at him with a playful gleam in her eyes. His heart bucked in his chest as she moved in closer.

"Wanna share?"

Hell yeah. Bodies.

"Absolutely."

It'd been too damn long since he'd been insider her. Too damn long. If it weren't for the fact Kerri was singing with Jordan and Cole later, Connor would've whisked her back to the ranch or her apartment or somewhere private along the way for their own bit of heaven.

"All right then, cowboy. Come get some."

His heart rocked in his chest as she sunk her teeth into the strawberry, careful not to bite all the way through then offered him the other end. Happy to oblige, he bit the berry, then took her mouth and shared the strawberry with her.

Hot damn, she tasted good. So damn good. His groin

Her Unbridled Cowboy

tightened and throbbed behind his zipper, and he classified the strawberry as the most erotic, tastiest one he'd ever shared. Nibbling at her lips, he took his time, lazily drinking every bit of sweetness she offered, quite happy to kiss the woman forever.

"Uhum."

The sound of several clearing throats and soft giggles had him slowing the kiss before they broke for air. He glanced at their interrupters.

Figures. His brother, Jordan and Brandi, who'd showed up in time for the cook off. The three stood by the truck grinning from ear to ear.

Cole smirked. "Sorry to break up your private party, guys."

Bullshit, he didn't look sorry.

"But we're due at the bandstand in less than a half hour, big brother."

Damn. He'd forgotten about that. Connor nodded, jumped off of the truck then turned to help Kerri. His groin tightened with a painful throb. The angle put him face to face with the tastiest part of her.

Jesus, he never had this much trouble controlling his desire for a woman before. But with Kerri? Shit. He was toast. A sap. Putty in her hands.

He swallowed a groan. That was the problem. He wanted to be in her hands, and have her in his.

At least the last part was doable.

Gripping her waist, he lifted her with ease and slid her down his hard body, enjoying her soft curves without moving a muscle. By the time her feet reached the ground, the need blazing in her eyes matched the size of the one ready to burst in his jeans.

"Okay," Jordan said. "Please tell me you have more of those strawberries, because…wow…that kiss was hot!"

Kerri stiffened up in his arms, and her face turned crimson, but she smiled and pointed to the cooler. "There's two left."

"Sweet." A second later, Jordan reached over the side of the truck, grabbed the cooler, then turned to her husband and smiled. "I think we just found the best dessert of the night. One for us and one for Brandi."

The quiet designer shook her head as she held up her hand. "No, I don't think so. Probably too much—"

"Only about thirty for half," Kerri said, cutting the woman off with a bunch of gibberish Connor didn't understand.

Brandi's eyes lit up. "Really?"

"See? There you go," Jordan said, handing the woman a strawberry...*his* strawberry, while she kept his other one.

Dammit. He'd had plans for them later.

Kerri's chuckle rumbled through him, and the look in her eyes told him she'd read his mind.

"Don't worry, I have more in my apartment," she told him in a hushed tone that had his dwindling erection at full tilt once again.

"So," Jordan said to Brandi. "You just have to find someone to share it with and you're all set."

Connor smiled as he caught sight of his friend approaching behind the others. "I think I see a volunteer now. How about Kade?"

Chapter Eighteen

"What about me?" Kade asked.

Connor watched as the designer's smile disappeared from her face at the sight of Kade rounding the truck. Had to be the uniform. She'd never looked at his buddy so cold before, and he was a little surprised by the designer's reaction. As soon as Brandi had caught a glimpse of the guardsman she'd stiffened, and the interest that had flared at the mention of his friend's name quickly disappeared from her eyes.

Yeah, very interesting. Her body language at the restaurant a few weeks back had been relaxed…interested. Not stiff and cold like now.

"Brandi needs you to share her champagne soaked strawberry with her like this," Jordan replied, then bit into the side of the berry and offered his brother the other side. They proceeded to demonstrate…

Christ. Is that what he and Kerri had looked like? His sister-in-law was right. It was hot.

Kade stepped toward Brandi and smiled. "I'd be more than happy to share your strawberry, Brandi."

The woman appeared frosty. And rigid. She glanced at Kerri who nodded and smiled. Brandi straightened her shoulders and turned back to his friend.

"No thanks." She shoved the berry into Kade's hand and stepped back. "It's all yours."

His buddy frowned. "Why? You have something against soldiers?"

Brandi shook her head. "Nope. I respect the military."

"Then what's the problem?"

Her chin lifted and eyes held a combination of sadness and flight. "I have something against *kissing* a soldier." The designer shifted her gaze to Kerri. "Congrats on your win."

"You're not leaving, are you?" Kerri asked.

"Yeah," Brandi said, moving backwards. "I've got to see a guy about…a…thing." She nearly tripped in her haste to get away.

By this time, Cole and Jordan had finished their strawberry and were watching the exchange with as much interest as him and Kerri.

His brother grinned at Kade. "Still got a way with the ladies, I see, man."

"Yeah." Connor laughed and jumped in for some ribbing. "You need to work on your follow through. She nearly broke an ankle trying to get away from you."

His buddy turned to them and the scowl disappeared from his face. "That just means I get the whole strawberry to myself."

Then the bastard ate *his* dessert right in front of him, and took his damn time, too.

"Come on, bro," Cole said, slapping his back. "We'd better get going. Why don't you walk with us, this way you and Kade can grab one of the few tables?"

Kade fell into step with them, placing his arm around Kerri. "And don't worry, I'll keep Connor company and out of trouble while you play."

"Good luck." Kerri's laughter kept the situation light.

Which is what it was. Light. Kade was just joking with him, but for a split second, even knowing this, Connor had experienced a burst of uncontrollable rage. Which was weird, because he didn't do rage. Up until

Her Unbridled Cowboy

last Thanksgiving, that had been a Cole thing.

Yeah, the woman he held hands with…she brought out all kinds of new feelings in him. Strong ones. And hell, he had no idea what to do with them. But that wasn't Kade's fault, so it was time he lightened things up.

"Get your own date," he said with a grin, wrapping an arm around Kerri's waist and dragging her closer. "Quit trying to steal mine."

Kade's brows rose. "Oh, so you and Kerri are on a date?"

Were they? He looked down at her and the hope in her eyes was exactly what his heart wanted to see.

"Yes," he replied, smiling at the pleased expression on her face. "Yes we are."

"Speaking of dates," Cole spoke as they continued to walk toward the bandstand. "Where's Kevin?"

Connor nodded. "Yeah, I haven't seen him all day."

"Are you kidding?" Kade chuckled. "He's in buckle bunny heaven."

Ah, yeah. Connor had forgotten how the venue was always a Kevin harem waiting to happen.

"But Kevin isn't part of the rodeo." Kerri frowned.

Kade snickered. "Tell that to the buckle bunnies. They don't seem to care."

They were still laughing when they reached the bandstand area. Connor stopped and turned to Kerri. He still couldn't believe she was enjoying the fair. With him. His date.

Monica wouldn't. His first fiancée had hated the dust and the dirt and the smell. Tiffany, his second, she didn't mind, but well, that's because she was probably doing half the rodeo contestants. But Catherine? Hell, his third…and worst. When he was a contestant, she would sit there and cheer and had him so damn fooled he hadn't trusted his judgment in years. Sure, she'd cheered and took a real interest in his life, and work and ranch...and bank account. Because he was her fiancé?

Oh, yeah, sure, but mostly because she'd planned to kill him and take over Wild Creek.

Christ. His gut still twisted into knots every time he thought about the conniving blonde. Thank God he'd overheard her talking about it, or who knows where he might be.

Probably six-feet under instead of walking on cloud nine, thanks to the beautiful, sweet, giving brunette next to him.

"I guess I'd better get going," she said, brown eyes warm with a flicker of apprehension. "Just not crazy about being up there as if on display, again." She smiled bravely.

Damn, she was adorable.

He wanted to pull her under the bleachers and show her just how adorable he found her, but well, not a good idea with hundreds of people around.

Standing toe to toe, he brushed a thumb over her lower lip and smiled. "You'll do fine, darlin'. I love to hear you play and sing."

She didn't do it often. Was more a Jordan/Cole thing, but he always loved her voice. Soft, sweet, sometimes with a punch. Kind of like the woman.

Kerri blushed, and then surprised the hell of him by cupping his face, lifting on her toes and initiating a kiss right in front of the others.

His chest swelled. Literally swelled at the action and what it meant. She admitting feelings for him, showing others he was important to her.

Yeah, he was definitely heading to cloud ten.

She drew back, and even though she was flushed and blushing at the same time, Kerri didn't shy away, didn't run, and that did something to his already swollen heart. Cracked it open a little more.

"Enjoy the show," she said, then turned and walked away with a smiling brother and sister-in-law.

Kade cleared his throat. "So, will you be holding the wedding at the ranch, too?"

Connor twisted to look at his grinning friend. "Very funny. It was just a kiss."

But Connor knew it was more. They'd staked a claim. Each of them. Right there in front of everyone. He rubbed his chest as he watched Kerri walking toward the stage. And, *Christ*, he was both elated and terrified at the same time.

"Hello, there."

He turned to see the sheriff making his way to them. George Hester had been sheriff for over seven years now, and a damn good one. With corruption increasing around the country, Harland County was lucky to have a straight shooter.

"Hi, Sheriff," Connor replied as Kade echoed.

The older man shook his hand and smiled. "Hello, Connor. You brought in some good looking bulls." He turned and held his hand out to Kade. "Nice to see you, son."

"Good to see you too, sir." His buddy shook the sheriff's hand.

George released Kade and looped his thumbs in his belt buckle. "As a matter of fact, I wanted to talk to you."

Eyes narrowed, his friend cocked his head. "Is something wrong? What did my cousin do now?"

"No." George held his belly and laughed. "Kevin hasn't done anything to my knowledge, yet." He sobered and cupped Kade's shoulder. "I wanted to talk to you about my retirement."

Shit. Connor exchanged a glance with Kade. Harland County had flourished under George's careful eye.

Kade voiced their surprise. "You're retiring? When?"

"Depends."

"On what?" his buddy asked.

"You," the sheriff replied. "Time to call it a day, son. But I'd feel much better if I knew my replacement was a respectable, law-abiding citizen like you."

Kade reeled back. "You want me to run for Sheriff?"

"Actually, I think that's a great idea," Connor said, in immediate agreement with the sheriff. Kade stood for everything George held dear. Loyalty. Commitment. Justice.

"I agree." The older man nodded. "See? That's one law abiding citizen already giving you his blessing."

Kade still wore a frown.

The sheriff smiled. "And as far as running for election, that won't be necessary if I appoint you to finish out my term. When that's up, then you'll have to run. By then, maybe you won't want to, or by then maybe no one will want to run against you." George rocked back on his boots. "I've gone unopposed twice now."

"That's because we like having you in office," Connor told him.

"Much obliged, son. But this old ticker ain't what it used to be, and the missus wants to travel."

Kade cleared his throat. "How soon are you talking?"

George smiled. He knew he had him, just as Connor knew the moment his buddy had uttered the question. Yeah, Kade was interested. And was certainly the perfect fit.

Responsible. Respectable. Helpful. Everything the county wanted in a sheriff.

"How soon?" The sheriff scratched his temple. "Well, as soon as I can talk you into it. You'd have to go through a process, but I've no doubt you'll do well. Why not stop by my office on Monday, and we'll get into more detail?"

Kade nodded. "Okay. Sure. I'll see you then, sir."

"See you then." The older man turned to Connor. "You boys enjoy the show."

Once they nodded, the sheriff turned and walked away.

"Well, now," Connor said, staring at his friend. "That was interesting."

Kade nodded.

"What are you going to do?"

His buddy shrugged. "Go hear what he has to say. But right now, I'm going to watch my buddy's girl take the stage."

Connor smiled. "Yeah, I can't wait."

They grabbed a beer and one of the few remaining tables and sat down to watch.

A crowd was gathering. Some would sit, others would stand, and others would dance. All and all, it was a good time waiting to happen.

And he loved good times. His pulse kicked up. And spending time with Kerri. *Hell yeah.*

Spending the whole day at the fair without complaining about dust, and animals and smells.

Kissing him for luck…without him asking.

Yeah, he could get used to this.

With her thoughts on Connor and getting back to him,

and her heart light, Kerri exited the stage after their set... and bumped right into Duke.

"Sorry, Kerri." He steadied her bare shoulders, and she had to fight the sudden aversion to him. Something had changed in the man. She couldn't put her finger on it, but something was different about him since their date a couple months back.

"That's alright."

He smiled down, still holding her shoulders. "I saw you with Connor earlier. You have any more strawberries?"

"Back off, Carver," Cole practically growled, stepping to her side, suddenly rigid and fierce.

But he wasn't the one the jerk needed to worry about. Heck no. Jordan had gone stalk still. Not good. Not good at all. Kerri had seen that look in her sister's eyes before. When two very big, very amorous, very drunk bikers wouldn't leave Comets after last call last year. Her former cop sister had persuaded the men. Their faces became acquainted, up-close-and-personal, with the bar. Twice.

So, yeah, Duke needed to heed Cole's warning before *his wife* made a move. Okay, maybe *she* better do something before the situation got out of hand.

"Nope, but I hear they're selling some over at the farmer's market section." Kerri brought her hand up between them to lightly tap Duke on the shoulder and break his grasp in the process.

Two strong hands clammed around her arms, and before she knew it, Cole pulled her behind him, shielding her with his body, forming a wall of hunk in front of her. Sweet. But unnecessary. She had a Jordan.

And, uh oh, her sister was stepping up to Duke.

"I'd like to make a suggestion," Jordan said, cupping

his shoulder. "If you're going to sniff around, go to the barn. My sister's taken."

Duke looked unconcerned. He even shrugged. "We'll see about that." Then he sent Kerri a look that said he wasn't finished yet, before he disappeared into the exiting crowd.

"Jackass," Jordan muttered under her breath. "He's lucky I restrained myself."

"No, he's lucky Connor wasn't here," Cole said. "He would've ripped Duke's arm off and beat him with it."

His brother and Jordan smiled, but Kerri wasn't amused. She was worried. What if Connor *had* seen that exchange?

Her gaze bounced through the crowd. There was a bit of a mass exit going on. Looked like a sea of cowboy hats.

"Hey." Cole dropped an arm around her shoulder and squeezed. "You okay?"

"Yeah, I'm fine. Just hoping your brother didn't see that."

Limb-ripping wasn't on her agenda for the evenings events.

After what seemed like forever, the crowd dispersed, no doubt to get ready for the main event at the arena, bull riding. His donated bulls would be crowd pleasers, but Connor had no intentions of watching. Once he met up with Kerri, he'd make arrangements for the bulls' transportation back to the ranch, then concentrate on the sexy cook for the rest of the night.

As he stood with Kade off to the side while the audience left the area, he spotted Cole and Jordan and the beautiful woman in his thoughts. His pulse picked up, then galloped when she spotted him and smiled. Her whole face lit up, and a soft blush crept into her cheeks, deepening the sparkle in her mocha eyes.

The urge to kiss her ripped through him so fierce, he had a hard time standing still and not rushing up to meet her. Out of nowhere, their parents appeared to congratulate the singing trio, but he only half heard, thanks to his still thundering pulse. When his gaze met hers, his whole body tightened, and he barely managed to hold back the groan. Heaven help him, she looked like she wanted to kiss him.

His buddy stepped forward. "Well done."

"Thanks," the girls said.

Cole slapped Kade's shoulder. "Maybe next year you'll give us something to cheer about in the rodeo?"

The Guardsman laughed. "We'll see. Right now, I'd better try to round up my Casanova cousin. I'll catch you later."

"See you later," he said, then turned back to Cole.

His brother thrust out a hand. "Thanks for staying, bro."

"Ya, goof." Connor shook Cole's hand and laughed. "You're not the reason I'm here."

Jordan patted Cole's chest. "Well, I'm here for you, sweetheart. Let's go buy some strawberries."

As he watched his sister-in-law pull his brother away, Connor rejoiced. Finally, he could get Kerri alone and…

A blur of blonde wearing a red shirt, short jean skirt and red cowboy boots pressed against him.

"Where've you been, stranger?" Ashley asked, then yanked his head down and kissed him with fervor.

Shit. Right in front of Kerri. He hoped she didn't think he was seeing the blonde.

He grabbed Ashley's shoulders and broke the kiss.

"Busy. Now if you'll excuse us, we have some celebrating to do." He detangled himself and chanced a look at Kerri. She didn't seem to be mad. No frown. In fact, she almost looked like she was smiling.

He dropped an arm around her shoulders, then led her away from a dumbstruck Ashley.

When they reached a fairly secluded spot by the 4-H building, he stopped and looked down at her. "Kerri, I'm sorry about Ashley. I—"

She put her finger to his lips and silenced him. "It's alright, Connor. I know *she* initiated that kiss."

He stared down, well, shocked. "You mean you're not mad?" He couldn't think of one women he'd ever been with who wouldn't have been.

"Of course not." A smile crossed her lips and lit her eyes as she glance up at him. Then her gaze narrowed. "As long as you didn't enjoy it."

"Well, now, I didn't say that." He grinned and she punched his arm.

"Hey…you're supposed to say, 'No, Kerri. I didn't.'"

Her playful tone and warmth in her eyes when she stared at him had his insides heating. God, she was wonderful. He backed her up against the side of the building and gently traced her chin. "No, Kerri. I didn't."

Her playfulness continued as she prompted with a smirk, "And, 'No one is as good as you, Kerri.'" Her eyes never left his while she ran her hand up and over his abs, then stopped when she reached his chest.

His heart tried to make a break for it and reach right for her palm. He couldn't blame it. That was where he liked to be. In her grasp.

His pulse increased as he watched her lift up on tip toe and nip playfully at his lips, always pulling back when he was just about to kiss her.

She laughed and didn't try to escape when he pressed into her and captured her mouth for a very hot, very deep kiss.

God, yes, this was what he'd wanted for the past hour.

He groaned at the first contact, the first taste of her kiss. It had been nearly two hours since he'd held her like this, which was four hours too long.

He pressed closer, but it wasn't enough. With one hand on her waist, he shoved the other under her hair, the soft strands like silk on his skin as he cupped her head, holding her at an angle best suited for possession of her mouth.

Her moan rumbled straight through him, testing his mettle. He would *not* take her up against the building. It was too public. But, oh hell yeah, he wanted to. She still tasted of strawberries and sangria, and when she sighed in his mouth, he nearly lost his resolve.

This kiss was more. Different. Unguarded. Was it the adrenaline from watching her sing on stage or something else? Connor didn't know. Didn't care. For the first time in years, he dropped his guard, too, and just went with it.

A small sound escaped Kerri's throat. Did she sense it? Could she tell he'd just knocked down all his walls and welcomed her in? She had an arm up around his shoulder, holding tight, while the other found its way to the back of his neck where she played with his hair. The light stroke of her thumb sent waves of heat straight down to his groin.

All too soon, or maybe just in time because he was lightheaded and so turned on he practically hummed, they broke for air.

He buried his face in her hair. "What do you say we leave this place?" he asked through ragged breaths.

Her hold tightened. "I'd like that."

Hell yeah, that was exactly what he wanted to hear. He drew back, and she opened her eyes and *hot damn*, they smoldered. His gut twisted with need.

"My place?" she asked, voice husky, gaze dark with the same need. "I have more strawberries..." She trembled in his arms.

"I love your strawberries," he said, forcing himself to release her, otherwise they'd end up back against that building. Instead, he captured her hand and brushed his lips over her knuckles. "I've got to go make transportation arrangements for the bulls I donated. Why don't you wait here? I won't be long, then we can head out. Is that okay?"

"Sure."

She smiled warmly, and it took him a second to remember what she was agreeing to.

He drew in a breath and smiled as he exhaled. "Okay. I won't be long."

Forcing himself to back away without kissing her, he turned around and rushed to the pens, as fast as his tight jeans would allow.

This interruption was good. Tonight was special. And he wanted to slow things down, not go off like a horny teenager. She deserved a slow hand, and he couldn't wait to worship every curve.

He entered the pen, oblivious to the activity, his mind intent on his task so he could get back to Kerri as soon as possible. A few signed papers and a quick talk to Pete who was there helping at the rodeo, and the transportation was taken care of.

Now, to take care of Kerri.

Smiling, Connor made his way through the crowd, stopping to shake hands with a few friends when it was unavoidable. *Christ.* He'd been gone over ten minutes now. His stomach tightened as apprehension skittered down his back. Maybe he shouldn't have let her alone.

Cutting across the fairway, he was passing the horse stable when a glimpse of lilac caught his eye. Kerri? He backtracked to find Ashley at the door.

The blonde placed her palm on his chest and blocked his entrance. "You don't want to go in there, Connor," she said, blue gaze soft with compassion. "I'm sorry. I know you thought she was different than the other city girls."

What the hell is she going on about?

He moved her aside and entered the stable. *Shit…no.* His heart slammed hard in his chest. It *was* Kerri. With Duke.

Shock stiffened his body while all the blood drained in a fierce rush to his feet. *Son-of-a-bitch…*She was kissing the bastard!

The stable spun slightly out of focus. He grabbed for the nearby stall and sucked in a sharp breath, but not much got past his tight chest.

Son-of-a-bitch! He fell for her tricks a second time.

They broke apart, and he watched Duke brush a strand of hair behind Kerri's ear, his gaze tender while he wore a shit-eating grin Connor wanted to wipe away with his fist. But not now. He was way too enraged to have the good sense to stop.

Air. Distance. Dammit, he had to get out. He turned on his heel and strode the hell away from the two-timing broad and her smiling prick. *The fuckers!* He lengthened his strides, brushing past Ashley and ignoring Kerri as she called after him. He did not want to talk to her. He was so furious at himself and her right now he had no idea what he'd say.

I'm a fool. Again.

God, how could he be such an idiot?

His hollowed gut twisted tight. He had all he could do not to double over as if the wind had been knocked out of him.

Christ. The two of them must've planned the basket auction, and he fell right into their trap. All it had taken was Duke's smug expression every time the bastard had bid. He took the damn bait and out bid the prick. *Jesus*, once again, he was the damn target.

Well, no more. Shards of pain stabbed at Connor's gut, but he kept moving through the crowd. He needed a drink. A big one.

What the heck just happened?

Kerri couldn't believe Connor just walked away. She'd turned around, relieved to find him standing there…and he'd walked away. Her insides twisted into a tight knot, and she rubbed her chest in an attempt to lessen the pain.

He left me with Duke.

And it wasn't that he hadn't heard her call his name because he'd glared right at her with so much anger and contempt she'd stopped dead in her tracks.

"Forget about him," Duke said from behind. "He's not worth your time."

Swiveling around, she stared at the bastard who'd just ruined something very special. And dammit, it was her fault to. She knew better. Her instincts told her not to trust the man who'd approached her a few minutes ago saying Connor had sent him to tell her to meet him in the horse stable because he was going to be a few minutes longer.

She'd walked in to find the building empty. Her mind had screamed this was a mistake, so she'd turned to leave and found Duke. Attempting to go around him, she'd asked him to move, but he said, "Sorry, this is for your own good," then spun her around and kissed her…exactly when Connor must've walked in.

It had all happened so fast, the twisting around, pinning of her arms to her sides, his mouth coming down on hers so hard she'd tasted blood, but within seconds his head had lifted and he'd pushed her hair behind her ear. That's when she'd heard a commotion from behind and had turned to find Connor glaring. She'd called out, expecting him to help, to…

Instead, he'd left her there, obviously thinking she'd been kissing Duke for pleasure. God…how could he think such a thing? *Especially* after the day they'd had…the kiss they'd just shared by the 4-H building?

"McCall is a pompous ass. You can do better," Duke continued, brushing an invisible speck off his shoulder.

Anger rushed through her in a fierce wave. "Enjoyed yourself did you?"

"Oh, honey you have no idea," he said with a ruthless laugh.

Chapter Nineteen

Before Kerri could think twice, she reeled back and her fist connected with Duke's jaw. He flailed backwards.

"That was for kissing me."

He rubbed his chin and took a menacing step toward her. "You bitch!"

Fury flowed free and rapid now. Before he reached her, she used her training and spun around, hitting the other side of his face with her foot, thankful her skirt allowed movement.

Duke staggered backwards and cursed.

"This is for Connor." Kerri pivoted in the opposite direction before he could right himself, and the force of her kick hitting his chest sent him crashing through a stall. The jerk landed in a combination of hay, dirt and manure.

Planting her feet, she grinned, but no amusement resided in her body. "Now, that's a look that suits you." Rage quivered through her limbs as she stared down at him. "If you ever come near me or touch me again, I'll call the police."

With that said, she turned and went to find Connor. She knew he was hurting. Knew he thought she was like the others. That she'd used him.

He should know better, her mind insisted, but given the amount of times he'd been hurt, she doubted he knew anything but mistrust.

The fair was hoping now. Throngs of people littered the fairway. God, it was going to be impossible to find him. Since her phone was with her stuff in his truck, she couldn't call him or text, although she doubted he'd answer anyway.

Kerri pushed through the crowd, glancing at every stand, tent and building she passed.

She had to find him. Pain wracked her body, both physical and emotional. She flexed her throbbing hand. Hitting Duke had been worth the discomfort. But now she had to find Connor. She couldn't just let him go like that, thinking she'd cheated.

He should know better, her mind insisted again. And was right. He should. Disappointment intensified her ache. He *didn't* trust her, and a relationship didn't work without trust. She wasn't going to worry about that now. She just needed to find him.

Heading to the next tent, the beer tent, she didn't have to go in and look because Connor waltzed out. Relief pulled some of the stiffness from her body as her steps slowed.

"Connor, there you are. I've been looking for you," she said, careful to keep the hurt from her voice. "Why didn't you wait?"

Smirking, he looked down his nose at her. "Why? Did you want to make it a threesome?"

She sucked in a sharp gasp of air, which backed up in her throat because her chest was so tight. He didn't bother to wait for her answer. He just turned to walk away.

Kerri lunged forward and grabbed his arm to swing him around. "Wait just a minute, Connor. What did you think you saw?"

She knew, but had to hear in order to disprove it.

A scowl darkened his face. "I saw exactly what I needed to see, Kerri. You are no better than the rest of them. In fact, darlin', you're worse!"

Anger and sadness mixed to form an emotional paste

in her chest. She could hardly breathe from the weight. "You know what, Connor? You are almost right."

A dark brow rose to disappear under his hair. "You admit you and Duke were up to something?"

"*Duke* was up to something alright, but I wasn't. All I was guilty of was waiting for you. But I highly doubt you'd believe me right now, so I'm not going to bother to defend myself to you."

God, she suddenly felt so empty. She wrapped her arms around herself, then winced when she inadvertently touched her arm where Duke had grabbed her.

Connor's gaze narrowed and searched her face, and for a moment, Kerri thought maybe, maybe they had a chance to get through this nightmare. But then he shrugged and his dark look returned.

"You're right, darlin'. I wouldn't believe anything you said. I don't even know why I'm bothering to waste my time with you now."

He would've continued on his way, but she ran in front of him and put a hand to his chest.

"Oh no you don't. I'm not done. I want to tell you what you're right about."

That got his attention. He stopped and folded his arms across his chest and waited.

She swallowed and pushed through the pain. "You're right to the extent that you did see what you needed to see. Or should I say, *wanted* to see. And you know what I think, Connor?"

Disgust curled his lip. "No, Kerri, I don't, and I don't rightfully care either."

"That's too damn bad, cowboy, because I am going to finish." Her heart hammered out of control. "*You* are afraid of commitment."

He reeled, arms dropping to swing at his sides.

"What? You can't be serious!"

"I am," she replied. "And you're afraid, too. Very afraid. That's why you unconsciously chose Tiffany and Catherine. You knew deep down there was something wrong and that marriage wouldn't take place."

His body shook as he stared down at her, and she knew he was barely holding on to his anger. Good.

"If you know so much about me and my love life, then how do you explain Monica?"

"Monica was the start of it all," she replied. "You did love her, and she did betray you. You never wanted to be hurt like that again, so you chose women who never held that power over you. I'm not saying those break-ups didn't hurt, but you knew the relationships weren't going to last almost from the start."

His jaw worked as he clenched his teeth and drew in a breath. "I see. So I asked Tiffany and Catherine to share my life knowing full well they were going to betray me, and I therefore wouldn't have to settle down. Is that about right, *Dr. Phil*? Did I leave anything out?"

He looked at her with so much distaste, she had to fight the urge to step back. "Not quite. And yes," she said quietly. "You left *me* out." Sorrow funneled into her chest and she had to stop to take a breath.

"You did that by yourself, Kerri, when you decided to scheme with Duke."

God, he was so clueless. She felt sorry for him.

"I did nothing with Duke, but because your feelings for me are getting too strong for you to handle, you saw what you wanted to see, so you could have a means for an out."

Dammit. Her vision blurred. She did *not* want to cry in front of him. He'd only think it was a ploy, anyway. She turned to walk away.

"Oh, hell no. Now it's my turn."

His hand closed over her, and he turned her around. Pain banded her arm. She winced and shook free. He'd grabbed right where Duke had. She rubbed the throbbing while he looked from her bruised arm to her face.

"Christ, Kerri. I'm sorry," he said, regret momentarily replacing his anger. "I didn't mean to hurt you."

She shook her head. "You didn't. It—"

"*Jesus!* I can see it plain as day." He cut her off, pointing to the discoloring, anger back to darken his gaze. "I've no idea why you're denying it."

She opened her mouth, wanting to finish telling him the bruise had been from Duke, but he held his hand up to stop her.

"Save it. You lie about everything. Duke, your arm…whatever. It's my turn," he rasped. "So, you're saying I saw you kissing Duke because my feelings for you are too strong, and I'm afraid of them."

She wasn't sure if that was a question or not, but she nodded. He shook his head and laughed without mirth.

"That's priceless. You're good. I catch you cheating and *you* turn it around to make *me* the bad guy."

She stepped closer. "It wasn't like that."

He ignored her. "Tell me something, Kerri…" He looked down at her, mouth thin, face pale, gaze full of hate and contempt. "Did you really ever stop seeing Duke? I obviously had it right the first time. You did sleep with him that night I walked out. You've been playing me all along. And damn, you were good, too. Pretending to be shy and inexperienced." He stopped, and his eyes narrowed as if he just thought of something. "You probably fucking lied about Lance being gay, as a way to make me feel sorry for you."

This time, Kerri reeled back as if slapped. "God, I can't believe you just said that." Her hand was back on her chest in a vain attempt to block the pain. It didn't work. She hurt. God, she hurt so bad her body was rapidly turning numb. "I don't see the point in discussing this anymore since we obviously don't have a future. Excuse me."

She pushed him out of the way, ignoring the uncertainty that crept into his eyes. He could think what he wanted. She didn't care at this point. She had enough trouble trying not to throw up.

Weaving through the crowd, she found a clearing and made her way to a tree. She was dragging in a few breaths when she heard someone call her name.

"Kerri, are you all right?"

She turned to find Brandi heading her way. Her eyes filled with tears, but she swallowed past her hot throat and nodded, then shook her head. "I thought you'd left."

"I did," her friend said. "But I had to come back to meet a client to look at some homemade furniture they wanted in their new den I'm designing."

Kerri nodded, fighting more tears threatening to spill over. "Can you give me a lift home?"

Brandi frowned. "Sure, but…I thought…did something happen between you and Connor?"

"Yeah." She hiccupped. Darn it. Air funneled into her lungs as she drew in a deep breath. God, she just wanted to get out of there.

"Come on. We can leave now," Brandi said, and they fell into step together.

The designer kept looking at her, but the woman never asked a thing. She was secretly thanking her friend when they found Jordan and Cole sitting at a quiet table, sharing a funnel cake.

Shoot. She didn't want to see them...or anyone right now.

"Hey you two," Cole said.

Jordan smiled. "Brandi, I thought you left."

"Had to come back, but now I'm leaving again," she said. "Kerri and I are both heading out."

Her sister's head snapped in her direction while Cole's gaze narrowed on her face, then glanced past her...probably looking for his brother.

"Where's Connor?"

Yep. She knew it.

She shrugged. "I don't know. Around I guess." Somehow she'd kept the tremor from her voice.

Jordan looked at her up and down, then slowly rose to her feet, her concerned gaze boring deep. "Kerri, what happened? What's going on, and don't say nothing because I know better."

Cole stood up to stand behind Jordan, his concerned expression matching her sister's. "Did you and Connor have a fight?"

A snort bubbled up Kerri's throat, but came out as another hiccup. *Darn it.* "Yes," she answered.

"Kerri, what's going on?" Jordan asked again. "Your dress is dirty, your arm is bruised and the knuckles on your right hand are swollen. Tell me what happened."

She should've known Jordan would take in all of those things so quickly. Once a cop, always a cop. She sighed.

"Jesus." Cole stepped closer to look at her arm. "Did Connor do this?"

She shook her head. "No. Of course not."

Her brother-in-law's eyes darkened so much she couldn't tell iris from pupil. "Who?"

"Yeah, Kerri, who?" Brandi stepped closer.

Then Jordan moved until she stood toe to toe. "Who did this, Kerri?"

"Duke," she replied, knowing it was useless to try to lie to her sister.

"Duke?" Cole and Jordan asked at the same time, both wearing a flush of anger.

Kerri nodded. Cripes. She might as well tell them and be done. "Yes. He grabbed me in the stable and kissed me."

Cole cursed. "I hope Connor beat the crap out of him." He shoved a hand through his hair and Kerri was hit with a fierce wave of sadness.

His brother believed her. *Why couldn't Connor have had this kind of reaction?* Silently her sadness spilled down her face as she shook her head.

"No, unfortunately your brother chose to think I was enjoying that kiss and was somehow scheming with Duke."

How could he think that of her after the wonderful day they'd spent together? After all the intimacies they'd shared the past few weeks?

She was just sick inside.

"Oh, Kerri, I am so sorry." Jordan gently placed her hand on Kerri's shoulder, and Brandi touched the other.

"That stupid jerk! I don't know who I am angrier with—Connor or Duke," Cole rasped as he paced back and forth then stopped. "First, I think I better go pay Duke a visit." He went to leave, but Kerri grabbed him by the arm and stopped him.

"Don't! I've already taken care of him," she pleaded, and he looked down at her in confusion. She managed a weak smile. "You don't think my cop sister wouldn't teach me a few things?"

A slow grin spread across his face. "I almost feel

sorry for Duke."

Jordan nodded. "You should. Kerri was top of her Kung Fu class and holds a 2nd degree purple belt." Jordan's pride showed in her smile. "Tell me what you did."

"Yeah." Brandi moved closer. "What did you do?"

Feeling as if it were all a dream, Kerri relayed the rest of the Duke/manure episode to them and managed a small smile at their laughter.

Her throat began to close up again, so she cleared it. "I'm leaving."

"Okay, hun," Jordan said. "Where's your stuff? In Connor's truck?"

Kerri nodded.

Jordan pushed a curtain of hair over Kerri's shoulder. "No worries. I'll drop it off tomorrow."

She hugged her sister. "Thanks."

"And I'll kick my brother's ass. In fact, I feel the need to do that right now."

Kerri pushed from her sister's embrace to grab Cole's arm and hold tight. Again. "Please don't bother Connor. He's feeling betrayed. He's hurting. He doesn't need a lecture right now."

Jeez, listen to her, sticking up for the man who was breaking her heart. But she understood him. Knew what motivated his harsh words. Didn't make him less of total idiot but she did comprehend.

"What about you?" Cole looked down at her, gaze warm and full of understanding.

She blinked and stepped back. "What about me?"

Jordan slipped her arm through her husband's and stared at her. "Kerri, you don't go kissing a man the way you did by the truck earlier today without having some deep feelings for him."

"I didn't say I didn't have feelings for him, but *he* chose to walk away, not me." Kerri sighed and swiped at the fresh trail of tears that spilled over at the realization.

Brandi stepped close and took her uninjured hand. "Honey, can't you do something about it?"

Kerri shrugged. "I tried. He wouldn't listen. And now, I don't think I should." At the trio of frowns that met her gaze. She pushed a lock of hair behind her ear then tried to explain. "Connor's whole problem with women is trust. He doesn't trust them, and I can't get involved with him if I have to worry about him mistaking things all the time."

Brandi nodded. "I see what you mean."

"Yeah," Jordan agreed. "Maybe he just needs time like Cole did, to come around to your way of thinking."

Cole kissed her sister's head and the happy couple smirked.

If only it were that simple.

"Well, if you're ready?" Brandi stepped forward, question in her eyes.

Kerri nodded. She wanted to get out of there so bad. Her head throbbed. Her arm throbbed. Her hand throbbed.

Her heart throbbed. And not in a good way.

She wasn't going to hold it together much longer. "Yep, let's go."

"I'll see you tomorrow," Jordan said. "If you need me, call."

She nodded. "Uh, yeah, except my phone is in my purse behind the seat in Connor's truck."

Cole straightened and pulled his phone from his pocket. "Do you want me to call him so I can get your things now?"

God, no. She couldn't take another meeting with

Connor now. She just couldn't. "No. Tomorrow's fine."

"Yeah." Brandi hooked her arm through Kerri's uninjured one. "She's staying with me tonight, so it's all good."

Kerri could've kissed the woman because her house key was also in her purse in Connor's truck. She glanced sideways at her friend and smiled her thanks.

"Okay, then tomorrow it is," Jordan said.

And with a wave, Kerri finally headed to the exit, her breathing a little easier by the time they made it to the field of parked vehicles.

"Just so you know, I don't have ice cream, but we can share some raspberry cheesecake yogurt," Brandi said, brown gaze apologetic.

Thank God. Kerri couldn't look at ice cream right now. It would only make her think about…

She inhaled and forced a smile. "Sounds good."

Darn it, Connor.

Bad enough the cowboy crushed her heart and clipped the wings she'd just started to spread, but did he have to take away her comfort food, too?

Chapter Twenty

The grand opening of *Texas Republic* was a big success. Kerri and Jordan were kept busy the whole week with prep and training and promo. Which worked for Kerri. It had been a tough week. Her chest still felt like it was in a vice. And she was sad. Very sad. The loss of what could have been hit her deeper than expected. For something that had mostly been a friends-with-benefits kind of fling, she was taking their break-up hard.

So the busy schedule, and the exceptionally busy opening day, was a welcomed distraction. The turnout was a huge success, and the band had started playing an hour ago. She could hear the laughter and clapping of the costumers all the way back in the kitchen.

It felt good to be in her element again. The past few months she felt off, floundering, but now she was where she belonged. Her domain. Pans, pots, skillets, cutting boards, knives, fillets, fresh vegetables…garlic. She loved cooking with garlic.

She was at home. At peace.

But still, Connor managed to haunt. She hadn't seen the cowboy since the fair, but his taste, his scent…and sometimes when she closed her eyes Kerri could almost feel his lingering touch. Especially in the dang pantry, her body would ache for him.

Stupid body.

Staying busy kept those feelings at bay. She went through her normal daily routine. And the world continued to spin.

Tonight was great, though. She welcomed the constant rush of orders the efficient wait staff brought her

Her Unbridled Cowboy

way. The two experienced assistant cooks she'd handpicked were perfect. They knew the basics of the operation, so Kerri only had to train them in the style of her cooking, and they soon established a good routine.

A two-night trial run had put the wait staff, kitchen, prep and bar staff through the paces. Kerri and Jordan had asked Kade to round up local service members and their families to act as guinea pigs in exchange for free meals.

It'd been a huge success. Not many ripples, and what little had surfaced were efficiently worked out. And a smooth opening was the product.

A tray of raw, marinated prime rib steaks was in Kerri's hands as she made her way out into the dining room toward the open pit. It was positioned safe from the costumers, yet where they could still see, smell and watch as their meals cooked. From the reaction of the crowd tonight, the pit was a big hit.

After handing the tray to the workers manning the pit, Kerri made sure nothing was needed. Satisfied all was going well, she headed back toward the kitchen when Jordan stopped her.

"Mom and dad just arrived with the McCalls," her sister informed, raising her voice to be heard over the band. "Come and take a break."

Her gaze drifted to were her sister pointed, and she stiffened at the sight of Connor settling down at the big table.

Jordan pushed Kerri forward. "You have to face him sometime," her sister said. "Might as well be where you know he'll be civilized."

True. It would be good to get it over with, too. The longer it took for them to bump into each other, the more apprehensive she'd become.

"Okay, but just for a minute. I need to get back in the kitchen." She brought a smile to her lips as they approached the table.

"Kerri! Hello dear." Her mom made to kiss her, so Kerri bent down to receive it.

"Hello." Smile still glued to her lips, she nodded to everyone at the table, including Connor, who gave her the same response. She sat down and sipped the ice water shoved in her hand.

"Looks like you're doing great." Cole grasped her free hand and squeezed. "Between your cooking and Jordan's head for business, you'll be packing them in like this for months."

Kerri returned his squeeze. "I hope so." She also hoped to be in California before summer's end.

"That's the idea, sweetheart." Jordan winked.

As always happened lately, when her sister looked lovingly at her husband, Kerri's heart suddenly felt empty. Her gaze involuntarily went to Connor's face, and she was startled to find a pair of brown eyes watching her intently.

With her pulse now cracking the sound barrier, she felt her cheeks heat despite her efforts to stop it. *Crud.* She really hated that he had the power to bring heat to her face…and body.

"Excuse me, Kerri," one of the waitresses said as she approached. "But there are a few customers who asked if they could meet the *wonderful cook*."

She felt her blush deepen as pride mixed with delight to brighten her mood. "Of course. Just lead the way." She stood and glanced at her family. "Sorry, duty calls."

Her gaze met and held Connor's for a beat before she turned to follow the waitress. His face and posture were full of indifference, but she'd caught a flicker of heat in his eyes. Kerri's satisfaction turned back to sadness. She wished the cowboy had had a clue.

Connor was aware of Kerri all night. Damn woman got under his skin and held tight. No matter how hard he tried not to, his gaze followed her as she made rounds to the tables before she eventually disappeared into the kitchen.

When his parents and the Masters had left, he'd moved to an empty booth with Cole to free up the big table, and they were eventually joined by Kevin and Kade. Connor deliberately sat with his back to the kitchen so he wouldn't have to look at her. Wouldn't have to add to the ache in his heart.

It hadn't helped.

Damn body knew when she'd return to the dining room before he'd catch sight. Awareness rippled down his spine and spread to his groin. Shifting in his seat, he silently cursed his body for betraying his mind and heart. He did *not* want to be attracted to a cheating woman, a woman who'd played him not once, but twice.

Too bad his body didn't seem to have such high standards.

"Oh great. Look who just walked in?" Cole's sour tone brought Connor's focus back to the room, and his gaze came to rest on the object of his brother's dislike.

Duke Carver.

The bastard's presence was enough to sour Connor's stomach. Duke was probably here to see Kerri and support her on her opening night. *Shit*. The knife stuck in Connor's heart sliced deeper. He still couldn't believe she did that to him. He thought she was different. Never in a million years had he thought she'd betray him. But she had, and he wasn't about to stick around and watch the two of them have a good laugh at his expense.

"If I had my way, I would have banned him." Once again his brothers' tone caught his attention.

Ban the man because of what he'd done to Connor?

The Dalton's both turned to see who Cole was talking about then twisted back, anger in Kade's eyes, while Kevin's gaze was full of humor.

"Man." Kevin grinned. "I would've given anything to have seen Kerri dropkick his ass into that stall."

At the mention of Kerri's name, Connor fastened his gaze on Kevin. His mind was trying to digest what he'd just heard when his brother spoke up.

"Serves that SOB right. I'll tell you, if he ever tried something like that on Jordan..." Cole shook his head and his eyes darkened with emotion.

Kevin laughed. "If he tried that on Jordan, he'd still be in the hospital."

Kade and Cole joined in the laughter as Connor tried to get his thoughts organized into something that made sense. He had nothing.

He turned to his brother and frowned. "What happened between Kerri and Duke?"

"Nothing I can talk to you about," Cole replied. "Sorry, bro, I promised Kerri I wouldn't."

Like hell. Now Connor's blood pressure started to rise along with dread. Had the bastard turned on Kerri that night? He glanced at Kade, then Kevin. Son-of-a-bitch! They knew something he didn't. He could see it. And neither Dalton was happy.

He grabbed his brother's arm as Cole lifted his beer. "So help me, if there's something I should know—"

"Oh, that's rich." His brother scoffed and drank his beer. "Hell yeah, there's something. And it's something you should've known without my help."

Christ, his brother wasn't making any sense. How many beers had Cole had?

"Duke assaulted Kerri in a stable at the fair, but she took care of him," Kevin explained, while Cole glowered. Kevin shrugged. "She made *you* promise, not me."

"*What?*" *Jesus!* Duke had assaulted Kerri? When? He'd seen them kiss, not fight. Connor felt all the blood rush to his head. "He did *what?*" Connor demanded hoarsely again, glaring at his younger brother.

"Don't look at me. You apparently had the perfect opportunity to intervene, but instead, you pigheaded idiot, you walked away and left her there with him."

He'd witnessed it?

As his brother's words sank in, Connor's mind went back to that night. "I saw them kissing, and all I could think was I had to get the hell out of there before I killed the prick."

"No, you saw *Duke* kissing Kerri," his brother corrected.

Connor blinked. Wasn't that what he'd just said?

"Look, Connor, think back to it," Kade prompted, leaning forward. "Where were Kerri's hands? In his hair? Around his neck?"

Christ, he didn't want to do this. Pain gripped his chest in a vice.

"Come on, Connor, think," Kevin urged.

Kade nodded. "It's important."

Fine. He closed his eyes and forced himself to recall that moment and Kerri's hands. They hadn't been around Duke's neck or back. They were…

"Shit…" He sucked in a breath.

"What?" Cole asked. "Where were they?"

Connor's eyes flew open. "Down at her sides, held in Duke's grasp."

The bruise...*Son-of-a-bitch!* That was why her arm had been bruised and what she'd probably been trying to tell him.

Fuck.

It felt like someone yanked the knot tangled in his gut as the truth of that night revealed itself in his head. He slumped back in the booth defeated by his own ignorance.

Cole folded his hands on the table and glanced at him. "I can't sit back and watch you do this anymore. Not all women are Monica. You have to learn to trust again, and until you can do that, you are going to end up alone."

Connor knew Cole spoke the truth, and he sat there for a full two minutes without moving as the magnitude of his own actions sunk in, along with his brother's words. He *should* have known better. In fact, deep down he *had*. Something had bothered him about that kiss, but he'd ignored it and walked away.

God...what had he done?

The words Kerri had flung at him replayed in his head. *"I did nothing with Duke, but because your feelings for me are getting too strong for you to handle, you saw what you wanted to see, so you could have a means for an out."*

Ah, hell. She could be right. Maybe that was what he'd been doing all these years, so he wouldn't get hurt. Only this time, it backfired. He got hurt anyway, and it was his own damn fault.

But worse than that...*my God*, Kerri *could've been*... Inhaling, he closed his eyes and grit his teeth, trying not to think about what could've happened to the sweet cook because of his stupidity. Doing so would drive him mad. The plain truth was, he'd walked away when she'd needed him most. He should've stayed. He should've protected her. His eyes snapped open.

He should've believed her.

Releasing the breath, he stared into his beer and fought hard to control the emotions whirling inside him. Never in this lifetime would he forgive himself. *Jesus,* he'd failed her. He'd failed her big time. Anger broke through his control, and he gripped his mug tighter. Anger for himself, for Duke, for Ashley, because it had not been a coincidence when he'd run into the blonde at the barn door right at that exact time. She'd helped the bastard. *Christ.* He'd fallen into a trap, all right. *Their* trap. Not Kerri's.

He was such a jerk. And so was his brother.

"Jesus, Cole," he said, his gaze snapping to his brother. "You knew this and weren't going to tell me?"

"Of course I was. But you were drunk that night."

"What about this whole week?"

His brother shrugged. "You were an ass. You deserved to suffer for the week."

Kevin laughed, even Kade's lips twitched into a grin.

Connor blew out a breath and sighed. "You're right. I deserve a lot worse."

"Don't you think you should apologize to Kerri?"

His brother's voice brought Connor's mind back to the woman he'd hurt. For the second time. "Yes. But first, I owe Duke an overdue visit," Connor said, and when he spotted the bastard across the room, he pushed against Cole to get out.

Kade leaned forward again. "I don't blame you for wanting to get even with that prick, but don't do it in here. Jordan and Kerri don't need trouble with the police."

"Especially on the night of their grand opening," Cole added before picking up the pitcher and refilling everyone's mugs.

Connor nodded and lifted his glass. "Fine. I won't do anything to him." He took a long swallow of beer. "At least, not in here."

He saw Cole exchange a glance with the Daltons, no doubt worried about the vehemence in his voice. Connor didn't care. He was most definitely going to have a *talk* with Carver, later. Right now, he had more important things to take care of. He had to apologize to Kerri. Again. He rubbed at the ache in his chest. *God*, he *needed* to apologize to her, to own up to his biggest failure, plead for forgiveness, although he didn't deserve squat.

Connor avoided Duke by remaining in his seat, talking about the calves that had been born that week, and the stallions he and Kade had bought. Conversation he normally enjoyed. Not tonight. Tonight it felt insignificant. Unimportant. It was just a means to help bide his time while he waited for the kitchen to close so he could finally talk to Kerri alone.

He didn't expect her to be receptive or to take him back. God, he would never ask her to. She deserved so much better. Someone with a clear head on his shoulders, who didn't jump to conclusions. Someone who had faith. Trust. And that wasn't him. At least, not yet.

Christ. He would never, ever forgive himself for leaving her with Duke. For saying what he'd said to her. His insides burned with disgust. And he doubted the burning would ever stop.

I left her there with Duke...

It's a wonder she didn't hate him. He wouldn't blame her if she did.

As Jordan approach and most of the kitchen staff came out to enjoy the music, Connor knew that the time had come.

He left the booth and found her alone by the sink, wiping the counter. He cleared his throat and she jumped.

"Oh, Connor, you startled me." She glanced at him quickly, but didn't hold his gaze, just turned back to her task.

"Sorry, didn't mean to." He slowly made his way to where she stood, wiping and re-wiping an already spotless counter, and he cursed himself for causing this awkwardness. "I just wanted to talk to you for a minute."

She stopped what she was doing and turned to face him, never quite making eye contact. "What's up?"

"I...It seems..." He swiped the hat from his head and played with the brim as he cleared his throat again. "It seems I owe you another apology."

She remained silent, but raised an eyebrow, so he continued. "I'm sorry I was such a jerk at the fair. That I jumped to the wrong conclusion...again. But most of all," he walked over to her, placed his hat down on the counter and put his hands on her shoulders and squeezed, until she finally met his gaze. "I am *so sorry*, Kerri, for leaving you in the barn with that...that..."

Anger resurfaced, and he fought to hold back on the bad language that threatened to spill. The thought of all the things that could have happened to her tore at his gut and tormented his mind.

It must've shown in his eyes because she placed her hands on top of his, and stared at him with understanding.

God, how could she possibly look at him with

anything but contempt?

"Thanks, Connor," she said. "It means a lot to me to know you don't think I'm capable of the things you accused me of."

He was about to make a remark, but she placed her finger to his mouth to silence him. It did that, and a whole hell of a lot more, as the feel of her flesh touching his lips sent a familiar shock wave through his body.

"…besides, I took care of Duke, so you don't have to worry about him." She smirked.

Agony tightened the invisible vice around his chest. "Kerri, I swear to God, if that bastard hurt you because of my stupidity…"

He crushed her close and closed his eyes, trying to convey what he couldn't say. Words escaped him. She deserved the words, but they wouldn't come. He promised himself, then and there, he was going to leave her alone. Just stay away from her. Forget his unending need to be near her.

He'd brought her nothing but pain, and she deserved better. If it hadn't been for him, Duke would've left her alone instead of using her to get revenge on him. Besides, Christ, he was so screwed up with trusting people that he'd hurt her more than Duke had.

And more than once.

How long they stood there, arms wrapped around each other, his head resting on hers, hers resting on his heart—a heart she completely owned—he had no idea. Connor only knew he needed her to be all right.

Soon, the comforting turned to something else, and his pulse picked up as his body remembered the feel of hers wrapped tight around him.

If he was to keep that promise to himself, he had to put a stop to this now.

He released her and stepped back, reaching for his hat to keep his hands from grabbing her again. "I'm sorry things didn't work out for us, Kerri, but I want you to know it was in *no* way your fault." Bending slightly at the knee, he caught and held her gaze. "You didn't do anything wrong. It was my entire fault and my problem. What you said to me that night at the fair is starting to make a whole hell of a lot of sense, but I'll be honest with you." He shoved a hand through his hair and shook his head. "I'll be damned if I know what to do about it." Guess he had some major soul searching to do. A slight smile tugged at his lips. "Anyway, I also wanted to congratulation you on tonight. It was a huge success."

She blushed. "Thanks. I'd forgotten just how much I missed the crazy, wonderful, madness of a busy kitchen." Her smile brightened the whole room with a radiance that reached into his hollowed gut and warmed some of the chill.

God, she's so damn beautiful.

Connor shoved the hat on his head and his hands in his pockets to keep from touching her. "Well, you did good." He smiled one last time. "Guess I'd better say good-bye, Kerri."

He searched her face to make sure she'd gotten his meaning. Some of her light disappeared as comprehension dawned in her big brown eyes, which, heaven help him, filled with tears.

She blinked them away and nodded.

It was best for both of them if he bowed out of their...*relationship*. She'd have a chance to find someone who would treat her with the respect and trust she deserved. Twice now, he'd shown her that person wasn't him.

With an ache in his chest, Connor touched his hand

to his brim, then exited the kitchen, leaving his heart in the hands of the sweetest woman he'd ever known. And the only one he'd ever fallen in love with.

The realization only strengthened Connor's resolve to leave Kerri alone to enjoy a normal life that didn't include him and his inability to trust.

Now, he had a few things to say to Duke Carver.

It was hard to believe it had been a whole year since the McCall's anniversary party. This year, they were having a family dinner with the Masters as the only guests. Mrs. McCall had asked Kerri to make her famous roasted vegetable orzo—a favorite of Mr. McCall's—and told her Emma would manage the rest of the dinner. So, Kerri was at the market, squeezing zucchinis, picking out the perfect one when a shadow fell across her cart.

"Kerri," a familiar voice said from behind.

Alarm raced down her spine in a stiffening move. Great. Duke. She hadn't seen him since the fair two weeks ago. She tightened her grip on the zucchini should he even think of trying something again, and slowly turned to face the jerk, only to be shocked speechless by his appearance. Dark glasses did little to disguise the tape on his nose or the bruising under his eyes.

She'd connected with his jaw, not his nose. And, although she'd knocked him around a little and he'd even crashed to the ground, she didn't recall him landing awkwardly on his arm, so the sling was as new as his broken nose.

"I just wanted to apologize for my behavior at the fair," he said before giving her a curt nod and walking away.

Okay weird. She glanced around, expecting to see Connor, or Cole, the Daltons, even Jordan putting the realtor up to that, but a young mother and her two children were the only other customers in the small store. *Yeah, really weird.* She shrugged, paid for her purchases and headed back to the apartment to cook.

It wasn't until later that night, when Connor walked into the celebration with bruises on his knuckles that her mind recalled her meeting with Duke. Her heart rocked into her ribs. She'd tried hard not to think about him the past week, but seeing him again brought all the longing and hurt to the surface again. Mostly longing. And just the thought of him searching out Duke to punish the jerk, made her feel all warm and fuzzy inside. It shouldn't. She should be appalled at the Neanderthal behavior, but she wasn't. Nope. She really wasn't.

Her gaze strayed to him often, and even though she was at her normal seat, right across from the cowboy, she couldn't catch his eye. All evening, the bugger avoided her gaze and direct conversation. If she hadn't known the reasoning, she probably would've been hurt or annoyed, but instead, she felt bad. Really, really bad. So much so, she cornered him the minute he left the room.

"Connor, wait." She rushed into the hall after him.

He stiffened and slowly turned to face her. *Jeez.* Her heart constricted and a small gasp escaped her throat. His jaw was bruised, too. Without thinking, she reached up to touch it, but he backed away.

"What do you want?" he asked, gaze as weary as his tone.

You, was the first thought that came to mind, but she curbed her tongue. Slowly lowering her hand, she hugged herself and drew in a breath. "I wanted to…I saw Duke today."

His chin lifted and gaze hardened. "Did he apologize?"

"So, you did have something to do with his injuries," she stated and opened her mouth to thank him, but he held up his hand in a stop gesture.

"I know what you're going to say, I shouldn't have. It was stupid, Neanderthal behavior, but I don't care. The bastard deserved it and much more."

"I agree."

"And if it…what?" He frowned down at her. "You do?"

She nodded. "Yes. Thank you."

"Christ, Kerri." He shoved a hand through his hair and cursed. "Don't thank me. You shouldn't have to *thank* me. In fact, I should've whipped his ass that night at the fair. You should hate me. I wouldn't blame you for hating me. I left you there. I failed you in the worst possible way—"

"Whoa. Wait a minute, Connor." She grabbed his arm and held him in place when he made to leave. God, the reproachful look darkening his eyes, sucking the life from his features made her physically ache. "First of all, you did *not* fail me. You were upset. You have a history of women disappointing you. I understand that's where you're mind jumped—"

"Stop it. Just stop it, Kerri." He shook her off. "That's just it. You shouldn't have to understand. Or thank me. I should've known right then, but I didn't." He let out a long breath, then turned to face her fully. "Look, I appreciate what you're saying. And I get it, darlin'. I really do, but I don't deserve it."

She grabbed his hand. "Well, that's where you're wrong, cowboy," she said, lightly brushing his bruised knuckles with her lips. "You need to stop beating yourself up. It's over. In the past. I forgive you, now you need to forgive yourself and move on."

His gaze softened, and he touched her bottom lip with his thumb. "You're something else, Kerri Masters."

She smiled and shrugged, warmth finally finding her heart for the first time in weeks.

"You deserve someone as understanding and open-minded. Someone who isn't...*me*," he said, sucking that newfound warmth from her heart. "Thank you for your forgiveness. It means a lot to me." He dropped his hand and stepped back. "But there's no way in hell I'll ever forgive myself."

With a curt nod, he twisted and walked away, similar to how Duke had left her in the store. Guilt ruled both of the men's actions.

But the two men were very different. One was honorable and one was not. Her chest tightened. That wasn't the big difference. No. The big difference between the two men who had fought because of her was the fact only one *held* her heart.

The novelty of the town's new restaurant hadn't worn off yet, and Kerri and Jordan were kept busy. The days had turned into weeks, and before she knew it, more than a month had passed.

She'd simply traded one torture for another.

She missed him, darn it.

Every night, Kerri found herself scanning the crowd for Connor's sexy, lop-sided grin, and went to bed with a longing she knew only he could satisfy.

He'd surprised her with that apology opening night, but what surprised her most was that he hadn't asked her if they could try again. Instead, he'd said good-bye and wished her well.

He'd ended it.

Boom.

Done.

She'd been dumbfounded, and if truthful, a little disappointed.

Despite his lack of trust in her, if Connor had initiated it, if he had crooked his little pinky at her, Kerri knew she would've given him another chance. Of course, it inevitably would've ended in disaster again—because without trust you can't have a relationship. Luckily, Connor had the hindsight to see that, and walked away. Which he did again at the anniversary dinner. She as much as gave him a second chance, but he didn't take it. Just insisted she could do better and walked away. Again.

That was over three weeks ago, and now as she drove to have lunch with her sister and the McCalls, Kerri couldn't help but wonder if she would get a glimpse of Connor today. She shouldn't want to see him. They'd left it in a good place. Amicable friends. A clean break. She shouldn't rock the boat. But…dang. She missed him. The uncontrollable urge to see him burned through her every day. What was with that? It was because of that urge she hadn't been to Wild Creek in weeks. Not since the anniversary dinner. Need would only cause her to do something stupid, and these days, it didn't take much.

Today, Jordan had enticed her over with the promise of one of Emma's famous enchiladas. She hadn't had the pleasure of one since childhood, and her taste buds were heightened in anticipation.

When she pulled up at the McCall Ranch, she noticed her sister and Mr. McCall standing by the fence of a corral where there was a lot of commotion. As Kerri neared, the excitement of a new horse being broken in explained the uproar.

She greeted her sister and Mr. McCall before turning

her attention to the cowboy, noting with relief it wasn't Connor, and ignored her increased pulse as her gaze found him on the other side of the corral.

Dang, the man was gorgeous. Tall and lean and perfect. He wore a denim shirt with the sleeves rolled up, tucked into a snug pair of faded jeans. His confident, easy-going presence was commanding, and she couldn't tear her gaze from his face as she watched him concentrate on the horse and rider.

Excitement and pleasure emanated from him, announcing to others that he loved what he did. Kerri recognized that immediately, because she held those same feelings for cooking for other people. There was nothing better than doing what you loved for a living.

As the beautiful gray stallion bucked the rider off, Connor quickly ushered the cowboy out of harm's way. She recognized the young man as the one who'd taken third place at the rodeo.

Then her *heart* bucked. Dear God, Connor was going to try to get on the demon. Kerri watched mesmerized as he circled the horse to try his luck.

Only a moment ago, she'd thought the animal beautiful with its gray coloring and black flowing mane. Now, with Connor as the rider, her outlook changed. Big time. This was a wild beast. Huge, and snarling.

Holding her breath, she watched Connor use his magic to get close enough to the horse to grab the horn of the saddle and pull himself on. The massive beast wasn't pleased, and she watched in fear as he was tossed forward and backward while it reared and kicked. His hat fell off and the horse stomped it mercilessly with its deadly hoofs.

Kerri gasped, and noted her sister's glance, but she didn't care. She refused to take her eyes off Connor.

With skill and determination, he stayed on the bucking horse.

As much as she wanted to leave because she couldn't bear to see him get thrown or hurt—or worse—Kerri stayed rooted to the spot. There was no way she could go until she knew the man she loved was safe.

The man I love?

Where in the world had that come from?

Kerri gripped the fence with white knuckles and slumped against it as her mind raced to understand what her heart had just revealed.

Holy smokes. When had that happened? And how?

Sure, she'd always loved Connor, but more as an older brother when she'd been growing up.

Kerri realized with a start that all that had changed last year. Her visit had opened up her mind to the fact he was an incredibly attractive and sexy male—who was *not* her brother.

When she'd arrived here last December and they'd kissed again, Kerri had started to see him clearly. The more time they spent together the past few months, the more she realized her heart had always known him, and their spirits were one in the same.

Wow…that was deep. And true.

Kerri *did* love Connor McCall, but was darned if she knew what she was going to do about it. There were several things she *could* do, but since he was the one who'd halted their relationship, there wasn't much of a point.

Finally, after what seemed like a millennia, Connor brought the horse under control, and Kerri breathed again. He was safe. The stallion's bucks had lessened in strength and height. She could leave…provided her legs were strong enough to carry her to Emma's kitchen.

"Well, I don't know about you, but I need a cool drink after all that." She tried to make light of the situation.

Jordan nodded. "I agree. That was some riding."

Kerri glanced one more time in Connor's direction and was startled to see him grin at her, then wave as he kept the horse moving under his commands.

With a tentative wave, she swallowed hard as she watched him through new eyes. Her whole body was warm and tingly and alive. She drew in a ragged breath and fought the urge to cough as dust entered her mouth.

I'm in love with Connor McCall.

Nope. Still sounded strange in her mind. But not her heart. No. In her heart, it made sense. Perfect sense. And felt good. Felt right.

Hoping Connor hadn't read her thoughts, Kerri turned to walk toward the ranch when her cell phone started to ring. She fished it from her pocket and frowned at the name on the screen. Lance.

Why was he calling?

"Hi, Lance."

Unsure if taking the call near the corral was smart with the unpredictable horse, Kerri decided to move toward her car. A few minutes later, after finding a pen and paper, she wrote down the number Lance told her then hung up, promising to let him know her decision.

Holy smokes. Kerri walked back to her sister in a daze.

"What's up?" Jordan touched her arm, dark eyes full of concern.

Kerri shook her head to clear it, then focused on her sister. "That was Lance."

Jordan grinned. "We already knew that. What did he want? Are you okay? You're standing there like you're in the fog."

"I guess I am." She shook her head again, then smiled. "He gave me Rene Bastille's phone number."

Jordan straightened and raised a brow. "From *Pierre's*?"

"Yes." Kerri nodded, heart beats increasing. "It seems Rene's head chef is leaving in a month, and he wants to know if I want the position. I've got one week to decide."

There. She said it and still couldn't believe it. *Top Chef at Pierre's...*

"Wow, Kerri, that's great!" Jordan pulled her into a hug.

"What is this *Pierre's*?" Alex McCall asked, still frowning.

"It's only the most posh and prestigious restaurant in Southern California. Kerri has always hoped to work there," her sister boasted.

"Oh. That's great, Kerri, but we would hate to see you leave. I thought you liked it here in Texas."

Mr. McCall turned an intent gaze on her. A gaze so strikingly similar to the one on Connor, who'd dismounted and was leading the horse around the coral, she was at a loss for words.

"Sure she does. It's just that this is something she's wanted most of her adult life."

Once again, her sister came to her rescue. Kerri blew out a breath. "Yes, and I do like it here, Mr. McCall, but I can't ignore the opportunity either."

"I guess you've got a big decision to make, then," he said.

She nodded and sighed. Guess she did.

"Wow," Hannah said, still trying to digest the news

about her daughter's job offer earlier that day. The McCall's had come over for supper and an emergency strategy meeting. "That was a major development. Kerri has *always* wanted to work at *Pierre's*."

Leeann let out a sad sigh. "What are we going to do?"

"Not to worry. I have an idea." Alex sat back in his chair and grinned. "All those two need is to be thrown together for a spell."

"Yes," her husband agreed. "They were doing pretty good there for awhile. But lately, they've been apart."

Hannah nodded. "Now, with the restaurant up and running, Kerri's busy there."

"And Connor's stuck at Wild Creek with his duties," Leeann said, turning to look at her husband. "Alex, the two of them are so busy right now. How are you going to manage that?"

"Not to worry, my dear." Alex patted his wife's hand reassuringly. "I'll take care of it."

Kerri took a five minute break at her family's table Saturday night at the *Texas Pub*. She watched them come in, and of course, her gaze was immediately drawn to the tall cowboy, then held fast. He looked tired and weary with slumped shoulders and a frown creasing his normally smooth brow. She could no more stop herself from approaching than she could stop cooking. Dropping into the chair across from him, she greeted everyone and asked him what was wrong.

Frustration clouded his gaze as he glanced at her. "Teddy, my cook, has an emergency in New Mexico and can't make the drive on Monday. I've called all my backups," he said, shaking his head, disbelief crowding his face. "It's strange. Not a one is available."

"I've struck out, too," Mr. McCall said. "Tough time of year, I guess."

From what she'd gathered, Connor couldn't postpone the drive either. These were the cattle he had to bring in for his scheduled spring auction next week, and he already had buyers lined up.

"How big is the herd?" Jordan asked.

"Little over five hundred head," Connor replied.

Her sister whistled. "Don't you have one in the fall, too?"

He nodded. "Yeah, but that'll be smaller." He stared at the glass of beer he twisted. "This one's the big one. Guess the guys will have to make do without a cook."

"Wait a minute." His father sat up straight. "What about Kerri?" Alex leaned forward and waited for his son's response.

Connor nearly spit out the beer he had in his mouth. Once he swallowed it safely down, he sat back in his chair and stared at her, gaze still weary.

She forced herself to stare back and her pulse picked up speed. Yeah, she didn't think it was a good idea, either. The two of them in such close proximity, despite the fact there would be other ranch hands on the drive, was not smart. She'd deliberately stayed clear of the guy the past few weeks because being near made her want things she couldn't have…

"Well?" his father prompted.

Without dropping her gaze, Connor shook his head. "Not a good idea."

"Why not?" Cole asked.

"Yeah, why not?" Her sister chimed in.

Great. She glanced down the table. Yep. Now the whole family was going to push her on the poor guy. Her attention returned to the silent cowboy, and she watched as a slight twitch tilted his lips.

"It's not her cup of tea," he replied.

Her brow rose. "Actually, I'm not crazy about tea, hot or cold."

He gave her a slight nod, but said nothing.

"I think he meant you couldn't handle it." Jordan lifted her glass and smirked. "That is an unwise assumption, my friend."

Kerri's gaze bounced between the two and settled back on the dimpled cowboy. *Huh.* He really didn't think she could handle it. And here, she thought he didn't want her to go because he couldn't handle *her*. Indignation lifted her chin. "Is that true?"

"Now, don't be offended, darlin'," he replied. "But the wide-open, barren range is not the same as the one you're used to cooking on." He chuckled into his beer.

Normally, she would've laughed, too, but for some reason, Kerri was galled by his amusement. "What's so funny?"

"You...a California cook on a Texas cattle drive." Now he laughed outright.

Kerri was still not amused. Her expression surely would've told him that if he hadn't been too busy shaking with mirth to notice.

"I don't think it's funny, Connor. I think you should consider her." Alex sent his son a stern look.

"Oh come on now, dad. You can't be serious?" Connor shook his head and took another swallow of beer.

"But I am, son. Kerri knows how to cook, and she knows how to ride. The way I see it, she's the answer to your prayers." Alex McCall sat back in his chair and folded his arms across his chest.

Both men were carrying on as if she wasn't there, and Kerri had just about enough. Sending a glare across the table to Connor, she ignored his sexy dimple before rejoining the conversation.

"I get the feeling, Connor, that you really *don't* think I can handle it." She told him with her gaze she was talking about the work, not their attraction.

He winked. "Then you'd be right, darlin'."

Sexy bugger.

"Then *you'd* be wrong," she corrected, sending him an identical look.

He sat stock still, and his eyes narrowed in a challenge. "Would I now?"

"Yep." She meant it.

"Seems to me the only way to settle this is for Kerri to go on this drive with you, Connor," Cole spoke up.

"Yeah," Jordan agreed.

Kerri looked from one brother to the other. "Sounds fair to me." She folded her arms and waited for Connor's objection.

It never came.

Instead, he surprised her by searching her face and looking at her thoughtfully. After only a minute of contemplation, he placed his mug firmly on the table.

"All right. Fine. Are you sure you want to do this, Kerri?" he asked, giving her one last chance to back out.

Not going to happen. Even though she was not sure, she told him the opposite. "Yes…I'd be happy to help you out," she replied, careful to let him know she was doing *him* a favor.

"Well, in that case, thank you, darlin'. Get plenty of rest tomorrow, because I want you at the ranch early Monday morning." He was still obviously trying to scare her off.

It didn't work.

"Fine. Is there someone who can fill me in as to

what you usually eat on these drives?" she asked as the whole table sat back with silent, grinning faces.

Connor nodded. "Stop by the ranch tomorrow. Cal will tell you what you need to know."

"Okay, I will. Now if you'll excuse me." Kerri got up from the table and her gaze swept the occupants before she continued. "My break is over, and I have to get back to work."

As she walked into the sanctuary of the kitchen, she took a deep breath and quaked like a mother inside. *Holy smokes. What the heck did I just do?*

She leaned against the back counter and drew in another deep breath. Cripes. Why did it feel like she was somehow hoodwinked into that cattle drive?

Judging by Connor's first reaction to her going, she didn't feel it was from him. No one was that good an actor. He'd been generally amused. She was just getting her mind around to Alex McCall when the swinging doors opened and Jordan breezed in.

"Good going, Kerri." Her sister smiled as she joined her by the counter, careful not to get in the way of the workers' busy pace.

"I'm not sure if it's good or bad yet," Kerri admitted as she washed her hands, then began to chop onions.

"It's good of course."

An odd look crossed Jordan's face as she glanced around the kitchen. Uh oh. Alarm raced through Kerri. Her sister was about to have a profound moment.

Jordan leaned in and spoke quietly. "If Connor told you he loves you and wanted you to stay, would you?"

Chapter Twenty-One

Kerri's heart rocked at the thought. "Yes." It was a no brainer. *If he said he loved me, I'd stay.*

Jordan nodded. "Well, now you'll have three days, or at least *two good nights* to get Connor to admit his feelings for you." Her sister grinned and folded her arms across her chest in triumph.

Kerri began to peel and chop all the onions until they were done. "I guess." She tossed them into a buttered pan on low heat to caramelize.

"What do you mean you guess?" Jordan followed her to the stove. "It's the perfect situation."

"I know. I'm just worried about this place." She turned and looked at her sister. "Who is going to cook while I'm gone?" she wondered frantically. "Maybe I shouldn't go." What if he didn't feel the same?

"Oh no. You *are* going, and this place will be fine. You hired good cooks." Jordan's hand swept around the bustling room, before she grabbed Kerri's shoulders. "They will do just fine, and I'll be here to lend a hand, so no more talk of not going."

"All right. I'll go. I'll go." Kerri relented. "I rather like the idea of being out under the stars with Connor," she whispered to Jordan. "I could do without the cattle and other eight men, but beggars can't be choosers."

"That's the spirit." Jordan winked, and they both grinned then got back to work as the third rush of the night began.

"I've got to be crazy," Connor mumbled to Cole as he

watched Kerri disappear into the stable to talk to Cal on Sunday afternoon.

"What are you talking about?" His brother joined him by the fence of the adjacent corral.

"For agreeing to let Kerri go on this cattle drive." He took his hat off, then shoved a hand through his hair.

Yeah, he had to be insane.

"No. That was a very smart thing to do," his delusional brother corrected.

"How do you figure?"

"I know what I've seen in both of your faces. The two of you are in love with each other, but are holding back. Why?"

"Even if she did love me, which she doesn't, she's better off without me," he stated, shoving the hat back on his head, never denying his love.

His brother's head jerked back. "Now how in the hell do you figure that?"

"Because I've done nothing but hurt her."

And he had to stop. He did stop.

Didn't he?

Cole walked over and grabbed his upper arms. "Connor, I have a very important question for you." When he remained quiet, his brother continued, "Do you trust Kerri?"

He stared into the dark, inquiring eyes and spoke the truth that went deep into his core. "Yes, I trust Kerri."

His brother's smile broadened. "That's great, man." Cole released him and smacked his arm. "So, what the hell's the problem?"

"The problem is I don't want to hold her back. If she knew how I felt, she might stay behind and always regret not giving that *Rene's* or *Pierre's* or whatever the hell it is, a try." He expelled his breath and looked down at his dusty boots, feeling as dirt-kicking-low as they were.

"If Kerri told you she loved you and didn't want to go, what would you do?"

Ah hell. Didn't his younger brother have anything better to do than hound him with painful questions? And, God, this was the most painful of all.

He sucked in a breath. "Cole, cut it out. Jesus! Don't you think I wouldn't die to hear her say that? That I, Connor McCall, was more important to her than her job?"

Christ. He longed to hear those exact words so badly from her sweet lips, he'd avoided her the past few weeks, knowing they'd never be spoken.

"It's settled then." Cole slapped his shoulder as they turned to walk toward the stable doors. "Kerri has to give her decision in one week, so that's how much time we have to get her to tell you she loves you and wants to stay."

His pulse kicked up. "Do you really think she'll do that?"

It was too good to be true.

"You bet I do. As a matter of fact…" His younger brother smirked. "I'd bet on it."

"And you think that will happen on the range?"

"Yes." Cole nodded. "Because, my dear brother, despite your busy days, your nights are a different story. Kerri will *have* to spend time with you."

"Yeah, me and eight other men." He stuffed his hands in his pockets and sighed.

His brother shook his head. "Not necessarily. There are a lot of wide open spaces, bro. I've been on your spring drives before and seem to recall some secluded spots." Cole grinned and slapped him on the back. "If you can get Kerri alone there by the creek and rocks, I'm sure you can convince her to stay."

Connor wasn't as sure, but knew it was worth a try. "I guess you're right."

"Of course I am. That girl loves you, why else would she brave a cattle drive and agree to cook for nine ornery cowboys?" Cole's grin turned sheepish. "She wants to stay in Texas. She's just waiting for you to give her a reason."

Hope fluttered like a piece of straw in a south Texas wind. "You really think so?"

"Yes, I do. You have two nights to give her that reason, Connor."

If she really did feel that way, then he'd be able to tell if they touched…

He straightened his spine and nodded. Two nights. He'd make them count.

What in the world am I doing, Kerri wondered silently as she found herself on the back of a horse very early Monday morning, riding with nine men an hour into her first cattle drive.

Her horse was loaded with everything Cal had reassured her she'd need to cook for them. And she'd even added a few of her own things. Including a bag of her special seasonings guarantee to make even a rock taste good.

Half of the men, plus Connor, Kerri knew from the ranch, the other half sent her begrudging looks. Seemed the older men weren't crazy about a woman tagging along, no doubt afraid she'd slow them down or get in the way. Kerri was determined to prove them otherwise. She'd nearly laughed out loud at their expressions when she showed up early and was dressed just like them and she'd easily kept up with the pace they set.

Knowing that despite the heat, you had to dress in layers, Kerri had on a T-shirt with a long sleeved, button-down red plaid shirt over it. She tucked them into well-worn blue jeans and pulled on her favorite old pair of cowboy boots. Her hair was secured at the nape of her neck in a ponytail before she donned a straw cowboy hat that was used during the warm months.

Judging by their faces, they'd expected her to show up in a halter-top, shorts and flip-flops. The urge to gloat had been there, but she'd suppressed it as Connor introduced her to each one individually.

She'd ridden this trail many times in her youth, and it was all starting to come back to her the more they pressed on. Settling back with a contented sigh, she enjoyed the brisk ride, and before she knew it, they stopped for lunch.

Thanks to Cal, she knew that lunch on the first day consisted of a cold sandwich. So, after work at *Texas Pub* last night, Kerri had made ten subs, which she doled out now.

The men offered murmurs of thanks, and a few raised their eyebrows at the sight of their meal. She just smiled and proceeded to hand out the water Cal had also told her was their usual choice of drink.

Once everyone else was taken care of, Kerri sat down on a rock and began to dig into her own sub. Suddenly famished, she was half way through when Connor sat down beside her.

As always happened when he was near, her heartbeats quickened and body warmed, and for the first time in weeks, she relaxed and enjoyed the sensation.

"How are you doing?" Warm, brown eyes looked at her with concern.

"I'm fine, Connor, honest. I'll let you know when

I'm not." She grinned and watched in fascination as his dimple appeared, then disappeared.

Holy Texans. He was looking at her lips. So, now, breathing was a problem. And a whooshing sound invaded her ears. The man was potent, and gorgeous and dang, she wanted very much to lean forward and take his lips with her own.

But she didn't. Kerri was well aware there were eight men watching them and didn't want to do anything to embarrass Connor in front of them. So, a mount-and-ride-fest was out of the question. *Too bad.* Because heaven help her, that was exactly what she wanted to do.

A low rumbled sounded in his chest. Yeah, he was getting the vibe.

With supreme effort, she brought her water bottle to her mouth and took a good long drink before getting up. "I'd better get the garbage together." She glanced down at him and had to force herself to move away.

Kerri was half way to her horse when she heard the unmistakable rattle of a snake. Stopping dead in her tracks, her gaze quickly scanned and found the culprit just off to her right.

Poised to strike.

"Kerri, don't move!"

She heard the terror in Connor's voice and saw a few men scrambling for a weapon.

Her heart was in her throat as her hand closed around the knife she had attached to her belt. In one fluid movement, Kerri slipped it out and threw the knife, decapitating the unsuspecting reptile.

Connor got to her just before the rest of the men. All eight just stared at the dead snake in front of them. But not Connor, he stared at her.

"Holy shit! Did you see that?" one of the men said.

"Sure did. She took its head clean off," another replied.

"Remind me never to get on your bad side," Cal joked, and several men agreed and laughed.

Connor, on the other hand, was not amused. He grabbed her shoulders and turned her to face him. "What the hell were you thinking?" he demanded, his face dark with anger.

She raised her eyes innocently at him. "Killing supper?"

"I'm serious, Kerri. My God…what if you'd missed? You could've been bitten and *died*." He let her go and walked in a frustrated circle. "I'm sending you back. We'll make do without a cook."

She rushed to stand in front of him. "No way. I'm perfectly capable of taking care of myself out here. I've spent more of my life here than in California. I don't know why you keep forgetting that." She stared up at him and shook her finger. "And I know for a fact you always bring a few vials of anti-venom with you on drives, so if I had missed and got bitten—" She ignored his sudden pallor. "—you could've easily administered it. So don't try to use this as a means to get rid of me because, cowboy…" She reached up and pulled his hat down on his face. "I'm not that easy to get rid of."

The rest of the afternoon went by even faster as the men asked her questions and Connor sent her begrudging looks.

"I have to know," Pete said, riding on her left. "Where in the world did you learn to throw a knife like that?"

She laughed. "New York."

Yeah, that got their attention. All nine men were now looking at her.

"At cooking school," she explained. "A few of us adopted it as a good stress relief activity."

"Throwing knives?" Cal asked.

Kerri nodded. "Yep. Throwing cooking knives at a picture of a certain instructor known for his sour moods and unfair marks. After one particular exam, believe me, I became very accurate at the game."

Laughter echoed across the range as they pushed forth.

All too soon, the afternoon was over, and they came upon the herd it would take two nights to move. Instructed to stay out of the way and follow behind once they had the cattle moving, Kerri did just that, in awe at the sight of the men at work.

Ropes and steeds ready should there be a breakaway calf, the cowboys controlled the herd, and one in particular, controlled her heart beats.

Connor was the epitome of tall in the saddle. His sure, swift, confident movement had her mind bringing up memories of him using those same attributes to handle her. Except the 'swift' usually started out slow and lazy…

Shards of heat shot low in her belly. Now, she was wet and turned on in the saddle. Which wasn't so bad. Every bump and rock of the horse enhanced her crazed state.

Okay, she took that back. It was bad. Very bad.

Kerri quickly and deliberately brought the image of that unpopular instructor to mind, which swiftly doused her flames.

She remained on her horse on their southeast trek, following the men at a leisure pace. Her gaze almost never left Connor's form as he'd closed in his side and kept the eight hundred and twenty five pound beasts moving.

He was simply magnificent.

Kerri admired the way in which he moved with ease and rose to the challenges that turned up. She watched in amazement as he brought his horse into a gallop to go after a stray a younger hand was having trouble with. But, instead of roping and bringing the calf in, Connor just kept the animal from getting further away and allowed the younger man the opportunity to gain control and usher the stray back to the rest of the herd on his own.

His unconscious actions had her heart swelling with pride and love. Lots of love. God, he just had to ask her to stay. She did not want to leave him.

For the next three hours, Kerri silently marveled at Connor and his men, until, finally, as the sunset lower in the sky, they came upon the first camp and stopped for the night.

While the men ushered the animals into the temporary pen, she got busy fixing supper.

Camp had a large pit surrounded by blocks with a big grate over the top. Using wood already there, she quickly started the fire, then pulled out the snake she'd secretly and quickly filleted that afternoon. She seasoned the snake meat and had it sautéing in a pan next to the pot of stew Teddy had made before leaving on his emergency. Thanks to the modern convenience of soft coolers, she soon learned cowboys no longer had to suffer with just beef jerky for food.

Although, she'd packed some of that, too.

By the time supper was ready, the men had washed up and had their bedrolls out. Having already added the snake meat to the stew, she spooned out liberal amount to each as they came up to her with their own plates.

She smiled when they moaned in satisfaction and complimented her between bites saying it was the best stew they ever tasted. Some even came back for seconds, and Kerri made sure to put a helping aside for herself before it all disappeared.

Connor sat down next to her again, and they ate in companionable silence. She had to admit, the men were right, the stew was very good, but she didn't know if it was the other cook's recipe or because she'd added the snake. She'd never had snake before, but heard it tasted like chicken. Now she could honestly say she had to agree. It was similar, just a little tougher. Still, with her seasonings on it, it was tasty.

"Miss Masters…"

"Kerri, please," she interrupted the older man.

"Kerri, what did you add to this stew? I've eaten Teddy's food for over a decade now, and although I can tell it was basically his concoction, I know you added something to liven it up." He grinned. "What was it? Chicken?"

"Well, not exactly." She grinned back, unsure whether she should reveal the secret ingredient to them for fear it might turn their stomachs.

"Yeah, Miss Mast…I mean Kerri, what did you do to old Teddy's stew?" another man asked, and soon she was surrounded by all of them wanting to know the mystery.

Even Connor raised an eyebrow as he waited for her explanation. Something in her grin must have given her away, because both his eyebrows shot up and his eyes widened.

"*Son-of-a-bitch*…you cooked up that snake, didn't you?" He stared at her in amazement.

"What?"

"I don't believe it."

"Did you?"

The men all stammered and looked at her as they waited for her answer.

"Yeah well, I thought it was about time we bit back." She smiled and was relieved when, instead of getting mad, they all started to hoot and laugh.

Connor shook his head, then sent her pulse into double-time as he gave her a heart stopping grin. "I can't believe you served us that snake."

"Seemed a shame to let it go to waste. I wouldn't have killed it if I didn't have to. But since I did, I figured we might as well eat it," she concluded, raising her shoulders.

"Only a Masters would do this."

Connor laughed and her pulse picked up again.

She winked. "You got that right."

His gaze suddenly sobered…and heated. And despite the falling temperatures, her body simmered.

After everything was washed and put away, Kerri opened up her bedroll near Connor's, then sat down. Someone was playing a guitar, and a few of the men were singing off key. She was invited to join in the fun.

Half an hour later, she got up despite their protests and left them to massacre the next song by themselves. She was getting some supplies ready for the morning when Cal ambled over, careful not to step on her scattered things.

"I just wanted to thank you for putting some fun in the day. Boss could use it," Cal said.

Kerri felt her face warm, but curiosity won over embarrassment. "Why?"

He shrugged. "He's been madder than a hornet lately. Even the bulls give him a wide berth."

Her Unbridled Cowboy

She laughed and went to step back, only to trip over her bag. Cal caught her and pulled her close to keep her upright.

"Thanks," she said, really embarrassed, more than likely beet red as she released her stabilizing grip on him.

"Everything okay?" Connor asked, appearing out of nowhere.

Her heart jump to her throat. Crap. Once again, this looked bad. And she didn't want to cause trouble between him and his men.

"Yes," Cal said, dropping his hold to turn to his boss. "She just tripped, and I caught her."

Kerri nodded, stomach churning. "Yeah, I'm such a klutz." She eyed Connor's face, bracing, waiting for him to fly off the handle, accuse her of God knows what...

He never did.

"Good job," Connor said, patting Cal on the back, his face friendly but concerned. Then he turned to her. "Be careful there, darlin'. You've got us all hooked. We wouldn't want to miss out on another meal."

To say she was shocked was the biggest understatement of the century. Stiffness eased from her shoulders when she let out the breath stuck in her dry throat.

"No worries," she managed to say, her staggered heart knocking her ribs when he smile and tipped his hat before walking away with Cal.

Yeah, okay, that was…good. That was real good. Smiling, she bent down and put away her things, happy to see Connor had made some serious progress. Now, she needed to do something about her dry throat.

Kerri headed to the cooler, grabbed a bottle of water and took a long drink.

"You never cease to amaze me, Kerri."

She didn't know what startled her more, Connor sneaking up behind her or his comment. Again, his voice wasn't angry; it was warm and did funny things to her insides.

"Ditto, cowboy." She winked at him, still euphoric over the fact he'd made some serious progress in the trust thing.

Her heartbeats were erratic and her thoughts erotic as she turned around to face him. He was so close she could feel his breath on her skin, and her hunger for him increased. A long-sleeved shirt now covered his red sleeveless top, and even though his yummy muscles were concealed, it did nothing to lessen his sex appeal. Noting some of the men taking an interest in them, Kerri gripped her water bottle tightly with both hands to keep from pulling him close. She wanted very much to show him just how amazing he made her feel, but refrained because of their audience.

"And if it weren't for those eight men over there…" she let her voice trail off and allowed him to fill in the blanks.

Never in a million years did she ever think she'd speak so brazenly to a man.

She heard Connor's intake of breath, but the darkness kept his expression from her as she strained to see him in the moonlight. Unfortunately, it was behind him and only served to illuminate her face for him.

"Christ, Kerri. Do you have any idea what you are doing to me?" he rasped out in a hoarse whisper.

His nearness and his words knocked her off kilter, and she had a hard time forming her thoughts. She wanted so bad for him to admit he loved her that if she could talk she would've gladly admitted her feelings first. Instead, when she opened her mouth all that came out was a breathy, "What?"

Just when she thought for sure he was going to say it, they were interrupted by the singing trio who came over for a drink.

"Don't mind us. We just need some water," the guitarist said with a grin.

Swallowing her disappointment, Kerri put a smile on her face and replied, "Sure. Help yourselves."

With the spell broken, she watched helplessly as Connor grabbed a bottle for himself, then smiled apologetically at her before making his way back to his bedroll.

After a mostly sleepless night, Kerri awoke feeling not so refreshed. She realized too late last night how foolish it was of her to put her roll so close to Connor's. All night, her body ached for him, and despite her exhaustion, it wouldn't let up. Finally at daybreak, she was relieved to get up and pack her things, then busy herself with breakfast.

All day, the torture continued. Too hectic to talk, they exchanged heated glances. Her body hummed, and she wasn't sure if she was relieved or upset when they reached the final camp. Just another half mile and the mare's rocking rhythm would probably have set off her tightly strung libido.

Kerri dismounted and stretched. Her whole body ached. For Connor. She hid it as best she could and cooked the men their dinner of chops and baked potatoes she'd wrapped in foil and placed in the fire. Afterwards, she served brownies for dessert and admittedly felt a little better herself having eaten a full meal. And chocolate. It gave her the energy to clean up with enough left over to pursue the sound of running water she could hear in the distance. Kerri had recognized the place, having spent many afternoons exploring this brook as a child. Now, she longed to enjoy its beauty and tranquility before the sun went down.

Connor watched Kerri clean up and wanted to go after her when she headed off in the distance, but wasn't sure if she needed the privacy or not.

All damn day, he silently cursed his brother and father for putting him in this hellish situation. Last night, he'd been about to ignore his brother's advice to wait for Kerri to say something and just tell her he loved her first, and let things take off from there, but when they were interrupted, the moment had disappeared.

Christ. All night long, his body suffered its own torment as Kerri lay so close to him he could have reached out and touched her. He nearly had. Several times. His hand had hovered over her hair, needing to feel its silky softness as if his life depended on it. His body remembered the feel of those sweet strands, her curves…her heat. To keep from reaching for her, he'd rolled away and stayed in that position for the rest of the night.

And paid for it in the morning.

Big time. He flexed his shoulder and fought a grimace. Damn thing was still stiff.

That morning, he'd never been more thankful for the break of dawn and the hard day's work ahead. Tough work would end his torture and keep him busy. Connor had been surprised when he heard her moving about early. He had to admit she was a hard worker and a welcome addition to his team.

Kerri knew how to do her job and didn't require anything from them except an appetite. If he weren't so

Her Unbridled Cowboy

attracted to her, he wouldn't even know she was there. His men took a liking to her too, and after only a few hours yesterday morning, she had them eating out of her hands.

When sunset began to close in, he began to get worried. Kerri hadn't come back to camp yet. *Shit*. What if she'd met up with another snake? He strode in the direction she'd disappeared and forced himself not to think the worst.

Chapter Twenty-Two

Connor had spent most of the day trying to figure out how he was going to get her alone near the stream, and now couldn't believe his luck as that was exactly where he found her.

Kerri sat in front of the rocks he and Cole had been discussing on Sunday. It was as if fate had read his mind and delivered her to this very spot.

Looking around, Connor was pleased to find they were completely alone. Not one to look a gift horse in the mouth, he eagerly took advantage of the golden opportunity and ambled closer.

"Kerri? Are you all right?" he asked quietly as he approached.

"Oh!" She jumped and twisted around, hand to her throat. "Yes. I'm fine." Her startled face lit up when she saw him.

This knocked the breath from him, so he decided to sit down next to her and lean up against the rocks until he regained his voice. Of course, her nearness was making it a hell of a task. His body was full of awareness and had been on fire since last night. The well-fitting jeans hugging her curves weren't helping his concentration either. He forced his eyes to focus on her averted face, not her lower extremities.

"Wow...incredible," she exclaimed.

It took him a moment to realize what she was talking about. Her gaze was trained on the horizon, now bathed in a dying ember glow. A deep blue faded into purple then into black, and swallowed the sun, making the millions of stars more visible overhead.

Her Unbridled Cowboy

"I envy you this, Connor."

Her voice, just above whisper, sent shivers racing down his arms and spine.

"No matter which way you look, and for as far as you can see…" she paused to smile at him. "You own all this. You're surrounded by such beauty."

He sure was, and her name was Kerri Masters.

She sighed and tipped her head back to stare up at the sky. "And the stars, wow. They seem so close here in Texas, not to mention that moon."

He watched as she reached her hand out as if to touch it.

God, she's adorable. His heart rocked.

"It looks close enough to pull down," she said in awe, then yawned. "Sorry." She half turned and stifled another yawn. "I think the two days are catching up to me." She grinned, then grimaced as she made to stretch her back.

"Here. Let me," he ordered gently as he scooted over. Stretching his legs out on either side of her, Connor began to massage her neck and shoulders.

"Mmm…that feels like heaven. Don't stop." He barely heard her plea as she yawned again.

His inner thighs burned where they came in contact with her soft rounded curves. His body swelled behind his zipper and the tightness in his lower abs increased as she slowly relaxed into him.

Damn. He wanted to flip her around, strip them both naked and thrust deep inside her. Connor closed his eyes and fought for control. He couldn't let his body's sexual hunger get in the way of his heart's need to communicate with hers. He had to know just where he stood with her, and what she was going to do about California.

When he finally got up the courage to ask, he heard

the unmistakable sound of a snore. "Kerri?" he ventured softly. Nothing.

Her breathing was now rhythmic and confirmed his observation. She had fallen asleep. He closed his eyes, leaned his head back against the rock and snickered.

Here he was, at the right spot.

At the right time.

With the right woman in his arms...and the poor thing was so exhausted she fell asleep.

He let out a breath and settled down more comfortably. Looked like it was going to be another rough night. Pulling her in closer, he smiled when she turned and snuggled into him, then mumbled his name before drifting off again. Never had he felt this strong sense of *right* before. He belonged with her, wherever that may be. Connor decided right then and there, even if it meant Kerri's place was in California, he was going to conform, commute, do whatever it took to keep her in his life.

Warmth and comfort cocooned Kerri, and she was loathed to open her eyes and break the spell. She hadn't slept so soundly in years and wanted to embrace it for just a while longer.

The sound of water softly lapping around rocks soon registered in her brain, and she slowly remembered she wasn't at her apartment in bed, but on a cattle drive...with Connor.

On Connor.

Kerri bolted upright when her brain kicked in just before her memory did. She was mortified. How could she have fallen asleep on this cowboy?

"Morning. Well, almost morning." His deep voice greeted her with a touch of amusement.

Turning around in the pre-dawn hour, she faced him. "Oh, Connor. I am so sorry. Are you okay?" She could feel her face fill with warmth.

He smiled. "That depends."

"On what?"

"On whether or not I still have legs. I can't seem to feel them anymore."

His laughter didn't ease her embarrassment.

"I'm sorry. Why didn't you wake me?" she questioned as she hastily stood.

"Because it felt great to hold you like that, and I didn't want to ruin it."

Startled and warmed by his admission, she smiled down at him. "Awe, that's sweet."

Grasping his hands, she helped him up enough for him to lean his large frame against the rocks, allowing the blood to flow down his legs.

"You big goof. You didn't have to lose the feeling in your legs for me. Well, maybe one leg, but certainly not two," she joked, and was rewarded with a grin.

"I'd do anything for you, darlin'," he said.

Her heart nearly fluttered right out of her chest. She stared at him a beat. "You sure are comfortable, cowboy." She patted his firm stomach, and he quickly captured her hand there.

Her insides stirred, and little jolts of awareness shot up her arm. Body in tuned with his, she couldn't stop from swaying closer.

There was so much she wanted to say, *needed* to say, but all the words stuck in her throat as she got lost in the desire smoldering in his eyes. She opened her mouth, but the only thing that came out was a moan as his lips captured hers.

Oh how she needed this. Wanted this…

She opened up to him, letting her body say all the things her heart wanted him to hear. Connor's heartbeat answered back under her palm as they kissed, deep and hungry and desperate. She was soaring. All was finally right with world. She was where she needed to be. Where she was meant to be.

When the kiss ended, he buried his face in her hair and inhaled as if trying to capture a piece of her. She trembled, and he pulled her in tighter.

"I've missed you," he said against her neck, mouth moving over her skin in a hungry rush.

"I've missed you, too."

He drew back, eyes raking over her face, searching deep. "God, I've been thinking about this for weeks," he said, hands on her hips, squeezing, causing heat to funnel in that direction.

Her knees began to buckle. God, she was so easy when it came to him.

He pressed her back against the tall rock and shoved a knee between her legs to keep her from falling.

"Easy there, darlin'."

That was the problem. She didn't want it easy. Right now, she needed it hard and fast. She'd been pent up for too long, and the past twenty four hours had been torture.

The still present moon must've cast enough light for him to read her face, because he growled and captured her mouth. Her insides quaked while her whole body trembled as his stroking hands and hot mouth took her toward that edge she'd been nearing for the last two days. He drew back, pushed her shirts up, and made a low, rough sound before he put his mouth on her cleavage playing peek-a-boo with her lacy bra.

More. She needed more.

Kerri tugged his shirts from his jeans and dipped her

hands underneath, letting them run up his, hot, quivering muscles. His hands and mouth found her nipples. She closed her eyes and gasped as need rocked through her. And still she needed more.

She let her hands skim back down, over his washboard abs, bellybutton, to brush even lower to the erection bulging out his jeans.

"I'm not the only one about to burst," she said, breath hitching in her throat as he sucked a nipple into his mouth, hard.

Her grip tightened on him, and he swore softly against her chest.

"Please tell me you have a condom."

He nodded. His hair tickling her skin. "Two." He drew in a breath. "And we're going to use them both, but this first time is going to be fast, because, darlin', I'm already there."

"Good." She shuddered against him. "So am I."

A minute later, in a series of fast, efficient moves, he had them both naked from the waist down.

His heated gaze raked over her, and he groaned. "I want you," he said, burying a hand in her hair as his lips met hers in a demanding, frenzied kiss. His other hand slid down her back to cup her butt, rocking hard against her.

Kerri moaned and clutched at his shirt. He was hot, on fire and she deliberately rocked into the large erection poking her belly.

He broke the kiss and gasped, hand trailing around her front, dipping low between her thighs, finder her wet and ready. "Christ, Kerri."

A soft, hungry sound caught in her throat. "Connor, I need…"

He released her, and she heard the sound of a

package tearing a few seconds before he sat down on the smaller, flat rock. "Come here."

She took his hand and climbed up, and with his help, straddled his lap, holding onto his shoulders as she sank onto his erection.

Their twin gasps of pleasure echoed in the pre-dawn air as he filled and stretch her in exquisite bliss. Kerri whimpered. He felt so good. So hot. And she was so wound it wasn't going to take long.

Three thrusts and she went off like a rocket. Connor followed right behind.

She slumped against him, face resting on his collarbone while he buried his in her hair. They stayed that way until their breathing evened out.

"I needed that," she said, pressing her mouth to his throat.

He made a choked sound, and his grip tightened on her hips. "Glad I could help."

"Me, too." She nodded, leaning back to look in his face. "You've no idea how close I was to becoming intimate with my saddle yesterday."

She felt his chuckle all the way deep inside. And just like that, heat started to build again.

God, she's adorable.

Not exactly what Kerri would want to hear with him still stuck inside her. Nor was this the right time to finally tell her he loved her. No. She'd only attribute the confession to hot sex. So, he leaned forward and kissed her while he brought them to their feet.

He drew back. "Time to move."

She nodded, a sad look crossing her face as she stepped back. "Yeah, we'd better get back. I'm surprised no one's come looking. We've been gone for hours."

"They won't look. And we're not going back yet,"

he told her, tracing a line from her temple to her chin, watching her eyes widen.

"We're not?"

"Hell no." He smiled, dipping down to kiss her neck. "I'm not done with you. We have one more condom."

She shuddered into him. "I'm all yours, cowboy."

At that, his heart cracked wide open, as open as the very ranch surrounding them. He cupped her face with both hands and stared into the heat and warmth of her gaze. She'd slayed him.

He took her lips, gently, softly. She could have anything she wanted. He'd give her anything and everything.

Again and again, he kissed her until a slow burn warmed, heating with frightening intensity.

Drawing back, he grabbed her hand and kissed it. "Stay here. I'll be right back for you." He didn't want her walking barefoot in the still dark, early morning.

Connor jumped off the rock, shook their discarded clothes, then quickly but carefully headed to the grassy area by the brook a few feet away. He dropped their things, peeled off his shirts and spread them on the cool grass before returning to get Kerri.

She was waiting by the edge, eyes full of anticipation and need, her half naked body making his knees weak. His heart caught and snagged.

He swooped her into his arms, his body growing hard at the feel of her soft curves in his hands and her warm breath against his neck. By the time they reach his make-shift bed, his whole body was throbbing with need.

Slowly, he let her feet touch the ground and turned her to face him. "Someone is over-dressed," he said, reaching for her top button.

Alleluia. She reached for the bottom, and two

seconds later, their fingers brushed in the middle and she shrugged out of the first shirt. Before he could reach for the second, she ripped it off and tossed it aside, standing there in only her white, lacy bra.

She tugged the straps down her arms and the cups loosened, teasing him with the glimpse of nipples. His body tightened at the sight, and he reached behind her to unhook the lace, his erection bobbing when her gorgeous breasts bounced free.

"God, you're beautiful," he said, taking in the sight of her standing naked and aroused before him.

He reached out and traced a line from her collarbone down to her tempting nipple, reveling in the goosebumps and hitched breath caused by his touch. She trembled and leaned into him, and he cupped the full weight of her breasts, brushing his thumbs over her tightened tips.

A moan sounded low in her throat as her palms traveled over his chest and abs, stroking a path to ground zero. *Oh yeah...there*. He sucked in a breath and closed his eyes, enjoying the feel of her hands working him. Damn, she felt good. And knew his rhythm.

She lifted her head and stared at him, the heat and longing blazing in her eyes ripped a groan from his chest. Burying a hand under her hair, he cupped her head and kissed her long and deep, thrusting his tongue into her mouth matching her tugs that were driving him wild.

Magical and talented, her touch made him sweat. He trailed his other hand between them, down her quivering belly, over her soft curls to the heat between her thighs. Jesus, she was wet. He felt himself pulse in her hand, and when he slipped a finger inside her, she broke the kiss to gasp.

Her hands shot to his hips, gripping tight as her knees began to buckle. He caught her and guided her down.

Kerri smiled up at him, running her hands over his chest. "You're so beautiful."

This startled him. "Me?"

Her grin widened, and she brushed her thumb over his jaw. "Yes, you."

He nipped at her thumb. "You and I obviously have different views of beautiful." Shifting onto his elbows, he glanced down at her body, blowing a breath over her nipple, watching it pucker tighter in the moonlight. "Now that's beautiful," he said, then bent down for a taste.

She moaned and arched into him.

Connor took his time, loving, touching, showing her just how he felt. He didn't want her to leave. He wanted to be with her, but if she was leaving, he'd make damn sure this was memorable for them both.

Starting at her throat, he kissed his way down her body, missing nothing, touching, tasting everything as she writhed underneath him. He was on fire by the time he got to her toes. But still he didn't rush. He started back up, stopping at her thighs, spreading her legs. His erection throbbed at the sight of her glistening pink warmth.

He nuzzled her thigh, and she made a low, hungry sound that nearly set him off. God, the woman was responsive, and he loved to make her respond. He glanced up and found her resting on her elbows looking down at him.

Holding her gaze, he ran his thumb over her wet folds. Her head tilted back slightly as she sucked in air.

He grinned. "I've been dreaming of this..." He used his fingers to open her before he leaned in and stroked her with his tongue.

Her whimper met his ears, and soon he was

sampling, and testing, checking her reactions. She moaned, thrust her hips and gasped. Even called out his name. God, he loved that. But when her fingers shoved into his hair, he knew he'd found the *oh, yeah, there* spot.

"You taste so good, Kerri."

She was trembling, panting, her hips rocking, and he wanted to give her more. He added a finger, and she let out sexy as hell sounds from her throat as she fell back and panted his name. She was wet and quivering and gorgeous, and he kept building her orgasm, wanting to make her scream.

And she did.

Connor brushed his thumb over her, applying the right amount of pressure and she cried out a low, throaty *yes* as she shattered. He lapped and laved, bringing her down slow, prolonging her orgasm before he lifted up to stare at the gorgeous, sensual woman.

Still panting, she crooked a finger at him, and he wasted no time crawling up her shaking body. Before he knew it, he was on his back, and Kerri was biting his neck, then kissing her way down his chest and abs. Licking and nipping, she tested his control, because he was about ready to burst.

When her finger stroked his erection, he set her aside. "I'm not going to last much longer."

"Good," she said, then rolled onto her back and a sexy, lazy smile tugged her luscious lips.

Ah hell. A growl rumbled in his chest.

With lightening speed, he fished the condom from his jeans, rolled it on and moved to kneel between her spread legs.

"Now," she purred, spreading further.

Christ. He sucked in a breath, grasping what control he could before pushing into her. Again, their twin sounds of pleasure hissed into the rapidly approaching dawn.

Grasping her hands, he held them by her head, leaned down until they were heart to heart, gazes locked...then he began to move.

God, yeah, this was heaven. This was home. Slowly, he pulled away then pushed back in, over and over, bringing her to that edge so they could plunge off into the depths together.

Her heart hammered beneath him, body writhed, fingers squeezed his hand, but she didn't close her eyes, her emotional gaze remained on his, and he let all his feelings, hopes, needs come to the surface so she would know *she* was his world. His home.

Tears spilled down her face, and she closed her eyes.

He slowed his movements. "Kerri," he said. "Look at me."

Her eyes fluttered open. The need and affection and hope within would've brought him to his knees if he'd been standing.

"I'm with you," he said, bending to kiss her slow and deep, and she moaned into his mouth.

All too soon, the need became too much. He began to move again, faster, picking up the pace. Kerri wrapped her legs around him, taking him in further.

It was too perfect.

Too good.

Too much.

He broke the kiss, and a second later, she called out his name, tightening around him as she burst and took him with her over that edge.

Kerri could barely feel her body as she floated back down to earth. Three times. Connor had given her three orgasms in the same amount of time it took her to make a tray of lasagna.

He was a much better cook than her.

She smiled and played with his hair as his ragged breaths washed over her neck. That was amazing. *He* was amazing. He made her feel. She felt him. And as soon as she could catch her own breath, she was going to tell him exactly how she felt.

Somehow, saying it while he took her to those gorgeous stars slowly disappearing overhead didn't seem like they'd be taken seriously. Throws of passion and all.

Because what Kerri felt was...real. Very real. And she didn't want Connor to doubt it.

He lifted up enough to look down at her. "Morning," he said, voice still low and husky.

She smiled and traced his grin with her finger. "And a good one at that."

"Mmm...hmm..." He nipped at her finger, then his mouth was moving over her throat, making her shiver. With a sigh, he drew back and stared into her face. "As much as I hate to say it, we should get dressed. It's getting light."

She nodded, and he helped her to stand. Kerri had a whole lot to say to the gloriously naked cowboy, but the naked part was a no-no if she wanted him to take her words seriously.

He shook out each piece of their clothes, and by the time the first rays of sun broke the horizon, they were pulling on their boots. Kerri stilled and sucked in a breath.

"God, it's so beautiful."

Connor nodded and moved behind her, banding his arms around her as they watched the beauty unfold in contented silence. She could happily stay there, in that moment, forever. It was perfect.

Well, almost perfect. They still needed to have their talk—get everything out there so they knew where they stood. Where their relationship was headed.

If they had one.

She inhaled and turned in his arms. "Connor, I…" The words got stuck in her throat as it swelled at the sight of his emotional gaze.

He brushed away a tear she hadn't even realized fell, then slowly lowered his mouth to hers. She shuddered and sank into him. She shoved her hands in his hair and melted.

Connor groaned. One hand around her waist, the other cupping her head, he kissed all thought, all reason…all agendas away. They were gone just gone. Which left *feeling* wide open, and *oh yeah*, she did…*feel,* wide open and didn't care because she felt him, too.

"Uhum."

They broke apart at the sound of someone discreetly clearing their throat.

"Sorry, boss, but it's getting late, and the men were beginning to wonder about breakfast," Cal informed, standing in the distance.

Kerri felt her face heat—*friggin' blush*—but kept the embarrassment from her voice. "I'll get right on that."

"All right. I'll tell the men." Cal turned away with a knowing grin and headed back toward camp.

Connor wasted no time drawing her back into his arms. "Where were we?"

If only they could continue…

She placed a hand on his mouth. "Whoa up there, cowboy." Drawing a hand lightly across the stubble on his chin, she sighed. "Sorry, but duty calls."

He groaned. "Duty sucks." He captured her hand before she could pull away. "We'll finish this later?"

His gaze darkened and held a promise she longed to explore, but they'd run out of time this morning…thanks to her three orgasms. Kerri really wanted to feel bad about that but failed.

A smile tugged at her lips. "You're darn right we will. You can't kiss a girl like that, then drop her like a ball and expect her to just bounce away," she admonished playfully. "Seriously, Connor, we do have a lot to talk about."

"Yes, we do," he said, tracing her temple as he pushed back a strand of hair. "But it's going to have to wait until later."

He released her, and together, they made their way back to the camp in a charged silence.

It was late in the day by the time they reached the holding pen at the ranch. Kerri was hot and tired and hungry, but felt so alive. Her heart was pounding in anticipation of their talk.

A talk with her cowboy.

That was how she came to look at Connor. He was indeed *her* cowboy, and she was going to do whatever it took to convince him he didn't want her to go.

She wanted to tell the men to take care of the cattle because she needed to steal their boss, but instead, she stayed out of the way and watched as the last of the calves were rounded up and secured inside the pen.

Her father and Mr. McCall were at the stables when they rode up. They stared at her and Connor, and she knew without a shadow of a doubt, they were indeed the reason she'd been on the drive.

The buggers.
Should I thank them now or later?

"Why am I not surprised the two of you are here?"

Her Unbridled Cowboy

She shook her head and smiled as she dismounted her horse.

"What? We just wanted to know how things went." Her dad kissed her cheek and grinned.

"Yeah. I bet." She grinned back and sent Connor a sly look as he joined them.

"Things are fine. All five hundred and fourteen head are in the pen, and we even got to sample some rattle snake for supper." He winked at her before he began to unsaddle his horse.

Her pulse accelerated and so did the heat low in her belly.

"Rattle snake? What are you talking about?" Mr. McCall questioned, but Connor just smirked and continued with his task.

Kerri shrugged. "I thought the men should taste real Texas cuisine." She bit back a smile as she turned to start unloading her equipment.

"I don't think we're going to get anything out of these two, Alex. We might as well go talk to Cal." Her father shook his head, then slapped his friend on the back, and the two of them walked off in search of the ranch hand.

"Those two are a piece of work." Connor looked over their horses at her.

She nodded. "That's for sure."

His eyes darkened and darted to her lips. "Kerri, I…" He stepped closer, and her heart rocked in her chest, pushing out her hitched breath.

Chapter Twenty-Three

"Connor," Hank interrupted as he came out of the stable with a phone. "One of the buyers wants to talk."

So do I, Kerri wanted to scream, but she didn't.

"Sorry, darlin'." He sent her an apologetic frown, then grabbed the phone and disappeared inside the stable.

Regaining control of her emotions, she finished her unloading.

"We'll take care of the mare. You've done enough," Pete said, ushering her away. "We all hope you'll be on the next drive. Your food tastes better than Teddy's…and you're better looking, too."

"Maybe." She smiled.

Kerri honestly didn't know where she would be by then. Hopefully, right here with Connor and her heart.

Two days later, Kerri pulled onto Shadow Rock Ranch for the Dalton's annual spring barbeque. It'd been two long days. She hadn't had a face to face with Connor since he'd disappeared into the barn the day they'd returned from the cattle drive. He'd called her several times, and they talked briefly, but between their busy schedules, they'd been unable to meet, until today.

Her pulse increased. *Finally*. God, she missed him. Had so much to tell him. So much to say.

Kerri and her sister took the day off of work to attend. She picked up Brandi and was parking her car when she received a call. Glancing at the caller ID, she grinned.

"Connor?" Brandi looked over at her and smiled.

Kerri nodded. "Hello, handsome."

"Hi, darlin'. You here yet?"

"Yep. Just getting out of the car. Where are you?"

"By the big oak. Hurry."

She laughed. "Okay. I'll be right there." She hung up and gave her head a shake, her heartbeats kicking up a notch in anticipation.

"Don't worry about me," Brandi said as they shut the car doors. "I want to go check on my horse before I join the party."

Kerri nodded. She'd helped Brandi board her mare here a few weeks back "Okay. I'll see you later."

She turned and headed for the big oak and her big cowboy, hoping today, right now, was the time they staked a claim. It was time. Past time.

But what if he doesn't say it?

Her rapidly beating heart nosedived into her ribs. Okay, that was not an option. After that night on the range, Connor had told her in every way but words that he loved her and wanted to be with her. And she had done the same.

This was just a formality.

And the perfect setting.

It had all started here at last year's party. Kerri remembered it vividly. Somehow, Jordan had gotten Cole to attend, much to everyone's surprise because he hadn't gone to any function in years. Not since the death of his first wife. Her sister had given the cowboy his space, but had remained close enough in case he needed rescuing.

Kerri also remembered how it had felt to be held by Connor.

It was the first time they'd ever danced together, and it had been his arms that had woken her up. Like a fog horn. *Holy smokes.* She'd realized with a start that night that she wasn't as fickle or prudish as her failed marriage had led her to believe. She'd felt a stirring for Connor back then, but was too confused to know what to do about it.

Not now.

Not this time.

Heck no.

This time, it would be much different. Kerri knew exactly what to do about it. All she needed was for the cowboy to show up.

And he had.

Her pace quickened like her pulse, and she wiped her palms on her aqua sundress when he finally came into view. God, he was so handsome. He took her breath away.

Dressed in a dark green, button down shirt, Connor had his sleeves rolled up to his elbows, accentuating his growing tan, all tucked into his snug, *wish-I-were-them* jeans. A pair of brown cowboy boots and brown hat completed his *Marlboro Man* appearance.

Kerri's heart skipped a beat as his gaze found hers and his face lit up with a smile.

"You look amazing, Kerri," he said, rushing forward to pull her in for a long, slow, delicious kiss. When they broke for air, he grabbed her hand and kissed it. "Let's talk before someone interrupts us, again."

She laughed.

He led her to the privacy of the trees, where he turned and leaned back against the big oak and squeezed her hand.

Funny. Kerri had so much she wanted to say to him, but now that the opportunity finally presented itself, she was tongue-tied. All she could do was stare into his

Her Unbridled Cowboy

handsome face.

He stared back, and his eyes told her he wasn't sure where to start.

"Kerri, I know how much that job offer in California means to you, and I know I don't have the right to ask you to stay but..." He took a deep breath. "I think you should know how I feel about you."

Her pulse raced, and her body began to sweat as she smiled and waited silently for him to continue. He dropped her hand to cup her face in both of his and tipped her head so he could stare straight into her eyes.

"I love you, Kerri," he said simply. "God, more than you could ever know."

Tears sprang to her eyes and she was powerless to stop them, just as she powerless to stop the rush of feeling warming her from within. She opened her mouth to tell him, but he put a finger to her lips and smiled.

"I have more I need to say." He brushed the tears away with his thumbs and continued. "All I want is for you to be happy. If it's that job in California, so be it. Take it. I just want you to know that we will work something out. Borrow Cole's jet. I'll commute. Move. Do anything I have to, because I am *not* going to let you get away."

The love and raw truth shining from his eyes stole her breath. Hope and love mixed, filling her heart so full the band restricting her chest broke and fell away.

He loves me. And *oh, God*...he offered to commute. Or move. *Move.* Leave his beloved ranch. His love, commitment, feelings for her staggered her very soul.

Kerri threw her arms around his neck and kissed him soundly. She pressed into him and held tight. Not ever going to let him go.

And he kissed her back, taking her breath and the

strength from her legs.

Never had she realized her heart had been off kilter. Needed to be set. Wasn't in position. Until her cowboy, with his big heart, big love and unbridled feelings, just clicked hers right into place.

A minute later, they pulled away panting and smiling.

"Connor," she said between breaths, unable to wait to tell him how she felt. "I love you, too. So much—"

And would've said more, but he cut her off with another kiss that curled her toes and destroyed all coherent thought.

Thinking was way overrated anyway.

Five minutes later, Connor forced himself to detangle the soft sweetness wrapped around him tight. Not that he wanted to. Hell no. He wanted to go on holding and loving the woman who was more patient and understanding than he deserved.

But someone kept calling her name, dammit. Apparently, their private moment was over.

She pulled away and stared up at him dazedly.

"Kerri?" *There it was again.*

She blinked, and his gaze roamed her features hungrily. God, he could hardly believe this beautiful woman loved him, but her eyes said it. Oh, *hell yeah*— with as much emotion and deep love as Jordan had for Cole. It humbled him. Made him feel blessed. Strong. Like he could take on the world.

"We need you, Kerri. Come on up."

Connor groaned. "That would be my brother with his impeccable timing," he said, turning her around to face the stage.

He was going to kill Cole later.

"Oh yeah, I forgot I promised I'd help them out with

a few songs." Kerri twisted back around and smiled apologetically.

His heart melted at the sight. "Go ahead. You know I love to hear you play and sing." He traced her lip with his finger. "And moan."

Color rushed into her cheeks, and he fell even more in love with her.

"There she is." Cole continued to sign his death warrant. "Kerri, I know my brother is hard to resist, but I promise, you can go right back to him when we're done."

Connor drew in a breath and dragged his gaze from Kerri's *oh so kissable mouth* to look at the stage in time to see Jordan swipe the microphone from his grinning brother.

"Don't listen to him, Kerri. You take all the time you need." Her sister winked at them and the crowd roared.

Kerri's blush deepened, but she smiled and held her hand up to wave at their audience. That was another thing he loved about her. Not just her strength, but her courage. Even if something intimidated her, she faced it head on.

She twisted back to him, her gaze suddenly serious. "I have a few things I need to say, too. I'm—"

Ah hell. Now the crowd chanted her name. Connor let out a breath and dropped his forehead to hers.

"Go ahead. I'll be right here when you're done," he assured and gave her a quick kiss before turning her around and pushing her toward the stage.

All the while she was up there performing, her beautiful gaze had stayed on him, letting him know she was singing the songs just for him. His chest couldn't expand any more. He'd never felt so happy. And so far away…

Connor moved closer, feeling warmed from the

inside out, needing to be near her. She was too far away. Much too far away.

And his mind raced with ideas and scenarios on how and where to get Kerri alone. They hadn't had the chance to discuss if she was taking the job. If she was moving. He only knew they loved each other. Which, was actually enough. Everything would fall into place. He'd make it work.

Finally, the third song ended, and he watched his brother place the guitar down. Anticipation rushed through his veins knowing he'd be holding his woman again soon.

And this time, he'd find a much more private spot. Shadow Rock Ranch was big. There were plenty of places where they could get lost and no one would interrupt. He'd make sure of it this time.

When his brother and Jordan hopped down, he expected Kerri to do the same. But she didn't. She remained. Lifting the microphone to her lips, she looked straight at him and his heart literally dipped.

"I'd like to say something before I get off the stage," Kerri informed and the crowd cheered. "I don't know if you all heard about the job offer I got from a prestigious restaurant in California."

Now the crowd suddenly moaned and groaned, and he understood their sentiment.

"I just wanted to let you know that Texas has once again captured my heart…and so has that cowboy over there."

Hot damn. She pointed at him with a grin so big and her heart in her eyes, he felt like an absolute king. Certainly the luckiest son-of-a-bitch in the whole state of Texas. Everyone hooted and cheered, and Kevin and Kade walked over to slap him on the back.

Her Unbridled Cowboy

"Way to go, Connor," Kade said.

His cousin nodded. "Yeah, you done good."

"So," Kerri continued when his gaze met hers once more. "That is why I turned down the offer."

He felt his mouth drop open as hope and love hit his chest with the force of a Brahma bull. *My God...she turned down California...*

She continued to smile at him, love shining in her eyes. "You see, no job is more important to me than you, Connor."

*Jesus...*that did it. His knees nearly buckled, but Connor fought through it and rushed the stage, needing to grab his woman and hold her tight. And he did. In front of a cheering crowd. Then he kissed her, thoroughly, and she kissed him back as the whole party looked on.

She loved him. Wasn't moving to California. And told him he was more important to her than her job.

He'd died and gone to heaven. This wonderful, sweet, giving, beautiful woman in his arms was his heaven. As long as he had her, he was home.

When they finally broke apart, Kerri's cheeks were wet. He cupped her face and gently brushed away her tears. "God, I love you so much I can't see straight."

"I love you, too," she said, caressing his chin, more tears spilling down her face.

He kissed them away.

Her smile turned mischievous, and she brought the microphone back up to her lips. "I just need to know one more thing, cowboy."

Gaze full of love, face glowing, she stole his breath and he couldn't take his eyes off her.

"Anything," he stated firmly, gazing down at the woman he loved more than Wild Creek or the south

Texas stars.

"Will you marry me?"

The crowd silenced, as if sucking in a shared breath.

Shocked speechless, Connor blinked at her a few times, slayed by her gusto before the smile in his heart found its way to his face.

"You bet I will, darlin'!" He pulled her in tight and spun her around, capturing her happy yelp with his mouth.

The microphone fell from her hands as she clung to him, body shaking with the emotions he'd seen in her eyes.

Wild cheers went up from the crowd, and happiness swelled in Connor's chest as he held everything that mattered most to him right there in his arms. When he stopped spinning, he looked down into her happy, jubilant face. Her smile suddenly turned saucy.

He quirked a brow. "What?"

"I just realized, you're no longer *unbridled*." She laughed. "Now you're a *brid*led cowboy."

Chuckling, he set his forehead to hers and kissed her adorable nose. "I can't believe you asked me to marry you."

Smile still tugging her lips, she reached up and brushed his jaw with her thumb. "Well, with your track record, I thought maybe *I'd* better do the asking."

Four pairs of eyes watched from their table in the far corner overlooking the party. They turned to each other and clinked flutes of champagne.

"Here's to two jobs very well done." Hannah gave the first toast.

"Here's to my happy boys and your wonderful girls for making them that way." Leeann's eyes filled up as the glasses came together again in celebration.

Nate glanced at the cousins. "So, now, our work really begins."

"Yes," Alex agreed, determination lining his shoulders. "What can we do about those Dalton's?"

The barbeque was in full swing and couples were dancing to the sounds of the southern rock band. Jordan and Cole barely moved as they slow danced together, and on the other side of the makeshift floor, Kerri and Connor fed each other strawberries.

Kade found himself smiling again. Normally, he would've been shocked by what had taken place on the stage five minutes ago. But being that Kerri is a Masters, nope, he wasn't surprised at all. But Connor had been.

"She sure got him good, didn't she?" Kevin asked, drawing up beside him.

He nodded. "Are you feeling all right?"

His cousin looked at him and frowned. "Ya. Why?"

"Because..." Kade shrugged. "You're not out there with some hot chick in your arms."

Kevin smiled. "Got to give the other guys a chance once in a while."

"You're some piece of work." He shook his head and tried not to smile.

"What are you gonna do, arrest me, Sheriff Dalton?" Kevin snickered.

"I'm not officially sheriff until Monday," he told him unnecessarily.

His cousin and everyone knew Kade had agreed to finish out the retiring Sheriff Hester's term. *One year. Shouldn't be too bad.* It was one of the smallest sheriff's departments in Texas. He had only two deputies under him.

"So, I still have time to raise a little hell this weekend," Kevin stated, not questioned.

Kade just shook his head. "You don't know the meaning of the word 'little.'"

"Sure I do. I can even use it in a sentence." Smiling, Kevin placed a hand on his shoulder and turned him to face the table where his cousin, Jen, was sitting talking to Harland County's newest designer. "I'm thirsty for a *little* taste of *brandy*."

He held himself rigid, despite the heat from images his cousin's words provoked. Images of tasting the full lips of the curvy, brown-eyed woman who occupied his fantasies. Until the fair.

"Go for it," he said, and watched Kevin raise his brows.

"Nah, man. Not me. *You*."

Kade scoffed. "No thanks. I'm not into Yanks."

"Since when did you care where a woman comes from?"

"Since she's a soldier hater."

After the way Brandi had reacted to him in his uniform at the fair, *no thanks*. Kade was proud of the Guard. Proud to serve, and didn't need some damn Yankee thumbing her nose at him.

Even if she was the only woman to spark his body to life with her mere presence.

Sparks were overrated.

**♥*

Stuffed Strawberries with Yummy Cream Cheese Filling

Main Ingredient:
30 fresh whole strawberries, large

Preparation:
Slice off the stem of each strawberry so the berries stand upright. Carefully cut each berry into 4 wedges, cutting almost to, but not through, the bottoms. (If you're a klutz like me, you may want to ask someone else to do that part.) Fan wedges slightly, taking care not to break; set berries aside.

Beat together until light and fluffy:
12 ounces cream cheese, softened
1/2 cup confectioners' sugar
1/4 teaspoon almond extract

Gently fold in:
2 tablespoons semisweet or milk chocolate, grated
(I'm partial to the milk chocolate and use a 'heavy' hand)

Fill the strawberries using a teaspoon or decorating bag with decorative tip if you're proficient. Sprinkle them with a little more grated chocolate, if desired. (Okay, I *desire* and sprinkle with a lot more grated chocolate.)

♥

Brandi left the east coast to start a new life in Harland County, Texas away from her overbearing stepfather's military minded ways,
and never-ending barrage of soldier 'suitors'. The only *boots* she wanted her man to wear were cowboy boots. So why did her heart flutter for the local Sheriff/part time National Guardsman?

♥

Please turn the page
For a preview of

Her Uniform Cowboy

Available Now

Chapter One – Her Uniform Cowboy

He left behind a fiancé and six-month old little girl...

Try as he might, Kade Dalton couldn't get that fact out of his head. The fact that he'd lost a soldier during his last deployment with the Texas Army National Guard, and the soldier had had dependants.

Grumbling a curse, he set his mug on the counter and strode for the back door. Just because he was up before the ass-crack of dawn, didn't mean he had to wake the whole ranch. Not that his cousins wouldn't be up in awhile anyway. Kevin usually left early for his commute to Houston where he was the vice president at McCall Enterprises. Jen would be up soon, too, thanks to her toddler, Cody, and Jen's husband Brock had Shadow Rock, the Dalton family ranch, to manage. But even though they would all be up soon, Kade quietly closed the door before heading to the stables. He had no desire for his family to realize how poorly he slept, or worse, to start his day with a lecture.

Yes, he knew it wasn't his fault the soldier had died.

He was just doing his job.

These things happen.

It's unfortunate, but a part of war.

Well, not on his watch. Not during his three previous deployments. *Christ*...He was the First Sergeant on the last two tours. He was responsible for the soldiers under his command.

The early June morning air was still somewhat cool and felt good on his heated skin. Kade closed his eyes and inhaled while he worked to get his mind out of

Afghanistan and rejoin his body back in the states. The scent of dirt and manure mixed with the fragrance of roses from a nearby trellis and he drew in another deep breath.

He was home where he belonged. In Harland County Texas. On Shadow Rock Ranch. His Guard family—minus one—was home where they belonged. He had people here who depended on him. Animals that depended on him. A community that depended on him.

Every morning he told himself this. Every morning he got out of bed and went to work. Every morning he felt like screaming. And that pissed him off. He wasn't weak, hated being weak. Almost as much as he hated being on edge. And he was on edge. Ever since that damn day.

Gravel groaned a muffled protest under his two-hundred pound stride. Keeping busy was the key. So, he helped out around the ranch. Worked with the horses. Went to auctions discerning which would make good stock horses. And being on edge was the main reason he'd agree to take over the Sheriff's position when the former one had approached him with the offer to finish out the man's term.

Harland County Sheriff?

Not something Kade had ever aspired to be. No. He liked horses and ranching and giving up one weekend a month and two and half weeks a year to Uncle Sam in the Guard. Never, had Kade ever thought about being a Sheriff. Yet, here he was, decked out in the tan uniform, weapons belt, badge and hat. Been that way for the past month. Harland County was fairly quiet, mostly rural, not much crime going on. Still, the extra job helped with his edginess.

So did sex, but his mutually agreed upon one-nighters had ceased once he'd accepted the badge. Didn't seem right. And looking for a relationship was out of the question. He wasn't about to stick some poor woman with his sorry ass. Hell no. Not until he got through some issues. Besides, relationships involved sharing more than a body, and his heart was off limits. Closed off. Locked up tight. In fact, no woman had ever reached his heart in over two decades. If it wasn't for the way he felt about his family and friends, Kade would question if he even had one.

Bypassing his truck, he headed for the stables on the far right. The quiet stable. The one where they housed the abused and abandoned horses. Currently, there were only two. Thank God. That meant most of his fellow Texans were taking their ownership responsibilities of these magnificent creatures seriously. Horses weren't toys you could ride whenever you felt like it. They weren't pets you paid attention to occasionally. They required work, maintenance, human touch…and son-of-a-bitch, he was edgy again. Nothing pissed him off more than a neglected or abused animal.

Stepping inside, he sucked in air heavy with the smell of more dirt and manure, but this time laced with the sweet scent of hay. The combination instantly calmed, took off some of that damn edge and he headed to the first of two stalls.

For several years now, he enjoyed working with the local vet to nurse the horses in this stable back to health. He'd made it Shadow Rock's practice to volunteer the stable to the humane society. It was a project of his, one he hoped to expand in the future. Now that he was more than likely home permanently, he needed to draw up plans. To…

He stopped dead at the stall.

Speaking of expanding…

Sweet mercy and Texas, that is a beautiful sight to behold.

Bent over, lightly rubbing down one of the horses legs was a local designer. God, she was curvy and hot and he wondered if she felt as soft as she looked. Something he would've discovered within the three months he'd known the woman if it weren't for two things. One, Brandy Wyne was not a one night stand, and two…she had an aversion to the military. The fact she was the only woman to spark part of him to life with just her mere presence didn't sit well with Kade. Hell no. So you'd think he'd be able to order his legs to slowly back out of the stall before being seen by the sexy woman with big brown eyes and golden streaks in her caramel-colored hair. Nope. He stepped forward instead.

Seems his legs took orders from a body part due south of his brain.

***
For announcements about upcoming releases and exclusive contests:
Join Donna's Newsletter
Visit me at: www.donnamichaelsauthor.com
***

Harland County Series

Visit my **Harland County Series Page** at my website www.donnamichaelsauthor.com for release information and updates!

Book One: Her Fated Cowboy
Book Two: Her Unbridled Cowboy
Book Three: Her Uniform Cowboy
Book Four: Her Forever Cowboy
Coming Soon
Book Five: Her Healing Cowboy

Become a *Cowboy Tamer!*

Drop me a line at donna_michaels@msn.com and request some Cowboy-Tamer swag!

***

Harland County Series
Book One: *Her Fated Cowboy*

NOR Reviewer Top Pick

L.A. cop Jordan Masters Ryan has a problem. Her normal method of meeting a crisis head-on and taking it down won't work. Not this time. Not when fate is her adversary. Having kept her from the man she thought she'd always marry, the same fickle fate took away the man she eventually did. Thrown back into the path of her first love, she finds hers is not the only heart fate has damaged.

Widower and software CEO, Cole McCall fills his days with computer codes and his free time working the family's cattle ranch. Blaming himself for his wife's death, he's become hard and bitter. When his visiting former neighbor sets out to delete the firewall around his heart, he discovers there's no protection against the Jordan virus. Though she understands his pain and reawakens his soul, will it be enough for Cole to overcome his past and embrace their fated hearts?

***

Harland County Series
Book Three: Kade/ Her Uniform Cowboy
Winner Best Cowboy in a Book/Reader's Choice-LRC
Awarded Crowned Heart of Excellence-InD'tale Magazine

Desperate for change after a verbally abusive relationship, Brandi Wyne leaves a symphony career, her family, and the Poconos to fall back on a designing degree and a chance to renovate a restaurant/pub in Texas. Even though part of a National Guard family, she'd sworn off military men when the last one proved less than supportive of her thyroid condition and subsequent weight gain. Too bad her body seems to forget that fact whenever she's near the very hot, very military local sheriff.

Texas Army National Guard First Sergeant Kade Dalton never planned on becoming Harland County Sheriff or the attraction to a curvy, military-hating designer from Pennsylvania. Heavy with guilt from the death of a soldier under his command during a recent deployment, and dealing with his co-owned horse ranch and a bungling young deputy, it's hard most days just to keep his sanity. But it's the Yankee bombshell who threatens not only his sanity, but tempts his body...and his heart.

Fighting their attraction becomes a losing battle, and Kade soon finds sanctuary in the arms of the beautiful designer. Does he really have the right to saddle Brandi with his stress issues? And if so, can he take a chance on the town's newest resident not abandoning him like others in his past?

***

Harland County Series
Book Four: Kevin/ Her Forever Cowboy
Hit both Amazon Hot New Releases list & Amazon Best Sellers list in Western Romance

Single mother, Shayla Ryan, longs to put down roots to create a stable environment for her baby girl and her younger sister, but the threat of her abusive, ex-con father finding them has made that almost impossible. Her newest residence in Harland County, however, holds a lot of appeal, especially in the form of a Casanova cowboy with eye-catching good looks and easy charm. Those two qualities took her down the wrong road before, and though the sexy cowboy interferes with her pulse, she can't let her heart get in the way of the safety of her family, or give it to someone who doesn't believe in forever.

If there's one thing software company vice president, Kevin Dalton, loves more than puzzles, it's women. Size, shape, race doesn't matter as long as they don't want a relationship—he's not looking to repeat the past, and more than happy to remain single. Until two beautiful redheads drop him to his knees—one with her cutie-pie smile, the other with her elbow. Too bad the elbow-toting beauty is both hot and puzzling. A killer combination too strong to resist. And without realizing it, the redheads slowly rewrite the code around his heart.

But when the danger from Shayla's past shows up, can he rise to the challenge to keep them safe...and really be what they need? A *forever* cowboy?

♥

Lisa was always the reliable, dependable rock to her family and friends, but it was time to put herself first and go after what she wanted. Starting with a certain green-eyed guardsman the family dinner has dealt with for years. The son of her mother's best friend. The gorgeous man who had a thing for her sister in high school.
It was time to supply the Bn. S4 with another option.

♥

Please visit the men who guard the Pocono Valley in this
Harland County Spinoff Series
Wyne and Dine
Citizen Soldier Series: Book One/Ben
Available September 2014

♥

***
Time-shift Heroes Series
Book One: Captive Hero
2012 RONE Awards Nominee Best Time Travel
2013 Reader's Crown Finalist

When Marine Corps test pilot, Captain Samantha Sheppard accidentally flies back in time and inadvertently saves the life of a WWII VMF Black Sheep pilot, she changes history and makes a crack decision to abduct him back to the present. With the timeline in jeopardy, she hides the handsome pilot at her secluded cabin in the Colorado wilderness.

But convincing her sexy, stubborn captive that he is now in another century proves harder than she anticipated—and soon it becomes difficult to tell who is captor and who is captive when the more he learns about the future, the more Sam discovers about the past, and the soul-deep connection between them.

As their flames of desire burn into overdrive, her flying Ace makes a historical discovery that threatens her family's very existence. Sam's fears are taken to new heights when she realizes the only way to fix the time-line is to sacrifice her captive hero...or is it?

Can love truly survive the test of time?

Time-shift Heroes Series
Visit my **Time-shift Heroes Series Page** for release information and updates!
Book One: Captive Hero
Book Two: Future Hero
Book Three: Unintended Hero

***

Cowboy-Sexy

Honky Tonk Hearts Series with The Wild Rose Press by Donna Michaels

4 Star RT Magazine Review*&*NOR Reviewer Top Pick

Finn Brennan was used to his brother playing practical jokes, but this time he'd gone too far--sending him a *woman* as a ranch hand, and not just a woman, but a Marine.

When Lt. Camilla Walker's CO asks her to help out at his family's dude ranch until he returns from deployment, she never expected to be thrust into a mistaken engagement to his sexy, cowboy twin--a former Navy SEAL who *hates* the Corps.

The Corps took Finn's father, his girlfriend and threatened his naval career. He's worked hard for another shot at getting back to active duty and won't let his brother's prank interfere. The last thing he needs is the temptation of a headstrong, unyielding, hot Marine getting in the way.

***
She Does Know Jack
A Romantic Comedy Suspense
by Donna Michaels

NOR Reviewer Top Pick

Former Army Ranger Capt. Jack 'Dodger' Anderson would rather run naked through a minefield in the Afghan desert than participate in a reality television show, but when his brother Matthew begins to receive threats, Jack quickly becomes Matthew's shadow. As if the investigation isn't baffling enough, he has to contend with the addition of a beautiful and vaguely familiar new contestant.

Security specialist, Brielle Chapman reluctantly agrees to help her uncle by going undercover as a contestant on the *Meet Your Mate* reality show. Having nearly failed on a similar assignment, she wants to prove she still has a future in this business. But when the brother of the *groom* turns out to be Dodger, the only one-nighter she ever had—while in disguise from a prior undercover case—her job becomes harder. Does he recognize her? And how can she investigate with their sizzling attraction fogging her brain? Determined to finish the job, she brings the case to a surprising climax, uncovers the culprit and *meets* her own *mate*.

***
Thanks for reading!

Made in the USA
Lexington, KY
01 June 2015